GUARDIAN
of AJALON

Books by Joan Campbell

The Poison Tree Path Chronicles

Chains of Gwyndorr (Book 1)
Heirs of Tirragyl (Book 2)
Guardian of Ajalon (Book 3)

Illustrated Collections of Short Stories, Reflections and Prayers

Encounters: Life Changing Moments with Jesus
Journeys: On Ancient Paths of Faith
Soul Search: Questions Jesus Asked

www.joancampbell.co.za

GUARDIAN
of AJALON

THE POISON TREE PATH CHRONICLES

———

BOOK 3

JOAN CAMPBELL

Guardian of Ajalon by Joan Campbell

ISBN: 978-1-991222-95-4 (Print)
　　　　978-1-991222-96-1 (eBook)

Guardian of Ajalon
The Poison Tree Path Chronicles series, Book 3
Copyright © 2018 by Joan Campbell

This is a work of fiction. Names, characters, places, and incidents are products of the author's imagination or are used fictitiously. Any similarity to actual people, organizations, and/or events is purely coincidental.

Cover design by Charles Bernard
Interior design by Beth Shagene
Ebook production by Book Genesis, Inc.

To Marinda, Marielle, Nicole,
Arno, and Ashlyn

Keep dancing with the king.

• • •

The LORD your God is with you,
the Mighty Warrior who saves.
He will take great delight in you;
in his love he will no longer rebuke you,
but will rejoice over you with singing.

ZEPHANIAH 3:17

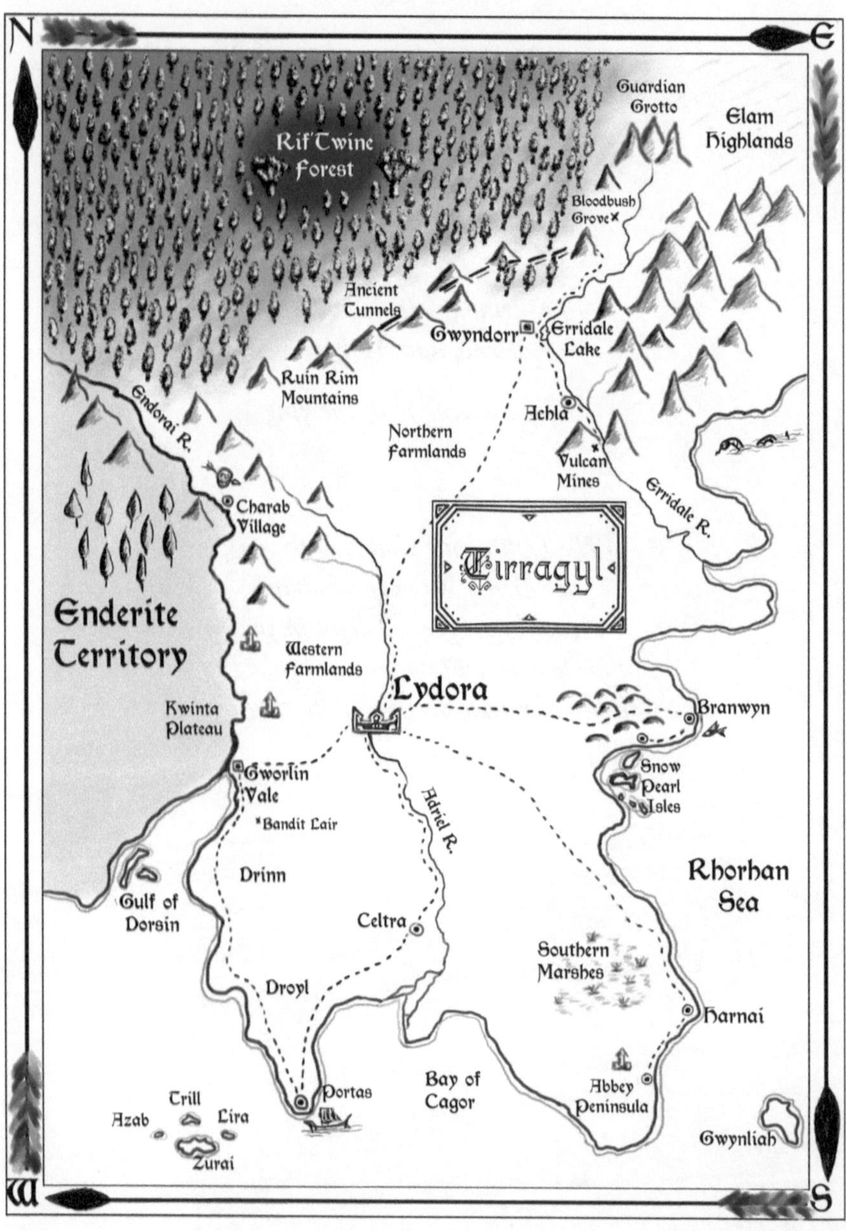

N
E
W
S
Rif'Twine Forest
Guardian Grotto
Elam Highlands
Bloodbush Grove
Ancient Tunnels
Gwyndorr
Erridale Lake
Ruin Rim Mountains
Achla
Northern Farmlands
Vulcan Mines
Gindorai R.
Erridale R.
Charab Village
Tirragyl
Enderite Territory
Western Farmlands
Lydora
Branwyn
Kwinta Plateau
Gworlin Vale
Snow Pearl Isles
Bandit Lair
Hdriel R.
Drinn
Rhorhan Sea
Gulf of Dorsin
Celtra
Southern Marshes
Droyl
Harnai
Bay of Cagor
Abbey Peninsula
Trill
Portas
Azab
Lira
Gwynliah
Zurai

Eastern Mountains of Tirragnl with Guardian Grotto
Triplet Peaks
Elam Highlands
Ruin Rim Mountains
Burrow
The Fissure
Deep Caves
Entrance
Ancient Tunnels
RifTwine Forest
Echo Pools
Rogue's Neck
Feyn River
Snow Barb Turret
The Fangs
To Winter Pass
Inner Peaks
Waif's Cleft
Outer Peaks
Errndale River
Jabal River
Cutter Crags
Two Plague Pass
To Bloodbush Grove

PROLOGUE

The Rif'iend moved effortlessly through the Rif'twine's Dark-zone, unhampered by the thick growth of trees, creepers, and vines. Crafted from darkness and malevolence, his essence was the same as that of the forest, making it as easy for him to melt through the Rif'twine as it was for dirt to mix into sludge.

He paused, breathing deeply of the death-and-decay–laced air, savoring the brief surge of energy that followed. He did not normally stray this far into the Darkzone. Most of his kind preferred to hover at the border of the Dark-and-Dimzone. It was there—where the forest pulsed outward to claim the southlands—that the Rif'twine's power was the greatest . . . and feeding the easiest. Until the south-erners started to fight the forest, he and his fellow Rif'iends had satiated themselves on all the Rif'twine devoured.

But the Rif'twine's power was declining, and the Rif'iends grew edgy. Now they tussled daily for the small scraps of death and pain the forest still stole. The fear and anguish of the rooters—especially the small ones—were a good source of food and power, but the Rif'iends were never satisfied for long. It was only when the delirea plant bloomed with death that the Rif'iends feasted as well as they had in the past.

He glided forward again through the silent forest. He detected the poison sap creeping deep in the towering trees and heard age-old echoes of the magic words that had called the trees to life and then death. The air was thick and cold. It enveloped him in its safe darkness.

But something was amiss.

He sensed a disruption in the darkness ahead of him. He slowed, approaching this strangeness cautiously. The air around him grew warmer. He quivered with disgust but forced himself forward to discover this source of heat.

Suddenly the Rif'iend found himself in open space. His eyes burned as the light scorched him with its brightness. Dread coursed through him, and he shrieked, fleeing back to the trees. How could this be? He was nowhere near the north, was he?

From the safety of the trees, he peered back at the open space—a clearing, completely free of trees, except for one. Flowers carpeted the floor around this single tree, a bright-green weeping willow, and water bubbled up from the ground below it. The creature wrinkled up his nose at the sweetness of the flowers and the freshness of the water.

Why had the forest not claimed this clearing with its foreign tree, flowers, and fresh water?

The creature backed away slightly, letting tendrils of his remaining power slither out into the Rif'twine, seeking an answer to this anomaly. Deeper and deeper those tendrils explored. He drew comfort from the Rif'twine's vastness. Of course, he skirted away from the north's intense glare, following his senses to the south, to Gwyndorr, where he perceived the answer lay.

Suddenly he saw in his mind's eye events he had not witnessed for a long time. For hadn't he been there when they had occurred, watching from the edges of the Dimzone? The time shift, he realized, had brought it to him again.

A crowd of southerners pulsing with excitement and a single poison tree. A gathering storm that meant the end of it all.

And finally the creature understood where he was and how this clearing had come to be. This was the place where the Rif'iends had scuffled over the ring, the one *he* had finally laid claim to. But why hadn't they noticed what was happening here, deep in the Rif'twine, while they fought?

He shuddered at the thought.

What power was so great, so frightening, that it could push back the very core of evil?

CHAPTER 1

The Old Magic that had veiled the Guardian Grotto for four hundred years had failed.

Failed.

Mikel must have spoken that ominous word aloud, for the scout standing in front of him looked up sharply.

"Sir?"

"Nothing." The High Commander sank down on the stool behind the map table. "Proceed with your report, Jeru."

The young scout had ridden hard. His hair was disheveled, his cloak wrinkled and dirt stained. The sharp smell of heat, exertion, and horse sweat warned Mikel that the news was so dire that Jeru had not yet taken the time to wash.

"Sir. Ruan and I were patrolling the Outer Peaks, past the Cutter Crags. That would have been" —his brow furrowed in concentration— "ten days ago."

"And?"

"From one of the high ridges to the west, you get a view past the Peaks."

"Yes." Mikel imagined exactly where his men had stood. He knew these mountains intimately, every crest and valley and slope of beloved hill. He had patrolled them once as a young Warrior and, even as High Commander, had led his men through them on more occasions than he could even remember.

"We saw movement, sir. Men on horseback at Two Plague Pass."

"*On* the pass?" Shock jarred through Mikel. This was worse than he had thought.

"Only a few men on the pass, but they have definitely found it."

"These men? Were they dressed in the colors of Gwyndorr's Lord?"

"No, Commander." Jeru looked down and swallowed. "They were dressed in the colors of Tirragyl. They were king's men."

By the abyss. Lord Lucian hadn't come alone. He had brought the royal army. And they had found the pass that had not been breached since the time of King Destaus, hundreds of years before.

"Did you get a sense of their number, Jeru?" Mikel's calm tone came from years of command.

"On the pass we counted about fifteen, sir. But . . ." Jeru's hesitation warned Mikel of the bad news to follow, "we climbed the western peak for a better view of the low ground."

"And?"

"Hundreds of men are massing there under the royal banner, sir. With more men and supplies arriving as we left to bring you the news."

"Thank you, Jeru." Mikel rose. "You and Ruan did well to bring the news so fast."

"Sir." The Warrior placed his fist on his heart and bowed slightly before turning to leave the war chamber.

When he was alone again, Mikel dropped back onto his seat, closed his eyes and imagined himself standing on the same windy western peak where Jeru had stood ten days earlier. Far below him the valley floor churned with the dark figures of soldiers, purple banners whipping above their heads. The Parashi's ancient enemy, the House of Taus, drew near.

He opened his eyes and leaned over the giant map stretched out on the table. His finger traced the line of the Outer Peaks until it came to rest on Two Plague Pass. A place of legend. Of victory. It was the pass that could not be found by the enemy, the pass that had kept them safe all these years. And on the single occasion in which it *was* breached, mythical foghounds had come to fight the enemy, or so the legends said. Even as a child Mikel had disbelieved the story. He knew that swords, not foghounds, fought Highborn invaders.

But the one thing Mikel *had* placed his faith in was the shielding power of the Guardian Rock. Until Shara had arrived. Fleeing Gwyndorr when Lord Lucian sought to bind her to his son in marriage, Shara had sought shelter at the Guardian Grotto. Her companions—the monk Andreo, the old man Eliad, and the groom Nicho—had not known that she carried with her a powerful and dangerous Cerulean Dusk Dreamer. Mikel had only realized it when Lord Lucian used the girl's dreams to briefly breach the Grotto's defenses. Although Mikel had confiscated the rock, he had not hidden it well enough, and its powerful allure had drawn Shara once more. In her final dream, Lord Lucian infiltrated the Guardian Grotto long enough to know exactly where it lay.

Mikel finally had to acknowledge with his heart what his head knew the day the Dusk Dreamer took full possession of Shara. Their Old Magic defense had been breached. They were no longer hidden, no longer safe. War was upon them.

Mikel's finger followed the Erridale River, the most likely route that the king and his army would take once they crossed the pass. At the confluence point, where the Feyn River split into the Erridale and Jabal Rivers, he stopped. Here the king could take two routes. One, the more direct route, followed the Feyn to Rogue's Neck, where the river cut through the Inner Peaks. From there it was mere days to the waterfall that veiled the Grotto. Mikel's eye fell on the other place where the Inner Peaks could be breached. Called Waif's Cleft, it had been discovered by a young Parashi boy at the time of the Hundred Year War. A narrow path winding between two tall mountains, it was even better hidden than Two Plague Pass. Once through Waif's Cleft, an enemy could make their way straight to the Elam Highlands. The Guardian Grotto had an opening onto this plateau.

Mikel had commanded the Parashi Warriors for many years. He had led raids on Highborn lands, fought royal troops in clashes when the old king's cruelty threatened the Parashi. He had protected his people, their ancient writings, and the Guardian Rock, here, in the depths of the earth. He had trained younger men to fight and protect. Yet Mikel knew that they were no match for the full force of the king's army. Had only Lord Lucian come with the men of Gwyndorr, they would have stood a chance against them. Even if they killed this army, thousands more would follow. The king could call every man in Tirragyl into service. The Parashi Warriors would be annihilated, the Old Writing destroyed, and the memory of the Parashi wiped from the face of the earth.

Mikel clenched his hand into a fist and smashed it down on the map over Two Plague Pass, wishing he had the power to crush the king's army with a single blow. If he could do that, he would not have to send his men to their deaths.

Pearce pushed open the door to the war chamber just as Mikel smashed his fist down on the map. Unease crept through Pearce. The High Commander was always in control and seldom vexed or angry. The scout's news must have been dire indeed.

"Sir?" he said quietly from the door. "I heard the scouts came with news?"

"Yes, Pearce." Mikel straightened, and instantly the control was back in his voice and posture. "Call the other commanders to the war chamber."

"Yes, sir."

Pearce hastened to the barracks and dining hall to call the other commanders to the war chamber. They returned to find Mikel quietly studying the map.

"Sit, men." Mikel waited for the commanders to find a place at the long table before he continued. "I have just heard from a scout that the king's army was gathering at Two Plague Pass about ten days ago."

Two Plague Pass? Pearce felt a stab of fear. The pass had not been found for hundreds of years. He saw the collective dismay on the other commanders' faces.

"It will take them time to traverse the pass with their supplies and horses," the High Commander continued. "But we must assume the worst. They could be as far as the Cutter Crags by now."

By the abyss! Their enemy had breached the Outer Peaks. It was unthinkable.

Mikel pointed to the map. "If they follow the river through Rogue's Neck, they could be here within two weeks. We cannot let that happen."

"What do we do, Commander?" Pearce asked.

"We must delay them in the mountains like our forefathers did when the Highborn invaders first came all those hundreds of years ago. We know these mountains better than they do. We use that to our advantage."

"Skirmishes, you mean?" Pearce couldn't keep the skepticism from his voice.

"Yes. We attack and retreat. We worry them like a fly worrying a grubear. We draw them off their path and into the hills where we can pick them off, and then we slink away again. We might not be able to push them back, but we keep them at bay, busy chasing their own tails. At least till winter comes, when the snow will hopefully force them to retreat."

"With respect, sir, it's the way cowards fight," Pearce said. "Let's fight them face-to-face. Give them a battle they will never forget."

The other commanders stirred in agreement.

"There are too many," Mikel said. "We will be slaughtered. Then who will protect the Grotto?"

"But we would all die like true Warriors, courageous and unconquered!" Pearce was on his feet, his sword above his head as he cried the words. "If all we do is chase them away, they will be back again."

"Sit down, Pearce," Mikel said. "This is not a discussion. It is an order. I am putting you in charge of three of our five units. You will take them into the mountains and keep the king's army at bay by employing skirmish tactics. The remaining men will stay to guard the Grotto and Deep Caves."

"You are not leading the Warriors, sir?" It made no sense to Pearce. This was the greatest threat the Warriors had ever faced, and they needed the High Commander to lead them, not hide in the Grotto with the women and children.

"I will be in charge of the men guarding the caves," Mikel replied, lowering his gaze to the map.

Pearce tried one more time. "Sir, I really think you should . . ."

"That's all," Mikel said sharply. "Ready yourself today. Tomorrow you lead the men into the mountains."

"Yes, sir."

"And, Pearce, station some men at Waif's Cleft. It would be a dangerous place for them to breach."

"Of course, sir."

As they rose to leave, Mikel said, "There will be another meeting in the gathering hall tonight. You are invited to attend."

"Invited or commanded to come?" Pearce had never spoken to the High Commander in such a tone, but he still smarted from Mikel's sharp words. And—truth be told—the High Commander had just dropped in Pearce's estimation.

"Invited." The High Commander's gaze held his own, and there was a flicker of sadness in it, as if Pearce's words grieved him. "During the Hundred Year War, Warriors were sent off with words of encouragement and hope on the eve of great battles. We will rekindle the old tradition."

As he left the war chamber, Pearce thought that words of hope were a useless substitute for what Mikel should be giving them: his sword.

The horses were restless this morning although Nicho whispered to them that all would be well. He suspected the animals sensed if you did not believe the words yourself. The Grotto had been a place of unease from the day he arrived back here with Jed, Rosa, Simhew, and the liberated rifters. No wonder, for they prepared for war.

Earlier two scouts had ridden in. Nicho could tell they had set a particularly grueling pace because their mounts, heads down and nostrils flared, showed signs of extreme fatigue. As he grabbed one of the reins, the words of reprimand were already on his tongue. But just then he looked at the face of the man leaping from his horse's back. His expression was strained, his eyes filled with apprehension. Nicho said nothing. The news the men bore was obviously urgent. Urgent enough for them to push their treasured mounts to the limit.

"Easy, boy." Nicho tried to soothe Crypin, Pearce's large grey stallion, who was snorting and pawing the ground. "Easy. You're a leader, boy. You need to set a good example." He stroked the stallion's broad nose and, for a moment, the horse stilled. "Good. Good. You're a warhorse, remember? Fearless, that's you."

"Ko?"

Nicho turned to see Jed standing against the stable wall, his serious face watchful and wary. How Nicho wished he could turn back time to when Derry was still alive. Then, Jed's face had lit up at the mere promise of a tickle from his father. Now, his father was dead and his mother lost in the backstreets of Gwyndorr. As much as Nicho and Rosa tried to fill the spaces in Jed's life, pain and mistrust were etched in those dark eyes.

"Jed." He bent down, fighting the urge to pull the boy into his arms. The boy did not like being held. "Do you want to give Crypin a stroke? I can lift you so you can reach."

Jed shook his head.

"I thought you were with Simhew this morning, learning your letters."

"Simhew is running arrows for Uncle Pearce."

"Errands, you mean?" Nicho smiled. "Did you find me all by yourself?" It was an impressive feat for a boy of less than five. The stables were far from the living area in the Grotto, near the back of the caves. "You've come such a long way, you might as well help me. Grab that bucket over there, and let me fill it with some feed."

The boy obeyed quietly, helping Nicho with the feeding. Nicho was pleased to see that he seemed unafraid of the horses looming above his head. They were gentle around him, responding to his innate stillness.

When they had done the rounds, Nicho sat on the ground and patted the straw next to him. "Time for us to have a little something too." He tore a piece of bread husk and gave it to Jed, who ate in silence. Nicho remembered sitting in the stable with Shara at Randin's house and eating bright-red apples, grown in the fertile land around Gwyndorr. He longed for fresh food and his mother, Marai's, aromatic cooking. The food in the Grotto was plain, unadorned, and seldom fresh. Food for soldiers.

"Do horses cry?" Jed's voice broke through Nicho's memories.

"Uh, no . . . but they do get sad."

"Is the grey one sadder than the others?"

"Ah." Understanding dawned. "No, Crypin isn't called that because he cries. It's just an old Parashi name. Like Lian." He saw the boy stiffen and realized his mistake. Lian was the name Jed had given to the last toy his father had carved him before he left for good. The toy that Hildah had sold when they were desperate for food. Nicho quickly continued. "We Parashi have the bravest horses in the world because we train them and treat them so well."

"So we can beat the bad lord when he comes?" Jed's dark eyes looked intently into his own, older and wiser than such young eyes were meant to be.

"We will try, Jed. We will be very brave, and we will try."

CHAPTER 2

Shara awoke. The dread that had been coiling inside her these last few days had tightened in her chest as she slept. Today they reached the Rif'twine, that forest whose evil darkness stole through Tirragyl. But they would do more than reach it. They would walk right into its heart, if Eliad was to be believed. The old man spoke of a path through the forest. He called it the poison tree path.

She lay a long time listening to his and Andreo's soft breathing. Nothing yet stirred to life, although a lightening on the horizon hinted that dawn was near. Shara rolled from under the blanket she shared with her companions and felt her way to the still-warm embers of the fire. She blew on them before carefully arranging some branches on the softly glowing coals. It took time, but finally small flames licked the dry wood.

She held her hands over the flames, trying to rub warmth back into her icy fingers. If it was this cold *out* of the forest, how would it be once they were trapped in that dark, shadowed world?

A flash of red and shimmer of gold caught the corner of her eye. Before she looked up, she knew what it meant. *The Gold Breast had come.* Trepidation and joy tangled uneasily within her as she hurried to Eliad's side and shook him by the shoulder.

"Eliad. Tabeal is here."

"Tabeal!" The old man sat up groggily, but his face lit into a smile as the bird came to settle on his shoulder. "You are just in time, my friend. Today we reach the path."

The majestic bird let out one pure note, and briefly joy broke through Shara's disquiet . . . until she remembered. The last time the Gold Breast had come to her, she had been caught in the endless dark dream brought on by the Cerulean Dusk Dreamer. Even though the Gold Breast had freed her that day, the damage had been wrought. Through her and the power rock, the Guardian Grotto had been breached, perhaps even destined to destruction. A familiar shame washed over her as she stared at the bird.

"On time for what?" Andreo pushed himself onto one arm, yawning as he rubbed his eyes.

The Gold Breast flew from Eliad's shoulder to the place where the book lay encased in its oilskin wrapping.

"Time for the telling, I suspect." Eliad stretched out and lifted the book to his lap.

Shara had taken many a turn carrying that heavy book from the Guardian Grotto. At times she cursed the day she and Nicho had uncovered it in the Silver Birch Grove outside Gwyndorr's gates. Since that day the book, written in the Old Tongue, had been nothing but a heavy weight to add to their already burdensome packs.

Yet every time she voiced these thoughts, Eliad shook his head. "At the right time, you will realize these words are not heavy but light."

She watched Eliad unwrap the book. As the oilskin fell away, the fire's growing flames glinted on the golden symbol engraved in its leather cover. The Old Script's emblem of freedom, Eliad had told her once.

Shara shuffled closer to Eliad and the book. Perhaps—if she was honest—closer to Tabeal. "We left the Grotto almost six weeks ago. Wouldn't our long journey have been the perfect time for this . . . *telling* of which you speak?" she asked.

Eliad looked at her with his usual gentleness. "We are on the edge of the Rif'twine, my love. The journey ahead is far more arduous than the one behind. It is for such a time that Tabeal has kept the book. In that dark forest"—his eyes roamed in the direction of the Rif'twine—"we will need its light. Tonight I will begin to read the words, and Tabeal will bring us understanding."

They set off as soon as there was enough daylight to see by. Eliad clutched his gnarled walking stick and led the way. Their time at the Guardian Grotto, and these last few weeks fleeing from it, had taken its toll on the old guide. His back seemed more hunched. His silver hair and beard were more matted, and his eyes—which had always held a youthful sparkle of mischief—had grown somber.

He was not the only one changed, Shara thought as she fell in place behind him. She was different too. No longer that fiery, dark-haired young woman who used to feel so deeply and speak her mind so freely, the one Nicho had fallen in love with. She had let the Dusk Dreamer's power into her life, and it had hollowed her out, stealing the best parts of her. Shara felt empty. Numb. Only regret and shame filled those deep places where once conviction and love had thrived.

Behind her Andreo spoke about the various plant specimens he had once gathered in the Rif'twine when he was a Brethren of Taus monk. His interest in creating healing potions and ointments had been against the Brethren's Code, which outlawed herbal alchemy along with all other Parashi practices. It had led to his Disgracing, where he was stripped of his monk's cowl, along with his name and position amongst his Brethren. He was forced to spend an exposed night on a plateau above the monastery. This was where the Gold Breast and Eliad had found him, rescuing him from the even worse fate still to come: the mind-altering powers of the Word Art Brothers.

Yet, it was clear from his uninterrupted account of the botanical wonders of the Rif'twine that his passion for healing plants was as strong as ever.

"Hush, my friend." Eliad silenced Andreo as they neared the road leading to Gwyndorr. How strange that their journey had taken them back to the very place they had escaped from months earlier. *Why did Tabeal not lead us to this path straight from Gwyndorr? Why take us all the way to the Guardian Grotto?* Shara had asked Eliad a while ago, thinking that if the Gold Breast had not led them to the Grotto, evil could never have breached it. *We had to go to the Grotto,* he had said simply. *Dark days lie ahead for them. The words of the book are their hope too.*

"Where does the path start?" Andreo squinted into the now-bright morning light, staring at the forest beyond the road. He knew better than anyone how prolifically the Rif'twine grew and had voiced his doubts a few nights ago as they sat around the fire. Even if the path they sought had once existed, it was unlikely to still be there. Creepers and vines would have claimed it by now.

But Eliad had remained resolute. *It is no ordinary path.*

"It used to lie right at the edge of the Rif'twine." Eliad glanced around to check that the road was clear before he continued across it. "But it is possible that the forest has grown around it. We might have to go into the Dimzone to find it. Perhaps even into the Darkzone."

Like all Tirragylins, Shara feared the Rif'twine, the forest that crept ominously closer to Gwyndorr, devouring everything in its path. Only the Rifter Gangs had kept it at bay in her lifetime. Within the forest grew plants that could strangle you, poison you with their berries, or draw you with their alluring scent before releasing their toxic spores. As they drew closer, the forest seemed brooding and watchful. It reached out an invisible hand that prickled her skin with fear.

The air was cool and the light murky as they stepped into the Dimzone, where the plants had not yet completely taken over. A smell like rotting meat accosted Shara and made her gag. She lifted her arm to her nose and tried to breathe through the fabric.

"You'll get used to it," Andreo said cheerily, patting her on the back. "So what are we looking for, Eliad? A poison tree, you say?"

Eliad nodded. He was already pushing deeper, towards the Darkzone, where the thick plant life made movement almost impossible. Shara hurried to stay by his side.

"What does a poison tree look like?" she whispered.

"It has a light bark with a milky substance on it and dark, shiny leaves. Look." He pointed to a tree that towered above the other plants. "But don't touch it. The bark is very poisonous in the Rif'twine."

"Is this the tree we seek?"

"No. It was younger than this. Smaller." He continued to move farther into the forest. "Although, in *this* forest, it could have grown a great deal since then."

They pushed a little way into the Darkzone before they could go no farther and had to turn back. Eliad carefully worked his way across the forest, checking around every poison tree for the start of the path.

Shara fell back to where Andreo picked some leaves. "What if this path is overgrown like you said it would be, Andreo?" She glanced to where Eliad thrashed at some vines with his walking stick. "Or what if it starts too deep in the forest for us to reach it? Where will we go then? We can't exactly walk back into Gwyndorr with Lord Lucian still on the hunt for me."

Andreo looked at Eliad, his forehead creased in thought. "I've wondered this myself. But Eliad has no doubt that the path is here. And he has never yet been wrong."

Shara and Andreo turned at the sound of the birdsong piercing through the ominous silence of the forest. Eliad's head shot up before he looked over at them, the old laughter back in his eyes. He didn't speak, merely pointed with his walking stick, and together they followed the sound of Tabeal's song until they reached, at the edge of the Darkzone to the west of where they had started, the poison tree.

"This is the one," Eliad said reverently, steepling his hands over his mouth as he stared at the tree.

It looked the same as the others but as Shara stepped around it, she saw that a path snaked through the forest from where the tree stood. It reminded Shara of a small tear on a long stretch of fabric, or a fine crack in a thick stone wall. The path seemed insubstantial with the trees towering above it and the undergrowth pushing against it, but some power seemed to hold the irrepressible forest at bay from that path.

"Well, I never," Andreo replied, staring slack-jawed at that path. "How is that even possible?"

Eliad came around the tree to peer at the path. "The poison tree path. The way to freedom."

Freedom. The word echoed through Shara, tried to take root. What did it even mean, this word? All her life, walls had hemmed her in. The very thing she thought would set her free had bound her even more tightly. In Marai's love, and later in Nicho's, she had felt a stirring of something free and lovely, yet they were both lost to her now. She did not know this freedom Eliad spoke of with such sureness. But one thing she knew: she wanted it. She would walk this path no matter how dark it got, no matter how long it stretched on.

"What are we waiting for then?" She stepped onto the path and looked back at her companions with a grin that hinted of her former self. Eliad laughed and nodded his approval.

And the three of them started down the poison tree path. To freedom.

CHAPTER 3

Mikel had seen the disdain in his men's eyes when he announced that Pearce would lead the units while he stayed to defend the Grotto. He knew his men heard only cowardice in those words, but he had no way to explain the weakness that had crept into his body since his last bout of illness. Since that night when Shara had found the Cerulean Dusk Dreamer and Lucian had breached the cave through her, the illness had lingered. Was it a sickness or the weight of what had happened that caused his body to fail him when he needed his strength the most? Even swinging a sword felt like an effort.

Mikel had left the war chamber and made his way back to his sleeping quarters, feeling out of breath by the time he reached its cool darkness. Now he lit a lamp with trembling hands before doing what he always did when the weight of his leadership pressed down on him: he turned to the ancient Parashi books. Reading how a remnant of his forebearers had held out against the invaders, always soothed away his restlessness. Poems of fealty to Ab'El were scattered amongst the accounts of battles. He read one of these now.

> *O Ancient of Kings,*
> *Greatest of Warriors,*
> *Only you can save us*
> *As the enemy draws near.*
> *Trumpets will sound your approach,*
> *And the enemy will scatter in fear.*

Come soon, Great King,
Come soon.

The words, filled with faith and deep longing, struck Mikel in a way they had never done before. An enemy was closing in on them now, too. He tried to imagine this Ancient King—one far more powerful than Tirragyl's Alexor—riding to their rescue. Hadn't his mother always told him stories of Ab'El and the vast land he ruled over? But the Ancient King had not come to the defense of the Parashi hundreds of years ago when the Highborn invaders first came. They had had to fight their own battles, as Mikel knew they would have to do now. His mother's faith had imprinted itself on him over the years. He believed there was a High King, but the king had forgotten about his Parashi subjects since the years of the Invasion, the Hundred Year War, and the Great Purge.

Unsettled by his thoughts, he closed the book and rose to put it back on the shelf. His trembling fingers made him clumsy, and as he pressed the book into its slot, another one—tucked away near the back—fell to the floor.

Mikel bent down and picked it up, recognizing it as the book that Eliad had left for him. He hadn't given the book a second thought since Shara, Andreo, and Eliad had left the Grotto. There had been too many pressing issues concerning the Grotto's safety. Now he carried it back to his seat and opened it, looking intently at the writing, so similar to Ancient Parashi. He recognized several words but could not decipher enough of the text for it to make sense. Eliad had said that the book held the key to the past and the future and that only the Gold Breast could unlock its words. That was another topic of his mother's stories, Mikel recalled. The Gold Breast. Eliad and Shara claimed that this bird had shown them the way to the Grotto. He had wondered about this at the time. Why had the bird left without showing itself to Mikel and the Warriors? He could almost hear Eliad's deep, laughter-filled voice saying, "Tabeal is always close and always just on time."

"If you're as close as Eliad thinks, now might be the time to come," Mikel whispered into the silence. "We really need you."

The prayer came from the same deep, broken place that the words about the Ancient King had touched earlier. It was a plea. A desperate cry.

Yet hardly a moment passed before there was a flash of red and gold in the doorway. Light seemed to rush into the chamber, pushing into the darkest corners. The bird alighted on the book that lay open on Mikel's lap. Its body was a rich red, its breast a radiant gold. A sense of deep awe settled on the High Commander as he looked at it. Awe and shame.

"I doubted," he said softly. "But help us now. Please help us now."

"The High Commander has called a meeting," Rosa whispered as she tucked a blanket around Simhew and Jed in their pallets. She blew out the candle in the chamber that she and the two boys shared. "We'd better hurry or we'll be late."

Nicho often found himself here as she put the boys to sleep. His own chamber lay down the passage. It was the same one he had shared with Eliad and Andreo, but Frintin and Gruel, the leader of the rifters he had saved fleeing to the Grotto, now occupied their pallets. Nicho still had an uneasy relationship with Gruel. The thought that he had knocked the rifter out cold continued to fill him with shame.

"What's the meeting about?" Nicho asked as they walked down the passage.

Rosa shrugged. "We'll have to go and find out, won't we?"

"Who else is going?"

"All the commanders, I hear. But anybody is welcome. Pearce isn't too pleased. Says he's got much to do before they leave for battle."

"Pearce?" Nicho looked up and thought he saw a slight flush on her cheeks. "Does he demean himself to talk to you?"

"We grew up together in the Gwyndorr slums. You know that, Nicho. You were there."

"I was much younger than the two of you. Still, I thought he'd forgotten about his days in the slums. Become a bit too high and mighty for us all." Nicho could not forgive Pearce for what he had done to Derry. Simple, good Derry would have followed Pearce to the Wailands if his brother had asked him to. He should never have taken him to the Grotto. To his death.

Rosa laughed. "Funny. That's exactly what he says about you."

"You're talking about me?" A sense of betrayal stabbed Nicho, and Rosa looked away for a moment. Rosa was one of his oldest friends. Back in the slums, she had risked much in allowing him to use her house to teach Parashi boys to read and write. He had rescued her son Simhew from certain death in the Rifter Gangs. They shared a history and an understanding. He didn't like having to share her with the likes of Pearce, who might well turn her against him.

When the conversation resumed, they found safer topics to talk about. Nicho told her how Jed had managed to find him in the stables and how the boy seemed to have a natural way with the horses. Rosa beamed with pride at the thought. How he valued that about her—that she could love the child of another like her own. He glanced at her as they entered the candlelit chamber where Mikel would address them. She was small and slight, built like a boy. Her short-cropped, dark hair added to the effect. He suspected he could have grown to love her with time, if Shara hadn't already stolen his heart.

"What?" She sensed his intense gaze.

"Nothing." He quickly looked away. The chamber brimmed with people. Pearce stood with the other commanders near the front. Nicho deliberately led Rosa in the other direction, finding them a seat on a bench between two of the other grooms.

"What's this meeting for?" he asked one of them. The man merely shrugged.

Voices quieted as the High Commander appeared at the entrance of the chamber. He was a tall, upright man with granite-grey hair and a face darkened by years in the sun, but there was a slowness in Mikel's step that Nicho had not noticed before. As the High Commander laid the book he carried on the table, Nicho saw the slight tremor in his hands.

Mikel looked up and let his eyes wander over the gathering. "My friends." The two simple words were laden with a lifetime of affection. "We stand on the cusp of war. Tomorrow our Warriors leave to fight the king's army. Fear has crept through our walls. I sense it in the cries of the children and the anxious looks of the women. Even the bravado of our men masks it." Mikel looked over at Pearce and the other commanders, and Nicho saw the ire on Pearce's face. "How do I know this, you ask? I know it because I feel the fear in my very bones. Some of you will deny it, and others will use it to fuel your hatred," again his glance seemed to find Pearce, "but let me tell you that I have found something to overcome it. Faith." Mikel flipped open the first page of the book and as he did so, Nicho sensed the shimmer of gold in the air. He knew instantly that it was Tabeal, even before the bird alighted on the book. The crowd gasped in wonder.

"It's the bird you called with that reed pipe." Rosa's whisper was filled with awe.

Nicho was already on his feet, pushing forward, intent on reaching the bird. Warmth pulsed into his chest. She seemed to be drawing him to her, and he went willingly until he stood a mere pace away from Mikel and the Gold Breast.

"Nicho," Mikel said softly. "I believe you two are already acquainted."

"What brought her here?"

"The book. And," he looked a little abashed, "my desperation."

"Yes." Nicho smiled, remembering the bird coming in his own dire situations. "Desperation does that. Is that . . . ?"

". . . the same book you and Shara brought with you. Eliad made a copy of it for us."

Nicho remembered Mikel showing it to him on the day he arrived back at the Grotto. "But I thought you couldn't decipher the script?"

"I can't. But I still have the sense that the Gold Breast wants me to try and read it, so let's see what happens." He looked up and spoke to the crowd. "My friends, this book is no ordinary book. It tells us about the past while showing the path to the future. It is a book of hope, and hope is just what we need in these dark times. So tonight I will read it, and every night following from this one."

There was a stir of excitement amongst the people. The Parashi loved stories. Nicho well remembered the ones his mother had told him as a boy.

"And this is how it begins . . ."

The words that came from Mikel's lips were strange and beautiful, and Nicho could see the looks of confusion on the faces around him. But he had known Tabeal longer than they had and so he closed his eyes, listening deeply, letting the words take him towards her and fill his mind until finally the pictures began to come.

He flew, higher than an eagle. Below him was a landscape of breath-stealing beauty—hills and valleys, rivers and villages. In the distance he could see high mountains covered in snow, and he sensed that this was where the journey would lead him—towards the royal citadel nestled in the mountain heights.

CHAPTER 4

That first day on the poison tree path stretched on and on. The monotony of that straight path, the pervading silence, and the dark denseness of the forest wall pressing in so close on both sides made Shara want to scream.

At times the path was a little wider and allowed all three of them to walk abreast. She would walk in the center then, as far away from the forest wall as she could get. Only Andreo's delight at all he saw broke that long day. He pointed out flowers and leaves growing on the side of the path, and the larger poison trees' buttress roots, which came almost up to Shara's waist. She tried to imagine a young child crawling through the forest to find these trees, tried to imagine the fear and desperation that the rifters must feel. No wonder so few of them returned. This forest might steal your mind as quickly as it stole your body.

Some time during that day, her thoughts turned to Nicho. What had become of him on his quest to save Derry's son, Jed? Had Randin captured him? If so, he might be a rifter in this very forest. Only now that she was free from the Dusk Dreamer's power could she allow herself to feel a tingle of grief at the love she had lost. Shame. Regret. Now grief. Perhaps such feelings were better than no feelings at all, than the numbness the power rock had cast her into these last few weeks. Would she ever feel something light and lovely again?

It was a strange day trudging along that soundless path, with no sense of where they were going or how far they had come.

Even Andreo finally fell silent under the cold oppressiveness of the Rif'twine. The small piece of sky they could see above them was reddening to dusk when they finally stopped to bed down for the night on a wide part of the path. Somehow Andreo managed to light a fire, and they huddled around it for comfort and warmth. When starlight had replaced the last glow of the sun, Tabeal suddenly appeared.

Eliad let out a throaty laugh. "I was wondering when we could start." He lifted the book and began to unwrap the covering.

Shara felt a small flutter of anticipation. "We're finally starting?"

He nodded as he turned past the first page, which Andreo had translated all that time ago. Shara could still remember the words:

This is the true story of Ajalon, the Great Kingdom, before it was split in two by the evil forces of Taus. It also tells of Tirragyl and the deception that Taus wove on this beautiful land. And of the great crimes committed against the King of Ajalon. I, Eliad, have written this in my own hand from the border pool in the Rif'twine Forest overlooking Gwyndorr, where you will find me on this day.

On the next page, Eliad's finger fell on the first word. He smiled, as if remembering. Then he began to read. The fire sizzled and hissed over the sound of his voice, and Shara had to lean in to hear the words. They sounded beautiful and strange to her ears, like the haunting music she had once heard a group of Warriors sing at the Grotto. She had not understood the lyrics of their song, as she did not understand these words. She only knew—in a deep part of herself—that the Warriors' words had been as lovely as the words Eliad now read.

She did not want the words to stop, but did Eliad know she could not understand them? Before she could interrupt, Eliad paused his reading and spoke softly. "They are heart-words, Shara. Close your eyes. Don't listen with your ears. Listen with the deepest part of yourself."

Shara closed her eyes and let the stream of words wash over her. Still they made no sense, but she stopped trying to understand them and, instead, relished in their beauty.

She opened her eyes in surprise. The words were forming pictures in her head. Had Eliad switched to speaking Tirragylin?

He was watching her, a smile on the corners of his mouth. "Now you are really listening. Let us start again."

She closed her eyes and let the words into her heart, where something remarkable began to happen. No longer were there mere images in her mind. She now heard sounds around her, felt the wind on her face, smelled freshness on the air, so different than the air in the Rif'twine. The words of the book, imbued with Old Magic, took her to another place.

She was flying, as an eagle would, over a landscape of incredible beauty. In the distance she saw snow-capped mountains while—below her—green hills and valleys took shape. A river wound lazily through darker green tree groves. Small villages were nestled in the folds of the valleys and along the river. Was this Ajalon, the kingdom the first page of the book mentioned?

Her journey continued towards the mountains. She was now closer to the ground, and she could see small figures tilling the earth or leading sheep to pasture. Children splashed in the river, where women were washing brightly colored clothes. On the wind she could hear snatches of singing and laughing, and she yearned to stop to speak to them or join them in their simple pursuits. But she did not have the power to stop. She could merely observe as she flew on in the warm sunlight towards the distant peaks.

After a while the landscape changed. She could now see craggy outcrops and deeper valleys where faster rivers carved out the earth. Here there were fewer villages, but she saw animals: an antelope with magnificent horns, deftly climbing to higher ground; a leopard lying on a rocky platform; rabbits scurrying for cover below her; a large grubear. The beauty she saw filled her with a carefree lightness—that feeling she had thought lost forever.

Finally, a magnificent palace appeared in her view. It was large, built of white marble, and—although it was bright—it had the warm glow of white cliffs at sunset. Perfectly symmetrical turrets reached gracefully upwards from a towering edifice, and she could see, from her aerial view, that it was built on many layers and that it contained multiple courtyards with fountains and gardens. The large gate was open wide in welcome.

She was suddenly no longer in the air, but standing in one of the courtyards. She could hear music and clapping coming from inside the palace. It was the joyful, fast music she associated with a wedding feast, music that made one's feet tap. Shara was moving towards it now, eager to see what lay inside the walls.

Through the entrance, she stopped in surprise. The large space was alive with people, all dressed in the same bright colors she had seen earlier. They appeared to be standing roughly in a circle, and each one of them was clapping and laughing, eyes straining towards the center. The musicians—with fiddles, tambourines, and flutes—were part of the same circle. They swayed as they played their joyful tune. A lone voice, deep and beautiful, carried the melody. Again Shara found herself longing to stop and be a part of this jubilant group. Instead she had the strange sensation of passing, completely unawares, among them, until she stood inside the circle.

Her eyes immediately found the tall man at the center. He had olive skin and a mass of thick black hair. Behind his full beard, teeth flashed with laughter, and his dark-brown eyes conveyed the same joy. He clapped his hands to the fast beat, while his legs seemed to move effortlessly in a complicated pattern that involved jumping, kicking, and spinning. For such a tall man, he danced with great style. With him in the circle were five children: four girls and one boy. The older three girls danced around the man gracefully and with obvious enjoyment. The younger boy and girl were holding hands and spinning around wildly, narrowly missing the others. Every one of their faces held an expression of complete delight.

"Come, Abba." The shrill voice of the smallest girl could be heard over the music. She let go her grip of the boy and tugged at the hands of an older man standing on the edge of the circle. "Come dance with us."

It was this man who had been singing, Shara realized, surprised. Not the tall man in the center. Yet this older man stood as tall as the one dancing inside the circle. In fact, other than the grey in his hair, he clearly resembled the other man. He allowed the girl to pull him into the circle as a loud roar of approval rose from the crowd. He laughed as the girl stepped on his feet, and he held her close and led her in a three-step dance.

Suddenly the music faltered. The clapping and laughter grew softer until it was all but quenched, and only a muted whisper swept through the crowd.

The two men stopped dancing and turned, as one, to focus on the opening that had formed in the crowd. Someone was pushing towards them. The older girls had stopped too, their eyes on the advancing man. Only the youngest boy was still spinning around, seemingly oblivious to the sudden change in mood. Finally he, too, halted, somewhat dizzily, to cast a wary look at the approaching man.

The man sank onto his left knee.

"Your Majesty," he said, addressing the older man. His head rose momentarily to look at the younger man, before dropping back down. "Prince E'shua."

"Greetings, Taus," the older man said. "Rise."

Taus stood. Shara wanted to study him. Was this the same Taus who she had been taught to revere for so long? But she found it hard to take her eyes off the older man, who she now understood to be the King of Ajalon. Everything about the king drew her gaze: his height—despite his age, he stood a head taller than Taus; his voice—deep and commanding; his eyes—full of laughter and a quiet knowing. In comparison, Taus seemed ordinary. He had a well-formed, handsome face, but on it was none of the laughter and joy that seemed so befitting of this castle. There was not even a hint of a smile as he spoke.

"My liege, I have come to report on the state of your security."

"Can this wait, my friend, till our council meeting tonight?"

"I think not, Your Majesty. I regret, of course, having to interrupt your . . . activities." He cast a disparaging glance at the children, who watched the interchange from just inside the circle.

"I will meet you in the council chamber. Let me call the elders together, and you can give us your report."

"I think it better if we meet alone, my liege."

"As you wish, Taus. E'shua and I will meet with you alone." The king sounded tired.

Taus's eyes flicked briefly towards the prince and, for a moment, Shara thought he would object to the prince's inclusion in the meeting, but he merely inclined his head in the direction of the king and said softly, "As you wish, Your Majesty."

The king's attention swept back to the children as Taus bowed in retreat.

"Well, aren't you all something?" He gathered the smallest girl into his big arms and swung her over his head. "Where did you all learn to dance like that?"

"Yana taught us," the boy shouted, holding out his arms for a turn to be picked up.

"Yana taught you? Isn't she too old to dance?" He swung the delighted boy high over his head now. "Yana even taught me how to dance, and you can imagine how long ago that was."

The older girls giggled at this, and the king winked playfully at them as he put the boy down.

"More, more!" the boy complained.

"Later, Aron. Run back to Yana in the nursery. E'shua and I must go see Taus now."

The children and crowd dispersed, and Shara followed the king and prince to the council chamber. She briefly wondered if they sensed her there, but then she remembered that the words had brought her here. She was seeing history—more vivid and real than she could ever have imagined—through the pages of the book, but she was not really living it as the king, prince, and Taus were.

Taus was already pacing the council chamber. At the men's entrance, he again dipped into a bow, but the king waved his hand with impatience.

"Be at ease, Taus." He beckoned Taus to sit at the long table as he took his place at the head, the prince seated to his right. "Tell me what you came for."

"My liege," Taus started, "in the last two months, I have organized all of Ajalon's men of fighting age into units. At your command, they can be called to take up arms within a day."

The king did not respond immediately, merely studying Taus's face as if he were seeing it for the very first time. The tiredness was back in his voice as he said, "The last time we spoke, I only commanded you to take a census of men, both young and old. What you have done was not part of my instruction."

"But at that meeting we discussed the need to increase the size of the army at your disposal, Your Majesty."

"You discussed it, Taus." The prince spoke for the first time. His voice had the same rich timbre as his father's. "The council agreed it was not necessary."

Taus's eyes narrowed as he looked at the prince. "It is a short-sighted approach." His voice carried a hint of menace. "We are a great kingdom, and there are many dangers against us."

"I think there are many more dangers within us," the king said, and Shara saw Taus flush.

"I hope you do not doubt my allegiance to you . . . both, my liege?" he said softly.

"E'shua and I have never given you anything less than our full trust, Taus. You know well that, aside from E'shua, you hold the most power of anyone in Ajalon. I would not have raised you to this position if I did not believe you to be capable and worthy of it."

"I was merely concerned about your security, my liege."

"Concerned with my security or your own power, Taus?"

In the silence that followed, Shara understood that the chasm of unspoken words between these men had formed long before this disagreement.

Taus finally spoke. "What would you have me do now, Your Majesty?"

The king sighed and ran his hand over his thick beard, his eyes never wavering from Taus's face. "My friend, I do not want to lose your counsel, but I will not tolerate your constant undermining."

Taus shifted uncomfortably at these last words and started to interject, but the king held up his right hand for silence and continued to speak.

"Too many times lately you have clearly gone against my commands, acting solely in your own interests and not for the benefit of Ajalon." The king pushed himself to his feet, towering over the still-seated Taus. "It is time, Taus, for you to decide. Are you with us or against us? You cannot be both."

The room started to fade. Shara fought against it, willing herself to stay there, desperate to hear Taus's response. But Eliad had stopped reading, and the silence carried Shara back to the path. She blinked, so fully in the other world that it was strange to be back in her own. She saw that the fire had burnt low—only a few glowing embers remained—and wondered how long they had been in the world of the book.

Her eyes sought out Eliad.

"Was that Ajalon?"

"Yes."

"And the king and prince? And Taus?"

"Indeed."

"And what happened after that?"

A smile crept onto Eliad's face. "To discover that we would have to keep reading, wouldn't we? It grows late. The telling will continue tomorrow."

CHAPTER 5

The tip of the sword found its mark on Elxa's heart.

"You are losing your touch, cousin," Klyden said, triumphantly flicking his sword away. "You lost your balance and didn't recover."

Nyla watched the two Charab men from the doorway of the cottage. Since Elxa's arrival on Azab Rock a few weeks ago, Nyla had been a constant witness to the two men's interaction and teasing. The family resemblance was obvious. They both had green eyes and dark hair and were well-built from years of weapons training. Elxa, younger by mere months, was shorter. His face was rounder, nothing like Klyden's handsome, chiseled features. But both men had the same quiet intensity and confidence.

Elxa winced. "What can I say? You win one and lose another."

"But always win the ones that count," the two men said in unison, with almost identical wry smiles.

"Another one of your tribe's proverbs?" Nyla asked. The men had an endless trove of sayings that she was not privy to.

"Indeed." Klyden sheaved his sword. "The Charab have one for every possible occasion."

"Especially ones that involve fighting." Elxa chortled.

Nyla turned away. There was something about watching the two men's close bond that left her feeling bereft. Initially she had thought it came from being the outsider—a woman and, even worse, their queen. They treated her with the distance and deference due a sovereign. Elxa even insisted on addressing her as "Your Majesty" despite her early requests for him to simply call her Nyla.

But it was more than that. Watching Klyden and Elxa's close connection churned up uncomfortable memories. Times when she and her twin brother Alexor had laughed at something that only the two of them understood. Other times when—as youngsters—they wrestled or played with wooden swords or, in later years, raced each other on horseback up the hills outside Lydora. Nyla fought to push these memories down because every one of them brought a fresh wave of pain, like fire in her chest. The very brother she loved so dearly had turned on her. Under the influence of Lord Lucian, Alexor had condemned her to death. He had stood impassively in the Adriel River as they drowned her, waiting for her portion of their shared soul to reach him. She could see his expression now. Cold. Distant.

"Is everything fine, Nyla?" Klyden had slipped into the cottage without her noticing.

"Yes."

"I will visit my father's tomb today. Elxa agreed to stay with you."

"Are you sure?" She glanced out the door to where the younger man was sharpening his sword. "You've never left me alone with him. He is an assassin after all."

"You may recall that is my background too?"

"It's different. Mada tasked you with keeping me safe. He came to kill you . . . or is your memory so short?"

"Not by choice. He was under the curse of Taus. I was his assignment."

"Well, maybe you still are," she said belligerently. "And maybe I am too. The Charab are after all under the control of King Alexor, are they not? The very man trying to kill me?"

The Charab had been the assassins of the Royal House since Taus first invaded Tirragyl. Once a royal messenger spoke the arming word, the Charab were compelled to obey their every command. Elxa had been commanded to kill Klyden and his sister, Lohlyn.

"For Elxa, the curse was broken the day he met the Gold Breast," Klyden said evenly.

"So you say. Pity this bird didn't stay around to change me too.

I heard Elxa's threats when he landed on the beach. I'm not quite as sure as you that people can change in the single beat of a heart."

"I will stay if you wish, Nyla."

"No." The deference in his voice annoyed her. "If you trust him, I will have to trust him too."

"I do. With my life."

A short while later, Nyla watched Klyden stride down the path that led to the beach and the forest where his father was buried. When they first arrived, he had made the pilgrimage almost every week, but he had not done so since Elxa came. Perhaps he, too, had not fully trusted his cousin, despite his words of assurance.

"Have you been to my uncle's tomb, Your Majesty?" Elxa asked from the courtyard.

"Just once. I felt like an intruder."

"They were always a close-knit family, even as children. Lohlyn, Klyden and their father. Theirs was a special bond."

He turned back to his sword. That was one thing she had come to know, and appreciate, about the Charab men—they were comfortable with silence. Nyla walked around the cottage to the tall sapling, pulling out the curved knife that Klyden had given her on their escape from her execution. She carved another deep notch into the tree.

"How many are there?"

She spun around. "Festering figs! You scared me."

"Sorry, Your Majesty." An apologetic smile flickered at the corners of Elxa's mouth. "We are trained to be quiet."

"Klyden does it all the time too." She fingered the notches—four groups of ten, and now another four. "Forty-four," she said. Forty-four days on Azab Rock, cut off from her kingdom and people and everything she had vowed to serve and protect. When they first came to the island, she had found the seclusion comforting. Now a deep restlessness was growing inside her.

"It's just a season, Your Majesty. You will return to your throne." Perceptiveness was another quality the Charab seemed to teach their children.

How could she ever return while Alexor sat on the throne, wishing her dead so that their shared soul could be united in his body?

"My uncle used to say, 'Time wears even the sharpest stones into pebbles,'" Elxa continued.

"Meaning?" she snapped.

"It takes time for things to be put right. For the rough edges of rocks to be smoothed in a riverbed. For evil to be overthrown by good. But eventually it does."

"You obviously didn't know my grandfather. Or my father. And now . . . ," she swallowed, ". . . now my brother. I'm not sure good ever overthrows evil. Evil always seems to prevail."

He bowed his head as if her answer weighed him down. The Charab still seemed uncomfortable to express an opinion different than her own.

"You have something to say? You know you may speak your mind freely."

"Yes, Your Majesty." He took a deep, steadying breath. "Until a month ago, I lived under the shadow of that evil. It forced me to do terrible things."

"Lohlyn, you mean?" It gave her a surprising amount of pleasure to see him flinch at the name. Klyden had told her how Elxa had cut her lady-in-waiting off the fire pole and finished her slow, painful execution with his own blade. He had almost managed to make it sound like a noble deed.

"Amongst other things."

"She was more than my lady-in-waiting and protector, Elxa. She was my only true friend."

"I know." His head was bowed again. "I am sorry, Your Majesty."

"So you *murdered* my best friend—your cousin. And still you think good triumphs over evil?"

"Yes." His gaze was steady. "Only good could overcome the power of that wicked curse. And the Gold Breast overcame it."

"Pity this so-called Gold Breast doesn't work for Highborn royalty."

"I suspect she doesn't really work for anyone. But she does . . . meet with you. If you allow it."

"I suppose we'll never know." Nyla waved her hand in a dismissal, and Elxa left her alone by the tree. She stood there for a very long time, gazing out over the dark waters that separated her from her kingdom. Elxa's words swirled through her mind. *Time will wear even the sharpest stones into pebbles.* How long did it take for a jagged rock to become a smooth pebble, she wondered. Far longer than a single lifetime. Far longer than Nyla cared to spend on this forsaken island.

A messenger gull from the mainland was waiting for Klyden when he returned from his father's grave. He broke open one of the closed mussel shells he had picked up on the beach that day and fed the bird the smooth morsel as he slipped the message from the case on its neck. Nowl's small, neat letters filled the tiny page.

> *King and Lord L attack Guardian Grotto. Mystery man*
> *asks questions in village. Perhaps he seeks queen? N.*

Ever since Elxa had found them on the island, Klyden had begun to question whether this was a good hiding place. If Elxa could track them down here, so could others. And as he had learned, the sea, which in many ways kept them safe, could also hem them in. Azab Rock had been a sanctuary for him, Lohlyn, and their father, and he had thought it could be that for Nyla too. But perhaps he had been foolish. Didn't his father's tomb prove that the island could be discovered and penetrated? His uncle, the new Charabian, had found it. Elxa had found it again. Ultimately the king would find it too.

The fact that the king's attention was elsewhere was a good thing, but could it be that he still had men scouting for Nyla? Klyden returned to the cottage that night feeling restless.

After dinner, Nyla retired to the room that used to be Lohlyn's. Klyden and Elxa made a small fire outside. This had become part of their routine. Occasionally Nyla would join them, but she often claimed tiredness and left the two of them to stare into the flickering flames and reminisce about their past. Klyden liked this time. It was something the Charab had always done. Every night, their tight-knit community came together around a large fire, to talk and sing songs and tell stories.

"Do you remember Uncle Swen?" Klyden asked after the two of them had stared silently at the flames for some time.

"By the blade! I haven't thought of him in a long time. He disappeared when we were but boys."

"I remember him well. My mother always said Swen was too soft for the Charab's harsh world, that the curse was too heavy on his slight shoulders."

"He was rather . . . unstable. I even remember him crying."

Klyden smiled. "Not something Charab men did."

"What made you think of him?"

"Just wondering where he went."

"The older boys thought he threw himself off the bridge."

"I don't think so," Klyden answered. "I was there on the night he left. He came to speak to my father. Said that if he didn't leave right then the curse would crush him alive."

"He should have known the curse follows you wherever you go." Remorse laced Elxa's words. "You can't escape it."

"My father said something strange, which I've been thinking about lately." Klyden's gaze followed the course of some rising sparks as they fled the fire. "He said there was a place that *might* be free from the curse's power. From the Rif'twine's dark magic. From death itself."

"Yes?"

"The tunnels of the Ruin Rim Mountains. Apparently there is a series of deep tunnels stretching all the way to the northeastern peaks."

"And they are free of dark magic? Somewhere the curse has no power?"

"It's what my father said. He gave Swen a rock. Said it was the key to the tunnels. One of only two, passed down from one Charabian to the next. All the way from Chaorlin himself."

"If this is true, why would the Charabians keep this to themselves? We could have gone to live there in freedom."

Klyden shrugged. "A freedom of sorts. But with no daylight or blue sky. My father said they were never meant as a home, only as a passageway. But it was Swen's one and only chance to live."

"What made you remember these tunnels, Kly?"

"I've been thinking where I could take Nyla. I don't think she is safe here." Klyden picked up a long stick and used it to push back a branch that had fallen out of the fire. "There was a message from Nowl. He says there is a man in the village asking questions about the queen."

"What kind of questions?"

"He doesn't say. But Nowl is worried."

Elxa was quiet for a while and then said, "This is a good place, Kly. Not easy to penetrate."

"Your father did." Klyden looked up at his cousin. "So did you."

"We are Charab, not merely king's soldiers. And," Elxa added softly, "we were under the power of the arming word."

"I know." Klyden wished he could have kept the hurt from his words. Yet the sight of his father's tomb was fresh in his mind. His father would still be alive if Elxa's father had not tracked him to the island. "All I'm saying is that it's hard to run from an island that is under attack."

"So you plan to take the queen to the tunnels?"

"Maybe, but not right away. I think we are safe for a while longer. The king's attention appears to be elsewhere. Nowl's message says he attacks the Guardian Grotto."

Elxa looked up in surprise. "The Grotto? It's part of the legend of our people."

"The base of the resistance. From which Chaorlin and Rabnin operated before Taus captured them."

"It's never been found. Is there still a resistance there?"

"Our distant Parashi cousins appear to still have a presence there."

"Why does the king attack it? Do you think he suspects you took the queen there?"

Klyden sniggered. "If he does, he obviously doesn't know how little love there is between the Parashi and the Charab. The Grotto is the last place a Charab would run to."

"Little love!" Elxa said. "They hate us. Think us on the side of the Highborn king."

"Well, yes." Klyden smiled wryly. "Being the king's assassins does make one some enemies."

CHAPTER 6

On their second day in the Rif'twine, Shara awoke to find Andreo gone.

"Eliad!" She shook the old man awake. "Andreo's gone." Eliad mumbled something incomprehensible and turned away from her. "Eliad!"

Only now did he wake up fully, looking first at her and then to the place where Andreo had lain. "Gone?"

"Yes, gone."

"But," Eliad looked around, "where could he have gone? There's nowhere . . ."

Just then Shara heard the notes of a familiar tune. Andreo appeared on the path, whistling cheerfully as if he were walking through the streets of Gwyndorr rather than in the middle of an evil forest. He was carrying leaves and roots and some relatively dry branches.

"Ah! Time the two of you woke up." He dropped the objects on the ground. "I'm about to make some breakfast."

"Where did you find all that, Andreo?" Eliad asked. "Didn't I warn you to stay on the path?"

"I always had at least one foot on the path, my friend. I had to walk some way but found a patch of grifling leaves growing right along the edge of the path. Makes a very nutritious tea."

"I remember," Eliad said with a slight grimace. "Bitter, but good for you."

"And the roots?" Shara asked.

"It's something the rifters boil and eat," Andreo said. "They call it *muus*. Their staple diet other than the scant supplies they are sent from Gwyndorr."

"It's pretty good actually." Eliad squeezed her shoulder. "You're going to eat a lot of it in the next while, so try to enjoy it."

Shara didn't draw much comfort from the grin that passed between the two men.

The muus and grifling tea turned out to taste much worse than she had even imagined, yet she forced as much of both down as she could because they were a source of warmth. The two men actually seemed to enjoy the meal.

"It grows on you," Andreo said, chewing on the stringy root.

"Somewhat like a fungus." Eliad laughed, washing away his last bite of food with the astringent tea.

That day, they kept up a steady pace through the forest, and by the time the gloom turned into darkness, they had settled down again around a fire. Andreo had found some fairly appetizing mushrooms during the day, which tasted surprisingly good compared to their earlier meal.

Now, Eliad opened the book again and began to read. This time Shara didn't struggle to allow the lilting words into her heart, and again she found herself in a world that felt startlingly more real than her own.

Oil lamps, hanging from hooks, cast long, dancing shadows on the stone walls. Shara was moving down a passage towards the sound of soft voices. She felt the cool air wrap around her as somebody pushed past in the same direction. She followed this cloaked figure into a dimly lit chamber where several men and women were huddled in conversation.

"Friends, please take a seat."

She recognized the king's voice instantly, and as the men and women sat down, she realized that she was in the same council chamber where the king, prince, and Taus had met. As her eyes adjusted to the low light, she could see the king and prince sitting in the same seats as earlier. Around the table she counted ten others: five men and five women.

"*Thank you for coming so quickly, my friends. It is a matter of utmost urgency. I would never have called you at this hour if it were not,*" the king started.

The voices had grown quiet. All eyes were on the king.

There was a very long pause before he spoke again. "*A rider came in less than an hour ago with news from my army commander, General Ga'abri. He sent word that a large number of his men have deserted.*" A murmur of disbelief rippled through the group of elders. "*He is counting exactly how many men are gone, but he estimates it to be about a quarter.*" Again there was a startled response from the seated men and women. "*It appears that they have taken a large cache of weapons with them—swords, bows, arrows. Even a wall-breaker.*"

A thin, elderly man voiced the collective shock of the gathered elders. "*My liege, how is this possible?*"

"*I know, Bedan. This is a blow to us all.*" The king's face was shadowed, but his voice sounded steady and strong.

"*There is one more thing.*" Finally his voice wavered, and Shara could hear the aching sadness in the words he spoke next. "*Taus is behind it. He has turned against us and taken many with him.*"

"*No, my liege!*" Bedan said, and the others loudly echoed his disbelief. "*It is not possible.*"

"*He wouldn't, Your Majesty.*"

The king allowed them to speak before he drew them back to silence and continued.

"*I have known for some time that Taus did not agree with many of my decisions. In the last while, he has even gone directly against my commands. But even I did not know just how deep his rebellion went.*"

The king rose, pushed aside his chair, and walked behind the elders, down the length of the table. He stopped when he reached Bedan and rested his hands on the old man's shoulders in a reassuring gesture.

"*A few days ago, Taus came to tell me that he had enlisted men into a people's army. This was so clearly against my instructions that I started to question his motives. I realized then that Taus is hungry for power. He wants my throne.*"

It was again Bedan that objected. "*My liege, you are accusing him of treason. This is not the Taus I know.*"

The king's tone was gentle. "Bedan, I know you have treated Taus as your own son. You have taught him much. You love him." He crouched down next to the old man now, eye-to-eye with him. "I love him too, Bedan. I saw all his potential and wanted to give him so much more. It's what makes his betrayal so painful."

The king straightened. He looked around, meeting the eyes of each person sitting at the table. "I told Taus to choose, and he did. I will ask each one of you the same question. Are you with us, or are you against us?"

A short man with dark hair and a close-cropped beard was the first to rise. Shara had the peculiar feeling that she had seen the face before.

"I am with you and Prince E'shua, my liege. To the death."

The king acknowledged these words with a smile and a slight nod. The next elder was already on her feet. One by one they pledged their loyalty to the king and prince, until only Bedan was still seated.

"Bedan?" the king asked gently.

There were silent tears running down the old man's face as he twisted around to look at the king. He pushed himself to his feet with some diffi-culty and stepped towards the king. He slowly sank down in front of him, gripping his ankles. The tears had turned into deep sobs now, which took some time to subside. When he eventually had control of his voice, he said, "You do not even have to ask, my liege. I am yours. Only yours."

The meeting continued, with the king, prince, and their council planning how best to fend off the threat of Taus and his rebels. Most of the elders recommended attacking the rebel army before they had time to organize and possibly garner support from their western neighbors. The prince, however, prevailed on the council to extend one chance for the rebel soldiers to return to the king's army.

Another messenger from the general arrived with confirmation that Taus was leading the rebel army and that they were moving rapidly in a southeastern direction. He also gave the exact number of men who had deserted. It was worse than they had thought. Almost a third of the army had followed Taus, and it appeared that many of Taus's recently enlisted "people's army" had also joined the rebels. The general estimated Taus's army to be over three thousand strong.

Additional oil lamps were called for, and a large map was brought out and laid flat on the table. The king, prince and elders leaned in to pore over it, and Shara had the strange sensation that she was now hovering above their heads, for she had a clear view of the map of Ajalon and its surrounding countries. In all the time that Andreo had tutored her, she had never come across the country called Ajalon. Her eyes were drawn to the southern part of the map, where a name caught her eye. The Rhorhan Sea. How was it possible? The Rhorhan Sea surrounded Tirragyl to the east and south, but if it was the same sea as on the map, wouldn't the land seem more familiar to her?

She was so absorbed in trying to understand the map that she did not follow the heated discussion of the council. Her attention was only brought back by the prince's finger punching down at a point on the map and his steady voice saying, "I believe they are heading for our southeastern province."

"But they will be trapped if they go there. It is surrounded by the sea on two sides and the mountains on the other," one of the women said.

Shara stared at the same point on the map, trying to make sense of what she saw. The town names were different, but she could have sworn that the shape of the coast was that of Tirragyl.

Now she recognized the islands in the Rhorhan Sea that were trade partners to Tirragyl, and a jutting peninsula to the southwest that was part of the Enderite Kingdom. Once she had absorbed these familiar geographic features, her eyes moved back to the north for she had never before seen this area depicted on a Tirragylin map. On all the maps Andreo had shown them, the Rif'twine was the northern border of Tirragyl, and since it was impassable, no one had ever determined what lay beyond it. Yet here, spread before her, lay a map that showed that Tirragyl was part of a much larger kingdom: Ajalon. There was something beyond what they knew. Shara felt excitement surge through her at this staggering discovery.

Ajalon was at least ten times larger than Tirragyl itself, and the Enderite Kingdom, too, appeared to be part of a much larger country. Shara's eyes roved hungrily over the map, taking in the names of towns, rivers, and mountains, trying to commit them to memory.

She wanted to object when the hands that had held the map flat started to roll it up again. She needed more time—a day or even a week—to absorb every part of it.

The discussion between the king, prince, and the elders seemed to have concluded, for they were leaving the council chamber in pairs or groups of threes, speaking in low, serious tones. Each of them had been assigned a task, and Shara berated herself for not paying more careful attention to the discussion.

Eventually only the king and Bedan remained.

"And me, my king. What do you want me to do?"

"Tell me about Taus, Bedan. You knew him better than anybody else."

"I do not know him at all," Bedan's voice was heavy with sorrow, "for I would not have thought him capable of this treachery."

"Many are capable of treachery. They deceive themselves that they are right and the person they betray is wrong."

"You have never wronged him, my king." The king was silent as Bedan continued to speak. "What I do not understand is how he could convince the other men to join him in this rebellion. What could they possibly have against you? Ajalon is a place where life is good, a place of peace."

"He told them lies about me. Maybe he promised them possessions or positions of power."

Bedan nodded wearily. "I am so sorry, my liege."

The king grasped him firmly around his shoulders. "Bedan, just because you loved him and treated him as a son does not make you responsible for the path he chooses."

"If only I had—"

"No," the king interrupted. "He has chosen for himself, just as you chose today. You could not have changed that. Love does not always break through to a prideful heart."

The older man's head dropped down, and his shoulders shook as silent sobs again racked his body. The king drew him into a tight embrace.

Shara looked away, feeling as if she had no right to witness this tender, personal moment. Unlike before, she was relieved when the room started to fade even though, surprisingly, she could still hear Eliad's voice. The words were now a soft, steady stream of sorrow, forming new images in her mind. Individual scenes flowed and mingled together, as if she were watching them all simultaneously. It reminded her of sitting in Marai's kitchen with the scullery maids all speaking at once. However, unlike in the kitchen, she could give each encounter her complete attention, as if she were completely present in them all.

She was in a stable where a smith was shoeing several horses. She was also in a cottage where a middle-aged man opened the door to a stern-looking soldier bringing news of his son's desertion. She was in the same cottage as the man comforted his crying wife. She was in the castle as the prince embraced the boy he had danced with and promised him that he would return again soon. She was in a lush green garden with a weeping man who she recognized as Bedan.

The words now did more than show her the people. They reached deeper than they had before, for she felt the father's shock of disappointment in his son, the fear of a little boy watching someone he loved going to battle, and the anger and loss from a friend's betrayal. Never before had she experienced another person's pain as if it were her own and, although she wanted to close herself off from their heartache, she could not. The words and emotions kept flowing.

Finally, just as she thought the pain would extinguish her very life, the words and images faded.

She found herself back in the forest with Eliad and Andreo. The words of the book had wrapped sorrow around them, and they sat in silence by their fire that night, until the tiredness claimed them.

CHAPTER 7

"Do you feel it too, Nicho?" Rosa asked. "How life in the Grotto feels . . . both dangerous but strangely . . . hopeful at the same time?"

Nicho was helping Jed lace his shoes, but he paused and looked up at his friend.

"Yes. Dangerous because only Pearce and his men stand between us and the king's army. But hopeful because of Tabeal and the book?"

"Sometimes I don't know if I should be cowering in fear or twirling in anticipation. It's the strangest feeling."

Nicho nodded. "Almost as if darkness is closing in on us, but we're closer than ever to the light."

"I do it." Jed pulled his other foot away and clumsily tugged at the laces.

"Look, Jed." Nicho guided his small hands. "You can make a loop with this hand. And another one with this. And then tie them in a knot. See?" He undid it again. "Now you try."

The boy bit his tongue in concentration but, with a bit of help from Nicho, finally managed a lopsided bow. He flashed a triumphant smile.

"Well done, Jed!" Warmth spread through Nicho's chest at that innocent smile. He glanced up at Rosa and the joy on her face told him she had seen it too.

"I do yours," Jed announced, pouncing onto Nicho's shoes.

"Good idea. You need practice," Nicho said indulgently as the boy worked on his laces.

"You know what the High Commander read last night? About Ajalon's king telling the elders about Taus's betrayal?" Rosa said.

"Yes?"

"Do you think that really happened? Or is it just a story someone made up. A myth? Like our mothers and the loretellers used to tell us?"

Nicho mulled over the words as Jed tied an awkward knot in his laces. "I don't know how it is for you, Rosa. But when the High Commander reads, it's as if I'm in that world. It feels more real than anything I've ever seen or heard."

"I suppose. But it could still be something the Gold Breast is conjuring in our minds. The way a dream sometimes feels real."

"Yes. Maybe. Still . . ." Nicho stretched out his other shoe to Jed. "It's also how valuable the book seems. How the Gold Breast led Shara and me to it. How Eliad used to speak of it. It had significance even before I'd heard a single word of it."

"It's just that Pearce . . . you know that first night when he was still here? After the High Commander had read, Pearce told me that he thought it was all nonsense. A distraction that Mikel had devised to keep everyone occupied while the enemy crept up on us."

Nicho snorted. "Typical Pearce!"

"Don't say that, Nicho. You know he was leaving the next day to fight the High Commander's battle for him, and—"

"The High Commander's battle?" Nicho interrupted. "Since when is it only his battle? It's all of our battle."

A flush rose on Rosa's cheeks. "Well, Pearce thought the High Commander should be leading all the Warriors and confronting King Alexor once and for all. He thought it rather cowardly for him to hide in the Grotto while an enemy approached."

"Cowardly? You know the High Commander is no coward!"

Rosa shrugged.

"He couldn't leave the Grotto unprotected. The women. The children." He lowered his voice, glancing over at Jed, who had lost interest in the laces and was now attempting to construct a house from the straw of the sleeping pallet. "You know how valuable the Guardian Rock is? What would happen if it fell into the king's hands?"

"I'm just telling you what Pearce said," Rosa said defensively. "And he's a real Warrior. He knows something about warfare, doesn't he?"

"A *real* Warrior?" Now it was Nicho's turn to flush with anger. "You mean not just a mere groom?"

"That's not what I said." Rosa stood up and grabbed the oil lamp. "Sometimes I wish you would be the Nicho I knew in Gwyndorr. At least there you didn't react every time I mentioned Pearce's name."

"I don't think you mentioned him in every sentence there."

"I'll see you tonight at the telling, Nicho."

"Commander. One of the scouts returns." The young Warrior whose voice dragged Pearce from sleep had been on early morning watch. "We think he's injured."

Pearce's hand was on his sword even before the full impact of these words hit him. "Injured? Only one you say?" He rose, fully awake, as only a soldier could be moments out of sleep. Around him his men stirred to immediate life.

"Where is he?"

"We saw him in the valley, sir, and signaled our position."

"Hard to tell if a man is injured from so far. But it bodes ill that his companion is not with him."

"It's Fritzin. He's usually as fast as a deer up a trail, but now he's just crawling up."

"Send someone to help him, you dolt. And bring him to me as soon as he arrives. Also, make sure he isn't being followed."

"Yes, Commander."

"Men." Pearce glanced at the solemn faces around him. "Eat something quickly and ready yourselves. The enemy must be nearer than we suspected."

Fritzin took another half hour to make his way to the camp. He was brought to Pearce immediately, pale and bleeding from a wound on his thigh.

"Sir." He grimaced as he stood before Pearce. "Dire news. The king's army is closer than the High Commander estimated. I came back fast through the hidden trails, but still . . . they can't be much more than two days behind me."

"Crif," Pearce called for one of the older Warriors. "Clean and dress this wound while we hear what the man has to say." He turned back to the scout. "How did you get injured? And what happened to Loryl?"

Fritzin grimaced, whether from the pain of Crif examining his wound or from the memory of the last few days, Pearce couldn't tell.

"We had just left the ravine path and stopped to rest the horses on the banks of the Feyn. Suddenly they were upon us. King's men. I didn't even hear them until they broke out of the bushes. Three of them." He looked away from Pearce. "The arrow took Loryl right in the center of his chest. A kill shot." Fritzin breathed in sharply as Crif unwound his crude bandage. "I managed to take down the one bearing down on me, with an arrow of my own, before jumping on Yorrel's back. I suspect they wanted me alive because the few arrows that followed were low, aiming for the horse. Thank the Ancient One it only hit my leg. Without Yorrel, I would never have made it back."

"Did they follow you?"

"One of them did. I suspect the other was seeing to the man I shot. But I lost him upstream, sir."

"Still, you may have left a trail for them to follow," Pearce said ominously. "Only three men, you say. You didn't see more?"

"No, sir. I think they were scouts like us."

"And right at the Feyn River already? By the abyss! We need to push forward fast to engage them or they'll be right on the doorstep of the Grotto."

Lord Lucian stood at a distance, warming his hands by the fire and watching Tirragyl's king and his inner circle of officers. Alexor sat on a low chest, his long mane of hair flecked with gold from the fire's light. Sparks of light danced manically in the king's eyes, perhaps a product of the fire's reflection; more likely, the result of the strong mead that he and his men had indulged in all night.

"Lucian!" the king said loudly, lifting his goblet in a mock salute. "Come have a drink, my noble lord."

"I fear I've had my fill, King Alexor."

"Nonsense! I haven't seen a single drop pass your lips. Have you, Zane?"

The officer to the king's right shook his head. "Not a drop, Your Majesty."

"Perhaps he does not approve of all our drinking and carousing?"

The king's words, spoken with an edge of insolent threat, were perceptive for one so drunk.

"Not at all, Your Majesty. After the long and swift journey here, a celebration is definitely in order."

"Ex . . . actly," the king slurred. "So have a drink, my wise advisor."

Lucian drew closer and allowed one of the king's officers to slosh mead into his goblet.

"Our prize is in sight, Lucian. The Grotto in our . . ." The king clenched his hand into a fist, watching it with the fascination of a young child. He regained his train of thought. "It's in our . . . grasp, Lucian."

"Indeed, sire. As our encounter with their scouts proved."

"Yesss." The king took a long draught of the mead. "We will crush them. Unshakable, that's what we are. And then the full power of the Guardian Rock will be mine. And with it, I will be able to find Nyla. Nyla will be mine too."

Lucian was not as sure as the drunk king. It was true that they had made good time reaching the mountains, pushing past the crags and into the ravine. It was a stroke of luck that their scouts had come across two of the Warriors at the Feyn River. Better still if they had taken one alive. Lucian was sure that the man would have cracked under the pressure of a Mind Rock interrogation. Instinctively his fingers found the dark rock lying in the safe folds of his cloak. The rock allowed him access into the minds of people in his vicinity. By some miracle, Shara—the girl he now pursued to the Grotto—

had possessed a Cerulean Dusk Dreamer. Only this power rock had given him access to her dreams, even though the distance between them was great. Their connection had led him past the defenses of the Guardian Rock and into the heart of the Grotto.

He looked up at the distant triple peaks, towering to the north. Darker than the night sky, they had a sense of strength and invincibility. It was at their base that Lucian sensed the Parashi had their last outpost—the fabled Guardian Grotto. But if the years of warfare between the Parashi and the Highborn invaders proved anything, it was that the Warriors, though few in number, would not be easy to defeat. In fact, Lucian thought, casting a wary eye around the camp where men were slumped either in sleep or drunken stupors, it wouldn't surprise him if the Warriors attacked at a time precisely like this. The Parashi would surely intercept them well before they reached the Grotto, and the attack would come when the king and his soldiers least expected it.

The king was leading his men in a rousing rendition of a tavern song. It seemed like the perfect time to slip away. The fire hissed its objection as Lucian emptied the contents of his goblet into its flames. It mattered little if the Warriors won an early, decisive victory over the king and his men. There were always more soldiers to draw on. Ultimately, the Warriors would not prevail against the sheer size of the king's forces. Lucian's only concern now was staying out of the fray.

CHAPTER 8

S how me how you do that thing where you flick his sword away, Klyden." Nyla had suddenly appeared in the courtyard, where he and Elxa were doing their daily thrusting and parrying. She held a long blade in her right hand.

"Really?" He couldn't hold back a small, derisive laugh. "Where did you find the sword?"

"My room." She lifted her chin in what Klyden was starting to think of as her defiant-queen stance. "And yes, I am very serious."

He recognized the blade now—Lohlyn's old practice sword. She must have kept it under her pallet, where Nyla now slept.

"Do you even know how to hold it, Nyla?"

"You tell me." She flew onto him with startling speed and thrust her sword towards his chest with deadly intent. Instinctively he jumped aside, swinging his own sword down on hers with a loud crash that must have jarred her fine fingers. Surprisingly, she retained her hold on the sword.

"Blithering blades!" Elxa exclaimed. "That was a vicious attack, Your Majesty."

"Thank you, Elxa." She shook her right hand with a slight wince.

"Indeed." Klyden couldn't muster up the same enthusiasm. "Where did you learn that particular move?"

"Lohlyn."

"*Lohlyn* taught you sword fighting? She was meant to pretend she didn't even know the tip of a sword from its handle."

"Well, Alexor and I had some lessons from the blade-master when we were much younger. Of course, Alexor always beat me. And I always cried." Nyla smiled. It was rare for her to speak about her past, even rarer for her to do so with some pleasure. "I clearly remember Lohlyn taking me back to my room and showing me how to hold the blade with both hands. *That's a little trick for us girls to know*, she said, *makes us as strong as the boys*. And then we practiced and practiced. It wasn't too long before I was beating Alexor, much to the blade-master's surprise."

"You have a strong grip, Your Majesty," Elxa said.

"And you never wondered where Lohlyn learned the ways of the blade?" Klyden asked.

"I was twelve, Klyden. It didn't cross my mind."

"What else did she teach you?"

"Well . . ." Nyla picked up the sword that she had dropped to the ground to shake the pain from her fingers. She held it just the way Klyden remembered Lohlyn holding hers, and lunged forward. "The thrust."

"Which we already saw," Klyden said wryly.

"The downward block. Side block. Sweep." She demonstrated each move with practiced care.

"Impressive." Klyden smiled, despite himself. He remembered learning the exact same sequence of moves as young children. "Did you carry on practicing them?"

"For a while, with Alexor. But as I grew older, Loh never wanted to practice with me. '*It's not ladylike*,' she used to say."

"She feared discovery," Klyden said.

"But she never taught me that move where you disarm your opponent. Can you teach it to me?"

"Why? When you have two of Tirragyl's finest swordsmen at your beck and call?"

"It feels important." She shrugged. "A monarch should be able to lead an army into battle, shouldn't she?"

"Well . . ."

"Not if she's a woman?" She thrust the question at him, faster than a blade.

"You're the first queen Tirragyl has ever had, Nyla," Klyden said gently. "It's never been needed. But if you wish us to teach you, we will. Right, Elxa?"

"Of course, Your Majesty." Elxa bowed his head.

"Good, that's settled then. And should Alexor suddenly appear, I can show him again how it feels to be defeated by his 'weak' sister," she said with forced joviality.

"At least he's nowhere near Azab Rock," Elxa said.

"Why?" Nyla looked up sharply.

"Well, with him attacking the Guardian Grotto, I mean." Elxa looked uncertainly at Klyden. "You didn't tell her?"

"It didn't seem important."

Nyla turned on Klyden. "*What* didn't seem important?"

Klyden sighed. "Nowl sent word a while back that the king's forces are attacking the Guardian Grotto."

"Why didn't you tell me?" Her face flushed again with the all-too-familiar anger.

"It matters little to us, Nyla." And—if he were honest with himself—perhaps he had known it would distress her to hear that her brother's rule continued unabated while she was stuck on Azab Rock.

"He attacks the Parashi resistance?" she said incredulously. "But how? Their position was always unknown."

"Nowl's message mentioned a lord. Perhaps *he* knew where it was."

"A lord?" Nyla's face furrowed in thought.

"The day they read the message from the Spy Master, the one exposing Lohlyn, there was a lord there who seemed to take particular pleasure in her fate," Klyden said softly. "Do you remember?"

"Yes. Lord Lucian! He was always at Alexor's side of late."

"Lucian?" Elxa asked. "It was he who sent the Raven to our village to discover if Lohlyn was a Charab."

"This Spy Master came to the village, Elxa?" Klyden turned to his cousin. "And you exposed her?"

Elxa dropped his gaze. "We were careful. Only mentioned her real name. And he came with the arming word."

"Still, it was enough to seal Lohlyn's fate." A sudden anger burned deep within Klyden. "And the queen's too."

"The Raven was a good man," Elxa said. "He had no intention of harming Lohlyn or the queen. But this lord was too clever for him. In the end he forced the Raven to sign the incriminating letter. "

None of them spoke for a long time. Klyden recalled that chilling instant in the palace's grand chamber. He could still see Lord Lucian's flush of triumph as he read the words. *An assassin in your midst. She goes by the name of Lohlyn of Lorren.* Fear had pounded through Klyden, momentarily stealing away his breath, his thoughts, his very reason for being. By the time Lohlyn grabbed Nyla to take her to safety, he had been back in control. But Nyla had not understood Lohlyn's intentions, and her resistance led to Lohlyn's arrest and, ultimately, her fire-pole death. That one letter, penned by the Raven, had unravelled every part of their lives. Klyden had lost his sister. Nyla, her crown. Tirragyl, a just and good ruler.

Nyla finally broke the silence. "Why would Alexor and Lucian attack the Guardian Grotto?"

"I hadn't considered it before, but do you think they might be searching . . . ," Klyden said, looking up at Elxa. His cousin nodded, and their voices—spoken in unison—rang with a menacing truth. ". . . for the Guardian Rock."

Cold shivered over Nyla's back as Klyden and Elxa chorused the two words. She had heard of the Guardian Rock—the most powerful Rock in Tirragyl—only once before. It was Mada, already old and frail, who told her of its existence in the palace. Her grandmother had lowered her voice as if imparting a great secret.

She could still remember the skepticism in her own voice. "A rock, Mada?" And then to humor the old woman, "Is it valuable?"

"Valuable?" Mada had spat out the word with scorn. "More than valuable, Nyla. It's *powerful.*"

Nyla's interest was piqued. "What does it *do* exactly?"

The old woman had shaken her head impatiently. "Nothing. It does nothing, Nyla."

"But—"

"It does nothing," Mada continued, "until it is joined to its companion rock. And then . . ." The old woman had stared up at the ceiling above her sleeping pallet as if looking far beyond the wooden beams. "Then, may Taus protect us all."

"Where is its companion, Mada?"

"Far in the northeastern mountains, Nyla. Well hidden." She had patted Nyla's hand absently. "Fear not. It will not be found. It is a rock that protects itself well."

"The northeastern mountains?"

"Yes. At the Guardian Grotto."

The cold shiver now reached deeper, lodging a knot of fear in Nyla's gut. "What do you know of this Guardian Rock, Klyden?"

He shrugged. "It's part of the lore of our people, dating back even before the time of our forefathers, Chaorlin and Rabnin. Still, it remains a mystery of sorts."

"Tell me what the loretellers said."

"I can't remember all that well, Nyla. My father, like all the Charab, was a practical man. His first goal was to teach us to fight and survive."

"But the old ones used to tell you stories around the fire at night," she persisted. "You told me that yourself. What stories did they tell?"

"I recall one story," Elxa said, "of how the Rock came to be at the Grotto."

Nyla turned eager eyes on him.

"Apparently, before the time of the Highborn invasion and the war that followed, there was a Parashi chief who ruled over the mountains. Chief Amrhan. In those days Tirragyl was but a small part of a much greater kingdom, one ruled over by the king of many titles."

"Many titles?" Nyla seemed unimpressed. "What was his actual name?"

Elxa smiled. "We children used to ask the loretellers the same question. This king was called by different names in different places. The Parashi knew him simply as Ab'El.

"This king gave Chief Amrhan the gift of the Guardian Rock.

Do you remember, Kly, the king's words as he presented it to the Chief?"

"I remember." Klyden smiled. "A story woven together by the loretellers to keep the attention of bored and wandering children. I doubt they were the king's actual words."

"Nevertheless, they were filled with a sense of impending danger, and it was not much longer before the invaders came."

Klyden said, "Yes, but—"

"Would you just tell me what the king said?" Nyla erupted.

"Sorry, Your Majesty, I will get to it. But first let me say that the loretellers told that when the Guardian Rock was one, it was the most beautiful power rock of them all. When you looked into it, you could see into its very depths, and it seemed to have no end at all, even though it was not much bigger than this." Elxa made a circle with his hands. "All the colors of the Old Magic swirled in that Rock, slowly changing course over time, like the stars in the sky. Few were allowed to lay eyes on it, in fact, because it was so mesmerizing. It could steal your attention for hours and yet you would think mere moments had passed."

"Was that the rock the king gave to the Chief?" Nyla asked.

"No. Well . . . not entirely. The rock the king brought to the Parashi was grey and plain. One day the king had entered his chambers and found that the Guardian Rock had begun to crack. It started only as one small fissure, but it grew and grew, and as that crack grew, the colors seeped away around it until every spinning orbit of rainbow light was gone. When the last colors had left, the plain grey rock cracked completely, apparently with such force that the two halves were thrust across the chamber in different directions."

"And it was one of these halves that the king gave to the Parashi," Nyla said.

"And the words the old king spoke were a prophecy of things to come," Elxa said.

"Spoken by loretellers *after* they had happened," Klyden added skeptically.

"The king said, *Darkness invades and color fades, yet the Guardian's strength stays true, and its power will protect you.*"

As Elxa looked up at Nyla, tears shimmered in his eyes. "And it did, Your Majesty. Even through the darkness of the invasion, there was an outpost that the invaders could not penetrate because of the power residing in that Rock."

"Until now," Nyla said. "Now the Guardian Rock may fail and the Grotto and its people fall."

CHAPTER 9

*A*s the words drew her back into their world, Shara found herself in a crush of horsemen, pounding hooves shaking the ground. The earthy smell of horses and leather filled her with a sharp pang of longing for Nicho. The air tasted of dust and danger, and a tingle of exhilaration replaced the memory of Nicho. After days of trudging the path through the Rif'twine, flying at the pace of horses felt exciting and fun. But the exhilaration died away when Shara spotted the prince at the front of the group. She understood then that they were in pursuit of Taus and the rebels, and she sensed that the battle to follow would be bitter indeed—prince against subject, brother against brother, friend against friend.

The group of riders was small—not more than fifteen, all dressed in black leggings, light chain-mail shirts and studded-leather doublets. Several of them wore metal helmets, but most had only leather helmets for protection. Sunlight flashed off the longswords that hung from their sides.

Their pace slowed as they urged their horses up a long slope, and when they had skirted the top of the small hill, they drew to a halt. Behind and below them lay a plain that stretched as far as the eye could see. Distant white-capped mountains bordered the plain in the direction from which they had come, and a river cut a lazy course into the green earth. Yet what drew Shara's eyes was not the natural beauty of the scenery but the dark mass that was gathered below them. Ajalon's army. From this height and distance, they looked like a nest of ants swarming over the ground, although as she continued to watch, Shara could see that they were clearly in units, moving forward in a disciplined formation.

At the front of each of these units, she saw a flash of red and, looking around at the riders she had accompanied, now spotted the same red banner. The Royal Banner's blood-red background was broken by a thick diagonal gold cross, reaching from corner to corner. A white crown sparkled in its center where the gold lines met.

On the prince's left was a thickset older man. His bushy eyebrows and moustache compensated for the complete lack of hair on his head. Despite his advanced age—or maybe because of it—he gave an impression of power and control. A military man of importance—this must be General Ga'abri. She also recognized two of the elders from the midnight meeting.

All eyes, including Shara's, turned in the direction the general now pointed. At first she could see nothing but the indistinct blue-grey of another far-off mountain range. The dark peaks shimmered like a mirage in the distant haze. Shara wondered if they were truly there or if her eyes were playing tricks on her. But then her attention was drawn to something else and, with growing understanding, she realized that this was what the general had seen: a cloud of dust.

It was the position of the rebel forces.

"They are trying to buy time, Your Majesty. That is why they are still moving south and not turning around to fight us." The general's words carried powerfully—a voice accustomed to giving commands.

"They are outnumbered," the prince said softly.

"Yes. Their only chance of gaining an advantage is to reach the high ground and fight us among the mountains. There they could set ambushes and do some damage. Out on the plains, they don't stand a chance."

"So we need to overtake them?"

"Yes, Your Majesty, but they are half a day ahead of us, and at the pace they are setting, they will reach the mountains tomorrow."

"We won't catch them?"

"No, my liege."

"What do you recommend?"

"Delay their progress and force the battle on the plains." The general pulled a small map from a leather pouch that hung beside his sword. "The key is the cavalry. If we ride our five hundred cavalry soldiers

through the night, skirting around them here," he pointed at the map, "we can cut them off before they reach the mountains and engage them while our foot soldiers come up from behind."

"Will five hundred men be able to hold back an army of three thousand?" the prince asked.

The general hesitated. "Our advantage is the element of surprise and their lack of organization and unity."

The prince thought for a long time before he spoke. "It is the only way. I will lead the cavalry and head off Taus. You will follow, leading the rest of the army, General."

"If I may be so bold, Your Majesty, I think it better if I lead the cavalry and you follow with your army. It is a dangerous mission, and the odds will be against us."

"No, General, it will be as I have said," the prince said simply. "I wish to have one last chance to speak to Taus's men. To grant each of them a chance to return home."

"Their behavior does not warrant a pardon, my lord," the general objected, "but if you will, allow me to speak on your behalf. I will not allow your life to be endangered."

The prince stared thoughtfully at him and then turned to the two elders and said, "Eli, Yaron, do you agree with the general that I should not grant them clemency?"

The short elder, the first to declare his loyalty to the king in the midnight meeting, spoke. "Their actions are an affront against your father, you, and all of Ajalon, my prince. I do not believe they deserve your pardon."

The second elder nodded in agreement. "Their treachery deserves death."

"Yes. Yet they have been led astray by Taus, and I wish to give them one last chance to reconsider who they will follow. Ajalon would not be the great kingdom it is, and my father and I would not be the rulers we are, but for our values of peace and mercy. We have all needed mercy at some stage, have we not, Eli?"

"Yes, Prince E'shua." Eli's small smile mirrored the prince's own in a shared secret.

"Allow me to speak for you," the general said again.

"No, General. I want them to hear my voice and look into my eyes as I extend them one last chance. Good men will fight by my side. Eli, Yaron, you will accompany me?"

"To the death," both men said simultaneously.

The cavalry set a fast pace throughout the night. First light found them in a riverbed, slightly below the plain where Taus and the rebels camped. The prince split the men into groups. One group would attack the rebels from the side, providing a distraction, while the others pushed ahead and cut the rebels off from the mountains.

As they moved silently out of the riverbed and into a small grove of trees, Shara caught glimpses of the rebel forces—men, horses, and the occasional flicker of a fire. The rebels were awake early, preparing for their final push to the mountains.

At a prearranged time, the diversionary group broke off from the others to take up position amongst the trees. The prince and his remaining men continued to skirt around the edge of the rebel camp. They stopped when the trees were too thin to give them adequate cover.

Shara was surprised at how quickly and ferociously the battle started. A signal must have been given, for behind her she heard hoof-beats as the diversionary group stormed onto the camp. There were shouts of alarm and then screams of pain, and then it was as if she gazed into the abyss. Horses plowed into the middle of the camp. Rebels were trampled by beasts or felled by swords. Men ran in confusion as awareness of what was happening rippled through the camp.

The prince waited a little longer as the camp's focus turned to where the cavalry had attacked, and then he gave the signal for his remaining soldiers to proceed. Stealthily they moved forward in three arcs. The men who curved in closest to the camp would take up position at the front of the near corner, but—once spotted—would fight to protect the other two units that were moving to take up positions in the center and farthest corner.

They had not gone far before they were seen. At the prince's command, the men broke into a gallop, desperately trying to reach their intended position. To her left Shara could see arrows raining down on the men in the first arc. Several hit their mark as men and horses fell to the ground.

"*Come on, men! We're almost there,*" the prince's voice broke through her shock.

Now the arrows were thudding into their group too. A man just behind the prince screamed as an arrow sank into his shoulder.

"*Stay on, Vins!*" *a fellow soldier shouted as the man's grip loosened, and he swayed in the saddle. His friend grabbed his reins and somehow held him up as they continued their wild dash forward.*

"*We're almost beyond the range of the arrows, men!*" *the prince shouted.*

Shara could see that they were now ahead of the rebels and that the rebels' arrows were falling short. The plan was working! They had managed to cut off Taus's men.

Three short blasts of the ram's horn were followed by the raising of a white flag. The prince requested an audience. For a while the fighting did not abate, but just when Shara thought Taus would ignore the cease-fire, a corresponding trio of notes sounded from the rebel camp.

"*Good,*" *the prince said.* "*This will buy us time and give Caleb's men a chance to fall into position.*"

The men from the diversionary unit were already making their way out of the trees. Shara was shocked to realize just how few of them remained. Already Taus's rebellion was taking its toll.

The prince broke from his men and rode towards the rebel camp, accompanied only by his banner bearer and Eli. He had pulled a dark-blue robe over his doublet. The long rays of the rising sun caught the crown of gold resting on his dark hair. Shara was struck by both his majesty and vulnerability as he approached the men who had betrayed him and his father.

The silence was tangible in both camps. Every eye followed the prince. Shara could hear the snort of a horse and the distant call of a bird. The prince had covered about two thirds of the way when there was move-ment in the rebel camp. The prince's men had seen it, too, for as several of them defensively lifted their bows, Yaron held up his right hand to warn against rash action.

Taus and two other riders emerged from the camp. As they covered the distance to the prince, Shara again experienced the floating sensation that had launched her into the book. She was no longer among the men but above them, moving towards the prince and Taus. She heard the first words the prince spoke, his strong voice laced with sorrow.

"What have you done, Taus?"

"Isn't it obvious, Your Majesty?" A thin veil of sarcasm covered Taus's voice. "Your father and you are no longer competent to rule this great nation, and the people of Ajalon wish you both to step down from the throne."

"You swore allegiance to us, and yet you betray us?" The prince's gaze shifted to one of the men that accompanied Taus. "Worse still, you cause others to do the same."

"They agree with me that you are not fit to rule." Taus's eyes also flickered towards the young man on his right, who gave a small, nervous nod of agreement.

The prince was studying the man. "You are Jotach's son, are you not? Nemar?

"Yes." The man looked up in surprise but quickly lowered his gaze.

"Your father is a great soldier—one of my most loyal men. What a sorrow for him that he needs to see this day."

"Why are you here?" Taus interrupted impatiently. "Don't you have important state business? Perhaps some children to dance with?"

"I wish to address my soldiers."

"My soldiers, you mean?"

"They took an oath of allegiance to me. They are still mine."

"They do not owe you their loyalty anymore. You and your father have jeopardized the security of this great country. Ajalon needs some-body powerful, somebody unafraid to develop and use the army when threats arise. Not somebody too soft to rule."

"No threat has arisen, Taus. Until today. And now you will see just how strong we are. We will not tolerate a rebellion that could tear Ajalon apart. We will not allow you to destroy our people.

Nemar's gaze was now firmly on the prince, a hint of fear in his eyes.

"They do not need to hear anything you have to say."

"I have traveled all this way to speak to them."

"I will not allow it," Taus said.

"Because you are afraid that they are not truly loyal to you?"

"They have made their stand, as have I. Nothing you say will change that."

"If that is true, you have nothing to fear," the prince said, pulling his horse to the left to make his way around Taus.

"No!" Taus drew his sword.

From the direction of the cavalry, a soft metallic sound carried towards them—the collective swish of swords being drawn and the twang of bowstrings being pulled taut.

"You don't want to do that, Taus," the prince said with a smile.

Uncertainty wavered across Taus's face. "Fine. Tell me what it is you wish to say, and I will pass on your words."

"I need to say it myself."

"I will let you speak to them on one condition."

"I do not negotiate with traitors." The words were as cool and hard as steel.

"I will let you speak to them if you promise us safe passage to the mountains," Taus said as if he had not heard the prince's refusal.

"No."

"Then I will not let you speak."

"How will you stop me?"

"With my sword. The way you should have been stopped a long time ago." Hatred thickened Taus's voice.

"And then my army will attack yours, and . . ."

". . . and there will be bloodshed," Taus sneered, "brought about by an incompetent king and his son, who will still not have spoken to my men."

The prince was silent before he said, "Your hatred and ambition will cost many lives, Taus. You have blinded these men to the truth, have warped their thinking with lies. I would have pardoned them had they returned. That was what I came to tell them."

"It only proves how soft you are." Taus laughed and turned his horse sharply. "If that is all, this conversation is over."

Jotach's son lingered a moment longer than Taus and the other rider. "I will tell them for you, my liege," he whispered to the prince before turning and urging his horse forward.

The prince returned to his men, his face creased with tiredness and sorrow.

Time again seemed to pass in some strange, condensed way.

The cavalry stood its ground, ready for the approaching battle.

Taus and the rebels, however, did not make a move.

And finally Shara saw the dust on the horizon.

"They have made good time," Caleb said. "They are less than an hour away."

Shara felt the relief of the men as they saw the rest of Ajalon's army approach.

"This may well be when Taus makes his move," the prince said tersely to Eli. "Look at their eastern and western flanks. Movement."

The prince's words proved true. Shara heard the long, mournful sound of the ram's horn coming from Taus's camp. Almost simultaneously, groups of rebels were running towards them.

"They attack. Sound the ready command!" the prince bellowed, and the ram's horn from their own camp wailed out a response.

Shara had expected the beginning of the battle to be filled with a cacophony of sounds: horses, weapons, and men readying themselves for action. But, surprisingly, the silence was only broken by the soft chord of bowstrings being drawn taut and the snort of horses objecting to the subtle tightening of reins. The soldiers watched in disciplined silence as the rebels approached.

"They are within range, sir," one of the unit commanders said, but the prince continued to hold up his hand as the rebels pushed forward.

The archers of the rebels were now pulling their bows from their slings, arming themselves as they ran. The front row dropped onto their knees to allow the men behind a clear shot. This was the prince's cue, and before the rebels' bevy of arrows could be released, he dropped his hand and shouted, "Now!"

The cavalry's marksmen were ready, and their arrows flew into the rebels' ranks. Arrows cut into flesh. Rebels fell forward. Others jumped over their bodies and kept running closer. Now arrows were thudding into the prince's men and horses. Shara watched in horror as men and animals dropped around her.

A lone voice cried out, long and mournful as the call of the ram's horn. "Nooooooo!"

She was back in the Rif'twine, and it had been her own voice that called out in lament.

"That is enough for tonight," Eliad said softly.

Even though the words stopped, her mind remained filled with the images she had seen. Her heart pounded as loudly as the cavalry's hoofbeats.

"The men . . . were they . . . are they . . . going to be fine?"

The question sounded foolish. She knew the answer, had seen it with her own eyes, but longed for Eliad's comfort.

Eliad was still looking at her, but Shara had the sense that what he really saw were other faces in a different time and place.

"No. They were greatly outnumbered. They fought bravely and stood their ground for as long as they could, but once the rebels breached their line, the prince sounded the retreat. He knew that it would cost all his remaining soldiers' lives, and even then they would not quell the overwhelming tide of rebels. It was not a price he was willing to pay. So many lives lost. All for one man's pride."

"Did Taus reach the mountains?"

"Yes. He and more than half his men. With the cavalry holding them back as long as they did, the general did manage to overtake the rebels' flank. Many of them surrendered. But the front troops and those rebels with horses managed to reach the mountains, where they dispersed."

"Couldn't they follow them into the mountains and track them down?" Andreo asked. "Once the general arrived, there were many more soldiers than rebels."

"They would have succeeded over time, yes, but Taus had one last weapon he would use, the most destructive one of all."

CHAPTER 10

Pearce and his men moved with the speed and stealth the Parashi Warriors were renowned for. Never before had so much hung in the balance. Never before had an enemy come so close to the Guardian Grotto. They needed to be stopped. Soon.

Only a sliver of moon marked their way as Pearce led his men over the final hill towards the edge of the Ravine. His thoughts turned again to the Highborn girl, the one Nicho had brought to the Grotto. Shara. For four hundred years the Guardian Rock had shielded them, yet all it took was one foolish Highborn with one illicit Dusk Dreamer, and their defenses crumbled.

Pearce had not truly believed their defenses were breached even when Mikel sent him and his men out a few days ago to ward off the king's army. Yes, the enemy's presence had reached into the Grotto through the girl's rock, but surely that was different than knowing exactly where the Grotto lay? It was only since Fritzin's return and the dire news that the king's army was making their way up the ravine path—straight to the heart of the Grotto—that Pearce had come to realize the truth: the Guardian Rock had failed. The enemy was closing in on them.

Crif tapped him on his shoulder and pointed silently down into the ravine. Pearce could not see anything, but he had come to rely on the older man's instincts. He halted his men and stared steadily to the place Crif pointed at. Finally he saw it: a flicker of a single flame amongst the dense trees.

They were high above the king's army here, with the cliffs particularly steep and impassable at this point. Already a plan was formulating in Pearce's mind, though. They would push on through the night, away from the king's army, and drop into the ravine at first light, tracking back to follow the king's men during the day. Surely, the king would expect an attack from the front and not from behind. It pained Pearce that his plan allowed the king to get one day closer to the Grotto, but there was no other way.

Tomorrow night the Highborn army would be stopped, if it was the very last thing Pearce did.

Nicho sat down next to Rosa as the High Commander opened the book.

"I thought you weren't going to make it," she whispered.

"Wouldn't miss it. You?"

"I guess not." She smiled—briefly. "It's the one thing I look forward to in my day since Pearce left."

The High Commander began to read. Nicho closed his eyes, letting the words weave pictures into his mind, drawing him deeper, away from his own world and into another. Last night the words had taken him into the heart of the battle between Taus and Prince E'shua. Today no battle sounds greeted him although, as he looked around, he realized he still stood amongst the soldiers of Ajalon.

"My liege." General Ga'abri bowed. "We have managed to capture almost two hundred more rebels, but the rest have made it into the mountains. Let us regroup. Fighting in this terrain requires an entirely different strategy. Our numbers are not an advantage anymore."

"Let your men recover tonight, and we will plan our next move." The prince's face was pale and drawn.

The general turned to leave and then seemed to remember something.

"There was a group of rebels waiting for us in the mountain pass. Claimed they wanted to surrender."

"Indeed?"

"Yes, my lord. They asked for an audience with you, but I told them they would rot in a dungeon before that ever happened."

"*General.*" The prince smiled. "*I believe royal audiences are solely mine to grant.*"

The general bowed. "*Of course. Forgive me.*"

"*Bring them to me after I've spoken to my men.*"

Nicho followed the prince as he moved amongst his soldiers. He saw the prince's embraces and small touches, heard his words of encouragement and sympathy, noticed the devotion shining from his men's eyes. What had made the rebels turn against one such as this?

After a while Nicho heard a commotion. The general led a group of bound rebels towards the prince. Loathing and anger was visible on the faces around them, and voices hissed "traitors" as the rebels passed by. It struck Nicho for the first time that these rebels had once been soldiers. Their betrayal was not only against the king and prince but against their own companions.

The general forced them to kneel in front of the prince, who studied each one of them in silence. It was sorrow Nicho saw on his face, not the anger of his men.

"*Who speaks for you?*" *he asked eventually.*

One face dared to look up and meet the prince's gaze. It was Nemar, Jotach's son.

The prince indicated for Nemar's hands to be freed.

"*Come stand before me, Nemar, son of Jotach.*"

The hisses started again.

"*Nemar, traitor . . .*"

"*No-good rebel . . .*"

The prince held up his hand, and silence fell. "*Nemar, why are you here?*" *he asked.*

Nemar shook violently. His words were jumbled and almost inaudible.

"*Bring him some water,*" *the prince said.* "*Start again, Nemar. Remember you speak not only for yourself but also for these others. Why are you here?*"

"*Your Majesty. You said . . . out on the battlefield, to Commander Taus . . . you said that you wanted to offer us a p—pardon. The commander didn't tell them. So I did.*" *Here he looked up at the prince, who nodded ever so slightly.*

Nemar went on. "I told them. These men believed me. We made a terrible mistake following Commander Taus . . . and so we wish to accept it—your pardon, I mean." He swallowed hard before he continued. "We know we will be punished for what we did, and we accept that . . . but we didn't want you to think . . . any of you to think," he looked up briefly at the men around the prince, "that we were for Taus anymore. We want to be for you, my prince. We made a mistake."

The words were not eloquent, but they were sincere.

The general spoke before the prince even had a chance. "Your treason has condemned you to death, Nemar. Death is the punishment for your mistake."

Nemar's head sank down in shame, but his voice seemed stronger. "We accept that, General. But please do not let the shame of our actions linger on our families. Let them know that we returned and once more pledged allegiance to the King and Prince of Ajalon."

"Nemar," the prince said, "I offered a pardon. You heard and accepted my words—I saw it in your eyes on the battlefield."

The prince turned to his soldiers and General Ga'abri. "The penalty for treason is death, but I offered one last chance to return. One last chance to undo a terrible decision. Sometimes each one of us needs one more chance. I will not condemn these men to death. They are free to go. I ask only that you do not condemn them with your words or actions. I have forgiven, and I expect you to do the same."

The prince turned back to Nemar and his companions, who were still kneeling on the ground. "Unbind them," he instructed. "Nemar," his arm went around the young man's shoulder, "well done for bringing my men back. Today, Jotach will be proud of his son."

The men were subdued as they set up camp for the evening. Despite the prince's words, the soldiers seemed to be avoiding the pardoned men, who huddled together at the edge of the camp. The prince and general had gone into the royal tent, planning their next move against the rebels.

Nicho, moving among the men in the camp, considered how strange it was that he could see them all so clearly and they couldn't see him. He wasn't sure he liked being invisible—he had an urge to tap a soldier on the shoulder and ask him all about the prince or speak to the pardoned men about why they had followed Taus. Instead he moved to the entrance of the prince's tent and quietly stood, admiring the red streaks of the sunset sky.

Suddenly a shout went up from where the pardoned men were pitching their tents. He couldn't make out the words, but the urgency in their calls was unmistakable. His first thought was that the pardoned men had infiltrated the camp to try to harm the prince, but then he heard another sound even more ominous than the shout: a low rumble coming from the direction of the mountains. The prince and general had pushed their way out of the tent, turning to the source of the sound.

"What is . . . ?" was all the general could manage. All around him Nicho saw soldiers with the same confounded expression on their faces. The noise was now a roar in his ears, yet the dread he felt kept him from turning to face Taus's final weapon.

Eventually, hesitantly, he turned to see the coming destruction.

There seemed to be a wave making its way under the ground to where they stood. It pushed the earth upwards, knocking over trees, rocks, and shrubs in its path and then crushing them inwards as it folded over itself. As he watched the cracks appear in the ground before the oncoming wave, he thought that he had never seen anything so strange or terrifying in his life.

The soldiers were powerless in the face of this onslaught. Several began to run. Nicho knew instantly that it was hopeless. The underground wave was coming at such a speed that they would never be able to outrun it before it swallowed them into the ground.

The prince was moving now, faster than Nicho would have thought possible for such a large man. But instead of running away from the wave, he was moving towards it. The general followed, and Nicho moved with them, although he wished now that the words would stop and take him to safety.

"What is it?" the general shouted over the roar, as he darted behind the prince through the chaos of the camp.

"Old Magic," the prince shouted back.

"But it is destroying, not creating."

"It is in the hands of evil."

The prince stopped and stood, legs slightly apart, bracing himself for the oncoming wave of destruction. He stretched out both his arms in its direction, palms facing outwards, closed his eyes, and started to speak.

The wave was now a mere hundred feet away by Nicho's estimation and would be upon them in less than a minute. It rolled towards them with such an inevitable power that any hope of escape died in Nicho. He watched its approach with the somber fascination of the condemned watching an executioner's advance.

The prince still spoke, although Nicho only knew this because his mouth was moving, for the words were completely drowned out by the deafening roar of the approaching wave. He could feel the earth tremble under his feet. Fleetingly, he wondered if this was to be his end or if the words would bring him back to the Guardian Grotto. He struggled to keep his own footing as the general was thrown to the ground.

The wave was larger than he had first realized—at least twice the height of a man. It was still coming straight for them.

Something was starting to change, however. The wave, now about fifty feet from them, was slowing down. It was difficult to tell, but Nicho thought that the noise may have died down a little too. Twenty feet . . . fifteen feet. Nicho threw himself onto the ground and covered his head with his arms, waiting to be engulfed by the earth. But his end never came. As the sound died down, first to a rumble and then to a mere whoosh, Nicho lifted his head and looked. About ten feet away, the wave had stopped.

In the eerie silence he could now hear the prince's voice. It was a mere whisper, like a breeze rustling the leaves of a weeping willow tree. Then another sound started, a hollow creaking as the wave started to move again. However, it was not moving towards them but away from them, and its motion seemed to have altered. It was slower than when it had approached them and flattened out, much like a wave washing over the beach. It also spread out sideways, and in its wake something seemed to be wriggling from below the ground. Nicho took a step back, for there were small green snakes pushing their heads through a multitude of tiny cracks on the ground the wave had rolled back on.

As he watched, they grew in size, and smaller snakes emerged from the sides of the bigger ones.

"Are those . . . ?"

"Trees," the prince said.

Nicho let out a long, pent-up breath. He wasn't watching snakes emerge from the ground, but young plants.

The general didn't seem as reassured. "Why are they growing so fast?"

The prince clasped the older man by the shoulder, and together they turned to make their way back to their men. Nicho could see the weariness etched on the prince's face.

"It's the result of the Old Magic Taus tried to use against us and which I reversed back in his direction. It was a Death Spell."

"Death? In Ajalon? That's not possible. Surely the Old Magic would have protected us?" the general said.

"He had more power than I thought. But he underestimated me."

"But the trees . . . ?"

The prince stopped, and the two of them looked back. Nicho turned too. As far as he could see to the horizon, in the direction of the mountains, the plain was now covered with small saplings about the height of his knee. It was unbelievable for it had been mere moments since the prince had stopped the wave.

"The trees, too, are the result of the Death Spell. Small seeds lying under the surface, some of which would have grown into large trees over hundreds of Ajalon years, are now under the influence of the spell. Anything—or anyone—in the path of the wave is under its influence."

"But the trees are not dead. They are alive." The general didn't try to hide his confusion.

"Yes," the prince said. "But ultimately they will die. They are growing steadily towards their inevitable end. And," he looked back one last time at the forest, "this forest will soon form an inseparable rift between us and the rest of my kingdom."

Nicho could not tell for sure why the prince's final words wound such a tangle of sorrow around his heart.

CHAPTER 11

Nyla was turning into a remarkably good swordswoman, Klyden thought with a measure of pride. Part of her success was that she insisted on practicing for hours on end. Now he watched as Elxa set up a target on a tree.

"It's too close, Elxa," Nyla called. "Hang it on the one behind it."

Klyden smiled. Nyla was a woman of contrasts. At times she was so quiet and pensive that when her steely will rose to the fore, it still surprised him. Lohlyn had always told him it was there. *Stronger than that brother of hers, that's for sure,* she used to say. And it was that very strength that had been such a threat to Alexor.

He watched Nyla carefully place an arrow in the bow and lift it to her shoulder. Elxa tried to correct her position, but she shrugged him away.

"This is something I've been doing all my life, Elxa. One thing my education did not lack was royal hunts."

She took her time, Klyden noticed, and when the arrow finally flew through the air, it was as true as any Charab arrow would be. It found its mark right in the center of the target.

"Good shot, Nyla." Klyden clapped and stepped forward. "I couldn't have done it better myself."

She nodded, accepting his compliment as her due. Another contrast, he thought wryly. That royal arrogance always at war with something fragile and unsure inside her.

"Well, we won't be needing to teach you the way of the bow, Your Majesty," Elxa said as he returned with the arrow.

"Except perhaps to work on your speed," Klyden said.

"What was wrong with my speed?" Her eyes narrowed on him.

"Only that it took you some time to set up and release."

"Time was not of the essence." She jutted out her chin. "But let's pretend it was."

She slipped an arrow into place, released it, and had the next one in place before the first even hit the center of the target. The second hit the mark right next to it and the third right below it, even as the second still quivered from the impact.

She turned back to him and smiled defiantly. "Still too slow for you, Klyden?"

"I stand corrected. Your speed is remarkable, Your Majesty." His bow was only partially in jest.

Nyla would later pinpoint three moments that brought light and clarity to the clouded confusion of the last few months.

The first was when Elxa told her that time smoothed even the roughest of stones. It was at that moment that Nyla first realized every day spent on this island was a day not ruling her kingdom and that she had been born to rule. She refused to hide away on an island forever.

The second was hearing about the Guardian Rock, and the memory it evoked of Mada's words: *may Taus protect us all*. Nyla sensed that nothing could protect her people if the Rock fell into Alexor's hands.

And, finally, that very afternoon when she had seen the respect on Elxa and Klyden's faces as she released the three arrows. At that moment she knew for certain that she was not weak, not a small remnant of Alexor's soul, as he and their parents would have her believe. She was whole and she was strong. And she was a queen.

That evening as she strode from the hut towards their fire, the two men looked up in surprise. Klyden was the first on his feet, Elxa close behind.

"Is everything fine, Nyla?"

"Yes, very fine." Klyden's expression held a question, so she continued, "Tomorrow we leave this island."

"Leave?"

"Yes. I am Queen Nyla, rightful ruler of Tirragyl. And I will not allow my people to be destroyed by Alexor's actions."

"But leave? What could you possibly—"

"Tomorrow I declare war on my brother."

"Don't be ridiculous, Nyla! You and what army?"

"Me and the best army in all of Tirragyl." Nyla smiled triumphantly. "The Charab."

"It can't be done," Klyden said for at least the fifth time, stirring the last embers of the fire to life.

They had spent the evening discussing Nyla's plan. No—he thought sullenly—they had spent the night listening to Nyla issuing instructions. They were to pack before dawn. Klyden was to prepare the boat. Send out a gull to Nowl. The old man was to find them mounts, fast ones, that would take them into the Enderite kingdom and over the bridge to the Charab.

"It can't be done, Nyla. And I'll tell you why. To begin with, if I set foot on that bridge, the first arrow that strikes will be straight into my heart." He looked to his cousin for confirmation. "Right, Elxa?" Elxa reluctantly jerked his head in agreement. "Under the curse, they are bound to kill me."

"Fine. Then only Elxa and I go."

"That's not how it works. These are not soldiers you can order around. They're assassins."

"And I am their queen. They will do as I instruct."

"They do only as the curse instructs," Klyden shot back, "but let us pretend that you even gain an audience with the Charabian and tell him this plan of yours. *I am Queen Nyla, and I require your men in my army.*" His last high-pitched words were laced with sarcasm and frustration. "Let us go one step further and imagine the Charabian takes you seriously. *Where do you require us to go, Your Majesty?*"

Klyden shook his head. "Do you know what he will say when you tell him it's the Guardian Grotto?"

"I don't know. Why don't you tell me since you have such insight into your uncle's thoughts?"

"He will say, 'When the Rif'twine has swallowed every last piece of Tirragyl.'"

"Meaning?"

"When we're all dead. The Parashi hate the Charab, Nyla. Why would we risk our lives for them?"

"Because you're related. You're from the same bloodline."

"With hundreds of years of killings and burnings and retaliation between us. A history like that doesn't get swept away by one queen's will."

"But the very existence of Tirragyl is at stake," Nyla said. "If the Guardian Rock falls into Alexor's hands—"

"*If!* Nobody knows what will happen," Klyden interrupted. "And the Charab have never been particularly interested in Tirragyl's existence or survival."

"Well, perhaps then I should use the arming word on them and *make* them a bit more interested."

The shock of her words jarred into the long silence that followed. Klyden looked at Elxa. His cousin had taken a step away from the queen, his face drained of all color.

"You wouldn't," Klyden said, almost in a whisper. "How could you even say such a thing? *Think* such a thing?"

"If it's the only thing that will save my people and my kingdom, then perhaps it's worth considering."

"It's a word of darkness, of utter evil, and if it ever passes your lips, Nyla, you will have gone the same path as your brother."

"You don't know the word, Your Majesty," Elxa's voice broke through the tension that rippled like heat between Nyla and Klyden, "do you?"

"Not yet," she said, casting Klyden one last disparaging look. "But I will do whatever it takes to save my people."

CHAPTER 12

Eliad had wondered often these last few days why the Rif'twine was so quiet. He had expected resistance. Of course, the very air they breathed—heavy with decay—seemed intent on holding them back from reaching their destination. At times, taking step upon step through that thick, oppressive air felt like trudging through mud. Still they marched steadily through every day, drawing strength at the end of each from the book.

But he had lived many years on the borders of the Rif'twine and knew too well what kinds of foulness roamed there. Where were the Rif'iends and the host of dark creatures that droned around them? Had they not been crafted from immortal darkness and given one command and one command only? To keep all living creatures from traversing the forest. So where were they? Was the power of the path too strong for them? Could they not even draw near it? Or had the light of the path perhaps disguised Eliad and his companions' presence in the forest? Eliad doubted it. The creatures had always been particularly perceptive, much like a spider knows the moment a fly lands in its web. In some ways their absence disturbed Eliad even more than their presence might have. Perhaps the Rif'iends had a more ominous plan, one that drew them deep into the heart of the forest—far from any hope of escape—before they attacked. No, Eliad shook himself from the gloomy thoughts. It was the darkness of the forest that filled him with such dread. They were safe on the poison tree path; nothing could harm them here.

"I am tired, Eliad." Shara's voice broke through his thoughts.

"It is early still, my love." He looked back at her. The journey's weariness was etched into her face. Every day in the forest seemed to age her more. "We have a good hour of light left. Let's push forward."

"A little slower perhaps?"

"Fine. And have another drink of water." He held out the water skin and watched her drink a few careful sips. The farther they penetrated the Rif'twine, the more difficult it seemed to find water. Andreo had managed to tap some every night from the bark of the frill trees, but last night's water catch had been significantly less than before. This, too, worried Eliad.

They set off again, and perhaps it was because of the slower pace that, nearing dusk, Eliad finally heard what he had been expecting all these days past: a rustling in the undergrowth. He looked back quickly at his companions. Their faces were a mask of grim determination. They had not heard it.

"Let us stop here," he said hastily, trying to keep the fear from his voice. Suddenly it seemed important to make a fire—light was the one thing the Rif'iends hated—and to open the book again. He suspected the Old Tongue words would work as well as fire to keep the foul creatures at bay.

Eliad seemed particularly keen to read that evening and, as he started, Shara closed her eyes and let the beautiful, unfamiliar words into her heart. This time the words transformed into swaying colors—reds, oranges, and yellows—and small sparks of light that carried upwards to the sky. Warmth drew her away from the cold forest. The colors in her mind blurred into a heat haze through which she saw the shapes of men.

It was night, and she sat by a roaring bonfire. Over the crackling of the fire, she could hear the prince's strong voice.

". . . for your bravery and loyalty."

She looked around, trying to find him. It was easy, for he was almost directly opposite her and he was the only man standing.

"What happened here today is hard for us all to understand."

There were nods and a murmur of assent.

"It is a shock to me too, but I will try to explain the parts I do under-stand. The parts I do not—the hatred that drove Taus to such drastic action—I will not speak of. Today is the saddest of days for our great kingdom. The day hatred tried to destroy love, and death tried to steal life." He paused. "The day a part of Ajalon was devoured by evil.

"Let me begin at the point you all know. Taus tried to raise a rebel army to defeat me and my father. He wanted to be King of Ajalon in our place, but you—our loyal army—prevented that from happening, and we routed him on the plains. He could not tolerate this defeat, and so he did the unthinkable. He reversed the use of Old Magic—always intended to bring life—and cast a Death Spell."

There were more murmurs around the fire. Shara could see by the solemn faces around her that the men understood the severity of what had happened here today.

"The spell was very powerful and would have instantly killed every-thing in its path. Taus, a trusted member of our council, had a great deal of power, but he must have drawn much power from the rebels."

The prince took a deep breath. "Only one course of action was open to me. To reverse the direction of the spell. By doing this, death turned back on Taus and his men. But also," he closed his eyes momentarily, "on the entire southeastern province that lies behind them."

The men absorbed this solemn news. The southeastern province of Ajalon. Few of them had traveled there. It was a harsh, mountainous area. Fewer still knew any people who lived there, for its desolate land-scape supported only a small population, all as tough and wild as their surroundings.

The general spoke their shared thoughts. "It is a tragedy, my liege. But most of our people have been saved for, of all the provinces, this one contains the fewest people."

The general's words seemed to bring the prince no comfort. "Losing a single subject is one too many, General," he said softly.

One of the elders asked a question too soft to hear over the crackling fire.

"Eli asks why the trees grew at such an unnatural rate," the prince *continued. "As I said, Taus's Death Spell was meant to bring instant death, but in the reversal I altered the one thing I could. Everything that falls in the path of the spell will indeed die. By our own measure of time that death appears to be very quick. But for every part of the province and every living thing touched by the spell, time will change too."*

The murmurs around the fire were questioning.

"The trees illustrate it well. The seeds lying dormant in the ground, which would have slowly sprung up and taken many Ajalon years to grow, were already saplings within mere minutes. Tomorrow they will be large, fully grown trees, and in three days' time those majestic forms will have died of old age, and newer trees will have taken their place. That is the view of the trees from our side, from Ajalon. But for anybody in the forest or on the other side of it, the trees appear to be growing at their normal rate. It is as if one day here is . . . maybe two or three hundred years there."

"If one day here is two hundred years there," the general frowned, "then the people affected by the spell have already aged half a century since the death wave hit them?"

"Yes, they have aged, but in their own time they have also had children, danced, sung. By tomorrow they will have died of old age, but in their own world they have had a lifetime. For now it was all I could do to diminish Taus's spell."

The talk around the fire continued and, although Shara tried to concentrate on it, she found herself lulled to sleep by the hum of the voices and the warmth, which finally displaced the chill in her bones.

When she awoke, it was quiet. She was lying curled up on the ground next to the fire. The men were gone, and the fire had burned low.

Initially, she thought she was alone, but after a while she spotted the silhouette of a man. She silently crept over to him, although she knew he could not see or hear her. It was Prince E'shua.

He was staring into the flames. The firelight cast a warm, shifting glow onto his features. His was a compelling face, full of strength, but smile lines around his eyes and mouth revealed a softness that she had seen as he danced with the children in the palace. She crept even closer. She wondered what would happen if she reached out and touched his arm or cheek. Would she feel flesh or only air? How she wanted him to turn those eyes on her, to see his face light up as he looked at her. But why would it? He didn't even know her. And she wasn't even really here.

Yet tentatively she reached out for his arm and said, "My prince?"

Before her fingers could touch the fabric of his robe, he shifted, and she withdrew her arm. Just for an instant, as he pushed himself off the ground, he looked her way. She froze. His eyes seemed to hold her own, although there was a faraway look in them and such pain that it brought an immediate jolt of grief to her. But in the next moment he was on his feet.

She now became aware of Eliad's voice again. The image of the fire receded. She didn't want him to stop reading, for then she would be back on the cold path in the Rif'twine. She wanted to stay near this fire and near the prince throughout the night.

Yet the words did not stop as she expected them to. Instead they sounded more somber and heavy than they ever had before. No new picture emerged, only a swirling darkness and an ominous sense of danger.

Eventually she heard the whisper of voices. The blackness had lightened a little into the natural darkness of night, and she could just make out the shapes of two horses moving slowly towards her.

She heard a woman's voice. "He said we were to meet him in the pass. Are we lost?"

"No! I know this area like the back of my hand." The man sounded angry.

"I am tired, Uncle Keros. I can't sit any longer. I want to stop," a child's voice whined.

"Shut up, boy! It's hard enough finding the pass without your whining."

The horses drew to a halt right in front of Shara. The man, with the boy sitting in front of him, slowly looked around as if trying to find his bearing. He let out an exacerbated sigh. "I don't understand. I've never seen this forest before."

"And yet you know this area like the back of your hand," the woman said.

"We are in the right place." The man sounded as if he was trying to

convince himself more than his companion. "The king's army is camped just to the west of us. We saw their campfires."

"I agree with the child. I think we should stop here."

"And have the prince find us in the morning with our precious goods? Are you out of your mind, Jezrel?"

The woman didn't reply.

"No, I am sure the pass lies only a short distance from here through this forest. We will leave the horses and go on foot."

The man lowered the boy roughly to the ground before jumping off himself. Then he reached up and took the large bundle of blankets, which Shara now noticed the woman holding, from her. She, too, dismounted before taking it back.

He staked the horses and slung a bag over his shoulder, grumbling under his breath. "Why he wants this useless, cracked rock, I really don't know."

Then, laden with their goods, the three figures slipped into the forest.

Shara tried to follow them, but her legs would not cooperate. Even as she tried with all her might to move towards the receding figures, she sensed that Eliad had stopped reading.

"No!" she said. "Who were those people?" But she was back on the cold forest path. "Couldn't you read a bit more, Eliad?"

He smiled at her. "We need to conserve the oil for the lamp. We have used our ration for the night." The lamp was sputtering. It would soon be out.

"It is a good time for us to sleep," Eliad continued, "for the prince's fire has warmed us."

"How is that even possible?" Andreo asked.

Eliad smiled, looking from one questioning face to the other. "My friends, you have much to learn of the ways of Old Magic. One of the first lessons you learn is to graciously accept its gifts."

CHAPTER 13

Lucian was not particularly surprised when the Parashi attack came. The closer they got to the Guardian Grotto, the surer he felt that the Parashi would show themselves, and another night of drinking and revelry had left King Alexor and his men vulnerable. As had become his habit, Lucian had separated himself from the army and was hidden in a small copse of trees as the shadows of the Warriors passed him by. He might have called out a warning if it hadn't meant giving away his own position. Instead he slunk deeper into the shadows and, in the light of the moon, watched the events unfold with a certain grim anticipation.

The Parashi, with the element of surprise and sobriety on their side, initially had the upper hand. Lucian could hear swords thrusting through sleeping flesh, startled cries cut short. Finally somebody called the alarm. Then there was panic and confusion as Alexor's men scrambled to their feet, floundering with their weapons. Some ran. Others clashed swords with Warriors. A group of men formed a circle of protection around the king's tent, although Lucian doubted that the Parashi would penetrate that far into the camp before being repelled, for they were greatly outnumbered. Still the fighting continued unabated.

Lucian suddenly heard men moving towards him. At first he thought they were Alexor's men trying to escape, but then he saw two Parashi. The taller of the two was young and flinched as he tightened a strip of fabric around his upper arm. He was injured.

"Why not call the retreat, Pearce? We've done well for one night's work, and the tide is turning. Also, I should take a look at that wound for you."

"I want their army flattened," the young one said through clenched teeth. "Not a single one of them must stand to attack the Grotto."

"There are just too many, and it's not what the High Commander told us to do. Worry them like flies, remember?"

"They draw too close to the Grotto, Crif."

"If we retreat now, we can still fight them tomorrow. If we don't, we might not have enough men left standing to do so."

"By the abyss, you are right." The one called Pearce took something from his pocket and blew on it. The instrument let out a deep, mournful call that resonated through the trees and into the camp of fighting men. His men heard it. They fell back, one by one running past Lucian and disappearing as effortlessly as only Warriors could. Pearce and his companion stayed until each one had passed them.

"Curse that Highborn girl," Pearce said as they turned to go. "May she die on that forsaken Rif'twine path they seek, just as my men are dying in the war she brought upon us."

Then they, too, were gone.

In the camp, men were moving about in a daze. The occasional soft whimper of a soldier cradling the body of a dead friend was drowned out by Alexor's angry shouts. Yet Lucian hardly noticed it, his mind only on the words he had just heard. Shara was no longer at the Grotto. If the Parashi spoke the truth, she was on a path in the Rif'twine forest. It made no sense. A path would be overgrown in a matter of days—no, hours. Nothing could withstand the force of the forest.

Nothing except . . .

No! It couldn't be. Hadn't he made sure of that himself? Well and truly defeated they were.

Unless . . .

A chill of fear crept through him as understanding dawned. He'd told the Rif'iends to get rid of the evidence. But what exactly had the fools done after he left?

The best Lucian could hope for now was that they at least stopped the girl before she reached her destination. They were particularly good at dealing with forest intruders, the Rif'iends.

"More troops. I need more troops." Alexor paced next to the mass grave his men were digging. Lucian suspected the king cared less for the loss of his soldiers than the loss of his pride that a group of Parashi could defeat him so decisively.

They had found only six Parashi bodies although some may have been taken by the Warriors the night before.

"Shall we bury the enemy bodies, sire?"

"No! Tie them to the trees and let the scavengers have their fill."

The men glanced at each other nervously. One did not hinder souls from reaching the Wailands and beyond by treating their bodies with disrespect.

"Do it!" the king shouted. "And send out messengers immediately. I want every able man here to crush this festering plague of Parashi resistance."

"You still have many men, Your Majesty. Far more than they do," Lucian said in as soothing a voice as he could. The last time he had seen Alexor this angry was when the king heard his sister had disappeared without a trace after she escaped her execution. "I counsel you to send for more troops, but at the same time push forward with the attack."

"I do not want my royal blood pouring out in these Taus-forsaken mountains." The king had lowered his voice so only Lucian could hear his words.

"But as you saw last night, my liege, we are vulnerable even if all we do is wait. Rather, attack. Eradicate them so they are no longer a threat. You have exceptional men around you. They kept you safe last night, did they not?"

"I suppose." The king scowled. "Better if they had stopped the enemy before they even set foot in our camp."

If they had been sober, perhaps they would have. Lucian said nothing.

"Once the Guardian Rocks are joined, I will be invincible, won't I?" The light of obsession shone in the king's eyes. Strange, Lucian thought, how those power rocks took ahold of you long before you even laid your eyes or hands on them.

"You will, my liege. None will rival your power then."

But even as he said it, the thought of a path winding through the Rif'twine pushed its way into his mind, and he wondered if the words were true.

Mikel had lived his entire life in the caves of the Grotto. He was accustomed to the lack of light, but as he made his way to the chamber for that night's reading, he thought that the Guardian Grotto had never seemed quite as dark and somber as on this particular day. He knew what had caused it: the arrival of two of Pearce's men this morning. Fritzin, limping and supported by a large Warrior, told Mikel how the king's scouts at the River Feyn had killed Loryl.

Mikel had known the young man well. His father had fought skirmishes alongside Mikel when they were both younger. He had sent for his old friend, Loryl's father, and had told him of his son's death. The father had borne the news stoically, but Mikel had seen the raw grief in his eyes. Mikel himself had felt this first loss to his very core, perhaps magnified by the knowledge that it was only the first of many. These fine young men, courageous and loyal, would fall defending the Grotto. Mikel knew this because the prophecy was burned into his mind.

> *The Guardian, once strong, grows weak*
> *As evil pierces through the Dusk*
> *Midnight darkness follows,*
> *And mountains shake at the wrath of the foe*
> *Before Dawn releases her light.*

The first two lines had already been fulfilled. Evil had pierced through the Dusk Dreamer, and the Guardian Rock's defenses had been breached. Now midnight darkness would follow, and mountains would shake as their enemy attacked. Would his idling strength last to lead his people back to dawn's light?

Help me, please help me. It was his constant refrain now, an acknowledgment of his own weakness.

The faces of his people turned to him as he entered the chamber with the book. On those beloved faces he saw anticipation, tempered by fear and weariness. The book was good for them. It was giving them the strength to get through every day. He began to read.

Mikel's voice wove a veil of grey mist around Nicho, through which the shadows of men moved.

"Halt," a commanding voice whispered. "I hear voices."

Instantly the men stopped moving, becoming as still as the larger unmoving shapes that Nicho realized must be trees. He, too, heard a voice a little way off now—a child's voice.

"I'm tired. I want to stop." Half whining, half crying.

"Not until we get to the pass." He recognized that abrupt tone. It was the man he had seen on horseback in an earlier reading, with the woman and young boy.

"Capture them." The commanding voice whispered, and the men moved stealthily forward.

Nicho heard a startled scream and a child's cry and the sound of men thrashing on the ground. Then the woman's voice rose hysterically. "Stop! It is me, Jezrel. We are here to meet Taus."

In the thinning mist, Nicho could see the woman now. A large man was holding her by the arm, pressing a knife to her throat. Her companion had been pushed to the ground, his arms twisted on his back. One man held his arms in place as another stood guard over him with a sword. Even the boy, wriggling wildly, had been lifted off his feet.

The man who had given the commands stepped towards the woman. Only now could Nicho make out his face. It was Taus, an incredulous expression on his face. "Jezrel?" She let out a startled cry as she looked at him. "By the abyss—how is this possible?" Taus said. "Let go of her, you idiot."

Instantly the large man let go of her and dropped the arm that had held the knife to her throat. Jezrel shakily closed the distance between herself and Taus, a bewildered expression on her face.

"Taus? What has happened to you?"

"To me? Nothing! What happened to you all those years ago? I waited there for two weeks, and you never came."

"Weeks? What are you talking about? We have come straight from the palace. We are only a few hours behind the prince and his army. They are still camped near here." She reached out and touched his face. "My love, your face. It has changed. And what are these streaks of grey in your hair?"

"What do you expect? It's been thirty years since I left. But . . . ," he looked at her in confusion, ". . . you haven't aged at all." Now his eyes took in the boy, who had finally stopped struggling in the man's arms. "My son? How is this possible? He is exactly the same age as when I left."

"That's because you only left the palace the day before yesterday, Taus."

Taus stood in stunned silence, staring at Jezrel and the boy.

Finally he spoke. "The Death Spell. The prince reversed it. Everything in its path should have died. But it didn't." He looked around frantically at his men. "I thought then that the prince had failed, that the spell had lost its power. But I was wrong. We are dying." His men's expressions were dazed. "We are all dying, but he has lulled us into thinking we aren't. He has cast a Time Shifting Spell on us all."

A strange silence gripped the group as they looked at Taus. Every one of their faces held a mixture of confusion and fear.

A man finally spoke up. "We are dying?"

"Yes. Dying. The spell meant for the prince has turned on us." There was a note of hysteria in Taus's voice. "I need to think." He strode away.

Jezrel, whose blank expression showed that she hadn't understood a word Taus just said, followed him, reaching out to grab his arm.

"My love, I did what you told me. I've got the child."

Taus's eyes darted to where the boy stood. He shrugged dismissively. "What good is he to me now?"

"Not him. Look!" Jezrel pulled apart the bundle of blankets that she carried. As Taus looked at what lay within it, his eyes widened. Slowly, a smile curled at the edges of his mouth.

"Maybe," he whispered, "I can still win this war after all."

CHAPTER 14

Nyla was the most stubborn woman he had ever met. And, because she was his queen, Klyden had no option but to give in to her wishes. Which is why, after an evening of telling her how dangerous and ludicrous her plan was, Klyden and Elxa had packed, closed up the hut, and rigged the sails on the boat that would take them back to Tirragyl's mainland.

The sea had been choppy that day, and Klyden was relieved to see the shore come into sight. He tightened the mainsheet and steered the boat towards the small bay where Nowl's boat lay anchored, smiling as he saw the familiar figure of the Wave Whisperer standing with his hands on his hips, pipe clenched between his teeth.

Once in the bay, he steered clear of the submerged rocks and anchored a few feet away from the shore. He glanced back at Nyla, whose white, perspiring face showed that the trip back had been as difficult for her as the trip to Azab Rock.

"This is as close as I can get us, Nyla. The water will reach your waist, but I can carry you to the land so you don't get wet."

"Don't be ridiculous. A bit of water never killed anyone." And with that she made her way to the side of the boat, swung her legs over the edge, and lowered herself slowly into the sea.

"Are you sure, Nyla? These waters are rather icy at this time of year."

He heard her sharp intake of breath and couldn't help but grin.

"It's rather . . . pleasant," she said through clenched teeth as she began to wade to where Nowl waited.

Elxa jumped into the water next, carrying his and Nyla's bags and weapons above his head. Klyden stayed behind to pull down the sails and loop the ropes before he, too, followed them to shore.

"I didn't expect you back so soon." Nowl, waiting at the water's edge, embraced him with one arm. "Is it because of the man asking questions in town?"

"No." Klyden looked to where Elxa and Nyla were drying themselves near Nowl's cottage. "The queen insisted. She wants to fight her brother."

Nowl blew out a long puff of pipe smoke. "That could get dangerous for those protecting her."

"Exactly."

Just then Klyden saw a man emerging from the woods behind Nowl's house, and he slipped his dagger into his hand. "Friend of yours, Nowl?"

"No. I think not." Nowl squinted. "But . . ."

Klyden began to move towards Nyla, grateful that Elxa stood by her side even though his cousin had not yet seen the stranger.

"Klyden." Nowl was suddenly behind him. "That's the man. The one asking questions."

Klyden began to run, drawing a circular blade from his belt just as Elxa turned in the direction of the man. His cousin let out an exclamation of surprise.

Klyden had closed the gap and, weapons in hand, stepped in front of Nyla just as Elxa said, "By the abyss. What are you doing here, Raven?"

The man stared wide-eyed at the blade and dagger in Klyden's hand.

"I think I've surprised you." He looked up into Klyden's face with a sheepish smile. "I should know better than to creep up on a Charab."

"Why are you here, Raven? How did you find me?" Elxa asked.

"Lydora's gate guards. They told me you were heading south." He shrugged. "You know what a good spy I am, don't you?"

Nyla stepped from behind Klyden. "This is Raven, the spy? The one who wrote the letter that set my brother against me?"

"Your Majesty. I am he." The Raven sank down on one knee, head bowed to the ground.

"Your letter brought all this to pass." Her voice was steel cold. "And you *dare* to come and bow at my feet?"

"Forgive me, Your Majesty. Lord Lucian threatened me. I had no choice."

"No choice but to betray your queen?"

"I did not know what he would do with the information. I thought he was only after your maidservant."

"*Only*? Her life was of that little value to you, was it?" The words were spoken softly, ominously. "This *maidservant* was my lady-in-waiting. My best friend. And," her eyes narrowed on the bowing man, "unfortunately for you, Klyden's sister."

The Raven looked up briefly and met Klyden's gaze. There was fear in his eyes.

"So, *Raven*. It's rather foolish of you to come here today. Rather . . . deadly." Nyla's voice was brittle with anger. "Avenge the blood of your sister, Klyden. Kill him."

Klyden looked at the man and tightened the grip on his blade. Lohlyn was dead because of him. The familiar grief swept over him, enticing him again to let sorrow harden into anger. But he resisted.

"Mercy, Your Majesty. I beg you." The Raven looked up, hands held up pleadingly.

There was no mercy in Nyla's eyes. Her cold gaze swept from the spy to Klyden. "Well? What are you waiting for? I gave you an order."

"Please don't, Your Majesty." Elxa also sank to the ground in front of her. "He is my friend. He is not evil. Not a murderer. He was caught in Lord Lucian's web, as we all were. Don't do this."

The queen was unmoved by the appeal. Her eyes found Klyden's. "He is the reason Lohlyn was on that fire pole, Klyden."

"I will not do this, Nyla." Klyden slipped his dagger back into its sheath.

"I am. Your. Queen. You will do as I command."

"You're not the queen I know and respect if you make me."

Nyla's face reddened as she stared at him. He noticed the small twitch in her cheek. Then she turned her back on him as if he was completely inconsequential in her life.

"Get up, Elxa," she spat. "And Raven. Thanks to my protector's insurgence, you get to see another sunrise. One I don't think you deserve."

With that declaration, Tirragyl's queen marched towards Nowl's cottage.

"Azab Rock changed her," Nowl said under his breath, gazing at the queen stroking the nose of the chestnut mare. "I see the strength but also the inner fire of a Vulcan Rock in her now."

Klyden looked up from his plate of fish. "It was always there, Nowl. But now I fear . . ."

"You fear . . . ?"

Klyden cast a glance to where Elxa and the Raven were sitting, overlooking the sea. They were not within earshot. "I fear that her need for revenge will consume us all."

"But is it revenge? Or a desire to protect her people?"

"Perhaps it is that too. But I fear she will go to any lengths to do it. You saw what she commanded me to do today." He took another bite of his fish and swallowed it hurriedly. "She even threatened to use the arming word on the Charab if they won't cooperate."

"Mercy!" Nowl's spoon clattered out of his hand. "She doesn't know it, does she?"

"*She* doesn't." Klyden's expression was grim. "But Elxa tells me the Raven does."

Nowl shook his head slowly. "But you leave for the Charab village tomorrow, and the Raven will go back to Lydora. That leaves only Elxa to tell her."

"That word will never pass Elxa's lips again, even if she commands it. He would rather drink poison."

"What of your safety, my friend?" Nowl stretched forward and gripped Klyden's arm. "You are still on their kill list, are you not?"

"If I walk over the Charab bridge, I am a dead man."

"Stay here, Klyden. Let Elxa take her if she insists on going." Nowl's eyes brimmed with love. And fear.

"You know I can't do that." He squeezed the older man's hand. "Her grandmother commanded me to keep her safe."

"And you've done that. You saved her from her own execution."

"She is still in danger. I will not abandon her."

"But what use will you be to her if you are dead? Let Elxa be her protector from here on if he is willing."

"I have the strange sense that our paths are still joined, Nowl." Klyden smiled sadly at his friend.

"You're the only one left." Nowl swiped angrily at a lone tear. "I couldn't bear . . ."

"I will be careful. I promise."

If it had been up to her, they would have left the moment they landed on Tirragyl's shore the day before, but Klyden had again overridden her decision and insisted they spend the night with Nowl. On reflection he had been right, for when they set off before dawn this morning, they were well rested and stocked for the journey ahead.

He had been right too, she now realized, in his refusal to kill the spy. Yet her command and his disobedience still hung in the air between them. They had hardly spoken a word to each other the day before, and even now, as he rode by her side, he gazed steadily ahead, refusing to meet her gaze.

Nyla turned her attention away from her protector to the feel of the mount under her. How good it felt to be riding again. It had been far too long since she had felt a horse's ripple of strength and joy of speed, so responsive to her touch. The mare was much smaller than her own mount in Lydora, but Nyla sensed her willingness to obey and give her best and for that she was calling her Sky, in honor of her own horse, Skybreeze. Now she pressed her heels into Sky's side and shifted her weight forward.

"Come on, girl." She urged the horse forward.

"Didn't I say we should go slowly till we are well away from the village and it was fully light?" Klyden reprimanded.

"I can see perfectly, and there's not another person in sight."

Klyden kept up with her then and said nothing more. She didn't turn to check the position of the other horses. From this point on she would decide the pace, and everybody would just have to keep up with her. She knew that the Raven would.

It had surprised her when the Raven had found her privately the night before, bowing low before speaking.

"Your Majesty, I would like to offer my services to you as you set out to speak to the Charab."

For just an instant she had had the urge to ask his forgiveness for her earlier treatment, but then she recalled again what had brought it about, so instead she had forced a haughty, royal tone. "Why would I want the killer of my best friend in my company?"

"I have skills. I know many people and many things. I could be an asset to your party."

She had finally told him flatly that she would rather drag a dead and festering pig around behind her than have him along. It was only early this morning, when she mentioned the spy's offer to Klyden, that she reconsidered. There was something significant in the hasty look that passed between Klyden and Elxa. And because Klyden opposed it so vehemently and she still smarted from his insolence the day before, Nyla decided to assert her authority in this one small matter. The Raven would come with them and be completely at her service, whether Klyden liked it or not.

Now as she galloped across the field, she fleetingly wondered why Klyden had been so very opposed to the idea.

CHAPTER 15

Shara had lost count of how many days they had been in the Rif'twine. The last several days had felt particularly difficult. Her mind seemed to be playing tricks on her. She kept imagining a soft rustle behind her, but when she turned, there was nothing there. Before, the air in the forest had been heavy and unmoving, since no breath of wind could reach through the thick trees. But now, at times, she sensed a movement of air, a whisper of a breeze that sounded a little like her name. Sssss . . . ara. That murmuring blew a cold ripple of fear over her skin.

Her companions didn't seem to hear it, for Eliad marched forward with the same grim determination as before, and Andreo was still distracted by his daily discoveries of new plants to be found only this deep in the forest.

She was starting to think she would never see the end of this path when she became aware that something had changed. It took her a while to realize what it was. The light—it was suddenly brighter than before. But there was something else too. The air. It no longer smelled of rot and decay. It smelled of flowers.

"What is that, Eliad?"

He turned puzzled eyes on her. "I do not know, child. Let us proceed with caution."

The aroma of flowers drew them forward.

"Do you think it could be the delirea bloom, Eliad?" Andreo asked suddenly.

"By the abyss." The old man stopped in his tracks. "I hadn't thought of that. But it only blossoms twice a year, does it not?"

"What is a delirea bloom?" asked Shara.

"A very poisonous plant. It draws its victims by its alluring aroma," Andreo said. "Unable to resist it, they are drawn right into its grasp. A carnivorous plant. Rather interesting. I saw one once although, of course, it was not flowering."

Shara knew all about objects that drew one close, that took over one's mind with powers. This smell did not give her the same sense. It was lovely but not as alluring as she imagined the delirea bloom would be. She pushed past the men, took a few more large steps . . . and found herself in a small clearing.

Her eyes feasted on what she saw.

It wasn't a very large clearing, but it was light and contained a single weeping willow tree, sun visible through its branches. Shara's eyes stung with the sudden brightness as she took in the tree and the array of wild flowers—yellow, orange, red, white, and purple—growing beneath it.

"Look!" She breathed in the sweet fragrance. "Look at this place. It's so . . . beautiful. Right here in the middle of the Rif'twine."

"It is beautiful," Eliad said, stepping into the clearing and looking around thoughtfully. "I wonder if . . ."

Shara was moving around the tree. She could hear water gurgling.

"Eliad, I think there's water here."

Slightly behind the tree a small brook bubbled from the ground, a ribbon of water winding out of the clearing from its source.

"Is it safe to drink, Eliad?" Shara let the water trickle through her fingers, cool and delightful.

Eliad bent over too, cupping some water into his hand and tasting it with his tongue. "Pure." He smiled. "Very pure indeed. A good place to replenish our water."

He and Andreo reached for their leather water pouches, but Shara kneeled next to the brook and let the water run into her cupped hands, drinking some of it and splashing the rest on her face.

"It's sweet! I've never tasted water like this," she said.

Both the men lay their water bags aside to sample the water, and

Eliad smiled. "I haven't tasted water like this since . . . well, for many years."

After they had drunk their fill, they lay their blankets near the tree and found some dry wood with which to build a fire later. Shara felt full and satisfied and, for the first time in days, safe. Sitting in the sea of color and fragrance, a stillness crept over her, almost like peace. The spell only broke when Eliad opened the book to read. Surprisingly, his words took her not away from the smell of the flowers but towards them.

That sweet fragrance seemed to swell inside her, filling every part of her with its loveliness. As she opened her eyes, she understood why the aroma of flowers had lingered. She was in a garden. It took her a moment to realize that this was the garden of the palace where the prince had danced with the children. She stood in the gardens of Ajalon's palace.

She meandered along the carefully laid-out paths edged by flowering beds, letting her eyes feast on the color and beauty around her. The air felt warm on her skin. Looking up, she could see small clouds being pushed by the same breeze that now caressed her face.

Shara heard a muffled sound. As she cleared a high hedge, she saw a woman in a fine silver-grey dress, sitting on a wooden bench. Her hair, almost the same grey color as her dress, was up in a large bun, but Shara could see no more of her than that for she held her face in her hands and wept softly.

Shara was drawn to the woman and the deep sorrow emanating from her. Forgetting that she was only an observer in this story, she moved forward to offer words of comfort, but before she could reach her side, she heard footsteps. Two men approached. One was Prince E'shua, the other the elder named Eli. The prince's expression was a mixture of rage and sorrow, and Shara felt a sudden fear for the woman he so purposefully strode towards. Was she the source of his anger?

The woman spun around. As she saw the prince, she rose off the bench, a flash of apprehension on her face. Then she sank to her knees, head bowed.

The prince touched her shoulder. Shara was relieved to hear gentleness in his voice. "Rise, Yana."

She did so, slowly and with the prince's support, and Shara saw that despite her tall, upright posture, she was of a great age. Her eyes were still filled with tears as she raised her head to look at the prince.

"Shua . . . I mean . . . my prince. You have heard?" Sorrow should not have weighed down such a light and musical voice.

"A messenger came last night from my father. I rode back as fast as I could. We have just arrived."

"I cannot . . . the grief I feel, it is too much to express. Forgive me, my prince, for bringing the king and you such unbearable pain." The unshed tears now welled over, and she bowed her head once more with the heaviness of her sorrow.

The prince drew her gently onto the bench, his arm encircling her.

"Yana. We do not hold you responsible, and we need your strength to comfort the children. So if you have any feelings of guilt, I need you to lay them aside."

She nodded almost imperceptibly.

"Also," he continued, "you must tell me all that happened, or at least the parts that you know, so that I can plan a rescue."

Hope seemed to rise for an instant on Yana's face. "A rescue? But Veron said that there is no way to . . ."

The prince held up his hand, and she fell silent.

"I believe there is a way. Tell me what you know."

"There is not much to tell, Shu . . . my liege. The children had bathed and were eating dinner in the dining hall. I had to help the little one, of course. She likes to feed herself, but she makes such a mess." Yana smiled at the recollection. "Then I went to tuck her into her crib. She doesn't fall asleep immediately. Sometimes she lies and gurgles to herself. But I always just leave her, and that's what I did the night before last."

The tears threatened to come again, and it took some time before she could continue. "I went to read fables to the older children. Even Marda likes to listen to them. Then I sent them to their rooms and went back to check on the little one. When I got there . . . something was different. The door was slightly ajar and, as I entered the room, I realized that the crib was empty."

The prince nodded for her to continue.

"Initially I did not worry. It was strange that somebody would take

her, but the first thought I had was that her old wet nurse had come to see her and taken her for a walk in the gardens. But when I found Rohanna, she said she had not visited the child at all.

"Still I was not particularly concerned. I know there are one or two others who enjoy playing with her, and I thought maybe they had her. I was ready to give them a good tongue-lashing, I was, but I thought she was . . . safe.

"But the longer I looked, the greater grew my anxiety. Nobody had seen her at all. I went back to her room. Had she crawled out of the crib and hidden in a closet? I looked everywhere. Then I told the Palace Guards, and they started to look in every section of the palace to no avail. Eventually I had to break the news to the king."

She bent her head over and wept again into her hands.

Eli spoke softly to the prince. "The Palace Guards tell me that one of the chambermaids saw a palace lady carrying an object in a blanket. And a lady, Jezrel, has disappeared, along with her brother, Keros. It is possible they were involved in the child's kidnapping."

"Jezrel?" The prince's expression was thoughtful.

"Yes."

"The mother of Taus's son?"

"Yes." Eli swallowed nervously. "They do have a son. He must be three or four years old."

"Is he also missing?"

"I am not sure, my prince. I can check . . ." Eli began.

"There is no time, Eli. Once they take her into the forest, the Death Spell will start to age her."

Yana looked up in alarm.

"We need to act quickly. It is possible they will try to hide in Ajalon for a while, but eventually they will be forced to flee through the forest to reach Taus."

The prince rose to his feet. "Issue a royal decree asking for anybody who has seen well-dressed travelers with two young children to come forward with information. Tell the general to send out his best army scouts for clues of their whereabouts."

"Yes, sire. And shall I tell the general to ready the army for an attack

on the southeastern province? If they defeat Taus, the child will be returned."

"No. The army will not go. If my father allows it, I will go alone."

"But it is too . . ." Eli appeared to reconsider his words as the prince started to leave. "My prince, may I accompany you on this mission?"

Prince E'shua stared long and hard at the elder before he answered. "I will be glad to have a friend at my side, Eli. Make the preparations for a lengthy journey. Now I must speak to my father."

Shara followed the prince into the palace. His pace was fast, and she had little time to marvel at the magnificent surroundings before they reached a massive double door encased in gold. Two guards stood watch outside it. As the prince approached, they bowed and swung open the doors to the throne room.

"Father." The prince dropped to one knee before the throne, where the king sat.

"E'shua." The relief was obvious in the older man's voice as he stepped from the throne and pulled his son into an embrace. He was dressed in a robe of gold, the edges of which glittered with red stones.

As they drew apart, Shara looked at the king. The grief etched on his face was so raw that it brought an instant lump to her throat. How different to the time before, when she had watched him sing and dance with the children. How contagious had been his joy and laughter then.

"Yana told me all that happened."

The king nodded solemnly. "And your messenger arrived telling of the Death Spell." His voice lowered. "You did well, my son, to contain the damage."

Both men were silent as they contemplated all that had been lost in Taus's bid for power. The prince finally broke the silence.

"They will take her to the southeastern province." He swallowed as if the next words were too cruel to voice. "There she will fall under the spell of death."

"I know, E'shua. We have little time."

"There is only one spell stronger than death, Father."

The king did not answer but turned away, head bowed in silent grief.

"Father?"

When the king finally looked up at the prince, his eyes were dark and unfathomable. Yet a silent message seemed to have passed between him and E'shua, for the prince spoke again softly. "I will bring her back. No matter the cost."

The king took his son into his arms and, heads bowed, their shoulders shook with silent sobs.

CHAPTER 16

Shara's sleep that night was restless. She woke with a start, her skin clammy with sweat and her breath uneven. It took her a while to remember where she was. One bright star shone above her. The dawn star, herald of the coming day. She lay for some time, listening to the rhythmic breathing of Eliad and Andreo. As her eyes adjusted to the dark, or maybe as the first light crept into the day, she could make out the shape of the weeping willow. She could even hear the soft gurgle of the stream behind it, and she had a sudden urge to go and wash in its coolness.

Carefully she pulled aside the blanket that Eliad or Andreo must have covered her with last night and crawled over the flowers, away from the men. She stood up once she had cleared the bed of flowers and carefully felt her way to the tree, following the sound of the water till she thought she had found the location of the brook. It seemed darker here, so she again went down on her hands and knees to feel for it. Now the sound seemed farther away again, as if it was coming from the other side of the tree. She stood, trying to feel her way back to the tree again. But this side of the clearing definitely was darker for, from here, she struggled to even see the large shape of the willow.

Another shape caught her attention, and she started to move towards it. But as she drew closer, she realized it was not a tree. It seemed to be moving and, as it slowly spun around, it gave off tiny trails of multicolored light. Beautiful and mysterious, it drew Shara ever closer to it as she tried to understand what it was. Yet no matter how much she closed in on it, it was always just out of her reach.

It was only when her foot caught on something and she took her eyes off the strange object that she grasped the danger. Her foot had caught on a tree root. She was no longer in the clearing. As she had moved towards the spinning object, it had moved away from her.

Panic filled her, and she quickly turned around to retrace her steps, but a voice stopped her—a soothing voice, soft and gentle as a harp. "Come, Shara. Let me show you something you've never seen before."

She turned back to where the shape had been, and in its place stood a woman. At least, she had the face of a woman, although her body was almost transparent and emanated a bluish-green light. Her face was pale yet beautiful, and her eyes were a light sky-blue that drew you into their boundless depths. Her hair was almost white, and it swirled around her face in a breeze that, strangely, touched nothing else. Around her neck, on a long chain, hung a rock that looked a lot like a Cerulean Dusk Dreamer. Shara had an urge to reach out and touch it.

"Come," the woman said again, this time beckoning Shara closer with a graceful sweep of her arm.

"I really should go back," Shara said, but she stood rooted to the spot, captivated by the mysterious woman and the rock around her neck.

"Indeed. You must be careful in the forest," the woman said, "but it won't take long, and you're safe with me."

Yes, Shara thought, she felt safe right now. And yet. "I . . . don't know. What do you want to show me?"

"Just something I have. It belonged to your father, but you are right. I think you'd better go back." She turned and began to glide away.

"Wait!" Did she mean the Cerulean Dusk Dreamer? How could she have gotten it? "Are you talking about my uncle, Randin? Do you have his power rock?"

"No. I mean your *real* father," she said breezily, still moving slowly away from Shara.

"Real father? I don't even know who he is."

"I do." Her laugher was soft and otherworldly, like distant bells. "So do you want to see your father's ring?"

"His ring. Of course. But how do you know him? Who was he?" Shara struggled to keep up although, as the woman moved, a path seemed to open up behind her.

"Come."

The gap between her and the woman grew although Shara was almost running now. Vines struck her in the face and tangled around her ankles. The air was heavy with Rif'twine spore. Behind her Shara heard a bird's call, but all her attention focused on keeping the woman in sight.

"You're going too fast." Shara was on the verge of tears. "I want to see the ring."

"Hold my hand, and we will go faster."

She reached out for Shara's hand. Her skin felt like a liquid caress, as if Shara had put her hand in a cool bowl of water. It was strange yet not unpleasant, and Shara let herself be guided, deeper and deeper into the forest.

Now that the woman held her hand, they moved with much greater ease. At times Shara almost had the sensation that they were moving straight through the trees or that the trees were bending out of their way, for she would see a tree right ahead of them, but although they carried on in the same direction, it wouldn't hinder their progress.

Shara's companion stopped abruptly.

"That's far enough, I think." She glanced behind her and let go of Shara's hand.

"Will you show it to me now?"

"What? Oh, the ring? I suppose I can." She drew something from inside her bluish-green cloak and laid it on Shara's hand. It was a thick gold band with an opaque stone inlay that sparkled with small, colored flecks of light. Shara slipped it onto her ring finger. It was far too large.

"This was my father's?"

"He gave it to his son. I took it from his finger myself."

"You took it off? How—"

"Shhh!" The woman put a finger to her lip.

"What?"

The woman smiled coolly and sang out one long, high note that warbled and reverberated in the trees around them. The strange echoes grated on Shara's nerves, reminding her of the sound of nails scratching a mirror. Suddenly she remembered Eliad and Andreo and realized how far from them she must be.

"I . . . I must go," she said, backing away from the woman.

"Really?" The woman arched her eyebrow in amusement. "Where will you go?"

"To the clearing."

"Then you're going the wrong way. It's that way." Shara took a few steps in the direction she indicated. "No. It's that way actually." The woman smiled.

Shara again changed direction, but a chill crept over her as she understood that the woman was toying with her.

"Maybe the others can help." The woman's tinkling laughter filled the air as Shara spun around to look behind her. "These are my friends," the woman said, sweeping her arm to indicate the dark shadows gathered in a circle around them. Shara could not make out their features in the wan light. They had the build of men, but their faces were hooded, covering their eyes and mouths. Their movements were strange—they seemed to glide rather than walk—and their presence filled Shara with fear.

The shapes were slowly closing in on her, for a growing coldness had crept into the air as they pushed towards her. Panic kept her rooted in place, watching their approach, unable to think or speak. As the cold increased, a numbness seemed to settle over her body and mind. It didn't matter anymore. They were coming for her . . . she would die . . . but it didn't matter.

A piercing call broke through the haze forming in her mind. A word settled into her thoughts: *Tabeal.* But she was so cold, so numb that she couldn't even remember what it meant. She was drifting away. Soon it would all be over, and she could rest. Again the call pierced into her consciousness and with it the same word, *Tabeal.* And another pressing thought, one that felt like a command: *Speak it.*

She didn't understand, but the urgency of the thought broke through some of the numbness.

"Tabeal . . . help." No more than a whisper. Little more than a thought. But at that precise moment a warm light flooded the cold and dark and, slowly, Shara became aware of her surroundings again.

The first thing she noticed was Tabeal perched on her shoulder, and it was from her breast that the warm, golden light was pulsing. Around her the black shadows cringed backwards, away from the light.

Only the woman did not move away, and she spoke with a note of belligerence. "You have no authority in the Darkzone. It was her choice to follow me."

Something like a breeze moved the air, and the sound of it rustling the leaves gave the impression of a voice speaking. So soft were the words that Shara thought she was imagining them. "She is not yours. She is mine."

Maybe the shock of all she had gone through this morning was playing tricks on her mind. She had heard a breeze, not a voice. But just as she had convinced herself that this was the truth, the mysterious woman answered.

"Don't you always let everyone choose their own way? Even beloved little Sarah?"

There was a long silence before the voice filled the air again. "She chose me when she called for help."

"If you always rescue her, she will stay the weakling she is." The woman's eyes, filled with disdain, were now turned on Shara.

"She is not weak. She is an Ajalon princess."

"Let her prove it . . . by defeating me."

"You are already defeated."

"Defeated?" The woman smiled triumphantly. "Have you forgotten the poison tree?"

"Silence!" The voice echoed through the trees. The black shapes shuddered farther into the shadows, and even the woman took an involuntary step back. "Leave," the breeze voice commanded.

The dark figures melted back into the trees until only the woman remained. "Be assured we will meet again, *princess*," she said softly before turning to follow the others, and Shara couldn't help but notice that her translucent body darkened and her white hair became a black hood.

Eliad and Andreo found Shara lying in that place, bent over double with her face to the ground and Tabeal guarding over her from a low branch. Shara's body was racked with sobs that did not stop, even after they lifted her up and hacked their way through the thick forest back to the clearing.

Eliad brewed some tea, coaxing her to drink until eventually her cries subsided. Now the two men sat watching her anxiously. Neither of them spoke.

"Thank you," Shara eventually said, "for bringing me back here."

"What happened, Shara?" Eliad asked gently.

"I woke up and followed this beautiful woman, and she led me away from you."

Shara threatened to break into tears again, and Andreo went over to her and placed his arm around her shoulder.

"She said she had my father's ring. My real father." Shara opened her hand to reveal the gold ring lying in it.

A shadow of emotion flickered over Eliad's face. "May I . . . ?" He reached out and picked up the ring carefully. He fingered it reverently before laying it back in her hand. "What happened then?" he asked.

"Then she let out this strange call, and these dark figures appeared all around me." Shara focused on Eliad's face, reliving the terror of being surrounded by the creatures. "I wanted to come back to you, but she wouldn't let me, and they were moving in closer and closer. And it got so cold that I could hardly think."

"Rif'iends," Eliad said. "They draw their life from the warmth and life of others."

Shara took a long, ragged breath before continuing. "I think

I heard Tabeal call to me, and then I called back to her. A mere whisper."

"That's all you need." Eliad smiled.

"And then the Gold Breast was there, and it was light and warm again. But there was this voice, Eliad." Shara turned questioningly to him. "I don't know where it came from. The woman wanted me to fight her, but the voice said that she was already defeated. She laughed and said something about a poison tree. Does that make any sense to you, Eliad?"

"You will understand when we read it in the book, Shara."

Finally, timidly, Shara spoke again. "One more thing. The woman called me Sarah." She swallowed and closed her eyes as if the next words were too much for her to absorb. "And the voice . . . the voice said that I . . . I am . . . a princess."

"Yes." Eliad nodded. "You are the one Jezrel stole from the palace. Princess Sarah, daughter of Ab' El, Ajalon's High King."

CHAPTER 17

Klyden could only describe the pace the queen set as "furious." Every day she insisted they leave at first light and push through the day with only a few short breaks to rest the horses. Fortunately, they were hardy beasts, working horses used to long, backbreaking days.

Dusk was nearly darkening to night when Klyden called her to rein in. She did so grudgingly.

"Nyla. It's time to stop. There's a town up ahead. Perhaps we can even find a tavern with a soft sleeping pallet tonight."

"It's Gworlin Vale," the Raven said, pulling his own mount to a halt behind them. "I know the tavern keeper at the 'Hog and Tankard.' The Bent Bandit used to supply him with friga-berry beer. He can be trusted."

"The Bent Bandit's berry beer?" Klyden arched a sardonic eyebrow.

The Raven smiled. "Best in the Western Cantref."

"Sounds like you have some history here," Klyden said. He had, against his good judgment, grown rather fond of the Raven these last few days.

"It's a tale to tell over a tankard of beer."

"Nyla?" Klyden asked.

"Fine. Lead the way, Raven." Even Nyla seemed to have softened towards the amicable spy.

Light and laughter spilled from the open door of the tavern the

Raven led them to. They stopped in a small, dusty courtyard where several horses were tethered. Klyden jumped off his mount and helped Nyla dismount her own. After a day of riding, it felt good to have his feet on solid ground again. He stretched the stiffness out of his body.

"Stay here. Let me go see if he has room," the Raven said, already halfway to the tavern door.

"How far are we from the Charab village, Elxa?" Nyla asked.

"This town lies on the Endorai River, Your Majesty."

"Elxa!" Klyden warned. Till now, Elxa's habit of referring to the queen by her title had mattered little, but here amongst people, it posed a threat. Nyla was dressed in the clothes of a merchant's wife, her distinctive light hair covered by a scarf. They had decided that her name would be Nola to complete the disguise.

"Sorry, Klyden," Elxa said. "The Endorai River is the border between Tirragyl and the Enderite Territory, Your . . . I mean Nola."

"Past the river it gets rocky though. Mountainous," Klyden filled in. "The horses will struggle. They're not used to it."

The Raven emerged from the door with a broad smile. "He has two rooms. And you won't believe it, but the Bandit is here. He's just delivered some beer and is staying the night."

"I don't like it, Raven," Klyden said warily. "He'll ask questions. We didn't come here to mingle."

"I tell lies for a living, Klyden. I find it's the best way to get to the truth." The spy had the audacity to wink at the queen. "Nola's secret will be safe with me. I promise."

"Let's stay," she said. "I need a good night's sleep after all the days on the road. And a tankard of that berry beer would ensure it, I'm sure."

"How right you are, *Nola*," the Raven said.

Klyden grabbed his and Nyla's bags and followed the others into the tavern. Why did the Raven have to be so very likeable? He was glad Nyla wasn't trying to kill the spy anymore, but he didn't exactly want the two of them to become friends . . . for friends might tell each other dangerous secrets.

• • •

Nyla felt light-headed and warm. The room spun slightly with men's faces, their voices sounding as if they came from a great distance. She felt like giggling.

"I think I've had just a bit too much beery bear," she said carefully so that the others wouldn't doubt her sobriety.

A bearded face with merry eyes swam into focus. "Not at all, Nola-love. One can never have too much 'beery bear.' Isn't that right, Raven-boy?" The Bent Bandit grinned at his old friend and poured the last drops of the flagon into the spy's tankard. "Be right back ta top ya up there, Nola-love!" He rose, his bent-over form weaving between the sea of bodies.

"I like him," Nyla said, watching him go. "No one ever calls me love."

"Neither have they called you Nola." Klyden's expression was stern, so serious, like a cold breeze. She wondered if she had the authority to *make* him drink his untouched tankard of beer, just so he wouldn't spoil her fun.

"Take a sip, Kly," she said. "Relax a bit."

"One of us needs a clear head tonight."

"Fine. You and Elxa can be the serious ones. Raven and I"—she put a jovial arm around the tall spy—"will enjoy ourselves."

"Better than trying to kill him, I suppose," Klyden said.

"Oh, Raven!" Nyla turned to the spy. "I was such a fool that first morning." She felt the tears prickle her eyes at the thought of what she had almost done to him. "Forgive me! Forgive me!"

"All is forgiven and forgotten, Your Majesty." The Raven smiled back at her, restoring the beer-induced fog of goodwill that Klyden's words had momentarily pierced through.

"Who's y'r majesty, Raven-boy?" The Bandit was back, reaching over the table to slosh beer into Nyla's tankard. For a heart-stopping moment nobody spoke.

"Just an endearing term I call my wife," Klyden said, putting his arm around Nyla. "Mainly because she always wants things her own way, like a true royal pain in the nether regions. Now *Raven-boy* here thinks he can call her that too." The coldness of the stare Klyden furnished on them even blew through Nyla's warm haze.

"To bossy women!" The Bandit laughed, raising his tankard. "They'll be the death of us all!"

"You've had enough," Klyden said under his breath, taking the tankard from her hands and emptying it behind him onto the stone floor. He stood up and lifted Nyla into his arms. "Me and the Missus are off to bed," he announced to the table.

"The berries will've made her soft as clay in y'r hands t'night, my friend, of that ya can be sure." The Bandit chortled.

"Elxa," Klyden said. "Get the Raven out of here too, before he spills his drink or anything else valuable."

Nyla laid her head on Klyden's shoulder and let him carry her up the stairs. "You smell nice, Klyden," she whispered. "So strong. Like horses and dust."

He took her to the smaller room and laid her down on the sleeping pallet.

"Kly?" She watched him undo her boots. "He's right, you know."

"Who's right?"

"The Bandit."

"Right about . . . ?"

"About being clay in your hands."

He stopped what he was doing and looked over at her with something that might have been longing. Or perhaps just sadness. Desire fluttered through her. Then he stood up roughly. "You're drunk, Nyla. And you're my queen. I wouldn't respect myself—or you—in the morning if I allowed that to happen."

He turned, closed the door, and left her alone.

For once it was well past dawn before Nyla awoke. Klyden sat at the same table as the night before, this time with some stale tavern bread and a goblet of lightly spiced mead. He watched her descend the steps. Her body stiffened as she saw him. Still, with the steeliness of her disposition, she forced her way across to him. He rose to greet her.

"Klyden." She dropped her gaze.

"Did you sleep well?"

"Yes. Good to be off the hard ground."

"Have some bread." He pushed it across to her. "Mead?"

She flinched. "I think I've had enough drink in this particular tavern."

"Potent stuff, the Bandit's berry beer . . . or should I say 'beery bear.'"

Her mouth curled into a smile. "Far too potent." She finally looked up at him again. "I'm sorry about . . ."

"It's fine. It was the beer talking, not you."

"A little bit me too." Her smile was wistful.

Now he was the one to drop his gaze. "It's forgotten already."

"And I'm sorry that the Raven and I almost exposed us with our foolishness."

"I think my lie saved the day."

"You mean the lie about me being a 'royal pain in the nether regions'?"

"Yes, that lie," he responded, smiling. "I see the berry beer did nothing to hinder your memory."

She took a piece of the bread and chewed on it for a while before swallowing it down. "I don't want to lose your respect, Klyden," she suddenly said. "It means much to me."

"You haven't lost it."

It wasn't long before Elxa, and then the Raven, joined them. Elxa looked worried, the Raven sheepish, as they sat down.

"Klyden. Nola." The spy dropped his voice and leaned in closer. "I said your secret would be safe with me, but it wasn't. I think I am more of a hindrance than a help. Perhaps we must part company?"

"Perhaps we should," Klyden said. He was aware of Nyla watching him, so he tried to hide his rush of relief.

"I think that is for me to decide. The Raven pledged himself to *me*," she said, with a touch of her old haughtiness. "And I say he stays."

"I think *you* are the one who needs to part from us, Klyden," Elxa interjected. "You know you cannot cross the Charab bridge. Gworlin

Vale already feels too close, but at least here you have a chance of evading the Charab."

"Only a chance?" Nyla frowned. "How would they know he was here?"

"It's their trade to know. No. More than that . . . compulsion to know. Like hunting dogs on a trail." Elxa shrugged. "It's hard to explain unless you've been under that arming word curse."

"You must turn back, Klyden," Nyla said suddenly. "I won't put you in danger like that."

"Then we should have stayed on Azab Rock," Klyden answered. "The moment I stepped back on Tirragyl's soil, I was in danger again." His indictment hung between them.

"It just struck me," Nyla said, "that you and I are not all that different. Both of us have kin after our blood. Both of us are hunted in Tirragyl. And now both of us need to choose our way." She took hold of his hand and squeezed it. "This feels right for me, Klyden, but that doesn't mean it's right for you."

"I was charged to protect you. For me, the promise I made your grandmother is more binding than a curse. I will stay by your side as long as I can, to fulfill my promise."

"But make me a promise too, Kly," she said. "That you will choose your dangers wisely."

"We don't choose our dangers. But I will try to be wise."

CHAPTER 18

Since their night attack, when they had managed to do some real damage to the king's army, Pearce and his unit had engaged in the traditional skirmish warfare that had, for decades, protected the Grotto. Attack and disappear in order to draw the enemy away. Distract and withdraw. Niggle at them like a horde of titan ants biting at the heels of a tsebee. Sometimes a young buck was known to trip and fall over, but not this time. This time the buck was ignoring the ants and moving steadily forward.

Still, Pearce could see no other way of engaging the enemy. They were outnumbered by more than three to one. The king's army was well armed and well trained, and since the night attack, on full alert. They repelled the Warriors with minimum losses and never took the bait to follow them into the mountains as all their previous enemies had done to their downfall. Instead they inched ever closer to the Grotto.

Pearce lay on his stomach and watched this dangerous enemy. They moved as one, disciplined and aware. At the center—well out of reach from Warrior arrows—were the king and his cavalry. Around them were the foot soldiers. Every second man held up his shield against an attack from above. Surrounding the foot soldiers were archers on horseback, and in the last few days, Pearce had seen the deadly accuracy with which they brought down his men in their hiding places. Besides the Warriors lost in the night attack and the three that had died after it, Pearce had lost another twenty-seven of his men in the skirmishes. A tenth of his men had died, and still the king gained ground.

"Where is their weakness?" Pearce asked Crif, lying by his side.

Crif furrowed his brow. "They are strong, Pearce."

"Still, there must be some way we can draw them away?"

"I don't think so. Skirmishes have worked before mainly because our enemies didn't know where the Grotto lay. Now they know, and nothing can lure them off their set course."

"The valley narrows soon. They will have to change formation."

"Maybe we have a chance at Rogue's Neck, but I fear we are too few to hold them there."

"I sent word to the High Commander after the night attack. When he realizes how close the king is, he will send more men."

Crif nodded. "But they will not be here yet when Alexor's army reaches the Neck."

"But the men we have stationed at Waif's Cleft could be! We need every weapon we've got."

"Are you sure, Pearce? The High Commander insisted we protect the pass at the Cleft."

"But we can see the king is going up the Feyn River to Rogue's Neck. What use are fifty of our men protecting a pass that's not under threat?"

"Fine. I'll send for them immediately."

"We have to stop our enemy at Rogue's Neck. It's our last chance."

Nicho looked around at the almost-empty stable and let out a long, weary sigh. Mikel had called for a hundred men to prepare themselves to leave the Grotto and join Pearce. They would take most of the remaining horses, and Nicho and the other grooms had worked the entire day preparing the animals. Most of their time had gone into checking shoes and fitting and forging new ones. Then they had put saddles and bridles on the horses and led them to the exit, ready for the men's departure.

Sorrow had stabbed through Nicho as he watched the Warriors and their sturdy horses navigate the craggy path of the Elam Highlands that afternoon. They were his friends—many of the men and all of the horses. How many would return?

There was little work left for him now at the stables, yet he found himself back there. He sank down into the soft straw and let the smell—a mixture of straw and dung and horse sweat—wrap its familiar comfort around him. The loss of today reminded him of the even greater pain he had felt on finding that Shara had left the Grotto. It was the kind of pain that punched into the core of you, stealing your breath away. The kind you pushed aside with work and people because it was so intolerable to think about. That way you didn't have to stare it in the face. But now the horses were gone. The people were gone. There was little left to distract him, and his thoughts returned to Shara.

He remembered the first moment he thought he might have feelings for her, the day she had come to Randin's stable to name Krola's foal. She had chosen the name Kharin, a Parashi name, and it was then that he had truly seen her for the first time. Not her Highborn position or the bossiness of her childhood. Not the unruly, dark hair or even the eyes that sparkled with such a zest for life. No, he had seen her heart, and something had melted in him right there in Randin's stable.

"She's gone, Nicho," he said out loud. "Forever."

That last word jarred through him. Until this moment he hadn't believed it. He had held to the hope that he might see her again. She was, after all, out there . . . somewhere. But war was upon them. Just over a hundred Warriors remained in the Guardian Grotto and another hundred or so with Kella in the Deep Caves. If the Warriors outside failed, could the remaining Warriors repel the vast army that marched towards them? Nicho would take up arms, of course, like all the old men who remained and the others: farriers, grooms, and blade-masters, who never had the makings of fighters. They would all take up swords in defense of the Grotto, its children, and the ancient dream of being free. Yet Nicho knew he was only a horse whisperer and that the day he picked up an unfamiliar sword to face the king's army would be his last.

The thought did not fill him with fear. Instead, strangely, it dulled the throbbing wound that the memory of Shara had opened up in him again today.

And for that Nicho was grateful.

Rosa looked at him searchingly as he arrived in the large chamber that night. "Difficult day, Nic?"

"You could say that. A lot of horses to ready." Yet he suspected Rosa knew him well enough to see that it was more than a physical tiredness. "The chamber is so empty with all the men gone," he said to divert her attention.

Indeed, when the High Commander began to read, his voice echoed strangely in the chamber. Nicho followed the pull of the words away from the emptiness inside and around him.

He was standing among three stone buildings on the edge of a forest. The structures had a neglected air about them. He could see blackened stones at one end of the largest building, the same end where the roof appeared to have collapsed. The smallest building had no door, only a gaping hole for an entrance, and through it he heard the murmur of voices.

He cautiously moved closer and stepped into the dark, cold interior. The smell of damp, rotting wood assaulted him, yet he kept moving forward, for the voice he heard speaking was Taus's, and he didn't want to miss a word of what he was saying.

". . . shouldn't be able to find us here. We will probably leave the day after next for that is how long I estimate E'shua will take to enter the forest."

"But why couldn't we go straight to your new home, my love, instead of putting ourselves in this danger?"

Nicho jumped at the sudden crashing sound. Although his eyes were still adjusting to the dark, he could see that Taus had risen and kicked a heavy clay pot across the room in the direction of Jezrel. Pot shards and porridge lay strewn across the floor.

"What a stupid woman you are, Jezrel! I have told you over and over

that we had to leave the forest and hide in Ajalon so that the Death and Time Spells wouldn't age us. Now pick up that mess."

Jezrel scurried forward on her knees, scraping the porridge into her hands, just as a baby's cry pierced the air.

"A stupid woman and a howling baby! Get that child quiet. I can't bear the noise."

Jezrel looked up at him, tears brimming in her eyes. "Let me clear this away, then . . ."

Taus turned. "By the abyss, I need the company of men." He strode out of the building. Nicho followed him out.

The building they entered was lighter than the one they had just left. Light streamed into it from the collapsed roof at the far end. The familiar smell of manure lingered here. This had been a stable or cattle shed at some stage. Men and their belongings were spread over the ground. As Taus entered, a few of them stirred warily, and one near the back rose to join him. It was Keros, Jezrel's brother.

"Morning, Taus. Sleep well?"

"Between my whining son and that screaming baby, it's a wonder I slept at all. I should have joined the men. Come and walk with me. I'm tired of speaking with children and women."

They left the buildings, walking wordlessly along the edge of the forest. Keros eventually broke the silence.

"Is Ajalon's southeastern province as wild as men say it is?"

"Its people are a different breed—independent and stubborn. And," he paused, "until I arrived and started to reeducate them, very loyal to the king."

"How did you change that?"

"By the sword of course, how else?" Taus laughed. "Over the forty or so years I was there, my army conquered their towns, and every citizen that didn't swear loyalty to me was either put to death or imprisoned." He pointed at the trees. "It helped that the king was cut off from them by this forest. Do you know that, except for the very edges of it, most of it is now completely impenetrable?"

"How did you come back to Ajalon then?"

"Old Magic." Taus chuckled at his companion's expression. "Surprised, Keros? I still have a great deal of power left."

"So is the whole southeastern population on our side now?"

"There are pockets of resistance. But they will be wiped out. Most of my army remained behind when I came back to scout out the position in Ajalon. They will have dealt with the resistance." He smiled arrogantly. "In addition, I have put in place an even better plan." He paused, waiting for his companion to question him, but when Keros said nothing, he continued. "I have set up institutions whose sole purpose it is to teach people that I am the rightful king. In a generation or two, Ab'El and E'shua will be completely forgotten and I, Taus, will be the one they remember. This brotherhood is charged with seeking every book that mentions the kingdom of Ajalon and destroying it. Clever, don't you think?"

Keros nodded hesitantly. "Forgive me, Taus, this is difficult to understand. But if we wait in Ajalon for two or three days as you suggest, won't a few hundred years have passed in the southeastern province? They won't remember you anymore. You will not have a throne to return to."

"If the Brethren of Taus have done their work well, I'll be more than a king. I'll be a god. In addition, when I left, I had a son of nineteen in the southeastern province, who would have taken over the throne. The line of Taus will rule in Tirragyl forever. But," he waved dismissively, "who wants to rule one little province when all of Ajalon is there for the taking?"

"Ajalon?" Keros laughed derisively. "You will never take Ajalon. You've tried before and failed."

"Don't underestimate me. What do you think the king will do when he realizes I have his daughter?"

Keros shrugged.

"I know exactly what he will do. He is so weak that he will probably send his son to come and look for her. He will put his own heir's life on the line for one helpless, useless child. That, my friend," he slapped Keros on the back, "will be the end of the great Prince of Ajalon. And then I only need to bide my time before I return to take what is rightfully mine, my claim to the throne strengthened by the fact that I have an Ajalon princess to marry my heir."

Nicho heard the distant hooves before Taus and Keros looked up.

"Word comes!" Taus said, turning back to the buildings that the two

horsemen approached. As the men reined in sharply, Nicho noticed the flared nostrils of the horses and the gleam of sweat on their coats. They had been ridden far and fast.

One of the horsemen spoke. "The prince is on the move, sir. I estimate he is less than two hours behind us. He is heading for the forest."

"What is it, Taus?" Keros asked.

"The prince nears the forest. We need to leave right away if we are to arrive back in Tirragyl before him. Tell the men."

The word spread quickly that they were leaving. The soldiers were ready in almost no time and, when Taus spoke the word, they marched as one body towards the forest. Nicho saw the wariness in their eyes. None of them wanted to return to what they now knew was a place of death. The bundle of blankets containing the kidnapped princess was again tied around Jezrel's body, and she supported its bulk with one hand while she held the hand of the boy in the other. They moved silently into the dark coldness of the forest, Taus in the lead. After a while he stopped, turned back to the men, and spoke in a soft, strangely soothing voice.

"Men. I have decided to give you, my loyal followers, a gift." Nicho was not concentrating on his words. Instead he found himself captivated by the light that seemed to shine in Taus's brown, gold-flecked eyes.

"I have enough power," his voice continued, almost as mesmerizing as his eyes, "to grant each one of you immortality. You will never die. Which of you will accept this gift?"

The men stood silently, unsure. Finally one of them spoke. "How will this work, sir?"

"I will transfer to you some of my Old Magic. You will have powers you can only dream of now. You will be able to kill with just a breath. And as long as you stay in the forest, you will live forever."

"We have to stay in the forest?" another man asked, looking around hesitantly at the trees.

"It will be your life source. It, and everything that ventures here." His lip curled up. "Or you can come to Gwyndorr and be dead in a few Ajalon hours. Your choice."

Nicho sensed the shift in the men. Their despondency lifted, and something of Taus's expression gleamed in their eyes, too, now. Power *and immortality—who could resist such an offer? Slowly men started to lift their hands for Taus's gift.*

When every man's hand was raised, Taus started to speak. The words were foreign to Nicho's ears, and they grated into him like the sound of a stone scratching glass. He wanted to block his ears and keep them out, but they kept coming, now crawling over his skin like hundreds of tiny spiders. He had the urge to scream, or run, or both.

The expression in the men's eyes had changed. Ambition gave way to fear. But it was too late. Already Nicho could see that their bodies seemed less solid, almost flimsy, like dappled forest shadows. They wavered, and just when it looked like they might disappear altogether, they seemed to return, darker and more menacing than before. As the creatures emerged, Nicho took an involuntary step backwards.

The shapes were fluttering and quivering in a chaotic frenzy, and a low wail emanated from them, growing steadily louder into a long screech that made Nicho cover his ears.

Still, Jezrel's wail managed to break through the black scream. "What have you done?" Jezrel, pressed in fear against Taus, still held the boy and baby. The four of them were the only ones unchanged. "What have you done to my brother?"

"Quiet!" Taus commanded the figures, and their sound diminished to a low hum, almost like a swarm of bees. He turned back to Jezrel. "I have granted him a gift, Jezrel. Unlike you, he will live forever."

"Where is he? Which one is he?"

"Does it matter? The Rif'iends will be my forest guardians."

Jezrel had sunk to her knees, sobbing hysterically. The boy, too, was crying, hiding his face from the frightening creatures. Taus looked languidly over at them both and then seemed to relent. "Very well. He was a rather good friend. I will give him some special powers. Keros come here."

One of the figures separated from the group and glided silently over to Taus. "Keros, you will be the leader and spokesman of this company of soldiers. I will grant you the gift to change shape and speak in any voice you choose."

As Taus spoke another incantation, Keros seemed to spin and change shape. The forms were there and gone so quickly that Nicho couldn't make sense of them all, but he saw a bear, an old man, a spinning, sparkling wisp of mist, and finally a beautiful woman with hair floating around her face. Then Keros was back to the black-hooded figure of the Rif'iends.

"Happy?" Taus looked over at Jezrel, who stared wide-eyed at what remained of her brother before doubling over with grief.

CHAPTER 19

Nyla, Elxa and the Raven stood on the edge of the gorge. Far below them flowed the Endorai River.

"Your people are definitely better with a sword than a saw, Elxa," Nyla said, looking reluctantly at the flimsy wood and rope bridge that spanned the chasm, the only way to the Charab village.

"We discourage visitors, Your Majesty," Elxa said.

"The greater deterrent is knowing that a Charab arrow is pointed at your head as you cross," the Raven added wryly.

"I think you are safe crossing with the future Charabian," Elxa said with a rare smile. He took a step onto the bridge. "One step at a time. And try not to look down."

Nyla watched him cross with a jaunty step. When he was about halfway, she took the first step onto the bridge. Her hands were clammy, and she had to fight the instinct to freeze. "Just one little step," she whispered. "And then one more." The bridge swayed menacingly, but she tried to quell the fear by deceiving herself that it was mere feet off the ground as she inched forward. As she neared the other side, she felt the jolt as the Raven alighted the bridge, and for a moment panic surged through her again. "You're a queen, Nyla. You want these men's respect," she admonished herself, and she pushed forward with even greater determination.

A bead of perspiration crept down her forehead as she stepped off the bridge. She quickly swiped it away as Elxa came to meet her, four men at his side.

"Your Majesty," he said. "These are my kin: Joyl, Eben, Kol and Aryeh." Each man dipped his head in acknowledgment, but Nyla saw none of the respect she had expected. "This is Queen Nyla, sovereign of Tirragyl," Elxa continued. Their expressions remained unchanged. They did not utter a word. Only Aryeh, a mere youth, showed a measure of wariness at her title.

"Shall I search her, Elxa?" Eben asked.

"That won't be necessary," Elxa said. "Your Majesty, you will be required to hand over your sword and dagger."

Annoyance flared through Nyla. The lack of respect was bad enough, but now they would confiscate her weapons? She began to object just as the Raven stepped off the bridge and said, "Better to do it their way, Your Majesty. These Charab are a law unto themselves."

The Raven handed his own knife to Eben and was rewarded with a quick smile. "How have you been, Raven?"

"Good, Eben. How is your young lad?"

"Much better." Eben held out his hand to Nyla and raised a challenging eyebrow.

She relinquished her weapons, then followed the men across a narrow path over rocky outcrops and into a thick forest. None of them spoke. Strange, for surely they had much to share with Elxa, who they had not seen for many months. Deep in the woodland, they finally came across a village of wooden houses.

"This is our village," Elxa said, turning to her. "Strangers are not permitted to mingle with the villagers until the Charabian has decided their fate. This means that you will stay in your own hut tonight, and maybe a little longer, until the Charabian can see you. Eben will show you to the hut."

"But this is ridiculous," Nyla sputtered. "I am the Queen of Tirragyl, and I demand—"

"Only the Charabian has any authority here," Eben said steadily. "Your hut is this way. Please follow me."

Nyla cast one last plaintive look at Elxa, whose expression was shielded. "Elxa. I'm not a stranger to *you*, and surely your words carry some weight around here."

"I will recommend my father see you soon, Your Majesty. But I cannot make any promises."

"Chin up, Your Majesty." The Raven smiled. "Happened to me too. At least they feed you well."

There was nothing Nyla could do except follow Eben.

At least the Raven was right about the food. A girl, whose face instantly reminded Nyla of Elxa, arrived near sundown with freshly baked bread and a thick vegetable broth. She smiled at Nyla as she put down the food but made no reply when the queen asked for her name. She came back half an hour later to fetch the bowl, again in silence, locking the door when she left.

It was not the reception Nyla had imagined, and only now did she recall what Klyden had said when he was trying to dissuade her from coming here. *These are not soldiers you can order around.* Had she made a mistake to find these people, putting herself and him in danger with this expedition? Would the king's assassins find Klyden's hiding place in the Enderite woods to the west of the gorge? Would they kill the last of the Old Charabian's line as her own grandfather had ordered them to do? *We're good at spiriting ourselves away,* Klyden had told her the day before. But suddenly she didn't feel so sure anymore. He might be good at hiding but, now that she had seen the Charab for herself, she had the sense that they would be just as good at tracking him down.

She stretched out on the pallet and drew a blanket up. Through a small, high window, she could see a patch of sky. Two stars blinked down at her like distant eyes. As she looked at those stars, a slow anger began to burn in Nyla's stomach. She was not a stranger. Not a mere visitor. She was as far above these villagers as those two stars were above their village. They should be bowing at her feet, not locking her up like a prisoner.

Tomorrow Nyla would show them who was really in control. *They do only as the arming word curse instructs.* She now understood that, of all Klyden's words, those had been the truest. And as they drew closer to their destination, Nyla had finally understood why Klyden had been so reluctant to let the Raven join them. The Charab would never have given up Lohlyn—one of their own—if the Raven had not come with the arming word. She had waited for a time to speak to the Raven alone and yesterday, as Elxa and Klyden studied the woodland hiding place, she had found her chance. The Raven had reluctantly admitted that he had used the arming word on the Charab. When she had demanded he tell it to her, he had wavered. *It's an evil word, Your Majesty. You do not want it on your lips.* She had reminded him then of his vow to serve her wholeheartedly and commanded him to tell her the word. He had.

"*Ra'aph-aqeb,*" she whispered now to the distant stars. It didn't sound evil to her. It sounded powerful.

"My father will see you now, Your Majesty." Elxa himself came for her in the morning. "Usually the wait is longer."

It had been one night too long as far as she was concerned, but Nyla merely nodded and followed him down to the river and across another feeble bridge. From here a small track wound through thick forest.

"Is this the Rif'twine, Elxa?" she asked.

"No. This is natural Tirragyl woodland."

"Did your father ask you about Klyden?"

"Not yet. He will interrogate all three of us at the Rondel."

"Interrogate? He can't interrogate *me*. I'm his sovereign liege!"

Elxa stopped and looked back at her. "Have you not yet realized that the Charab do not give anybody their allegiance? Remember what the Raven said." A fleeting smile crossed his lips. "A law unto ourselves."

"You've always treated me with honor."

"Yes, but I am not curse-bound anymore. The curse, it . . ." He struggled for the right words. "It takes away one's will to pay honor. Especially to anybody related to Taus, who cursed us in the first place."

Nyla thought about this as they walked once more in silence. She had grown up believing that respect and honor were her birthright. How strange to be in a place where nobody thought highly of her. Where, in fact, her position was held against her.

"Do you think they will find Klyden's hiding place, Elxa?" she asked eventually.

"Yes," he said after only a moment's hesitation.

"But we agreed we would tell them Klyden stayed on Azab Rock, right?"

"My father is not an easy man to lie to."

"Have I sealed Klyden's fate then?" Her voice wavered. "Did I doom him in this senseless quest of mine?"

"Maybe." His gaze was solemn. "But Klyden is the son of the Old Charabian. One of the best. He will not be easy to track."

She said no more for tears threatened to spill, and the last thing Nyla wanted was to be crying when she met the Charabian. Elxa led her to a large clearing where a huge wooden platform had been built in the trees. Two knotted ropes dangled down from above, and Elxa showed her how to climb, hand over hand, to the top. She struggled, and eventually he had to pull her onto the platform himself. It was a most undignified arrival, and she couldn't help but think that it gave the Charab men—waiting in silence on the platform—a few moments of amusement, although their faces remained unreadable.

"Come, Your Majesty," Elxa drew her to her feet. "My father awaits you in the Tribunal Rondel."

This turned out to be an enclosed wooden structure in the middle of the giant platform. The door was low, and Nyla had to duck to enter it. There were already several people inside.

A short, powerfully built man sat on a platform. His greying hair was curly and his beard thick. There was intelligence, even cunning, in his green eyes. At his feet sat the girl who had served Nyla her food yesterday, and in her lap lay a pillow with a beautiful opaque rock on it. Two younger boys stood by the older man's side. Several other men formed a semicircle around him. She recognized the four men who had escorted them from the bridge the day before. The Raven, too, was present, chatting amiably to one of the men.

The older man rose to his feet as she entered and inclined his head ever so slightly.

"Queen Nyla. Welcome to the Charab Tribunal. I am the Charabian."

Nyla was unsure what the required response was to this, so she, too, dipped her head and said, "Thank you for granting me an audience."

"Let me introduce you to my kin. My daughter, Frey," he pointed to the girl at his feet, "and my sons Sira and Brun." He proceeded to introduce each of the men in the circle before concluding with, "and you have had the pleasure of meeting my son Elxa and our friend, the Raven." His eyes seemed to narrow on Elxa as he said, "It is not every day that one of our own disturbs the sanctity of our village by bringing a stranger to our midst."

"He did it on my command," Nyla said, a note of steel in her voice, "and in respect to my position as his sovereign."

"We do not owe our allegiance to Tirragyl's crown."

"That's not what I've heard. For generations you have been the assassins for my forefathers."

"Not by our own will as you undoubtedly know."

"Yes. But I come with a request." She cleared her throat, wanting every word to come out the way she had practiced it. "You may know that my brother Alexor wants me dead. He has now turned his attention to attacking the Guardian Grotto, coveting the Guardian Rock that has protected it for so long. If he lays hands on it and unites it with the Guardian in his own possession, I fear that the forces he unleashes will destroy all of Tirragyl."

Her words were impassioned and powerful, and she sensed a small stirring of emotion amongst the men. Yet the Charabian remained impassive.

"So what do you want from us, Queen Nyla?" he asked.

"An army. To help protect the Grotto and the Guardian, and ultimately keep all of Tirragyl safe from the harm that will be unleashed when the Rocks are brought together."

"An army to protect the Parashi, who consider us the worst of traitors?"

"Not just them. All of Tirragyl needs our protection."

"We do not involve ourselves in Tirragyl's concerns."

"The destruction of this entire nation, including your own

village, is slightly more than a mere 'concern,' wouldn't you agree, Charabian?"

"No, I would not agree. If Tirragyl falls and we fall with it, I will thank the Ancient One with my dying breath that he has finally seen fit to bring destruction on the House of Taus."

The silence that followed his words smoldered with the rage of generations.

"You would welcome the death of innocents just to see my hated house destroyed?" Nyla's words were soft, filled, too, with a quiet anger.

"Judgment falls on the heads of the guilty and the innocent. It has always been thus. And my people are not guilty of bringing it on. That guilt lies squarely on your own shoulders."

"*My* shoulders? Was I there when Taus invaded, when he placed a curse on you? I bear no guilt in this."

"The guilt is in your blood as the curse is in mine."

It was then that Elxa stepped forward. "Father, we can be free of this curse and this guilt and this hatred between us. There is a bird that—"

"Take this spawn of Taus back over the bridge with you, Elxa," the Charabian interrupted coldly. "And never bring another stranger into our midst."

"But, Father, I am free. The Gold Breast—"

"*Now,* Elxa! Before my kindness runs out and I give Sira the command to kill her."

"*Kill me*?" A cold rage pumped through Nyla now. "*Spawn of Taus*? How dare you—"

"Do not speak anymore, Queen Nyla. Your audience has come to an end."

"Well, then I think only one thing remains to be said." She had hoped it wouldn't come to this, had hoped she would be able to reason with the Charabian, but now she knew there was no other way. "*Ra'aph-aqeb.*" The word quivered from her lips.

Nyla watched in amazement as the Charabian's face twisted, in pain or surprise, and he stumbled to his knees as if an invisible force pushed him to the ground. His eyes, so full of defiance a moment before, were suddenly filled with anguish, and he dropped his gaze to the floor as if merely looking at her filled him with more pain than he could bear. All around the room, men dropped to their knees. Only the Raven and Elxa remained standing.

"No, Your Majesty, no!" Elxa whispered.

Yet strangely it was Klyden's face she suddenly saw in her mind. On the day she had commanded him to kill the Raven, she had seen the disappointment in his eyes and heard it in the words he had spoken to her: *You're not the queen I know and respect if you make me.* That day had diminished her in his eyes, and the day she had been drunk at Gworlin Vale had diminished her a little more, despite his assurances that he respected her still. Once he knew what she had done here today, not a shred of respect would be left, and the thought of that tore deeply through her.

The Raven had been right. Now that she saw what it did to men, Nyla knew that that single word spoken by Taus generations ago over the Charab was the most evil of words. And it had passed her own lips too—Nyla, the spawn of Taus.

CHAPTER 20

"*Ra'aph-aqeb.*"

For a moment Elxa could not understand that the word of the curse was shrieking off Nyla's lips. Nyla, who he knew was nothing like Taus or her forefathers. Yet when his father and brothers and every man in the room, except himself and the Raven, fell to the floor in subservience, his mind finally admitted that it had to be true. He looked at Nyla then. Her face was a mask of shock; her normally pale skin had taken on a deathly pallor.

"No, Your Majesty, no!" he whispered, and she turned large, frightened eyes onto him.

"I . . . I had no idea." She backed away towards the entrance of the Rondel. "It's not how I wanted it to be."

She stumbled from the Rondel, and for a moment he thought of following her, but his sister's voice, high with fright, drew him back.

"Elxa. You are standing. The curse has no power over you. How . . . ?"

"The Gold Breast, Frey," he whispered. "Its power is greater than the curse."

His eyes found the Raven. The spy was holding his head in his hand, slowly shaking it from side to side. "Raven?"

The spy met his gaze. "She demanded it. I made a vow to her. Forgive me."

Around the room the men began to push against the weight

of the word. His father was the first to wrestle it aside, lifting a reproachful gaze at Elxa.

"You bring . . . an heir of Tirragyl to taunt us?" he asked through clenched teeth.

"She didn't *want* to use the word." Anger surged through him at his father's behavior. He had never seen his father treat someone with such contempt. "You forced her to it when you called her a spawn of Taus."

His father lurched to his feet and sat down heavily on the platform. His brothers and some of the men were still on their knees, looking around warily for Nyla.

"Yet were my words not proven true?" his father asked. "Where did she go?"

"I will go and find her."

"No. Let the Raven go. I want to speak to you, Elxa."

"Yes, sir." The Raven's relief was evident as he slipped out the door.

"So." His father appraised him for a long, uncomfortable time. "It is true that this curse can be lifted. First my brother. Now you. Tell us how this happened."

And Elxa told them about Lohlyn on the fire pole and her dying words about the Gold Breast. He told them about Azab Rock and Klyden's arrow, which should have killed him. Finally he told them about a bird so beautiful that it almost hurt your eyes to look at it, of the warmth that had spread through him at the bird's call, taking away the cold, commanding voice of the curse, and replacing it with freedom.

By the time he was finished, there was longing on every face around him. They yearned for such freedom.

Nyla stumbled from the Rondel. Even on the platform, the guards were doubled over. The sight of them filled her with fresh shame. She ran to the rope and clambered down. *Away. Away.* All she wanted to do was get away from the Charab and their disdain and the evil that she had unleashed on them.

She found the path that Elxa had led her on this morning and ran wildly. Branches caught her face and grasped at her clothes. Roots clasped at her feet, but she continued to run, only catching her breath at the small bridge that led to the village. By now a rough plan had formed in her mind. She would try to get back to the main bridge and cross over to the Enderite Territory. Here she would pay one of the locals to take her to Gworlin Vale. She wouldn't try to find Klyden. Doing so would only lead the Charab to him. That and the fact that she never wanted to see the disillusionment in his eyes once he knew what she had done.

The village was quiet although several children scuttled into a doorway as they saw her. One woman, hanging up washing, startled as she saw the queen.

"Where is the hut where I was kept?" Nyla asked her breathlessly.

The woman hesitated. Then she pointed to one of the huts. Nyla smiled her thanks and ran to the hut to collect her bag, cursing when she remembered that her weapons had been confiscated. When she returned, the woman was still there.

"The path to the main bridge?"

"I'm not sure I should . . ."

"Please. I used the arming word on the men, and I just . . . I just have to get away."

The woman looked afraid. She pointed again. "That tall tree. Just next to it."

"Thank you."

Nyla found the beginning of the trail and forced herself to slow down, for every now and then a path snaked off the main one and it wasn't always easy to see which one she should take. She always chose the path that seemed the most worn, and finally she broke through the forest and onto the plateau. She began to run.

There were guards at the bridge, new ones that she didn't know. The oldest stepped up to her.

"Let me pass," she said in her most authoritative voice.

"We can't do that unless the Charabian allows it."

"Tell me. How do you think I got away from them all?" The man shook his head. "I'll tell you how. I used the arming word on them. And if you don't let me pass I will use it on you too."

His eyes widened in fear. "I am under orders to—"

"I don't want to say the word, and you don't want to hear it. I can tell you now that the Charabian will be glad to see the back of me. I am the spawn of Taus, if you did not know."

"I know who you are, but . . ."

She pushed past him then. If they laid a hand on her, she would say the word, but no sooner than that. They did not try to stop her.

The bridge swayed from side to side. *Don't look down.* Steadily she crept forward. It crossed her mind then that they could still stop her. All it would take was a single arrow. One arrow and the enemy they loathed would fall down, down, deep into the ravine below. She deserved it after what she had done to them. It would be quick at least. They knew how to make a kill shot, the Charab. But no arrow came.

When she finally reached solid ground, she sank to her knees and wept. Then, emptied of all but her will to survive, she stood up and began to run.

"Father, please let me go too."

"No, Elxa. Kol and his men will go. They will bring her back."

The Raven had returned a little earlier, accompanied by one of the bridge guards, with the news that the queen had crossed the bridge and now roamed, unarmed, in Enderite Territory.

"But what if she uses the arming word on them again? They'll be immobilized."

"If the girl is daft enough to do that, perhaps she doesn't deserve rescuing."

"She's far from daft, Father. She's afraid and ashamed. But she trusts me."

"You will stay, Elxa." His father's mouth was set in a line he knew all too well. He would not change his mind. "There are things we need to discuss."

"Let the Raven go then at least," Elxa pleaded.

"Fine." The Charabian motioned for the spy to join the search party. Elxa and his father were left alone in the Charabian's dwelling. It was the home he shared with his second wife, not the home Elxa had grown up in. Elxa knew it was a deliberate decision. His father did not want him to be at ease. When Frey slipped into the room a moment later, carrying the Verity Gem, he knew his father was particularly serious.

"You don't trust me anymore, Father?" The realization stabbed through him. "You think I would lie to you?"

"You *did* bring an enemy to our village," his father said stonily.

"She's not our enemy!"

"Anybody with the curse on their lips is an enemy."

"You didn't treat the Raven like this even though he spoke the word too," Elxa shot back. "And you treated her like an enemy long before she even said it."

"It's about intention."

"You angered her, Father. Insulted her beyond anything she had ever experienced before. She had no intention to use the word for evil. Doesn't her disappearance prove that? She could have had you marching on your head by now, otherwise."

"Enough! You will answer my questions." The Charabian nodded curtly at Frey, who cast an apologetic glance at Elxa.

"Fine. And if the stone goes grey, does one of your sons kill me? It's how you threaten all outsiders, is it not, Father?"

"If the stone goes grey, you will have proven what you found so very repulsive earlier—that I cannot trust my own son anymore."

Elxa could find no answer to that. His father's words were true.

"Did Klyden come with you into the Enderite Territory?" It was the Charab way. Direct. Go in for the kill.

"Yes."

"Is he near?"

Elxa looked down. *Far too near.* He had tried to dissuade Klyden from coming this far.

"Is he near, Elxa?" The first note of gentleness came through in his father's voice. It reminded Elxa that the Charabian didn't want to do this either. It was the curse, after all. Elxa could still remember the taunting voice of that curse, the pressure and pain that clenched at everything in you.

"He is near," Elxa finally said, casting a glance at the clear Verity Gem.

"Where is he, Elxa?"

"I will not tell you that, Father. I do not wish you to harm Klyden—for his sake and your own. I will protect you both."

He and his father both stared at the gem in Frey's hand. It remained clear. The truth had, after all, been spoken.

Finally his father smiled. "You remain a true son and a true Charab, Elxa." The Charabian nodded at Frey, and she wrapped the gem in a cloth and stood up. "You will stay in this house. My men and I will find Klyden."

Half an hour later, Elxa stood at the door of the Charabian's second home and watched his father and five fully armed men march to the path leading to the bridge. He tried to swallow away the lump of grief that rose in his throat. He may not have told his father everything, but he had told him enough. Enough to lead six of Tirragyl's best assassins to his cousin, his friend.

Frey crept beside him in the doorway, placing her warm hand into his icy cold one.

"Tell me again how you found the Gold Breast, Elxa."

"I didn't find her. She found me."

She drew him from the door to the rug, letting go of his hand to sit, cross-legged, on the floor.

"Well, let's pray to the Ancient One that the Gold Breast will find Father too. And soon." The childlike faith in her eyes momentarily lifted Elxa's despair. He sank to his knees next to his sister, and together they whispered out their hearts to the Charab's long-forgotten God—their only remaining hope.

CHAPTER 21

After what Shara had gone through with the Rif'iends, they decided to rest a few days in the clearing. Shara was relieved. The thought of going back into the forest filled her with dread now that she knew the black figures were there. They had been there all along—she had even heard their whispers—but now that she had seen them and experienced the strange numbing effect of their presence, she balked at the idea of going back into the Rif'twine.

The clearing, on the other hand, was light and filled with color and a sense of peace. Shara again sat in the middle of the flowers in a shaft of sunlight as Eliad started to read.

She had the sense that she was rocking slightly, as if she rode on a horse. The first thing that came into sight was the sky—a deeper, more beautiful shade of blue than she had ever seen before. Then she became aware of the men riding alongside her: Prince E'shua, Eli, and a third man. Despite the fast pace, she still had time to marvel at the beauty of the landscape. Towering mountains, forested dales, waterfalls, and fields of flowers. Ajalon was a feast for the eyes.

Shara had been drawn to the prince that first day she had seen him dancing with the children. But now as her gaze fell on him, something deeper tugged at her, something that left her feeling a confusing blend of joy and sorrow. The sense of belonging to someone vied with a sense of loss and anger that he had been taken from her life. If Eliad was telling the truth, E'shua was her brother, torn away from her fourteen years ago.

As they approached a small hamlet of houses, the prince slowed to a trot just as several children poured out of the houses, shouting loudly, "It's the prince!" Adults, too, emerged, waving and smiling.

The prince slowed to an unhurried walk, speaking and waving back at the people on the side of the road. A small girl of about five or six pulled away from her mother's grasp and darted into the road right in front of his horse. He reined in tightly and smiled down at her.

"I'm sorry, sire!" The mother hurried forward to grab her child.

"No, let her greet me," the prince said, laughing. "Lift her up here."

A man lifted the little girl up onto the prince's knee. He held her gently with one arm and asked, "What is your name?"

"Esther," she replied shyly.

"Have you ever been on a big horse like this?"

She shook her head.

"He likes it if you stroke him here." He patted the stallion's neck, and the girl's little hand followed tentatively.

He lowered his voice in a conspiratorial whisper. "Esther. I'm going to tell you something important. Will you remember it?" She nodded solemnly. "You're special and strong and loved." Her face broke into a smile that showed two missing teeth. As the prince handed her back to the outstretched arms of her mother, he whispered, "If anyone tells you otherwise, remember that a prince knows best."

Shara's eyes swam with tears. As the prince had lifted up the girl, she had imagined what it must feel like to have those strong, safe arms around you and hear your name spoken with such tenderness. She was ashamed at the pang of jealousy she felt.

They traveled on over hills and valleys and followed the course of the river winding through lush plains. At every hamlet they reached, the prince received a warm welcome. But all too soon, Shara saw a vast forest stretching ahead of them, and her mood dampened. The prince was on his way into the forest to rescue the princess. To rescue her.

At the edge of the forest, the prince and Eli dismounted and untied their saddlebags, swinging them over their shoulders. Then they handed their reins to the third man before turning towards the trees.

Prince E'shua looked solemnly at his companion. "You know the

Death Spell is at work in the forest, Eli. I will not see it as a weakness if you choose to stay in Ajalon."

"Do you remember when your father asked us to choose who we would follow?" Eli asked. "If you go into the forest, my liege, and I do not follow, I am untrue to myself."

"You are a great man to have by my side. Thank you, Eli."

In the forest, Shara sensed the familiar cold oppressiveness. Dread coursed through her as she thought of the Rif'iends. The prince set a fast pace, using his powers to move through the inhospitable forest. There was little talk between him and Eli as they concentrated on moving forward.

Eli eventually broke the silence. "Where are we heading, sire?"

"In a southeasterly direction. I suspect he will take her to one of the larger towns. Perhaps Lydora or Gwyndorr, where they can hide her without too many questions asked."

"How will we find her there, my prince?"

"I am not sure we will, Eli," he said, and there was sadness in the words. "But there is something I can do. Not only for her but for every one of my subjects. I need to make a way back for them through this forest. Already it is a barrier nobody can breach except with Old Magic powers."

"I don't understand." Eli frowned. "Are we not trying to find Princess Sarah?"

"We are. But it could be that Taus took her into the forest right away. She might be an old woman by now or . . ." The unspoken words weighed heavily between them. "Even if she has not been exposed to the Death Spell for long, Taus will guard her carefully. She will be difficult to find and reach."

The words halted, and slowly Shara became aware of the light and warmth of the clearing.

"We have nowhere to walk to today, Eliad, and no oil to ration," Andreo said. "Could we read a little more?"

The old man looked up at her questioningly. "There is much to take in here, Shara. Do you want me to continue?"

He was perceptive, Eliad, for as much as she wanted to be with the prince and Eli on their journey, fear had begun to creep in too.

When Eliad had first started reading the book, it had been just another story. Even though he had told her it was true, she had felt removed from it. This was a story about characters leading lives very different to her own, like the fables and legends of other books. But now she understood that *she* was a central character in the book. The prince was trying to rescue her, and this single thought filled her with both hope and dread. It meant that she was more loved than she could ever have imagined, yet also that she was the reason the prince was in danger.

Eliad and Andreo were looking at her expectantly. "Shara?"

"Yes, carry on, Eliad," she said after a while. "But it does take some getting used to, becoming a princess at my age."

Eliad opened the book and again began to read.

Shara's heart sank when she heard the single word that Prince E'shua spoke.

"Gwyndorr."

She slunk forward to where he and Eli stood and peered through the trees at the familiar city walls she had thought far behind her, now conjured by the book's words. The prince and Eli had reached their destination.

"What do we do now, my prince?" Eli asked.

Both men looked disheveled and tired. Eli's short, neatly trimmed beard had grown wild and bushy.

"We will go into the town and determine whether Taus is here," the prince said. "Let's start by finding a place to board."

Shara wandered with them through Gwyndorr's streets, bustling with traders and craftsmen. The stench of the sewers and the constant drone of voices jarred her senses after the beauty and peace of Ajalon.

"This is a dirty place," Eli whispered.

"Before the rebellion it was a city of great charm, with the majestic mountains as a backdrop." The prince looked around wistfully. "It was one of my favorite places in Ajalon. There was no wall because the people were safe. There was much music and dancing then. And horse parades." He laughed. "Gwyndorr was known for its magnificent horses and its skilled horse whisperers."

Several men pushed in close to them, giving them hostile stares.

"Let us find a tavern, Eli. We are drawing some unwanted attention."

They found one near the city gates. Its proprietor, a short, chubby man, greeted them effusively.

"Welcome, welcome, friends. My name is Yamiel. You are not from these parts?"

"No," the prince said.

"What parts are you from then?" Yamiel's smile didn't waver.

"Very far parts. Do you have a room, Yamiel? We will be here quite some time."

"Yes, yes. You have the look of important traders. Are you here for the Summer Fair?" he asked as he led them up the narrow stairs.

"We will stay for the Summer Fair," the prince answered.

"For you, my special guests, only the best room will do," Yamiel said as he swung open a door. It was dark and dirty, with a small hole in the wall to let in some light and air, although from the stench, Shara suspected the room looked directly over a rubbish-laden street. On the floor were two straw pallets, a large bowl of water, and a chamber pot.

Eli started to object. "This is not acceptable, Yamiel. We shall not—"

"It is a fine room," the prince interrupted. "We will take it. What is the price?"

Yamiel's smile faltered for an instant before it returned even more broadly.

"For you, I will make a special price. For I know you have come from such far parts. Three sovereign for the week."

"Ridiculous!" Eli sputtered.

"Fine. We will pay you now for four weeks," the prince said, taking out a pouch and laying five silver coins in Yamiel's outstretched palm. "I believe that is the equivalent of at least twelve sovereign?" For the first time Yamiel's smile reached his eyes.

"Ah! A man who knows quality when he sees it. You will be most comfortable, my friend. Most comfortable."

As he backed away, he said, "You can throw your refuse out of the hole in the wall. And you call me if you need anything else. I can arrange anything you need . . ."

"Thank you. We do not require anything more than this," the prince said, catching Eli's eye with a smile.

"Oh, but where are my manners? What shall I call my esteemed travelers?" Yamiel asked.

"I am . . . Shua, and this is . . . Eli . . . ad. Eliad," the prince said.

Shara startled when she heard the name. Eliad? She looked carefully at Eli's features. It was easier seeing the image of Eliad in his face now that he had such a bushy beard. And hadn't she thought he looked familiar the very first time she saw him in the king's council chamber? Yet Eliad's beard was almost white now, while Eli's was dark.

While she pondered over this new revelation, she had the sense that time was passing in the book. Several images flowed together.

She was with the prince and Eli walking on Gwyndorr's streets.

They were eating in a tavern and talking to an old man.

They stood watching a wrestling match at the Summer Fair.

They slept on the dark, damp floor in their tavern room.

They sat around a small fire in a house, surrounded by people listening intently as the prince spoke.

Finally, she stood with them in Yamiel's dark, narrow passage.

"Another twelve sovereign for the month, Yamiel?" The prince held out the coins.

Yamiel's eyes were drawn to the money, but he did not hold out his hand. Instead he said, "Ah, but my friend. You remember I gave you a good price for the room these last few months, for I knew you had come such a far way. Now the price will be the normal fare of twenty sovereign for the month."

"Ridiculous!" Eli sputtered. "We can find a much better room for a quarter of that price."

"Yes, but my friends, I am giving you so much more than a room." Yamiel's smile slipped slightly. "There are many people asking questions about my two guests from far places. But I am a loyal man and always good to my friends, so I have not told them anything."

"Are you threatening us?" Eli leaned menacingly towards the shorter man. The prince laid a restraining hand on his shoulder.

"No, no, my friends. I am just saying that you are safe here, under

Yamiel's care. That is worth many sovereign, don't you think?" The smile was back.

"As you say, Yamiel." The prince pulled the additional coins from his pouch and placed them in the man's now-outstretched hand. "But we do require something more from you."

The smile became thoughtful. "For you, Shua, Yamiel will find anything you need. A beautiful woman, maybe? A horse? You are too esteemed to walk on foot. What is it you need?"

"Information," the prince said.

Yamiel's chest seemed to puff out even more. "Anything, anything. Yamiel knows much that goes on in the city. In fact, there is no better man to ask. Nothing happens in Gwyndorr that is unnoticed by Yamiel."

"I knew you were the right man to ask. What I need to know is whether any other strangers besides us have entered the city in the last few months."

"But there are so many people coming and going. Surely you have seen this for yourself? Gwyndorr is a busy trading city."

"The person I seek could have two children with him. The older, a boy, and the younger, a girl. I believe his intention will be to stay in the city, to establish himself."

Yamiel's smile was calculating. "Why do you seek such a traveler?"

"I have business with him."

"Of course, of course. Where are my manners? I will try to find out if such a man has come into the city. It may be costly, though. People speak more freely when they hold a sovereign or two in their hands."

Eli watched stonily as the prince handed over another ten sovereign to Yamiel.

"Thank you, Shua. With this Yamiel will make a start."

The door had hardly closed behind him before Eli spoke. "My prince, I never question your actions, but please allow me to speak my mind now."

"Of course."

"That man is a snake in the grass! He is charging us far too much for this rat-infested dump, he is threatening us, and now you have even told him our mission in Gwyndorr. You cannot trust him!"

"You are right."

"And the money will reach no one's hands but his own," Eli continued.

"I know, Eli."

"And he won't keep his mouth shut either. He'll be telling the first person who asks what we are here for."

"It's true. Absolutely true."

Eli's tirade dried up as he realized the prince was agreeing with him. "If you know this, why did you give him so much information to use against us?"

"Well, because I do need information," the prince said, sitting down on his straw pallet, "and I actually believe Yamiel when he says he has his finger on the pulse of Gwyndorr. And because I am not trying to hide my presence here. Taus knows I will come for Sarah. One of the easiest ways for me to find him is for him to find me."

"Forgive me for speaking so bluntly, my prince, but that makes no sense whatsoever."

The prince laughed heartily. "I suppose it doesn't. But Eli?" His tone grew serious. "Trust me. I do have a plan."

CHAPTER 22

There had been no Warrior attacks today, and Lucian took it as a bad sign. It meant that the Warriors were planning something big. His eyes scanned the peaks ahead of them. They were not as tall as the distant triple peaks, but they were still an imposing barrier between the king's army and the Grotto.

"Lucian." Alexor's voice broke into his thoughts. "I think we have scared those Parashi back into their hill holes."

"Possibly, sire," Lucian said, taking the tumbler of tea that one of Alexor's men held out to him. No longer under attack, the king had called a halt at midday to give the horses and men a rest. Lucian's gaze fell on the army commander, Rillon. His own skepticism was mirrored on Rillon's face.

"What do you think, Commander?" Lucian asked. "Have we scared them away?"

"I fear they may be regrouping and planning an attack, Lord Lucian," Rillon said, looking uncomfortably at the king. Lucian knew well that Alexor could react unpredictably to news he did not want to hear. Yet they had to face the facts. Their lives depended on it.

"Pah! We have dispelled them at every turn. They are no match for us," the king said.

"Let us not forget what they did to us that first night. Since then they have only engaged us in small skirmishes, sire. I fear they are capable of much more," Rillon said.

"You *fear*?" Alexor turned on the commander. "The commander of my army fears a group of Lowborn rebels?"

Lucian watched Rillon's face contort with humiliation and anger. Finally he said, "I do not fear them, sire. But neither do I underestimate their abilities. They have, after all, resisted the kings of Tirragyl for more than four hundred years."

Now it was the king who flushed. For a moment Lucian thought that his volatile anger would flare up, but then Alexor seemed to take stock of the men's assent with Rillon's sentiments. Lucian was surprised at the king's next question. For once, it showed a measure of humility. "So where would you plan such an attack if you were a Parashi, Rillon?"

Rillon pointed to the peaks ahead of them. "The narrow point where the Feyn River cuts between those two mountains, sire. We'd be at our most vulnerable there."

"But there's no other way to the triple peaks. We have no choice but to push through it."

"There might be another pass somewhere through that chain of mountains." Rillon let his eyes sweep eastwards over the imposing range.

"But we will be just as vulnerable at any pass, won't we, Rillon?" the king asked.

"Not if there aren't any Warriors there, sire," Rillon answered, "because they're all protecting this particular point here."

"I sense a plan, Commander," Lucian said with a knowing smile.

Pearce had expected the king's army to reach Rogue's Neck that afternoon. His men were all in position, waiting for his command to attack. But the army had stopped along the Feyn River, at least a two-hour march from the Neck, and had not moved since. From his position on the eastern peak above the Neck, Pearce could just see them, like a throbbing army of titan ants.

"Pearce, the men have returned from Waif's Cleft," Crif said from behind him. Pearce turned to see Nezer, a fellow Warrior commander, striding towards him.

"Your men rode fast," Pearce said with a smile. "I'm glad you made it."

"What in the abyss did you call us here for?" Nezer retaliated with a scowl.

"Well. Good day to you too, Nezer! You might care to take a look down the ravine." Pearce moved aside so that Nezer could see the king's army for himself. "I've lost too many men these last few days, and I need all the Warriors I can get. This," Pearce pointed to the narrow Neck below them, "is where we stop the king's army once and for all."

Nezer let out a low whistle. "It's a huge army, Pearce. But I was there when the High Commander told you to position a unit at the Cleft. I was unhappy to leave it."

"Alexor's entire army is *here*. All you'd be doing at Waif's Cleft is swatting away fru-flies. A waste of those great archer skills, wouldn't you say?"

Finally, Nezer's face broke into a smile. "You're right. Let's get these Highborn pigs. They won't know what hit them."

"Right. I have men positioned all along the Neck on the eastern and western peaks." Pearce pointed to his units, well hidden on the mountains. "I want you and your men to take position at the base of the mountain, as the Neck widens again. Take down anybody who makes it through."

Nezer's expression was serious again. "It's a dangerous position, Pearce."

"I know, Nezer. But we'll throw everything—and I mean every-thing—at them on their way through. The ones that make it will be dazed and battered and no match for a Warrior's arrow."

"As you say, Commander," Nezer said with a grim nod. "May this battle go down in glorious Warrior history." They gripped each other's arms in firm Warrior style.

Over the next hours, Pearce watched Nezer and his men nimbly make their way down to the ravine bed. They were in position before nightfall.

The king's army still had not moved.

• • •

As in the previous nights, Mikel's voice echoed through the nearly empty chamber, filled only with women, grooms, blade-masters, and a small remnant of Warriors. The words of the book again took Nicho to the familiar streets of Gwyndorr, streets he had hoped never to see again.

Time had passed, for the prince and Eli had arrived in springtime, but now the air had a bite of winter in it. Nicho followed the prince, Eli, and Yamiel up a steep street. Yamiel was panting so heavily for breath that, for once, he wasn't smiling.

"Are we almost there, Yamiel?"

"Yes . . . yes," Yamiel huffed. "At the top."

Nicho realized they were approaching Lord Lucian's manor. The last time he had been there was when they had rescued Shara.

"Here?" the prince asked, pointing at the imposing gate where two men stood guard.

Yamiel nodded, leaning his hands on his knees and trying to catch his breath. After a while he straightened up and spoke.

"This is it. Lord Poldyr's manor house. The finest in all of Gwyndorr."

"It is fine," Eli said, peeking at the mansion through the gates. A guard moved towards them.

"And according to your informant, today is the wedding day of the lord's granddaughter to a foreigner?" the prince said.

"Yes. My cousin's wife has a brother who works for Lord Poldyr. Apparently a foreign man has asked Lord Poldyr for his granddaughter Tessor's hand in marriage. This is not so strange for she is an heiress to a huge fortune and a title. I would just about marry the ugly wench myself." Yamiel laughed. "What is strange though is that they have agreed to it. Over the years she has turned down many such requests. Believe it or not, the old man actually asks her opinion."

"What do you want?" a gruff voice asked. The guard was standing opposite them at the gate.

"I am looking for Urda. It is Yamiel, his sister's cousin."

"He is busy. Come back tomorrow after the wedding feast."

"No, no. He said I must bring a scribe to record the betrothal agreement." He gestured towards the prince.

"Lord Poldyr has his own scribe."

"It has to be a town scribe," Yamiel countered.

"That's not the town scribe. He looks like a foreigner. Now get out of here."

"You don't want to make Lord Poldyr angry, do you? But here . . ." Yamiel held out a pouch with some coins in it. "We won't be long. Half an hour, no more."

The guard quickly pocketed the pouch as he glanced towards the guardhouse. "Fine," he said. "You and you. The other one," he pointed to Eli, "stays here. Urda is in the hall, putting up the tables. Come back as soon as you are finished."

"Thank you, thank you, my friend. Urda will be most pleased." Yamiel and the prince slipped through the narrow opening in the gate and walked over the cobbled stones towards the house.

Nicho looked around with interest, for it looked different than how he had remembered it. The gardens were beautiful and colorful. The men working in them waved at the prince and Yamiel as they passed them. Where the strange statues had stood, there were ponds joined by small streams filled with gliding fish. It felt peaceful.

At the door they were welcomed by a friendly older man, who directed them to the hall where Urda was supervising the household staff as they laid out tables and benches for the wedding banquet. Despite Yamiel's prediction, Urda did not seem particularly glad to see them.

"It's a busy day to visit, Yamiel. I am surprised they let you in."

The rebuff did not deter Yamiel. "It is good to see you again, dearest cousin. This is my good friend, Shua. He just wanted to ask you some questions about the foreigner who is to marry Lady Tessor."

"Why?" Urda eyed the prince with suspicion. "What's it got to do with him?"

"He has come from far places to find his foreign friend. It will be worth a few sovereign to you to help him know if this is his friend or not. This is not too much to ask, is it?" He smiled as he laid the pouch in Urda's hand.

"I have little time and will answer only a few questions," Urda said. "But this is not a good place."

He led them outside behind the stables.

"What do you want to know?" Urda turned impatiently to the prince.

"Tell me this man's name and how he came to ask for Lady Tessor's hand in marriage."

"Sir Lucian. He did not say where he came from, but he is darker than our people and speaks a different way." Urda added thoughtfully, "Somewhat like you."

"Did he have anybody with him?" the prince asked.

"No, only a few men were in his attendance. There is a rumor among the servants that he has a young son hidden somewhere in the town, but it must be kitchen gossip. Nobody has seen him with a child."

"And a baby?"

"No. Is that all?"

"Why did the lord and his granddaughter agree to this marriage?" Yamiel asked with genuine curiosity. "She's turned down countless men over the years, hasn't she?"

"True love, apparently," Urda said. "The two of them look like young lovebirds. They can't keep their eyes off each other. He is, of course, a fair bit older than her, but it seems he is as besotted as she is herself. So do you think this is the friend you seek?"

"I feel it may be," the prince answered. "When do you expect him to arrive today?"

"He is already here," Urda said with some surprise. "He and his men have been staying here this week. In the eastern wing." He pointed to the rooms above the door through which Shara had escaped.

"Is there any way we could see him?" the prince asked.

Urda shrugged. "Not unless he comes down soon. You can't stay till the wedding banquet."

"What if you call him down for some reason?" Yamiel suggested.

"I am little more than a houseboy. Why would he come down on my request?" Urda asked. "I need to get back."

"Tell you what . . . ," Yamiel thought quickly. "We will stay hidden here for another half an hour. If in that time you can manage to get Sir

Lucian to come down to the stable, we will give you . . ." He looked at the prince.

". . . five more sovereign," the prince finished.

"Ten," Urda said.

"Seven," Yamiel said, "and your cousin's undying devotion."

"Cousin through marriage only." Urda scowled. "I'll see what I can do."

They stayed hidden behind the stable for more than half an hour. Yamiel had just signaled to the prince that it was time to go when the manor door swung open. Two men emerged. The front man was tall and greying at the temples. It was Lord Lucian, younger than when Nicho had seen him last, but Lucian no doubt.

Nicho stared long at his bearded face, and finally the truth jolted through him. This man was both Taus and Lord Lucian. They were one and the same man. How it was possible, Nicho did not know, but it was true. And Taus now stood a few feet away from the prince, the man he wanted dead.

Yamiel turned eagerly to Prince E'shua and whispered, "Is this the man you are seeking?"

"It is him," he answered softly.

CHAPTER 23

Klyden woke in the dark of night and listened. It was so quiet that he could almost hear his heart beating. Too quiet, in fact. His body prickled with a sense of danger. He told himself that nobody could see him here, tied into the fork of a tall woodland tree, yet he knew it was something every Charab was taught: *when you're alone, without a watchman, the safest place to sleep is in a tree.*

He lay, unmoving, for a long while until he was sure nobody was near. Then, as quietly as he could, he untied the ropes, lifted his pack from a higher branch, and shimmied down the trunk. *Listen to your instinct*, his father used to say, and his instinct was telling him to move.

He moved west, deeper into the Enderite woods, feeling his way from trunk to trunk in near silence. At the sound of a soft rustle or twig breaking, he froze, but each time it was only a small quill hare or buck, caught off-guard by the unobtrusive human.

By the time pale light spilled through the canopy of trees, Klyden again pulled himself into the branches of a tree. He was tired, but he could not sleep now—not in the light. He dug in his pack for some of the edible roots he had gathered yesterday and chewed on one of these as he watched and waited, bow in hand.

He sensed them before he heard or saw them. The Charab sense is a fine-tuned instrument, and he knew if it was working for him, it was working for them too. He initially thought there were only four men, but after a few moments he realized there were six. They were moving in a paired formation that told him they did not yet know exactly where he was. But it was only a matter of time.

Clinically, his mind formed a plan. Shoot man one and man two, who would both be in his clear line of vision within a few paces. Drop to the ground while throwing a blade at man three and man four, who should instinctively move closer. It was the last two men who would prove difficult. They would have time to pinpoint his position and draw an arrow on him. Yet even a Charab occasionally made a mistake. *If* he was still alive by the time man four hit the ground, he could change position and, shielded by the tree, take out man five with the blade in his left hand and man six with the blade in his right. He estimated there was a one-in-four chance of survival.

His arrow was in place as man one came into his sight. It was the face that undid him—the greying hair and dark beard so like his father's. Was this how his father had felt when this same man—the new Charabian—came for him on Azab Rock? Was that why he had taken his own life rather than loose an arrow into the heart of his beloved younger brother? Klyden could not hesitate any longer; his plan hinged on this first arrow reaching its mark. He drew it back.

Don't shoot him. The voice filled his mind, strong and commanding. *They are destined to be mine. You are not to harm them.*

But they are curse bound. They will kill me.

You are mine too, and I will not let them harm you. Reveal yourself to them. Klyden hesitated. *Now, my son.*

Klyden knew the voice well enough, although it had never before spoken with such clarity. He knew there was only one thing he could do: obey. Yet fear gripped him at the thought.

He dropped his bow and arrows and all the blades from his hiding place in the tree before sliding to the ground, hands above his head in surrender.

"I am here, Uncle," he said, staring at the Charabian's face, even as his uncle's sword tip pointed at his heart.

"Klyden, you fool." His uncle's face crumpled with grief. "You are my assignment."

"I know."

The five other men were now all silently in position around him, swords in hand. Klyden knew each one of them by name.

His uncle looked down at the pile of weapons at his feet. "You could have taken us, Klyden. You probably had a one-in-four chance."

"The Gold Breast wouldn't let me. Said you were destined to be free of this curse, just as I am."

"Gold Breast?" His uncle's eyes roamed the trees hungrily. "Is it here?" Even as he said the words, a shudder struck his body, and he clenched his jaw in pain. "The curse . . . it . . . it won't . . ." He tightened his grip on the sword. "I'm sorry, Kly . . ."

"You *can* be free!" Klyden cried. "You and all your men. This curse is weak compared to the strength of the Gold Breast."

"Nothing weak about it." There was resolve in his uncle's gaze now. He wanted this distasteful deed behind him.

"Look at me," Klyden said. "I look just like your sons. Wouldn't you fight this curse if you had to plunge a sword into their hearts? Wouldn't you fight it with all your heart if Elxa stood in my place? Or Frey?"

The girl's name unleashed emotion in the Charabian's eyes, undid the curse's power for an instant. "Frey," he whispered. "Not Frey."

"Frey doesn't want you to do this," Klyden said. "She called on the Ancient King to save us both." How did he even know that? he wondered fleetingly. The words were filling his mouth before they even reached his mind. "Frey and Elxa loosened the curse's power with their prayers. You just have to *believe* and *act* as if it is defeated."

"Generations, Klyden. It's bound us for generations," the Charabian groaned.

"No! My father was free. I am free. We are not bound by one pitiful man's curse any more. We owe our allegiance to One far greater than him!" Klyden felt the warmth of the Gold Breast within him now, and it washed away all his fear. "We are the beloved of Ab'El, not the puppets of Taus."

The words were infused with the Gold Breast's power. He watched them settle on his uncle, whose eyes widened in surprise, then understanding, and finally joy.

His sword dropped from his hand, and he stared at Klyden in amazement.

"We are not bound anymore. We are free," he declared with certainty.

All around Klyden, swords clattered to the ground, and men sank to their knees with joy-filled tears. Free. Finally, truly *free*.

Hardy Enderite horses awaited them outside the woodland. The nearest villagers to the bridge were always prepared to supply them, fearing what the Charab might do if they were denied. The joy Klyden saw on the Charab faces around him was matched by his own joy at riding amongst his kin. They set a fast pace. By midafternoon, the horses had been returned, and Klyden was making his way across the bridge to the home he had never expected to see again.

The guards on the far side stared in amazement at him as he leapt off the bridge, before turning questioning eyes to the Charabian, who had crossed just before him.

"It's quite a story," the Charabian said. "There will be a gathering at the Rondel tonight where I will explain it all. Tell me, did Kol and his men return with the queen?"

"The men returned, sir, but without her. She has vanished without a trace."

"The queen?" Klyden looked at his uncle sharply. "You mean Nyla isn't with Elxa in the village?"

"She bolted."

"Bolted? Past the bridge guards?"

"She threatened to use the arming word on them." His uncle pursed his lips. "And given that she'd used it on the rest of us, she probably would have too."

"By the abyss!" Klyden's mind reeled at this revelation. Nyla had used Taus's curse on his people. How could it be? He had thought he knew her heart. He had been wrong.

"Let's get back and hear from Kol," his uncle said. "I don't like the thought of her out there alone."

"I am her protector," Klyden said, glancing back over the bridge. "I will set off immediately and find her."

"Come to the village and hear from the men first, Kly. Then you'll have a better idea of where she might be."

One of the bridge guards must have gone on ahead, for word had already reached the village by the time they got there. *One of their lost sons had returned. The curse was broken.* Men, women, and children spilled out of the huts and ran to the path as their group arrived. A cheer arose amongst the men, and a host of voices picked up an old Parashi battle song as the men passed by. Children, sensing the festive air, darted around joyfully. Frey ran forward with a tear-stained face and threw her arms around her father. Elxa was close behind her, his face beaming as he embraced Klyden.

"The Gold Breast came?" he asked.

Klyden nodded. "Your prayers were heard." The surprise on Elxa's face gave way to a solemn frown at Klyden's next question. "But what of Nyla, Elxa? Your father says she isn't here."

"She left two days ago. Kol and his men set off almost immediately. Maybe she had two hours on them, no more. But they can't find a single clue as to where she went."

"She used the arming word?"

"At the Rondel," Elxa said. "That's when she ran. I don't think she understood its power till then."

"I wouldn't have thought her capable of it," Klyden said softly.

"My father"—Elxa looked to where the Charabian stood speaking to his wives—"he treated her with contempt. It angered her. She had no intention of using it, I think, but . . ."

"Still. It reminds us of who she is."

"Kly. You weren't here. It wasn't like that."

"I am under oath to protect her, no matter what she's done," Klyden said grimly. "I will set off now. Will you come, Elxa?"

Elxa nodded. "If my father allows it."

"How much longer to Gworlin Vale?" Nyla asked.

"Before sun sink," the one called Drul answered. He was the

older of the two Enderite traders who had come across Nyla an hour after she ran from the Charab bridge. Small but stout, like all his countrymen, Drul's face seldom broke out of a scowl. Still, Nyla preferred him to his leering younger brother, Pry. Curse those Charab for taking her weapons and leaving her so vulnerable!

"Why you go there?" Pry grinned. "You come to Harnai and be our good omen for to sell."

She still struggled to understand their accent and strange sentences. It wouldn't surprise her if Pry had actually just suggested they sell her at Harnai.

"No. My friend waits at The Hog and Tankard," she lied. The Raven had said the tavern keeper was a decent sort. Perhaps he would help her from there. She couldn't wait to get out of her present company.

Nyla would happily forget the last three days. When she stepped off the bridge, her only goal had been to get as far from the Charab as she could. Yet, on joining the traders, she had soon realized that she may have jumped out of the cauldron and into the fire. When they came upon her, Pry had looked her up and down the way one might assess a horse, and she had sensed he was a man to stay away from. Yet, she had had little option but to give them five silver coins and to tell them that her friend would double the amount on her safe return to Gworlin Vale. Drul's eyes had lit up at the sight of the money and the promise of more to come.

She had slept restlessly the last few nights, her hands around her money pouch. Last night she had awakened in the dark and watched the two men sitting at the fire, arguing and casting sidelong glances her way. Were they discussing how to rob her, sell her, dispose of her body? Nyla did not sleep again after that, even when she heard their rhythmic snoring.

"You take turn on toes." Drul's growl broke through the disturbing memory.

She slid off the back of his horse and grabbed the reins of the heavily loaded donkey that he held out to her. Not a very gallant people, the Enderites. She was definitely doing a lot more walking than they were and had to listen to a constant stream of grumbling about her slowness.

Drul's words proved true for, an hour or two later, well before sunset, she caught sight of the Endorai River and—beyond it—the Tirragylin town of Gworlin Vale. The rush of relief that swept through her was so great that she did not notice the look that passed between the two men.

"My good companions," she said, feeling remarkably amiable, "you have done as you promised and brought me to Gworlin Vale. Here your reward awaits."

"Reward too small," Pry said. "Need more."

"More! Ten silver coins is a lot. I do not have more."

"Not coins," Pry said. "You."

If his words were unclear, the look he gave her was not. The fear that had lain dormant in her these last few days unfurled deep inside her.

"Drul," she said, her voice betraying her fear, "you will not receive the coins I promised if anything happens to me." Surely his greed would overcome Pry's lust.

"Coins in your cloth," Drul said mildly, pointing at her robes. "We take for us and slow three days."

Pry had climbed off his horse and was coming towards her now. She let go of the horse's reins and began backing away from the leering Enderite.

He merely smiled, and his gaze seemed to consume her. "You like, pretty one. I good."

"No." She threw all her old authority into that single word, but it did not stop him.

She turned away from him then and began to run. It was hopeless, of course, and she knew it, but still she ran, trying to ignore the heavy panting behind her that proved he was close.

He reached for her, grabbed at her robe. It tore away in his hands, and he stumbled backwards, giving her a little bit of ground.

It was then that she heard the distant beat of hooves. She saw two riders in the distance, and she stopped running and began to wave.

"Help me! Over here."

"Enderite horsemen." Pry grabbed roughly at her arm. She could smell his rancid breath as he leaned in close and whispered, "They not care for Tirragyl's wench. Maybe they have you too when I fi—"

His word was cut short by the arrow that hit him in the center of his chest. He looked down at it in surprise, then at her, almost pleadingly, before falling heavily to the ground.

One of the horsemen galloped past her as the other reined in sharply. She was too afraid to look at this new Enderite captor.

"Sir, I have nothing. I—"

"Nyla. It's me."

"Klyden!"

Her protector slid off the horse's back and turned his dark eyes to her. "Did he harm you?"

"Not yet. But . . ." Suddenly it felt as if her legs could not hold her anymore. Klyden reached out for her as she began to wobble. He drew her into an embrace, smelling of wood smoke and mountain heather. When her body was no longer shaking, he pushed her away.

"Can you stand?"

"Yes. How . . . how did you get here so fast?"

"We rode through the night and swapped horses this morning at another village so we could keep up our pace." He looked up as Elxa returned. "Did you deal with him?"

"He begged for mercy. Said he had no intention of harming her. I tied him to the tree." Elxa dipped his head towards her. "Good to see you again, Your Majesty."

"Let him go. It was his brother," she cast a quick look at the dead man on the ground, "who had the bad intentions."

"Fine." Klyden mounted his horse and effortlessly lifted her off the ground, placing her in front of him. "Let's go get a meal and some rest."

This time Nyla sipped slowly at the berry beer, remembering well how intoxicating it had been the previous time they were at this tavern. They spoke little, although Elxa did tell her how the Gold Breast had saved Klyden's life and lifted the curse off the Charabian and his men.

"But the bird didn't appear?" she asked.

"No, but she spoke through Klyden with as much power as if she were actually there." Elxa grinned. "Isn't that incredible?"

"So you are free to return to your village now, Klyden," Nyla said, glancing his way. He had hardly spoken to her since the rescue.

"Yes." His gaze was guarded, unreadable. "But as long as you are in danger, the vow I made to your grandmother binds me to you."

"Perhaps I should free you of it."

"It doesn't work that way."

"So I'm stuck with you then?" she teased.

He didn't smile. "It appears we are stuck with each other."

"Well, don't look so happy about it." Nyla's anger flared up. "I'd rather not have you by my side if you're going to be so morose."

"Because you fare so very well by yourself, don't you, Nyla?" His brief gaze was dark, unsettled.

"I would have fared better if the Charab hadn't stolen my weapons and left me completely defenseless."

"Yes. And rather a waste of time on their part, to take away your weapons when there was only *one* you really needed." Now his eyes flashed with anger too.

This was all about the arming word and the generations of kings who had kept his people captive, just as she had tried to do when she spoke that cursed word. A fresh wave of shame filled her at the memory.

"I shouldn't have used it, Klyden. I had no idea what—"

"Of course you didn't have any idea," he interrupted. "None of your forefathers ever thought of the terrible pain they were inflicting either. It was always just about what they wanted. What *you* wanted." He pushed himself up from the table and looked at his cousin. "It's been a long few days, Elxa. I am going to bed."

She didn't watch him climb the steps. Elxa gave her an apologetic smile before taking a hasty bite of the bread husk the tavern owner had brought them. Nyla's hunger was suddenly gone. She gulped down her rising tears with a long draught of berry beer and let the horror of what she had done to Klyden's people wash over her afresh.

CHAPTER 24

Shara was, as usual, the first to wake, but since that frightening day in the clearing, she always stayed in the safety of her blanket. It was not long before Eliad stirred awake. Andreo slept soundly next to them. Shara had the impression that he had fallen asleep much later than they had, for she had woken once in the night to find him pensively staring into the fire. The realization that Lucian and Taus were the same man had knocked Andreo hard. All his life he had worshiped a mere mortal, and a cruel one at that. The disillusionment that had started with his disgracing at the monastery had crept ever deeper. He was questioning the very foundations of his life, growing quieter and quieter as he did so.

Shara and Eliad prepared some food and packed their blankets quietly in preparation for the journey, although Shara still felt some trepidation about setting off again.

"Every day I am afraid to walk deeper into the forest, Eliad," she said softly as they worked alongside each other. "Are they always there? Or will they leave us alone now?"

"I won't lie to you, Shara. They are there, waiting for their chance to draw you away. But the One with us is much greater than they are. That is what we need to trust in."

"The One with us?" Shara tried to make sense of his words. "Tabeal? But she's just a bird. And she only appears every now and then."

"A remarkable bird, don't you think? And never far away."

Shara nodded, thinking back to the feeling of peace whenever Tabeal sat on her shoulder, of the light and warmth piercing the cold fear, of the direction and comfort the bird gave when she was there.

"When Tabeal is with us, it is as if the king himself is here," Eliad added.

"I don't understand."

"In the Rif'twine, with its confusion and deception, these things make little sense. But one day it will be as apparent to you as your face's reflection in a crystal-clear pool."

Shara asked no more questions. Her thoughts already spun with all that she had learned. *Nothing is as it seems*, Andreo kept muttering lately, and Shara felt the same struggle to make sense of all the new insights.

Once Andreo woke up and they had eaten some breakfast, they set off again. Since leaving the clearing, the monotonous landscape of the forest had started to change. No longer were they making their way across flat land, but the path wound through terrain that became more rugged the farther they went. Initially, Shara had noticed only the increased slope of the ground, slowing them down and tiring them out, but now they found themselves skirting around cliffs and traversing valleys. Once the path had led down to a river, and they had been forced to half clamber, half slide down the steep embankment in order to cross it. This river, which—Eliad said— had its source high in the mountains, was stronger and deeper than the little stream they had followed out of the clearing. It had been a challenge to keep their balance on the wet, slippery rocks under the water's surface, and several times Shara had almost lost her footing before Eliad reached out to steady her. Once across, they had to climb up a steep incline on the other side of the river and follow an equally winding track parallel to the river.

Shara enjoyed the change of scenery. Back in Gwyndorr, she had liked the view from the small windows in some of the bedrooms, where she could see a small part of the distant mountains. Trapped as she had been, she had sometimes imagined what it would be like to walk amongst those majestic cliffs and had wondered what lay on the other side of them. Now she was in the northern part of that very same mountain range, according to Eliad. These were the mountains, he said, that the rebels had escaped to after their battle with the king's army.

That night they stopped at a small clearing overlooking the river. Shara enjoyed the sound of the gurgling water. After the clearing with the flowers, this was the most peaceful place they had found in the Rif'twine. They went down to the river in the early evening and drank deeply from its sweet water. Shara also washed and, sitting by the fire that night, felt more refreshed than she had in many days. Andreo had found two silver fish caught in a small pool, and the aroma of them roasting on the fire filled her with a pleasant anticipation.

"They'll take a little while," Eliad said. "Let's make the time pass faster by reading, shall we?"

Andreo nodded eagerly, but Shara felt the familiar anxiety that had been gnawing at her lately. Every night Shara was emotionally torn as the words transported them back to Gwyndorr and the prince's determined search for her. Observing him felt like a gift. Yet as the story progressed, a sense of dread had crept into her that she carried with her long after Eliad closed the book. For as easily as the prince had tracked down Taus, she feared Taus would track down the prince. And she kept wondering about the words the Rif'iend had spoken about his fate. The one thought that she could not shake was that if the prince were still alive, he would be here now, leading her home.

"Shara?" Eliad asked gently. "Do you want me to continue?"

She knew she could not stop or change the end of the story. She nodded. Maybe knowing would be a relief.

The words took her back to the streets of Gwyndorr. Again Yamiel led the way. This time she knew exactly where they were for it was her own street that they walked on and Randin's house that they approached.

Yamiel was speaking. ". . . or so they say. It is hard to believe really, for the captain is a man as hard as nails. His wife, too, is not the type to take pity on a child."

"And yet they have taken in their cousin's destitute child," the prince said thoughtfully.

"That's what Yamiel hears on the streets," Yamiel said.

As they walked past Randin's house, two guards moved closer. If Yamiel's intention had been to engage them in conversation, their expressions must have deterred him, for he did little more than greet them and move on. The prince and Eli both looked briefly through the gates to the courtyard before following Yamiel. At the top of the street, they headed down a small alleyway and wound their way back to the tavern.

Back in their small room, the prince and Eli discussed the latest information.

"How do we find out if it is her, my liege?" Eli asked.

The prince thought for a while. "We won't be able to gain access to the house. It is more closely guarded than the town prison."

"Probably why Taus chose it," Eli said, "but how would he have convinced a man as hard as that to take in a child?"

"You must remember that in the last few months, Taus, or Lucian as he is now called, has become the most important man in this town. Marrying Lord Poldyr's granddaughter gave him status, and with the lord's death, he took over his land and title."

"Death! Just over a week after the wedding? I am sure Taus had a hand in it."

"Suspicious, indeed," the prince agreed. "Randin is a man motivated by wealth. Yamiel says he is quick to take a bribe or two."

"Taus could be paying him to take in the child?"

"That's what I suspect."

"What a terrible place for the princess to be," Eli paced to the window. "And she's been there more than a year already!

"I am sorry, my prince," Eli said hastily as he saw the sorrow on E'shua's face. "I just feel an urgency to rescue her."

"I do too. But the time and the manner are not as you would wish. This is not just about Sarah. I want to rescue every one of my subjects from Taus's curse. I want to make a way back to Ajalon. For all of them."

"Back to Ajalon? How, Prince E'shua?"

"You will see soon enough, Eli. The time is near. But now let us find out if this child is our Sarah."

He took a small reed pipe out of his pocket, brought it to his lips, and blew on it. No sound came from it, but Shara had seen the pipe before, when Eliad had given it to Nicho. She knew who he called.

Hardly any time seemed to pass before Shara saw the familiar red-and-gold flash at the prince's window.

"The Gold Breast, my liege," Eli said in surprise. "How did she get here so quickly from your father's court?"

The prince laughed heartily. "You have been gone from Ajalon too long, my friend. You have forgotten the ways of Old Magic. Tabeal is not bound by time as we are here." He stretched his arm towards the window, and the bird flew to him and perched on his hand. He moved her close to his face and whispered to her. The bird twittered in response, and the prince again laughed.

"Apparently, all is well in Ajalon. It is little more than half an hour since we left.

"I have an important job for you, Tabeal," the prince continued. "Go to the house of the Captain of the Guard and tell me if Sarah is there."

Again, almost no time passed before she returned to chirp in the prince's ear.

This time he looked up solemnly. "As we suspect, Sarah is in the house."

"What do we do now?"

"We wait, Eli. Already plans are set in motion. It is just a matter of time before they reach their fulfillment. And I have many things I need to tell you, for you and Tabeal will have to undertake a part of Sarah's rescue alone."

"Do we go for her right now, my prince?" Eli's face lit up.

"You have not listened, Eli." The prince's words were sorrowful, not angry. "Come, let me explain it all."

Eli and the prince sat together, and Shara strained to hear their conversation, but the book's words pulled her away, towards the door.

Now she found herself in the dark, dirty passage of the tavern, feeling her way down the stairs. These led abruptly into a room full of loud men sitting at wooden tables laden with tankards of mead. Shara recoiled at the smell of alcohol as she pushed invisibly past the men. They reminded her of Maldor and his friends at her wedding feast.

She spotted Yamiel standing by the tavern door, giving instructions to a young barmaid. His eyes flicked over the room, lingering on the entrance to the stairs from which she had just come. He turned and pushed open the door and went out into the night. Shara followed him. The air was cool and pleasant after the stuffiness of the tavern.

He seemed purposeful as he hurried down Gwyndorr's dark roads and alleys. Shara looked with interest at the people loitering in the shadows. Their eyes followed Yamiel appraisingly. Some scantily dressed women called out for his attention, but he ignored them. She remembered Nicho telling her that Gwyndorr could be a dangerous place at night, that few went out alone. Yamiel must have serious business to take the risk.

She almost lost sight of the tavern owner as he ducked around a corner. She followed him into a narrow alleyway where he stopped abruptly by a door, glancing around as he knocked. Shara heard a muffled voice from inside, and Yamiel answered with a single word.

As the door swung open, a muscled man beckoned Yamiel inside. Shara slipped inside before the door slammed closed. She followed the man and Yamiel down a dark passage into the back of the house. Here the passage opened into a sparsely furnished, candlelit room. Shadows danced on the walls. Two men sat on wooden stools, and as the one with his back to her slowly turned around, shock shuddered through her. Lord Lucian.

He spoke in his languid voice. "Ah, our informant. Take a seat, Ya . . . ?"

"Yamiel, my lord." He hastily sat on the wooden stool to which Lucian pointed.

"So, Yamiel. You have news which may interest me?"

"Yes, my lord. I know the whereabouts of someone you seek." Yamiel spoke quickly, his smile nervous.

"Who?"

"A traveler from far. He calls himself Shua and his companion is Eliad."

"And why would I be interested in them?"

"They were seeking you. And the child now with Captain Randin."

Lucian's hands clenched—almost imperceptibly—into a fist.

"Leave us," he said to his two companions.

When they were alone, Lucian's tone was soft and dangerous. "Tell me, Yamiel. Why would you inform me about these men?"

"I know you are a man of considerable power and wealth and . . ." Yamiel floundered, and it was Lucian who finished his sentence.

"And you think I should pay you for this information?"

"If it is of value to you, m'lord."

"Of course. What amount did you have in mind, Yamiel?"

"Thirty silver coins," Yamiel answered hesitantly.

"The price of a slave." There was contempt in Lucian's voice. "Do you even know who it is that you give over into my hands?"

Yamiel remained silent.

"Very well." Lucian took a pouch from his side and counted out the coins into Yamiel's hand. "Where is he?"

"My tavern near the town gate. The Lantern Tavern."

"Go back. We will come for him later tonight." Lucian called the men back into the room. "Let out our guest."

Shara watched him leave, fear lodged in her throat. She wanted to run down the streets of Gwyndorr, back to the prince, shouting at him to leave and never return. But she could not. She was trapped in another time, with eyes but no voice. Powerless.

As the door closed behind Yamiel, Lucian turned to the other man.

"Send for Randin. Tell him we have word of a dangerous criminal in town."

The scene melted away into darkness, and now Shara became aware only of the sounds around her. Boots, many boots, thumping on the ground; men's voices, hushed but excited; the clatter of swords and shields. The sounds of Randin's men going to capture the prince. As Yamiel's tavern materialized, the fear and sorrow that had lodged in her body broke out in a wail of despair that nobody could hear.

Guards poured into the tavern, shoving out the surprised late-night drinkers. Yamiel stood at the entrance, face strained and—for once— unsmiling as he directed the men towards the stairs.

Shara was caught in the melee and confusion of men pushing in while others tried to get out. She was acutely aware of the sound of boots on the stairs and the smashing of the door as they reached the prince's room. After that there was a small period of quiet and, for an instant,

Shara hoped that Prince E'shua and Eli had escaped and were far from this hideous tavern. But as a cheer started, first upstairs then carrying around the room, she knew her hope was in vain. She looked on with trepidation. She did not want to see the prince, who loved her enough to come and find her, being manhandled by Randin's coarse men. Yet, conversely, his face was all she did want to see, all that might bring her comfort at this time.

It was not long before he appeared, hands tied in front of him. The young guard by his side smiled gleefully at his companions.

She looked into his face. Already a red welt on his check showed where one of the guards had hit him. Yet his eyes reflected no shock or anger at what was happening. There was a quiet knowing in his expression, a strength she had seen there before.

One of the tavern drinkers near her asked, "Who is this man?"

"A spy and rebel, come to overthrow Gwyndorr."

The prince was pushed through the crowded room. As he reached her side, Shara put out her hand, longing as never before to touch him, to draw from, and maybe even give, comfort. But, as before, there was only the strange sensation of moving air, reminding her anew that all she now witnessed had already taken place.

The thought brought no comfort.

CHAPTER 25

Pearce watched the sun steadily moving across the sky and felt the anxiety gnawing inside him. The king's army had been camped in the same location for two days already. It was obvious that they were expecting—and preparing for—an attack in Rogue's Neck. The day before, Pearce had sent out scouts to report on the king's activities. They should have returned by now.

Move, you Highborn fools. Pearce watched the portion of the king's army that he could see from his position on the western ridge. Waiting was always difficult for him. It was when he began to doubt every decision and move.

"I wish they would get here," he said.

"Wars are won or lost in the waiting." Crif shrugged. He was shorter than Pearce, and sitting for long times in cramped places did not seem to bother him.

"Scouts should have been back by now."

"By this morning at least. Should I send someone to look for them?"

Pearce considered this. Usually he knew exactly what to do, but now doubts assailed him. "What do you think, Crif?" he asked eventually, feeling the weakness in his words.

"Let's give them a little longer," Crif said. "If they haven't arrived by late afternoon, we'll send out two men."

By late afternoon the scouts had not returned. Pearce sent out two more.

Nicho spent the day alone. Now that so few horses remained, there was little work for the grooms. Most stayed with their families or friends or played Garrison and Gallows at the long, empty tables in the eating hall. Some had taken to practicing sword fighting; Nicho had joined this group the last few days, but he saw little improvement in his sword skills. He was still too cumbersome on his feet, too slow to block, and too hesitant to attack. Pearce had been right all along. He didn't have it in him to be a Warrior.

Today he found his way to the back of the caves, to the Burrow, which climbed up to an opening onto the plateau. The two guards on duty there looked surprised to see him.

"High Commander know you're here?" the one asked.

"Sure," Nicho lied. "Just struggling with murk malady. Need some light and air."

He made his way over the rocky plateau until he saw a small vale of lush green. Here he found a spring that gurgled into a stream. Nicho followed it right to the edge of the plateau, the point where it cascaded over the edge. It was here that Nicho spent the day, looking down over the mountains and valleys below, soaking in the warmth and the beauty and the space around him.

Yet nothing could still the turmoil inside him brought on by Mikel's reading last night. It was the moment when Yamiel, the prince, and Eli stopped outside Randin's gate that Nicho realized the shocking truth. He should have seen it earlier, of course; it had been right before his eyes. *They have taken in their cousin's destitute young child.* The prince's words rang in Nicho's mind. *As we suspect, Sarah is in the house.*

The princess that Prince E'shua sought had grown up in Randin's house. She had played in the mud with Nicho. His own mother had loved her like a daughter. She had run to Marai every time she didn't get her own way. He could see her now, her dark, wild curls and flashing eyes full of indignation. The child that Taus—Lucian—had stolen had been brought to the very place where Nicho lived. She had been his friend, and then she had become much more—the one he loved. Yet also, he thought with a stab of sorrow, the one he left behind and lost because of his decision to return for Jed. Shara was no ordinary girl. Sister of Prince E'shua. Daughter of the High King. Shara—*his* Shara—was Princess Sarah of Ajalon.

Strangely, this realization left him feeling even more bereft than before. If Shara had found the path that would take her home, and if he ever had the chance to follow her, even then they could never be what they had been before. A Parashi in love with a Highborn had been impossible enough. A Parashi in love with a princess? Ludicrous.

The sun was gliding towards the western horizon by the time Nicho made his way back to the Grotto. One last look at the deep valleys and folds of mountain below him reminded Nicho of what lay ahead. Deep in those valleys, King Alexor and his army moved ever closer to the Grotto. Nicho suddenly hoped with all his heart that Shara would reach the safety that awaited her in Ajalon. He would never join her there. His fate lay at the Parashi's last battle for the Guardian Grotto. Nicho knew he was unlikely to survive it. He just didn't have the makings of a great Warrior. Yet he would be with his people, just as Shara would be with hers. The thought brought him a measure of comfort.

Nicho was late reaching the chamber where Mikel read. He could hear the lilting, foreign words as he slipped into the back and sank down onto a bench. He closed his eyes and let the Old Magic words transport him back to Gwyndorr.

He was in a large crowd thronging outside an imposing gate, which he recognized with a start—the gate to the Barracks. It was where he had gone to rescue Simhew when the boy had been taken for the Rifter Gangs. Through the iron bars, he caught a glimpse of the large quad and, across this parade ground, he could just make out Prince E'shua tied to a wooden stake. All around him voices buzzed.

". . . say he is here from a distant country."

". . . a spy and after the merchants' wealth . . ."

"My brother is a town guard and says the man was plotting to overthrow Gwyndorr."

"Yes, I heard he's already infiltrated the town and turned some to his cause."

"Apparently he has a heavily armed troop of men waiting just outside the gates."

As the stories grew in intrigue, Nicho sensed the crowd's restlessness increase, so that by the time Randin appeared on his horse, they were uncharacteristically belligerent towards him.

"How can your men have let this revolutionary into our midst?" a voice shouted.

"Aren't your guards meant to protect us?"

Randin lashed out with his whip, forcing a path through the heated mob. Several people spilled into the quad as the gate opened for Randin. The guards thrust the crowd back, but the words took Nicho forward. He followed Randin as he dismounted and paced across the quad towards the prince.

"Well, well. What have we here?" Randin circled the prince slowly and thoughtfully. "I do not like being awakened in the middle of the night and told there is an enemy in my town. What is your name?"

"Shua." The prince met his gaze steadily.

"Where are you from?"

"Ajalon, the kingdom beyond the Rif'twine."

Randin threw back his head and laughed. "Nothing lies beyond the Rif'twine."

"So Tirragyl believes."

"Even if it did," Randin's eyes narrowed on him, "how would you breach the forest?"

"My power is greater than that which created it."

"Power?" Randin stopped pacing. "So you admit you have power? An army? Weapons? Where?"

"There is no army. Just me."

"What of your companion? Where is he?"

For the first time Nicho saw disquiet on the prince's face. Randin saw it, too, for he pressed in again. "Where is he, Shua?"

"He left before your men arrived, but he poses no threat. Lucian wants me, not him."

"Lucian wants you?" There was surprise on Randin's face. "Why?"

"Perhaps you should ask him yourself."

Nicho turned to see Lord Lucian striding towards them. His eyes, glinting with excitement, were fixed on the prince. His smile was a twist of triumph. He drew so close to the prince that, for a moment, Nicho thought he was going to greet him with a kiss. But he merely lowered his voice and hissed, "Welcome to my kingdom, sire."

Lucian looked at the captain. "You have questioned this prisoner, Randin?"

"I just started."

"Good. I sent for the elders so we can get this trial over with soon."

"Trial? I have not yet found any rebellion warranting a trial."

"You will, of course." The words were a veiled threat.

"He may be a little deranged," Randin frowned at the prince, "but what exactly has he done?"

Lucian ignored the question. "Ah, perfect timing. Here are the elders and witnesses."

Issor, Randin's second-in-command, led seven men towards them.

"Is this him?" one of the elders asked, studying the prince disdainfully.

"Indeed. The one who comes to overthrow Gwyndorr," Lucian answered.

"That has yet to be proven, Lord Lucian," another one replied. Nicho recognized him as Aknor, Randin's father-in-law. "We cannot question him, or any other witnesses, here," Aknor continued. "Is there a room in the Barracks that we can use?"

"Certainly. I will have one prepared." Randin beckoned for one of his men and gave instructions in a low tone.

The prince was led inside. Nicho followed him and the elders to a cell with bars on the windows and several chairs against the walls. The prince was shoved to the floor.

"While we wait for the witnesses, we might as well hear the prisoner's side of the story," one of the elders said. He kept looking impatiently at a timepiece tucked under his robe. "Who are you and where are you from?"

The prince spoke clearly, telling them of Ajalon and how he had come through the Rif'twine a few months earlier in search of his sister, who had been kidnapped.

"See how he lies," Lucian interjected. "He's obviously covering up his real intentions."

"Just because he lies doesn't mean his intentions are to overthrow Gwyndorr." A red-haired elder spoke for the first time, staring intently at the prince.

"If his intentions were not evil, he would not need to lie."

Several elders nodded at this statement, but the red-haired elder stood silently, a troubled expression on his face.

There was a shuffle in the passage outside and a town guard appeared, followed by Yamiel and his cousin, Urda.

"Sir, the witnesses have arrived," the guard announced.

"Good. Let us continue," the impatient elder said. "Lord Lucian?"

"Thank you." Lucian smiled charmingly. "I have only recently become aware of this man Shua's presence in our city, but I managed to piece together his plans against Gwyndorr. It appears that he and a companion entered our town about seven months ago, and the two of them have been involved in some very unusual activities."

"Such as . . . ?"

Lucian frowned at the interruption. "He established his base at the Lantern Tavern, near the city gates, and apparently kept a close watch on the gates, monitoring the arrival and departure of visitors and becoming familiar with the routine of the Town Guards. He also befriended several townsmen and questioned them about the town's defenses."

"Are any of these men present?"

"Randin's guards are searching for them, as well as this man's accomplice," Lucian said. "He also seemed particularly interested in infiltrating my own household, gaining access to Lord Poldyr's homestead just before my wedding and speaking to one of my household servants." He beckoned to Urda. "It's my belief that he poisoned Lord Poldyr and that I am his next intended victim. In disposing of leaders and turning the townspeople against those who remain—including all of you—he plans to take the entire town by force."

"You have proof of this, Lord Lucian?" Aknor asked. "Signs of an army?"

"He is clever. His army lies hidden in the outskirts of the Rif'twine, awaiting his command. But I think it best for my household servant to *explain firsthand the plot Shua was hatching." He indicated for Urda to step forward.*

Urda came to stand in front of the elders and haltingly answered their questions, glancing every now and then at Lucian as he answered. At first the questions revolved around his position in Lucian's household and how the prince had come to speak with him. But as the elders asked about the prince's words and intentions, Nicho realized Urda was telling a fabricated story. Glancing at Lucian's face, he had no doubt as to its source.

"You say this man was very interested in the whereabouts of Lord Lucian?"

"Yes. He offered me money to draw Lord Lucian out to the stables."

"Why did he want him there?"

"As he showed me the money, he whispered that he would rid the household of Lord Lucian and later Lord Poldyr. Then we would all have our freedom."

"Did you take the money?"

"No, sir."

"Did you tell Lord Lucian?"

"No, sir. I was scared just for having spoken to the man."

"And did you see the accused again at the estate?"

Urda again glanced quickly at Lucian. "Yes. He was at the estate again just before Lord Poldyr's mysterious death. I didn't think much of it at the time, but afterwards I spoke to the steward, and he said that he had seen the man go into the kitchen just before the dinner at which Lord Poldyr became mortally ill. He must have slipped some poison into his wine."

"How did he gain access into the estate and the kitchen?"

"I suspect he bribed one of the staff. That, or they are one of his own people."

The next witness was Yamiel, and he told of covert meetings between the prince, Eliad, and several townspeople, and how the prince had forced him to reveal the location of Randin's house.

"He was assessing the strength of the town's defenses and planning to kill Captain Randin."

Nicho saw pain in the prince's eyes as he looked at his betrayer. Yamiel did not meet his gaze.

"We will deliberate now," the senior elder said finally, drawing the other six men into a group. It did not take long before he rose to speak.

"Gentlemen, the elders have reached a decision with regards to this man. Shua stands accused of evil intentions towards Gwyndorr. Conspiracy is a serious charge and, as you are aware, carries the death penalty. Therefore, the evidence needs to be convincing and the verdict unanimous." He looked nervously towards Lucian as he continued. "Neither of these conditions apply. The evidence lacks credibility and we are divided . . ."

"What?" Lucian rose to his feet, enraged. "How much evidence do you need? We have a dangerous man in our midst, and you wish to pardon him? You bunch of old, senseless fools!"

Aknor rose too, a flush on his cheeks. "Lord Lucian, I suggest you take more care with your words. Treating elders with contempt is punishable by—"

"You threaten me, Aknor?" Lucian's tone was soft. "I could destroy each one of you in the blink of an eye. I know your comings and goings. The visits to prominent ladies . . ." he stopped in front of the impatient elder, who quickly diverted his eyes. "The bribes from merchants . . ." Now he glared at another elder. "And the corruption at the heart of this group. I could bring each one of you down." He returned to his seat. "Maybe you require a bit more time to reconsider."

The elders, momentarily stunned, stared at Lucian. The impatient elder whispered something to Aknor, who again rose to his feet to speak.

"This is unacceptable, Lord Lucian. You would bribe us to sentence a man to death? We will not allow this miscarriage of justice."

"Really, Aknor? And yet you once signed a man's death warrant merely because you wanted his property and he refused to sell it to you."

Aknor paled. "That's . . . that's not true. He, he was . . . who told you that?"

"Does it matter? The more important question is who will I tell?" Lucian's lips curled into a smile. "I suggest you give this verdict some more thought and reach the right conclusion. Besides the personal dilemmas you face, there is also the small matter of the crowd." Sounds of

chanting wafted through the window. "You do not wish to incur the wrath of the people, do you? They don't seem to share your doubts about this criminal."

The elders conferred again, with a greater sense of urgency. Nicho glanced at the prince. He stared quietly ahead, surprisingly calm in the face of the life-and-death decision hanging in the air. The elders spoke intently to the red-haired man, who had earlier spoken out in defense of the prince. He kept shaking his head. This one man stood between Prince E'shua and death. Stay strong, Nicho willed him.

Yet—in his heart—he knew the outcome even before Aknor stood to announce their final decision. The prince, he realized, had known it from the beginning. Hadn't Nicho seen it in his face as they pulled him down the tavern stairs?

As Aknor spoke, the single word echoed around the room and deep into Nicho's heart.

Guilty.

CHAPTER 26

They had barely broken camp, and Elxa was already caught in the middle of an argument between Nyla and Klyden. Since they had rescued the queen from the Enderite traders, the tension between the two of them had been bowstring taut.

"How am I meant to fulfill my vow to your grandmother if you insist on being so headstrong and placing us all in danger?" Klyden snapped.

"I've told you, you're free to go, haven't I? Consider the vow fulfilled and go back to—"

"I'm not going back. I didn't make the vow to *you*."

"Well, Mada's dead. She's not going to hold it against you now, is she?"

"My people are a people of honor, Nyla. Our words mean something and—"

"Are you saying I'm not? That my words are empty and without honor?"

"Well, not *all* your words are empty, as we well know."

Elxa downed the last of his tea and rose, clearing his voice to interrupt the barrage of words flying around him. "It's well past sunrise. I think we should go."

"Good idea, Elxa," Nyla said. "You and Klyden go *that* way to Droyl and your beloved Azab Rock, and I will go *that* way to Lydora."

"Don't be a fool. You are *not* going to Lydora."

"It seems you have forgotten to whom you speak, Klyden." Anger always brought out her haughtiness. "I happen to rule this country. And *you*, in fact. I don't need your permission to go to my own royal citadel."

"You rule this country, do you? I don't think so. That privilege rests solely on the shoulders of your brother, who every man in Lydora bows to now. You would set foot in a place that will be the death of you?"

"Klyden, you seem a bit dimwitted lately. I will explain this again slowly so that you understand it. When my brother—"

"No matter how many times you explain it, it doesn't lose its idiocy. You think that when your brother hears you are in Lydora, he will rush back, leaving the Grotto and Guardian Rock alone."

"Ah, I see you do understand the plan." She clapped mockingly.

"That part I understand. What I don't understand is just how you are planning to escape from his clutches once he is back. I will be on my *beloved* Azab Rock, remember? Not diving into the Adriel River to rescue you as they push you under a second time."

"Pay attention, Klyden. I'm only going to say this one more time. I. Don't. Care. Alexor can take my soul in that cursed river. He's taken it already. I'm nothing anymore. This might just be the last thing I can do for my people. It's the only way I can keep them safe a little longer, to keep the Guardian Rock from falling into his hands."

"Your Majesty, I—" Elxa tried.

"And you call me dimwitted! As soon as he has killed you, he will return for that Rock anyway."

"Klyden, there's something you should—" Elxa said.

"Well, I'll have given Tirragyl a few more months at least. It's the best I can do."

"You will have—"

"Stop it, both of you!" Elxa exclaimed loudly. They looked at him in surprise. "You are so busy fighting that you are missing something very important."

"What's that?" Nyla asked.

Elxa pointed.

Klyden and Nyla turned to look. Riders were galloping towards them from the north, with more and more horsemen spilling over the horizon behind them.

Nyla watched warily as they drew near. She recognized the short, muscular man in the center of the group before he reached them. The Charabian. Now that he was free of the curse, had he come to avenge his people for all she and her forefathers had done to them? Would Klyden step in to protect her, or was he too angry at her for using the arming word?

The Charabian reined in his horse and, with great agility, jumped from its back. He turned to her and covered the distance between them in three strides, pulling his sword from his scabbard as he walked. Klyden, Nyla noticed, did not draw his own sword in her defense.

The Charabian stopped and sank onto one knee, laying his sword on the ground between them. "Your Majesty. I come to pledge my allegiance, and that of my men, to you. Our swords will henceforth be your swords in the battle for Tirragyl."

For a moment Nyla was too stunned to speak. Then something stirred to life in her again. She was still the Queen of Tirragyl. Alexor had not taken that from her after all.

"Please rise. I accept your allegiance with immense gratitude, Charabian. I do not feel worthy of it," she continued softly as he rose to his feet, "after what I did to you in your own village."

His eyes crinkled into a surprisingly warm smile. "Elxa told me afterwards that I had behaved rather shamefully to my royal guest. I must apologize."

"No, no. It is I that must apologize. I acted in anger. I did not intend to hurt you or any of your men when I spoke the word. But—"

"It is infused with evil." The Charabian nodded. "Still, you had us completely in your power, and you did not use it. I've thought about that a great deal these last few days, and over time something dawned on me." He paused. "The fact that you did nothing with that power tells me that you are very different than your forefathers. And that you are the first sovereign of Tirragyl I would willingly follow."

Nyla swallowed away the lump in her throat. "Thank you. But I fear we are too late to defeat my brother. They are many weeks ahead of us. My only hope remains that I reach Lydora before the Grotto is defeated. Perhaps then Alexor will turn back. He is desperate . . ." She cast her eyes to the ground and swallowed. "Desperate for my soul."

"I think there is another way, Your Majesty." The Charabian drew a rock and thinning parchment from his robe.

"What is it?" Elxa stepped forward to look.

"A map drawn by Chaorlin, our forefather." He unfolded it. "It shows the entrance to the ancient Ruin Rim Mountain tunnels."

"Tunnels? I've never heard of them," Nyla said.

"If the stories about them are true, they are no ordinary tunnels. They lead directly to the northeastern mountains and can only be accessed by this." He laid the almost-triangular rock in her hand. It pulsed with warmth. "It's a key."

"So it's a shortcut to the Grotto?" Nyla felt hope pulse through her. "That will reduce the time it takes to get there."

"More than that," the Charabian said. "Legends say that the tunnels are untouched by dark powers. That Old Magic permeates it. And that in the tunnels, years dwindle to mere seconds, and death itself is held at bay. If this is true, we could enter the tunnels and reach the other side almost immediately." The Charabian looked up at her intently. "I am a simple man. A man of the sword. I do not claim to understand such things. But for you—and for Tirragyl—I will seek the tunnels and the Guardian Grotto." He smiled wryly. "For that's another place shown on Chaorlin's map."

"Thank you." Nyla grasped the Charabian's arm tightly before looking up at the solemn faces of the still-mounted men. "Thank you all. Now, let us ride to save Tirragyl."

Nyla and the Charab army covered good ground on their first three days of riding, setting a fast pace across the flat western farmlands. To their west lay the mountain range marking the border between Tirragyl and the Enderite Territory. Their own village lay tucked deep in those mountains. But the men's eyes were trained on the distant northern peaks, at first nothing more than a small, shimmering mirage, yet growing steadily larger and more solid as they pounded across the plains.

They rode until even their night-trained eyes could no longer perceive the features of the terrain. Then they quickly set up camp, watering, feeding, and brushing their horses, before sitting down around their fires to eat their own meals.

Klyden sat some distance away from Nyla, watching her laughing heartily with Elxa and a group of his kin. He couldn't recall ever seeing her laugh so. When he first came to the palace seven years earlier, she had been a mere child. Already she had had an air of seriousness so at odds with the flippant attitude of her twin brother. The gravity had only grown once Nyla was crowned queen, and the opposition began. Since Klyden had rescued her, she had seldom even smiled. Always those light-blue eyes seemed to be filled with memories and regrets and concerns. She had approached fleeing from her home and hiding on Azab Rock with a gritty courage Klyden admired, but throughout that time there was a heaviness and sorrow in her that would not shake free. Only now did Klyden see a different Nyla—one filled with purpose. Perhaps even peace.

"She is young to be queen." The Charabian slipped into the open space next to him and followed Klyden's gaze. "You have done well to protect her all these years."

"Lohlyn did most of the protecting."

"I'm sorry about Lohlyn, Kly," he said gruffly. "I'm sorry about your father too. He was already—"

"I don't want to speak of my father." Sometimes it surprised Klyden just how raw his grief still was. It was not true that time healed heart wounds as it did flesh-and-blood ones.

His uncle did not speak again. Klyden, ashamed of his sharp tone, eventually broke the silence. "I worry about taking her to the Grotto. She would be easier to protect if we took her back to the Charab village."

"True, but it is not for you to decide. She is queen and sets her own course even if it leads to danger." The Charabian watched Nyla across the fire. "I admire her for not shirking from the risk. Tirragyl needs a courageous sovereign."

"Courage she has in abundance. But like you say, she is young. She acts rashly sometimes." Klyden thought back to Nyla, drunk on berry beer. To the desire in her eyes. "Sometimes she needs protecting from herself."

"Not this time. I sense here something larger at work. Not merely a young woman on a quest. This feels . . ." The Charabian struggled to find the right word. "Ordained. Purposed, if you will. It's why I brought my men to serve her."

"I was astonished to see you." Klyden looked at his uncle. "I did not think you would so quickly excuse what Nyla did."

The Charabian nodded thoughtfully. "You know her better than I do. But I sense in her something good. Right motives, even though her means to achieve them were wrong. No?"

"I considered her the best sovereign Tirragyl ever had. I wouldn't have thought her capable of using the arming word." Klyden's gaze slid back to the queen. "I had a choice of who to save—Lohlyn or Nyla. Perhaps I made a mistake choosing the queen. Perhaps she was not worthy of it."

"You did not save her because she was worthy, Kly. You did it because you had taken an oath to protect her. You had to be true to the oath. To yourself."

"Yes." Klyden nodded. "But my oath cost Lohlyn her life."

"Lohlyn wouldn't have wanted it any other way."

"It was just easier to accept when I thought Nyla a good queen. Now . . . well, I can't recall anybody who has disappointed me more."

They watched her together, her white hair sparkling in the firelight. She sensed their scrutiny for she glanced up, and her eyes locked with Klyden's. A shadow seemed to pass over her; the lightness that had been there moments before was suddenly gone as she looked away.

His uncle turned to him, brow furrowed. "Assassins and protectors must guard their hearts, Klyden. Feelings only get in the way of doing our jobs."

"My disappointment with Nyla will not prevent me from protecting her."

"It's not only disappointment I'm worried about."

CHAPTER 27

As Lucian rode beneath the towering mountains of the Inner Peaks, he smiled at the memory of the Mind Rock interrogation he had performed two days earlier. It had been a long time since he had used the Mind Rock with such deliberate intent on someone who was actually present. He had forgotten how thrilling it could be.

Several soldiers had dragged a bleeding Parashi into the camp. "We brought one in alive, Commander." They pushed the man before Commander Rillon. "A scout. His companion is dead."

The king, Rillon, and several of his men had taken the prisoner into a tent for an interrogation, but after an hour and a half, the king had stormed out, followed closely by the commander. "Useless! It will take far too long to break this man. Time we don't have."

"Even if we had days, I doubt we could break a Parashi, sire. They are known to be stoic and can withstand excessive pain," Rillon said. "But we do not need his information, my liege. I have already sent men east and west to look for a pass. If the Parashi are lying in wait on the cliffs ahead of us, as I suspect, we can stay here another few days. They are unlikely to move."

"Could I have half an hour with the prisoner?" Lucian had asked mildly. "I am rather skilled at interrogation."

The king had laughed derisively, but the commander had shrugged and said they had nothing to lose.

Lucian had found the prisoner in the tent, bleeding not only from the arrow wound in his shoulder, but also from the soldiers' rough interrogation techniques. He gave Lucian a contemptuous look, and red spittle flew onto Lucian's gown as he hissed, "Give up now, you Highborn pig. I will tell you nothing!"

Lucian had carefully wiped the man's blood from his robe before sitting down across from him.

"Don't fear. You will not have to *tell* me anything." As he took the black rock from its deep pocket, he had felt a surge of heat through his fingers. It had been too long. He was going to enjoy this.

The prisoner had glanced nervously at the rock. "Is that a power rock?"

"Indeed. One of the most powerful of all, a Mind Rock. There are different ways for me to use it. Usually I do it when people are asleep. Gently, so they don't suspect." The rock had felt soft and smooth in Lucian's fingers. "But there's another way. Far more interesting and direct. More damaging to the mind, but it matters little in this case." The Parashi had blanched in fear. "You didn't expect to survive this, did you?"

Lucian had wasted no time after that, so keen was he to experience the rush of rupturing another's mind. He had watched the young man's face as he entered his mind, had seen the shock and terror before his eyes rolled back in his head and his body began to convulse. Lucian had closed his eyes then and focused solely on the man's mind, proceeding more gently to give the thoughts and images time to settle. He had seen the Grotto, familiar from his time in Shara's mind. He had edged the man's thoughts towards the High Commander, pleased to see the strain on Mikel's face when he spoke of the approaching king's army. Lucian took note of the man with the scarred face too, the one called Pearce. It was he who had sent this young scout out from their hiding place in what they called Rogue's Neck.

Lucian had probed around for memories of the mountain and its layout. The young Warrior had many memories of sorties around the Grotto, but there were fewer in this part of the mountains. Still, somewhere he must have heard of a pass, even if he hadn't been to it himself. Skillfully, Lucian found the threads of a story that the young man had been told as a child. It was the story of another boy in another time, a brave boy who had grown up to be a great Warrior. The threads of the story were hazy and tinged with a dreamy glow. This young man had aspired to be as great a Warrior as the boy in the story. The boy had discovered a narrow pass between two peaks. For a while an older man's face swam into view, that of the grandfather telling the story. His voice crackled with age. *It's called Waif's Cleft, Zeren—the only other place besides Rogue's Neck where the Inner Peaks can be breached. Troyin found it when he was not much older than you. It's so narrow that only two men can go through it at a time. An enemy won't find it unless he knows where to look although it's right there between the two peaks. Snow Barb Turret and The Fang.*

Lucian followed the name Waif's Cleft to another more recent memory. The young man was lying on the cliffs above Rogue's Neck, watching a group of men slowly picking their way to the river floor. What did these men have to do with Waif's Cleft? Lucian probed gently, and the answer—when it finally came—thrilled him. The one called Pearce had made a mistake. He had called these men away from protecting Waif's Cleft, to lie in wait at Rogue's Neck. Waif's Cleft was unguarded.

After this Lucian had roamed roughly through Zeren's mind, no longer taking care to keep it intact. He had gazed into the sad eyes of a beautiful, young woman and had roughhoused with two younger brothers. One of the last untainted memories had been of Zeren whispering tenderly into the ear of a light-brown mare. After this, the Parashi's mind had become too fractured. Confusion and terror brought on a creeping darkness.

The Parashi was barely conscious when Lucian withdrew from his mind to tell the king and commander what he had discovered. They decided to send half the army east to Waif's Cleft and leave the remaining half as a decoy at Rogue's Neck. As long as the Warriors could see a portion of the king's army in the Feyn River Valley, they would remain in place, expecting the army to move. The king, Rillon, Lord Lucian, and about half the soldiers had set out almost immediately to find Waif's Cleft.

Commander Rillon fell in next to him, his voice breaking

through Lucian's memories. "How many days to this Waif's Cleft, Lord Lucian?"

"The Parashi had never been there himself so he couldn't tell me for sure. But he did tell me the names of the two peaks between which it lies: the Fang and the Snow Barb Turret."

The commander furrowed his brow. "Not much to go on, is it?"

Earlier that day, they had met their scouts returning from seeking out a pass. They had not found one. On hearing this, the commander had seemed reluctant to continue. He was diverting half the king's army based on a Parashi's dying words—words he hadn't heard himself.

Then a soldier rode up to them. "Commander, we have spotted snow barb eagles hovering around one of the peaks ahead. It may be the place."

Rillon looked at Lucian for confirmation.

"Fine. Head that way."

The commander rode off with the soldier, leaving Lucian to his own thoughts again. He looked up at the mountains and the small, hovering shapes high above them. Could that tall, single peak be named for the birds that nested there? As he rode ever closer, another two-pronged peak came into view. Perhaps this was The Fang.

Lucian was growing impatient. Already he knew that the true prize he sought—Shara—was no longer at the Guardian Grotto. All he could hope was that the Rif'iends had managed to stop her on this so-called path through the Rif'twine. Still, two other rewards awaited him at the Grotto. One was the Guardian Rock, which would finally be complete again, with all its pure power his for the taking. The other was the knowledge that the Parashi rebels, the thorn in his flesh from the time he had first invaded this country, would be annihilated once and for all.

Which is why, when Lucian finally heard the triumphant shout and the excited babble of soldiers ahead of him as they discovered the pass, he closed his eyes and let the pleasure of imminent victory rush through him.

• • •

"At least half the army is moving east."

The words of the returning scout chilled Pearce to the core. He had always coveted leadership, had sought it out and fought for it and claimed it with pride. But these last few days, waiting for the king's army to come through Rogue's Neck, had changed him. Suddenly he understood the great weight of leadership. Lives were in your hands, destinies at your fingertips. All Pearce wanted now was to hand over this terrible mantle to another.

"Any sign of Zeren and Jeol?" he asked to mask his panic at the news.

"Jeol, yes," the scout answered somberly. "Shot. We brought back his body. But no sign of Zeren."

"They took him alive." Crif, always so unflustered, sounded worried. "If they interrogated him, and he told them about Waif's Cleft, that would explain why they are on the move."

"Impossible," Pearce said. "We are Warriors. We die before we whisper a word into those pigs' ears!"

"He was young, Pearce. Fear does strange things to men," Crif said.

By the abyss! If Crif's words were true, Pearce had doomed them all. The High Commander had told him to station men at Waif's Cleft, but he had called them back, leaving the way through the Inner Peaks open. From that point it was an unhindered march to the plateau and the back entry of the Grotto.

Even worse, the additional unit he had sent for from the Grotto had arrived the previous day, meaning that fewer than two hundred soldiers remained to defend the caves. How Pearce wished that Mikel were here. He would know what to do. But it was all up to him now. He had to make this right.

"Send for the commanders," he told Crif softly after the scouts had left. "If we do not act immediately, I fear I may have doomed us all."

It took nearly two hours for Crif's message to reach the two commanders stationed at the base of Rogue's Neck and on the western cliff. It took another two for Nezer and his companion to make their way back to where Pearce spoke in urgent tones to Crif and the other commanders.

They sat down to a low murmur of greeting.

Pearce wasted no time. "I have made a mistake, one that may cost us the Grotto if we do not act immediately." He looked at Nezer as he said, "I fear the king and more than half his army are on their way to Waif's Cleft."

Nezer's fist went to his mouth as if to block the curse on his lips.

"I'm not sure," Pearce continued, turning his gaze to the others. "Perhaps they will not find it. But our scouts say they move east with great speed. The king is at least a day and a half ahead of us. And," he shook his head desolately, "they took one of my men alive. He may have revealed the Cleft's location."

"What do we do?" Nezer asked, and Pearce was grateful that the commander did not berate him again for his terrible slip of judgement.

"Nezer, take your Warriors back to Waif's Cleft. If the king has already breached it, stay there to prevent the rest of his army from following."

Nezer nodded his approval of the plan. "I will call my men and set off right away."

Pearce turned to the others. "The unit that arrived from the Grotto yesterday will return to it immediately, warning the High Commander that the Inner Peaks may have been breached and that the Grotto might come under attack from the Elam Highlands."

"If the king's army is already through Waif's Cleft, I doubt we will reach the Grotto in time to defend it," the commander of this unit said grimly. "Or even to give them warning."

Pearce knew it was true, but he had no time to dwell on that now. "Izra, you and your men will stay here to defend Rogue's Neck. Split your men over three groups and position them on the cliffs as well as at the base where Nezer's men were." Izra nodded solemnly as Pearce continued. "It will be difficult to hold the Neck with so few men, but it can be done. A battle worthy of a minstrel's song, right, Izra?"

Izra smiled fleetingly at the weak jest.

"My men and I will cut across to Winter Pass," Pearce said. "If the king's army has breached Waif's Cleft, that's where they will ascend to the Highlands. Perhaps we can catch them yet. Questions?"

The men shook their heads and rose silently. They knew what they needed to do and what was at stake. They needed to move, and move fast. To fight, and fight fiercely. They needed, above all, courage to face the greatest threat the Grotto had ever known. The Warriors' future rested on their shoulders.

CHAPTER 28

The journey through the Rif'twine stretched on and on. At times Shara could hardly remember what it felt like to have open space around her. Always that ominous wall of trees pressed in around her. Always the voices of the Rif'iends taunted her or tempted her. If not for the terror of her last encounter with the magical creatures, she might have listened to the latest alluring voice calling her to an open place. *I will show you fields and a vast sky,* the voice whispered. She could almost see it in her mind.

"No! It's a lie!"

"Shara?" Eliad stopped in his tracks.

"Sorry. Did I speak out loud?"

"The voices again? What do they promise this time?"

"An escape from these walls." She smiled wistfully. "Fields. Open sky."

"You will have all of that and more in Ajalon."

"It feels so unreachable, Eliad."

"Every step takes us closer, dear one." Eliad dropped his pack on the ground. "It grows late, and weariness makes us more susceptible to their wiles. Let us stop."

They ate a hurried meal so that Eliad could read again. Shara feared knowing what the elders' guilty verdict meant for the prince, but Eliad seemed almost impatient to reach this part of the book. *The very heart of the story,* he had called it. As soon as the words began, Shara felt the familiar, powerful pull into the past. She first became aware of the chanting voices, and even though she couldn't feel the press of bodies, she realized—before she saw them—that she was in the middle of a crowd.

She could tell by the long shadows that it was early morning. The noisy crowd she was a part of thronged down a road. Behind them lay the walls of Gwyndorr. The prince was nowhere in sight, and for a moment she thought that meant the elders had released him after all. But as she looked at the faces around her, she knew this was not the case. These people, who had been angry last night, demanding punishment for the supposed spy in their midst, now looked excited and triumphant.

Ahead of her the crowd was chanting. The people near her now took up the refrain, so that it echoed all around her. She struggled to make out the words. It sounded like . . . poison tree.

Poison tree.

A cold dread crept through her body. If the book's words had not drawn her along, she would have been paralyzed on the spot. Suddenly even breathing felt difficult. Now she knew. She knew what was to become of Prince E'shua. He would be tied to the poison tree, the death Gwyndorr reserved for its murderers and traitors.

Unbidden, her mind evoked an image of her cousin Ghris, returning from watching a poison tree execution. "I've never seen a man writhing with such pain." His words came back to her now. "It must be the worst way to die."

The throng suddenly came to a halt. There was a murmur of complaint, but as the people realized that the front of the crowd had reached the edge of the Rif'twine, they pushed outwards, scrambling for a good view of the execution. Shara did not want to see it, but the words carried her forward regardless, right through the crowd, the way they had the first time she had laid eyes on the prince dancing with the children in the palace. The fleeting joy-filled memory brought tears to her eyes.

Soon she stood in front of the people, who had spread themselves into a large semicircle of several layers. The Town Guards, brandishing swords and threats, held them back.

Her eyes scanned the group behind the guards. She saw Randin, Lucian, several of the elders, and more guards. But finally she found who she was looking for. The prince—held up by two large guards— had been stripped down to the waist. He looked exhausted and frail, so unlike the strong figure she had come to expect.

Next to him, several guards were huddled on the ground. It appeared that something significant was happening for the crowd was cheering them on and laughing as if they were at a Spring Festival. The guards were drawing lots. One young man, crouching with the others, let out a triumphant "Yes!" and rose to his feet, showing the crowd the long stick he had drawn. This elicited a cheer from the crowd. Another let out a groan, which brought forth a loud laugh. He was the one who went over to the small metal box on the ground and took out what appeared to be thick gloves.

It had fallen to him to tie the prince to the tree, a task dreaded by the guards. Again Ghris's words came to her mind. The tree's bark is so dangerous that if the guards have a small wound and touch the tree, they could end up poisoning themselves.

The unlucky guard, pulling out a small dagger from his belt with his gloved hands, grimly approached the prince. What came next shocked Shara—Ghris had not told her about this. The guard grabbed the prince's arms and cut deep slits on the top of both his hands. This was where the poison would enter his body. The crowd met the prince's gasps of pain with a cheer. For them the entertainment had just started.

The prince was pushed down onto his stomach as the guard quickly made two more incisions just behind his ankles. Shara watched as the blood poured from the four wounds. The men holding him roughly hauled him up again, and they thrust him in the direction of the tree.

Shara now looked, for the first time, at the tree that would seep its poison into his blood. It stood alone at the edge of the forest, smaller than the trees around it. Its bark was coated in a milky-white substance, which—Ghris had told her—was what made it so toxic. The tree con- sisted of a base trunk that split, fairly soon, into three thick boughs that thrust their way upwards, there dividing into smaller branches, where the foliage of thick green leaves started.

The two men holding the prince stopped warily a step away from the tree, waiting for their companion to arrive with the ropes. Another guard brought a large wooden stool, which was placed at the base of the tree.

The gloved guard tied the prince's hands and feet with long pieces of rope, which trailed behind E'shua as he was pushed with his back towards the tree. The executioner now climbed onto the wooden stool and pulled the prince's left arm above his head, tying it around the first of the Y-shaped boughs as the two guards cautiously held the prisoner in place. The process was repeated with the right arm, and then the legs were tied around the thick base of the tree.

When he was finished, the guard carefully arranged his hands and feet so that the bleeding wounds would be directly in contact with the tree's bark. Satisfied, he stepped away to admire his handiwork, and the crowd loudly applauded his bravery. The guard who had earlier won the draw now brought a bucket of water. The gloves were removed and the executioner carefully washed his hands of any poison that may have unwittingly found its way through cracks or holes. His task complete, he waved and smiled at the crowd and drank heartily from a flagon of wine that somebody thrust into his hand.

Shara watched all this not because it interested her, but because she was too afraid to look into the prince's eyes. She suspected that if she looked, she would be unable to control her tears.

She looked around her at the people in the crowd. Many had brought food and were sharing it around with their friends. There was an air of anticipation as they waited for the poison to take its deadly toll on the prince's body.

Ghris's voice came to her again. "Slowly, steadily it enters the blood, to be carried to every part of the body. Do you know what that means, Shara? Every part of that man's body was on fire with pain. He was breaking down before our eyes."

As always when caught in the words of the book, Shara could not judge how long she had been there. The sun now seemed higher in the sky, the people more restless. She stood, her head bowed down, not lifting her eyes to the prince.

A thought came to her then. If he was here on this tree because he had come for her, didn't she owe it to him to look into his eyes, to share just a little of his pain? She forced herself to lift her head and look at him then, hanging on the cruel tree, and even though sorrow pierced through her, she continued to look, willing him to know that one person in this crowd saw him differently. One person cared.

His pale face showed pain, although he hadn't uttered a single sound since his initial groans. Within the confines of the ropes, she could see him squirming. His eyes squeezed closed, and his jaw clenched at—what she thought must be—a wave of pain.

The crowd noticed too. There was a stirring of excitement. Voices shouted out, "It's starting! Look!"

"See what happens to Gwyndorr's enemies!"

More time passed, but Shara's eyes never left Prince E'shua's face. Now she could hear his rasping breaths. Every one of them sounded like an effort. Between breaths his mouth appeared to be moving, as if he spoke to himself.

"What does he say?" a voice shouted from the crowd, and a guard went closer to try to make out the words but shrugged his shoulders at the crowd.

Finally the level of pain broke through the prince's silence, and a long, low moan escaped from his lips. To Shara it was a heartbreaking sound, and even the unsympathetic crowd subdued somewhat.

"Usually not more than an hour from this point," one of the older guards said quietly to a younger one standing by his side.

Shara watched. Every moment of Prince E'shua's anguish, she saw. Eventually he writhed in agony, although he never raised his voice to more than a low moan. He didn't look at her, yet she continued standing watch over him, sending him her love over the eight large steps and span of years that separated them. He had come for her. He hung on the tree because of her. That knowledge was too heavy for her. It pulled her down into the depths. For her.

She was watching his face so intently that she only became aware of the approaching storm when a loud peal of thunder broke above her head. It startled her. She looked around. It was dark for the middle of the day. The clouds overhead were a heavy steel-grey. A cold wind lashed her, menacingly shaking the leaves in the trees of the Rif'twine.

She realized that the crowd had diminished. Most of the people must have left when they saw the storm clouds building up.

"Come quickly," a man was saying to his sons. "At this rate we won't reach the town gate in time."

None of the elders remained. Randin, too, had left, but Lucian stood in a huddle of guards, in serious discussion.

The huddle broke up, and Shara watched as they quickly gathered up the tools and the wooden stool they had brought with them. All but two of them, the most junior it seemed, left hastily with the last of the crowd.

Still Lucian remained.

It seemed impossible, but it grew darker still. The clouds were so thick and black that almost no light crept through them. The wind suddenly died. It was eerily still. To Shara it felt as if all of nature was bracing itself for what was to come. The air was charged, and she felt the hairs on her arms rise as a primeval fear warned her to escape the storm's wrath. Yet, even if the words had not kept her there, she would have fought the urge to run. She did not want her brother to die alone.

She could tell it was almost over. His body had stilled, exhausted from the poison's assault. The occasional involuntary twitch was all that showed the last sparks of life. His breathing had changed. It sounded like a rattle in his chest. The end was near.

She would have cried if there had been anything left inside her, but she felt as empty and hollow as a worn-out stump. Numb. No tears.

The storm broke around her with a fury. Initially, single, large drops thrashed the ground, kicking up the dry dust at her feet, but soon sheets of water broke loose from the sky, lashing at everything that dared to stand up in its path. She felt its vengeance and fell down onto her knees, head bowed down, arms covering her head for some protection. Lucian had retreated into the cover of the forest. The two guards, torn between their fear of the storm and their fear of the forest, edged down the road in the direction of the town gate.

The storm raged on.

When Shara finally felt the rain ebb to a steady rhythm, she rose. The words now pulled her closer to the prince, and as she approached him, she knew it was over. The labored rising of his chest had stilled. His head—a mass of dark, storm-washed hair—lay cradled on his chest.

She stood before him, trying to memorize every part of his beautiful, broken body. She looked at his feet, coated in blood; his legs, powerful and dark; his arms and hands, chafed by the ropes. She longed to run her hands through the dark, wet curls, to feel in them the last softness of her brother's life.

Finally her tears came, as if the storm had filled up her reservoir of grief. She wept into the rain, her voice rising above its steady pulse. "Why? Why? Why?"

After a while a numbing cold edged over her body, and she froze. Only once had she felt ice creep into her body like that, and she knew without looking that the Rif'iends were near.

"You're not really here," she told herself. "The book brought you here. They can't see you. They can't touch you." Yet it took all her courage to look up and see the mass of black shapes that flittered out of the forest towards her.

They slunk closer and closer to where she stood at the poison tree. Occasionally one or two darted forward more boldly but then fell back again. A low hum emanated from the group, growing steadily louder. Eventually, one slunk right past her and reached the prince, gingerly sweeping up against his body as the mass stopped humming and flittering for a moment. The bold one emitted a loud shriek that seemed to excite the others back into action. Now they all leapt past her onto the prince's body in a wild, loud frenzy.

A languid voice broke through the chaos. "Yes, he's dead."

Lucian strode from the forest. At his approach, the dark shadows slunk silently away from the body on the poison tree.

"I have a task for you," Lucian continued as he reached the body. He took a knife out of his belt and slashed at the ropes around the prince's legs. He indicated for one of the black shadows to lift him up so that he could cut the ropes around the prince's arms too.

The body crumpled in a heap at the base of the tree. Lucian stood over it and smirked. "So falls the mighty Prince of Ajalon. How easy he was to defeat." He turned away towards Gwyndorr, casually calling over his shoulder, "Get rid of his body."

Shara could only watch as the Rif'iends fell onto Prince E'shua's body once again, like fru-flies to a carcass. Slowly his body, covered in their black mass, started to move towards the Rif'twine. No, she thought, how could this be happening? How could even his body have fallen into the hands of his enemies?

They reached the forest's edge and slowly started pulling him deeper into the trees until she could no longer see him. As she stared into the forest depths, trying to catch one last glimpse of him, she felt an overwhelming sense of emptiness and loss. They had won. They had killed him and even had his precious body.

The words changed pace now, becoming lighter, and as they did, she felt herself lifting off the ground. At any other time it might have been exhilarating. Her journey into the book had started this way, flying over Ajalon. Now the words lifted her slowly above the Rif'twine. It lay stretched out beneath her as far as she could see, foreboding, even from a bird's eye view. She searched the horizon, hoping to catch a glimpse of Ajalon, but from this angle the forest seemed never-ending.

Her eyes roved over the trees. For a small instant, she thought she saw movement, but it was difficult to pinpoint its source in the homogenous green landscape. She stared for a long time at where she thought she had seen it. Yes, there it was again, near the forest's edge. Could she be seeing the Rif'iends with the prince's body through that thick canopy? No, surely not. She continued to gaze intently at the place. But it wasn't the Rif'iends she saw. It was something stranger still. It looked like a small split in the thick, impenetrable fabric of the forest. Her eyes followed the pale line back to its source. It started from the place where the poison tree stood, the place where the Rif'iends had pulled the prince's body into the forest.

And finally Shara understood. As the prince's body was dragged through the forest, a path was being formed. A path back to Ajalon.

CHAPTER 29

The day before, Shara had stood with Eliad and Andreo on a high bluff where the trees of the Rif'twine could find no grip. It afforded them a rare view. What Shara saw stilled her and filled her with a yearning so painful it almost stole away her breath. Below them lay a vast green plain. Beyond a fringe of trees, a river wound through the beautiful land and—as it caught the dusky colors of the sky—appeared to flow with molten gold. Ice-capped mountains rose in the distance.

"Ajalon." Eliad's voice had resonated with joy even as he wiped away his tears. Shara had thrown her arms around him and let her own tears flow too. She was almost home.

Now Shara woke with the light of dawn. Her first thought was of Ajalon. She had an overwhelming desire to see it again, and so she rose and followed the path back to the bluff on which they had stood the day before. This time she sat down on the ice-cold rock and watched the sky lighten and Ajalon unfold below her. The river now reflected the red of sunrise, looking like an artery of blood. Eliad had told her the day before that they would follow the river to the very heart of Ajalon—the palace—and to the king. Her father.

Will he really want to see you? The thought came unbidden. She glanced around nervously. *His most beloved son would still be alive if it weren't for you. When he lays eyes on you, he will remember all he has lost. You will only add to his sorrow.*

It was true. She hadn't thought of how it would be to walk into the palace that had once resounded with joyful music and children's voices. Now that the crown prince was dead, it would be a place of mourning. Would the king and his subjects look at her with resentment for causing the prince's death?

Perhaps if you were like his other daughters, it would be different. They are worthy of his love. Perhaps even worthy of their brother's sacrifice. But you . . . he will look at you and know you are worth neither.

No, she wasn't worthy of such love or such sacrifice. Hadn't she stolen the Cerulean Dusk Dreamer and let its darkness into her life and into the lives of those she loved? The Guardian Grotto might already be destroyed because she had let Lucian find it through her.

You don't really belong in that palace, Shara. You will always be an outsider. Like us. The voice sounded soft and sorrowful. Concerned, even.

"Are you a Rif'iend?" she asked.

No, we are not the dark creatures. We are The Banished, living on the outskirts of Ajalon, never daring to come into the presence of the king. Do you know he demands nothing less than perfection?

Perfection! Now Shara knew that she could never set foot in the king's palace. She glanced up at the distant snow-capped mountains, and sorrow tightened around her heart. All this time trudging along the poison tree path she had yearned to look into her father's eyes. Yet to look into them and see disappointment would be worse than never looking into them at all. And wouldn't living on the outskirts of Ajalon still be a much better life than she deserved?

You will be happy with us. It's where you belong.

Eliad woke up afraid, the call of the Gold Breast still ringing through his dreams. He looked around. Andreo lay curled in sleep, but Shara's blanket was empty.

"Andreo," he whispered, struggling to his feet. "Shara's gone."

"Mmm? Too wide to cross," Andreo mumbled.

"Wake up."

Andreo sat up. "What? What is it?"

"Shara isn't here." Eliad stumbled forward, heading for the bluff where they had stood the previous evening. He had seen the longing in Shara's eyes as she looked at Ajalon, her home, but why would she have gone on without them? "Shara!" he called. "Shara!"

Then he saw her. She was walking down a hill just to the west of him. Eliad's relief was short-lived, for almost immediately two things dawned on him. Shara was not on the poison tree path, and huddled silently on the top of the hill where she walked was a throb of Rif'iends.

"Shara! Come back!"

She turned and waved, unaware that the Rif'iends above her quivered into life. Eliad watched helplessly as a black weapon materialized between them. Their trembling chorus of excitement filled Eliad with terror.

He began to run towards Shara.

The tender voices of The Banished were calling Shara away. She heard another call too, a long, sorrowful one that she recognized as Tabeal's. She dipped her head to the side to hear it better, but as she did The Banished called to her with even greater urgency.

The bird is as perfect as the High King. She has never failed him as you have. She cannot understand. Do not listen to her.

Another voice rang through the morning air. "Shara come back!"

Eliad. She looked up and saw him standing on the bluff above her. Only now did she realize she had left without saying farewell. Perhaps she should go back and explain that she was one of The Banished. Shara lifted her hand in a wave and began to turn back.

They will force you to stand before the king. You will see nothing but disappointment and pain in his eyes. He will never let you stay. Why put yourself through such humiliation?

"I'm just going to say goodbye."

At that moment, she sensed movement above her and heard a soft swish through the air. She had no time to consider what it was or where it came from for, just then, something thudded into her with such force that it knocked her to her knees. She cried out in surprise.

A deep, sharp pain pierced her side. As she looked down, she saw an arrow shaft sticking out from her flesh. Only a trickle of blood was visible.

Eliad was half running, half sliding down the hill towards her. Even from this distance she could see the shock on his face and wanted to reassure him that she was fine, that there was almost no blood.

Before she could speak, however, another arrow sliced into her, just below her collarbone. She stared at it, uncomprehendingly, wondering how it had come to be there. Its end was made of bright red feathers: a beautiful red, the same color that now spread over her chest.

Eliad reached her just as she sagged to the ground. Behind him Andreo came running. She felt their hands on her and heard their voices, but their words made little sense. A dark terror stalked the edges of her mind. *Was she going to die?* Her friends' wide-eyed expressions reflected her fear. *It must be true then. She would die. So close to home. How could it end like this?*

Yet the soft, gentle notes of a bird's song reached into her and hushed her as a lullaby stills a child. The beautiful sound wove a veil of lightness and calm over the place where the terror scrambled for a grip. *Tabeal is here. All is well. All is well.*

Searing pain wrenched her away from the place of peace. Hands lifted her. A fire of agony burned in her chest, pain so great that Shara feared it would keep her from taking her next breath. They were carrying her, the whole world swirling with colors—blue sky, grey cliffs, red hands, gold feathers. Through the stranglehold of pain, Shara still managed to marvel at the mixing colors and light.

After a while the jolting pain and voices began to fade. She could now hear a gurgling sound, like the brook in the clearing had made. It was near her. No closer than that—*in* her, a thick, wet sound. But eventually even that quieted, and a strange hush enfolded her, only broken by a pulsing deep inside her.

The colors grew dimmer. She tried to pull herself back to them, sensing it was important to stay. An urgent voice from very far away was calling her but—although she wanted to—she couldn't follow it.

The pulsing slowed now. Darkness encroached. Finally she stopped fighting its pull and let herself slip into the quiet blackness.

Together Andreo and Eliad carried Shara back to the poison tree path. The eager squeals of the Rif'iends turned to shrieks of rage and, glancing up, Eliad could see a tussle being waged for the black bow. Finally one of the Rif'iends had hold of it and fired an arrow in their direction. When it missed, the tussle commenced with even more screaming than before.

"Lay her down here," Andreo said quietly when they finally reached the path. Shara groaned as they lowered her to the ground.

"She lives," Eliad whispered, although the front of her tunic was soaked red and his hands coated with her blood.

Andreo felt for the pulse in her neck. "Barely. I need to stop this bleeding, Eliad. Tear strips from your garment."

Eliad did so as quickly as his shaking hands allowed. He watched Andreo press them around the arrow wound. "We need to get her home, Andreo," he said urgently. "Death cannot take her in Ajalon."

"How far is it?"

"Half a day, no more. We can make a stretcher."

Eliad saw the hopelessness on Andreo's face as he looked down at Shara, but he would not allow such a thought to take hold. He could not have brought his king's beloved daughter this far only to lose her now.

"You tend to her while I find some branches and vine for a stretcher," Eliad said.

Once he had the branches and vine, Eliad used them and a blanket to craft a stretcher. The Gold Breast alighted on Shara's chest as they lifted her onto it. Andreo had staunched the bleeding, but Shara's face was as colorless as a midnight moon.

It had been difficult terrain to traverse when they were merely walking it, but now—carrying Shara between them—it was almost impossible to edge their way down the hills. They stumbled and slipped, but by sheer determination reached the last fringe of forest that separated them from Ajalon. Here they rested for a short while before pressing on.

Live, Shara, live, Eliad pleaded silently as they walked the path created by another's blood.

Every part of Eliad's body ached, especially his arms, but other than occasionally changing positions with Andreo, he refused another rest. The men did not speak, both lost in their own silent thoughts and fears. Ajalon. In Ajalon Shara would live. Just a little farther, just a little farther.

Eliad was so deep in concentration, coaxing his body forward, that he did not immediately sense that a change had occurred. Andreo had slowed and, when he stopped altogether, Eliad looked up.

Andreo was looking at him, sorrowfully. "Eliad. It's . . . over."

Eliad looked at Shara. She lay unmoving, as she had been these last two hours, the bird still perched on her chest. She didn't look different. She didn't look . . . His mind refused to even think the word. Andreo was wrong.

Yet as he was about to tell Andreo this, the Gold Breast let out one long, pure note. Beautiful. Sorrowful. And Eliad *knew.* Shara was dead. Everything had been in vain. Taus had won.

Eliad sank slowly to the ground next to Shara's lifeless form. He studied her pale face, marveling that it looked as beautiful in death as it had in life. It occurred to him, for the first time, that with the dark curls she closely resembled Prince E'shua, her brother. He wished he had noticed it earlier and had told her. It would have made her happy.

Too numb to weep, he looked up at Andreo. The monk's eyes brimmed with unshed tears as he stared at the princess's body.

"She was so happy last night at the thought of reaching Ajalon," Eliad said dully. "How did this happen?"

Andreo knelt next to Shara's body. "Couldn't the Gold Breast have stopped them?" His face was etched with confusion and grief.

They sat in silence, holding Shara's hands, feeling the warmth of her life slowly drain away. When her skin chilled his own, Eliad carefully laid her hand down.

"Let us carry on, Andreo."

They both took up their positions again and slowly shuffled towards Shara's homeland. The urgency was gone, yet every step required all their strength and determination.

This is how they finally arrived in Ajalon, not with the joy they had anticipated, but weighed down by a sorrow heavier than the body they bore between them.

CHAPTER 30

The highest peaks of the Ruin Rim Mountains towered above the riders as the Charabian held up his hand to halt them once more.

Nyla felt a surge of impatience. They had traversed this particular stretch three times already looking for the entrance to the tunnels.

She watched as the Charabian unrolled the map. Elxa and Klyden drew alongside him to study it again, but Nyla didn't join them. She had done her share of staring at that ancient document over their six-day journey and knew that the tunnel's entrance lay somewhere near what was marked as the "Fading Fall." She glanced up again at the strange phenomenon they had just discovered—a fine spray of water cascading over the edge of the cliff yet never reaching the ground, as if some magic drew it away.

Surely this was it. Or could there be another this strange?

"My queen," the Charabian called. "I think we should set up camp here for the night."

"But there is still light," Nyla objected. "We should keep looking." Every day they wasted seeking the tunnels, Alexor drew closer to the Guardian Grotto.

"My men will search for it on foot. That will be more thorough than from a horse."

Nyla saw the truth in his words and followed the others in dismounting, tethering her horse and laying out her blanket. She intended to join the men in the search, but the Charabian came over and laid a hand on her shoulder.

"Sit a while, Your Majesty. We've set a grueling pace this last week. It's been difficult even for my men, and they are used to such hardships. If the entrance is near, they will find it." He looked to where Klyden and Elxa were already leading several men across some rocks. "They are exceptional scouters."

"I know." Nyla smiled briefly. "I've been with them long enough."

She had come to like and respect the Charabian these last few days and sensed the feeling was mutual. He treated her with a mix of esteem and fatherly protectiveness. His men followed his lead and were courteous and kind. All except Klyden. Her protector avoided her and kept his distance wherever he could. They had hardly spoken more than a few politely strained words to each other this last week.

"Looks to me like there is a mountain storm approaching." The Charabian pointed to the east where dark clouds, lit up by the occasional flash of lightning, massed over the mountains. "They are the fiercest of storms. Thankfully, rather rare." He frowned. "Let's hope we find the tunnel before the storm breaks for the horses will be spooked by the lightning."

They sat in silence after that, sipping steaming cups of origo that one of the Charabian's men brought them. Nyla watched the storm draw near. The cold wind whipped angrily against her face. The air was charged and ominous, setting the horses to restless pawing and nickering.

"Is there nowhere we could shelter?" she asked finally, feeling the beasts' anxiety as her own.

The Charabian didn't reply. He was looking past her and, as his face broke into a smile, she turned to see Elxa running towards them.

"Father! We have found it."

"Thank Ab'El." The Charabian was already on his feet. "Come, Your Majesty. We don't have a moment to spare."

The Charab men broke up camp and led their horses to the tunnel entrance with their usual speed and efficiency. Nyla's heart pounded as the Charabian placed the triangular rock over the matching-shaped indentation in the face of the cliff.

"By the abyss! How did you find a triangle that small on a mountain this big, Elxa?" she whispered.

"We're trained to be observant." He grinned. "And I suspect the Ancient One helped, for there was a shaft of light right on it as I walked past."

Something was happening. A metallic clanging sound was followed by the deep grating noise of stone sliding against stone. A crack appeared in the cliff, slowly widening to reveal a dark opening. The entrance was tall—the height of four stacked men—and wide enough for three horsemen to ride next to each other.

Nyla felt a shudder of apprehension as she stared into that gaping blackness, but next to her Elxa pounded his fist into the air.

"It's all true! Chaorlin's map. The key that opens the tunnels." He turned to her excitedly. "And if that's true, then the Old Magic part of the legend must be too."

Nyla wasn't so sure, but she followed the men as they mounted and urged their horses towards the tunnel. The animals went willingly enough, their fear of the approaching storm greater than their nervousness of the dark entrance.

"Festering figs, it's dark up front," she whispered to Elxa when they were a few paces into the mountain. Far ahead of her a man had lit a torch, but its light hardly reached Nyla and Elxa.

The Charabian entered last. As he placed the triangular rock on the corresponding indentation inside the tunnel, there was once more a click and a loud grating noise as the door slid closed, shutting out the last of the daylight.

Yet with the final clanging of the doors, the tunnel suddenly lit up.

Around her the men's gasps reflected Nyla's own amazement. Rows of Vulcan Rocks lit up both sides of the passage, casting a warm glow in the tunnel as far as the eye could see.

The Charabian smiled proudly at her. "The ancients knew a thing or two, didn't they, Your Majesty?"

"Did Chaorlin do this?" she asked wonderingly.

"They say Ab'El had the tunnel made to traverse this part of his kingdom with ease. Perhaps it is why the Old Magic still lingers here, sealed for hundreds of years." He urged his horse forward. "Now let us go find this Guardian Grotto."

Pearce had seldom seen a storm so violent. Earlier, the dark, massing clouds had stolen all the light from the sky, forcing him and his men to slow to a mere snail's pace. Before long, the first torrents of rain had lashed down on them, and they had no choice but to seek shelter. Now they were pressed together under a narrow overhang at the base of Winter Pass, with little room for the men and their horses. Water gushed over the lip of the ledge, soaking them in icy coldness. Lightning cracked around them, so deafeningly close that they felt its vibrations through the ground.

The horses reared in fright with every new thunderclap, landing heavily on men's feet in the confined space. There were sure to be a few broken toes.

And this cursed storm couldn't have come at a worse time.

The king's army had indeed breached the Inner Peaks at Waif's Cleft and, by the time Pearce and his men followed in pursuit, were already more than a day and a half ahead of them.

Still, Pearce had believed he and his men could catch them. They knew these mountains. Their horses were used to the rough terrain, and the king's army was large. It would take the king's men longer to pick their way across the mountain trails than it would the Warriors.

Pearce and his men had ridden hard, resting only briefly to water and feed their horses and themselves. They had steadily gained on the king's army until only a little more than half a day separated them.

Today, a few hours before the storm broke, the king's army had climbed Winter Pass to the Elam Highlands. Fear clenched deep inside Pearce at the thought. The king drew dangerously near to the Grotto. Six hours of solid riding and Alexor and his army would be at the Burrow entrance. Pearce had hoped to follow them up the pass before nightfall and overtake them on the Highlands in the course of the next morning.

But then the storm broke.

At least, Pearce consoled himself as he watched the lightning flash, it would force the king to a halt too. And as soon as the rain lightened, Pearce and his men would set off. It was not too late to stop their enemy. His mind skirted around the truth that they were vastly outnumbered. Less than a hundred and fifty men rode with him, and he had seen the vastness of the king's army. But they were Parashi Warriors, used to beating the odds. Skilled fighters with one burning desire: to save the Guardian Grotto.

With the dark clouds moving away, the rain weakened a little. Pearce pushed his way over to Crif.

He still had to shout to make himself heard. "Crif! I think we should set off again."

The older man turned his eyes to the sky and pointed to a new bank of clouds moving in from the east. "This isn't over yet, Pearce!" As if to highlight his words, an ominous rumble broke through the sound of the beating rain.

"Do you think we'll still get up the pass before nightfall?" Pearce shouted.

"Even without the storm, there's no more than three hours of daylight," Crif called back. "The horses will struggle with the rocks so wet and slippery. We'd have to lead them over the steeper parts." He shook his head. "It's foolishness, Pearce!"

Crif's words confirmed what Pearce already knew. But with so much at stake, perhaps they had no choice but to be foolish. To take a life-or-death risk. Pearce stared angrily at the rain lashing down from the sky.

"*Why? By the abyss! Why now?*" Pearce flung the words into the sky, but the storm's raging voice drowned out his own.

CHAPTER 31

Andreo stepped off the poison tree path and into Ajalon. Warmth dispelled the Rif'twine cold. A soft breath of air caressed his face.

Andreo bent down to lower the stretcher bearing Shara's body, then straightened and gazed around. What he saw filled him with quiet awe. They stood on a plain of downy grass strewn with flowers swaying joyfully in the breeze. Their sweetness perfumed the air.

After the deathly quiet of the Rif'twine, the sounds of life delighted him. He perceived it all as he never had before, distinguishing the individual insect-hum and birdcall even as his heart beat to the rhythm of the jubilant combined chorus. The light, warm and gold, bathed everything around them in its soft radiance. No harsh shadows broke the scene, only a clarity that showed every blade of grass and flower, the river and distant mountains in all their splendor. Andreo thought he could stand here forever and never tire of the sight.

"Welcome home, Andreo." Eliad sighed contentedly, a smile spreading across his face.

Home. Andreo had only ever thought of Ajalon as Shara's home, never his own. But in that instant he felt the truth of the word. Suddenly he knew that this ancient kingdom had beckoned to him long before he even laid eyes on its name in Shara's book.

For a moment the splendor of Ajalon had stolen away his sadness, but the emotion battered into him again as he looked at the body of the princess. Shara should have been here with them. The light and joy of this place should have reflected in those dark, expressive eyes. He closed his own eyes at the thought, feeling guilty that he could see what she never would.

"Andreo?"

"I'm fine." He shook away the thought of those brown eyes. "Let's be on our way. I imagine we have a long way to go."

As he stooped to pick up the stretcher again, Eliad said, "There's no need. Look."

He was pointing to a copse of trees near the river, where a group of riders emerged. They were still some way off when the front one lifted his arm and, with a whoop of joy, spurred his horse forward.

Tabeal, who had been perched on Eliad's shoulder as they stepped into Ajalon, flew towards the horsemen, and Eliad—with a joyful shout of his own—set off after her.

Andreo watched from afar as the front rider jumped to the ground and embraced Eliad. Soon the others were clamoring around the old man too.

After a while, they turned and led their horses to where Andreo stood. He counted eleven men, recognizing the front one as General Ga'abri from Shara's story. Two of his companions were familiar too—elders from the king's council.

The general greeted him with a wide grin. "Welcome to Ajalon, Andreo!" Accompanying the booming voice, a trunk of an arm encircled Andreo around his shoulders. The others came, one by one, to shake Andreo's hand as heartily as they would an old friend.

General Ga'abri dropped to his knees next to the stretcher and let out a long, sorrowful sigh as he looked at Shara's body. The men grew quiet, drawing around the stretcher, heads bent as they looked at their king's slain daughter.

After a long silence, the general issued an instruction. Two men ran to where the horses stood, returning with a gold-handled stretcher. They reverently transferred the princess's body, then lifted it between two horses with saddles adapted to carry it.

Questions churned through Andreo's mind. Why had they brought the stretcher? Had they expected an attack? But he did not ask. The moment was too solemn as the general, the two stretcher bearers, and an additional two men mounted and set off slowly in the direction of the distant mountain peaks.

"Aren't we leaving too?" he asked.

"We will follow shortly, but there is no haste," one of the men said. "We knew you would be hungry, so we brought some food."

They spread blankets on the ground and laid out ornately carved silver goblets and plates before passing around bunches of grapes, red plums, fresh figs and olives. Andreo thought grief would have robbed him of his appetite, but after weeks of eating little more than muus, the simple bounty delighted him. The golden juice they poured into his goblet tasted of summer and sunlight and quenched his thirst as only the water in the clearing had done.

When they had eaten their fill, the men presented Eliad and Andreo with horses. Andreo's mount was a beautiful chestnut mare, gentle and responsive to his touch. They set off at a trot and Andreo took pleasure in the journey. There was much to see and marvel at as they wound their way down to the river and rode along its banks. He saw trees bearing fruit he had never encountered before and birds that appeared completely unafraid as the horsemen passed by. His Ajalon guides delighted in answering all his questions and sharing their vast knowledge with him. They finally stopped at a shady place on the riverbank and dismounted.

"You can wash here," one of the men told him. "We have brought towels and new garments for you."

Andreo looked down at his clothes and felt a pang of shame. He looked pitiful. His outer robe was filthy and ripped, and suddenly he longed for the refreshing feel of water on his skin.

Eliad had already stripped off his outer garment and was wading into the river. "Come, Andreo," he said, laughing.

He had expected the water to be cold, but it was soothingly warm as he followed Eliad into the river.

"Come under." Eliad laughed, splashing him with water. Strange, Andreo thought. Eliad no longer seemed old in Ajalon.

"I don't swim."

"The water is filled with Old Magic. You can't drown in it. Try it! There are some wonderful things to see."

Hesitantly, Andreo took a deep breath, scrunched his eyes closed, and ducked under. His arms and legs seemed to move of their own accord, and the gentle river current drew him along.

Something tapped against his arm. He opened his eyes to see Eliad pointing at the brightly colored pebbles lining the bottom of the river. Andreo marveled at the clarity of the water. Small, brightly patterned fish glided past him. Something larger—almost birdlike—dived around him playfully. He saw intelligence in the creature's eyes.

Then he saw the water plants. Andreo pushed towards them, wondering at the wide array of leaves—broad, sleek, wispy—swaying in the current. Their colors were as varied as their shapes—red, green, purple and yellow. Truly, life thrived in Ajalon.

He took his time, examining each one closely. When he finally looked up again, Eliad was nowhere in sight. He pushed to the surface to look for his friend, wondering briefly how he could have stayed under so long without taking a breath.

He made his way back to the shore to find Eliad sitting with the others, his beard and hair dripping water onto a deep purple robe. The men brought Andreo a thick towel and blue robe made of silk, which felt cool and soothing against his skin.

Contentment settled lightly over Andreo as they set off again. His needs had been seen to with kindness and forethought. He had feasted, bathed, and was now clothed in a princely garment. His senses delighted at the sights and sounds around him. The men had welcomed him as warmly as a friend—perhaps even a brother.

Eventually, the contentment may have coursed through him and transformed into a deep peace. But its flow was blocked by a large, unmoving stone of grief that he doubted even Ajalon could smooth away.

CHAPTER 32

How long had they been riding through these endless tunnels? A look of confusion had passed over the Charabian's face when Nyla asked him the question earlier. He shrugged. "I . . . I really don't know, Your Majesty. Days? Weeks?"

"*Many* weeks," Klyden had added. "It's a long distance between the Ruin Rim and northeastern mountains."

Riding next to Elxa, Nyla thought back to the moment when they had first entered the gaping chasm in the cliff and the Vulcans had lit up the path before them. Deprived of daylight, they had lost all sense of day and night. They rode until they tired. Then they stopped, ate, and slept before riding on.

Besides the light of the Vulcans, the ancients had provided well for the needs of travelers using the tunnels. Troughs brimmed with water, ingeniously channelled from the droplets seeping from the limestone rock. The occasional large chamber had been carved out and straw—still surprisingly fresh—laid down for bedding. In adjacent chambers, bales of straw fed the horses.

Were it not for the monotony of the tunnels and Nyla's burning impatience to reach the Grotto, she might have enjoyed the ease with which they moved, the small luxuries of soft bedding, and the companionship of the Charab men. Yet Nyla's thoughts churned constantly on Alexor attacking the Grotto and Mada's ominous words: *If the Rocks are joined, may Taus protect us all.*

She consoled herself with the thought that, had the Guardian

Rocks already been joined, they would have felt it. Perhaps the earth would have rumbled, boulders broken loose from the tunnel walls, and the light of the Vulcans been extinguished. No, Alexor had not yet reached the Guardian Grotto, she told herself. They still had time to defeat him.

Nyla's horse came to a stop as the riders ahead of them halted. She strained her head to get a better view of the blockage. Was there a rockslide again? They'd had to clear one away before. She heard the animated voices of the front men and looked questioningly at Elxa.

"I think we're at the end of the tunnel," he said excitedly.

They heard the grating sound that had started their journey through the tunnels, and Nyla sensed the air around them lightening. The men let out a loud cheer.

"By the abyss!" she exclaimed. "We're really here?"

From where she stood, she could see the top part of the tunnel's entrance and make out a blanket of dark clouds.

They spilled out of the tunnel into a soft drizzle of rain. Ahead of them lay a lush valley through which a fast-flowing river ran. Its roiling, muddy water dragged branches and even small uprooted saplings along on a wild current.

Nyla pushed forward to where the Charabian stood. She breathed deeply of the fresh, rain-washed air. "Looks like we've just missed the brunt of a huge storm," she said. "Strange that we entered the tunnels just as one was about to break."

"Not strange at all considering it was the same storm, Your Majesty." The Charabian smiled.

"But you said yourself we have been in the tunnels for weeks."

"Yes, by our own understanding of time. But with Old Magic, time dwindles and death is halted."

"So the legends are true!" Hope coursed through her at the realization. "The tunnels really are infused with Old Magic."

"Let us hope the map is just as true." He dismounted and gave the reins of his horse to one of his men. Nyla dismounted and followed him back to the entrance of the tunnel, where they knelt down to study the map together.

"We're here." He pointed. "And this river's source is on the Elam Highlands, here. If we went upriver, we would find the waterfall."

"And the Grotto's entrance lies on these Highlands?" She pointed to a place marked with an ancient word.

"Yes. That word translates as *warren* or *burrow*. There seems to be another entrance at the base of these mountains," he pointed, "shielded by a waterfall. But it's farther away and the terrain looks difficult to cross."

"So we need to get onto the Highlands and find that burrow entrance?" She stared at the towering cliffs beyond the river. "How in the abyss do we get up there?"

The Charabian shook his head, looking uncharacteristically defeated. "It seems the ancients had a way." He pointed to another word marked on the map.

"What does that mean?"

"The Fissure."

"Well, let's go find it," Nyla said.

They left the horses in the care of the youngest man in their party and followed the course of the river on foot, in search of the ancient way to the Highlands. The rain had finally stopped as the dark clouds rolled southwards. But night approached. They would be forced to stop soon.

This time it was the man called Eben who pointed to the cliff. "Do you think that could be it, sir?"

If Nyla had hoped to see a path or steps carved out of the smooth rock wall, she was sorely disappointed. All that was visible was a deep crack about the width of a fist, cutting the cliff into two.

"Interesting." The Charabian put his head back and gazed upwards. "Does it run all the way to the top?"

"I suspect so." Elxa followed his father's gaze.

"How high do you think the cliff is?"

Elxa let out a low whistle. "Maybe four hundred feet?"

"More than that." Klyden stared upwards. "Closer to five."

"Either way, cousin," Elxa said, laughing, "it's a bone crusher of a fall."

"How can a crack in a cliff be the way to the top?" Nyla asked.

"There's rotting wood at the base," the Charabian said. "The ancients must have jammed stakes into that crack and used them for hand and footholds."

"But the stakes are gone. There's no way up. We'll have to find the other entrance." Nyla couldn't quite keep the relief from her voice.

"Perhaps." The Charabian's gaze was still on the cliff. "Or we climb up right here in the morning."

"How in the abyss . . . ?" Nyla exclaimed.

"We tie together all our ropes and use that to pull ourselves to the top," the Charabian said.

Nobody spoke as they contemplated the difficulties. Eben finally asked the question on all their minds. "But who takes the rope to the top?"

Nyla knew the Charab did not lack courage, so the long silence that followed Eben's question showed just how dangerous this task would be.

"I'll do it." Klyden stepped forward.

Nyla's heart lurched at the thought of Klyden climbing the cliff with his bare hands. The Charabian seemed to have similar misgivings. "Are you sure, Kly? It might be easier for a smaller man to do it."

"I've always liked a challenge, Uncle."

They set up camp on this side of the river, deciding that it would be easier to cross in the morning once the raging waters had subsided. There was no dry firewood, but the men huddled close, laughing and telling their old tales.

Nyla usually enjoyed this part of the day, but her thoughts kept returning to what lay ahead the next morning. Klyden would climb the cliff. *A bone crusher of a fall.* Elxa's words took shape in her mind, filling her with dread. She looked at Klyden in the light of a flickering torch and felt the familiar tightening in her chest. From the time he had rescued her from the Enderite traders, Klyden's disdain for her had been evident. He could not forgive her for using the arming word. On the rare occasion that he spoke to her, it was either with forced politeness or subtle sarcasm, and she often caught his angry glares when she laughed with Elxa and the others.

How different it had been on Azab Rock, when she had seen respect in his eyes and heard it in his voice. What she wouldn't give to earn back that esteem.

"Could I be so bold as to make a suggestion, Your Majesty?" The Charabian interrupted her thoughts.

"Of course."

"Speak to him."

"Who?" Even though she knew.

"Klyden."

"He hates me. Can't forgive me for using the arming word. I'm the last person he wants to speak to."

The Charabian smiled. "I suspect his feelings are more complicated than that."

"What good will it do? We near the Grotto. After the battle everything will change . . ."

"Yes. But it is for this very reason that you need to speak to him. If there's one thing a Charab knows, it is that death steals the confessions and farewells from our tongues. Better to speak them now. You might not get the chance again."

"You don't think Klyden can make it to the top?" Nyla tried to keep the fear out of her voice.

"Yes, I believe he can," he said solemnly. "But it is very dangerous."

Death steals the confessions and farewells from our tongues. A sudden sense of urgency filled her. If Klyden fell tomorrow, her chance to say what she needed to would be gone.

She watched her protector closely the rest of the evening for a chance to speak to him alone. When he finally rose and headed for the river, Nyla followed him to where he stood on the riverbank, staring silently at the dark shape of the cliff. He sensed her behind him of course.

"Nyla." He looked at her fleetingly before turning back to the river.

"We haven't spoken for so long," she said as she came to stand next to him. "And I never really explained to you what happened at the Charab village."

"I know what happened." His words were clipped.

"But you didn't hear what drove me to it. Your uncle was—"

"Blaming my uncle might alleviate your guilt. The royals have been doing that for generations." In the dark he couldn't see the effect his iron-tipped words had on her. "But it doesn't change that you are just like them. A Tirragylin royal to the core."

Briefly her old pride surfaced, indignant at his words, but she pushed it down again. If this was to be their last conversation, she wanted it to count.

"For once the Queen of Tirragyl has nothing to say?" Bitterness laced his voice as he said, "Lohlyn thought the world of you. But she sacrificed herself for just another power-hungry heir of Taus. A wasteful, empty sacrifice."

Grief. Suddenly Nyla understood. This was all about his grief. It always had been. Even with the insight, his words still wounded her. But after a long silence she spoke the words she had come to say.

"I'm sorry for so many things. For using the arming word. For being the cause of Lohlyn's death. For not being the queen you hoped me to be. I'm sorry that you and your family are still putting your lives in danger for me. And I wish, with all my heart, that I had trusted Lohlyn when she tried to save me. I'd ask for your forgiveness, but I can hardly forgive myself. I'm deeply sorry, Klyden."

Then she turned and walked away. At least the confession had not died on her tongue.

CHAPTER 33

In Ajalon, time wavered and changed course. In fact, Andreo reflected, it did more than that. The very concept of time flowed away like the water of the river they now followed through the mountains—gliding past but never running dry.

At first he had queried his guides often.

How far is it to the palace?

How many days had they been traveling?

How many more until they reached their destination?

Their replies told him nothing of what he wanted to know, but perhaps everything he needed to.

They would reach the palace at just the right time.

They had traveled long enough to see many a wonder in Ajalon, but not long enough to see them all, and—they added with a chuckle— nobody ever could.

The destination was wonderful, but he must not miss the joy of this journey.

At first their answers annoyed Andreo, but as they wound their way along the river, stopping to admire a flower or taste wild berries growing along the bank, he found himself drawn into the gentle, unforced rhythm of Ajalon life.

Once, knowing his love of plants, his guides took a wide detour to show him gardens that contained the most ancient trees in Ajalon. He had been mesmerized as he stood at the base of the towering trunks and stared up at the light filtering through their leaves. He had leaned against one of the trees and closed his eyes, listening to its rustling whispers.

Perhaps here he could judge the passing of time, he thought fleetingly. As leaves died and fell and returned and died again, he would know a year had passed. He thought his guides would agree to a year of watching leaves, but a small remnant of Tirragylin impatience balked at the idea. Instead he sat for as long as he chose before setting off again with his companions.

They spent much time around fires, speaking and listening intently to each other. One night Andreo spoke shakily of his deep grief. Eliad drew alongside him and pulled him into an embrace, and the other men came closer, two of them weeping openly with him. In that moment Andreo sensed a small lump of grief breaking away and a little peace trickling into his heart.

Only later did he speak of his anger towards the Gold Breast. *Why didn't she stop Shara's death?* he had asked. Andreo expected them to defend Tabeal or berate him for his thoughts, but they did neither. Again they drew around him and agreed that the Gold Breast could have saved the princess, admitting that they did not understand why she hadn't.

But the bird is the king's. She is good and everything she does is good.

Those words wove into Andreo's mind and, although he could not see what was good about Shara's death, the thought of Tabeal's goodness restored a little of his lost love for her. And with that even more peace seeped into his heart.

They rode now along a narrow mountain pass, and Andreo looked back often to the land of Ajalon stretched below them. But it was as they crested a hill and he turned his gaze forward that he saw it.

The palace.

Built on a cliff, it towered above them and was built of white marble, reflecting all the warmth of the Ajalon light. The buildings stretched up but also along the cliff, in a beautiful symmetry of walls and towers.

"Incredible," Andreo exclaimed. Next to him Eliad gazed at the palace with an expression of delight and awe. "Why didn't you tell me we were this close, my friend?"

"Because seeing a newcomer's expression when they first see the king's palace is one of our greatest pleasures," Eliad said, laughing. "Even for us the sight doesn't cease to amaze, but there's nothing that compares to that first glimpse."

"It's even better from inside," one of their companions said, smiling. "Come, let us go in. I see the banners on the wall inviting all to gather for the king's banquet. We'll have just enough time to prepare." He winked at Andreo. "Didn't I say we would arrive at the right time?"

A banquet? Andreo thought it strange that the king would throw a feast during a time of mourning. He had just lost his daughter. Andreo's grief for Shara remained a raw wound. Wouldn't her father's sorrow be just as great, if not greater?

But he kept the thought to himself as they made their way up the road to the palace. Finally they rode through an imposing gate and into a beautiful inner courtyard filled with fountains and large pots of flowers. Music wafted from inside the palace, reminding Andreo of the time he had seen the king dancing with his children.

People drew around them in a warm Ajalon welcome. As they dismounted, they were given goblets of fresh, cold water. A boy brought out warm water, cloths and towels to clean away the dust of their long journey.

A young man came running from the door to throw his arms around Eliad. "My friend! It's good to see you again."

"Daric, you old rascal." Eliad laughed. "Did you manage to keep this place running without me?"

"It wasn't easy." The man chuckled, turning to Andreo. "Welcome to the king's palace, Andreo. If you would follow me, I will take you to the rooms prepared for you. They are very near Eli's, in fact. The king invites you both to dine at his table tonight."

Eliad flushed with pleasure. "As always, it would be a great honor, Daric. But come, let us first show Andreo his new home."

He linked his arm into Andreo's and led him into the king's palace.

CHAPTER 34

Mikel had planned the battle for the Guardian Grotto, running the scenarios through his head. Most likely, the guards stationed near the Echo Pool would send word that the king's army was near. This would give Mikel time to place Warriors in position between the Echo Pool and waterfall. From these hidden positions, the remaining Warriors, though few in number, could inflict some damage to the king's army. Ideally, the king's army would fall back to regroup, but if they did push forward, they would still encounter the arrow traps at the waterfall that guarded the Grotto's entrance. The traps would eventually run out of ammunition, but Mikel would have more Warriors stationed behind the waterfall to shoot at any soldiers that made their way through.

The important part of Mikel's plan was that it gave him enough time to move the children and most of the women through the Burrow exit, out to the Highlands, and into the Deep Caves. He had contemplated moving the children earlier, but he knew the separation from parents would be difficult, so he delayed it as long as possible

Mikel knew that they would not be able to hold off the king's army indefinitely, but they would fight with the courage of true Warriors. The Grotto might ultimately be taken by their enemy's sheer force, but a seed of hope remained that the king would not discover the location of the Deep Caves. The Deep Caves would keep their greatest treasures safe: their children and heritage, their ancient writings, and the Guardian Rock. And his own precious daughter, Kella.

Mikel was eating breakfast when a commander burst into the dining hall. Instantly the clatter of knives and forks stilled and voices grew silent. Mikel was on his feet by the time the commander reached him.

"Not here," Mikel growled. "Meet me in the war chamber."

"This can't wait, sir," the commander answered. He dropped his voice so that only Mikel could hear. "The enemy has breached the Burrow. They are pouring in like water."

"By the abyss!" Mikel glanced around the dining hall. Every face was turned expectantly towards him. His mind reeled at the implications of this news. The king's army must have found and breached Waif's Cleft. And—the thought sliced through him like a knife—they wouldn't be able to bring the children to safety at the Deep Caves.

"The Warriors in the upper barracks are engaging them, but they are few, and I fear they will soon be overwhelmed."

"Take your unit of men and try to delay the enemy as far back in the upper passages as you can." Mikel spoke calmly, even as he thought that, unhindered, the king's men could be in these very chambers within an hour. "Send one of your men to call the acting commanders to the war chamber."

"Yes, sir." The man ran back to the exit.

Mikel looked around at the solemn faces of the people he loved, who trusted him to make the right choices. He had failed them, never foreseeing an attack from the Highlands. What could he say now to prepare them for what lay ahead?

"My beloved people." His voice echoed through the all-too-empty chamber. "The moment we have been preparing for has come. The king's army has attacked, not from the waterfall as we expected, but from the Burrow."

He saw the shock on their faces, but only a few murmuring voices broke the silence.

"I need just two things from you all now. To stay calm and to follow orders. Everyone knows where you are to meet your assigned leaders. Go to these places immediately, quickly but calmly, and await your instructions.

"Let us take our stand with courage." He placed his fist on his heart. "For the Grotto and the Guardian!"

Everyone was on their feet, fists to their hearts. Their voices rose in unison. *"For the Grotto and the Guardian!"*

By the time Mikel reached the war chamber, his acting commanders were already waiting for him. He wasted no time.

"We have been breached at the Burrow. Sirla and his men have already left for the upper passages, where they will try to slow down the enemy. Eni, take your men to the middle cavern and passages leading off it and engage in the cave-warfare tactics we've prepared. Luan, your front men will support Sirla's unit, while the others cover the mid-passages. Go now!"

He wished there were time to draw all the Warriors together and speak of the bravery that would be required in this, their final battle. He would tell them of the ancient Parashi courage he saw in each of their eyes, and he would remind them that they would die as they had lived. With dignity and freedom. But there was no time. Instead, swallowing down the lump of sorrow in his throat, he watched the commanders leave.

Only Mikel's oldest commander, Jabur, remained. He had been placed in charge of those that were not battle trained: the grooms, blacksmiths, older boys, and the women prepared to fight.

"We've spoken of this moment before, Jabur."

"We have, sir," the commander replied grimly.

"But we have much less time than we had thought. And the fact that we cannot reach the Deep Caves changes everything." Mikel shook his head. What a fool he had been to delay getting the children to safety. "Your unit will now have to accompany the children and women to safety through the waterfall."

Surprise showed on Jabur's face. "You mean you want us to *leave* the Grotto? You don't want us to fight?"

"You might still need to fight in the protection of the children. They can't fend for themselves, and they won't have the safety of the Deep Caves as we had planned."

"Sir, may I speak bluntly?"

Mikel nodded.

"My unit may not have much training, but they are as passion-ate about saving the Grotto as every battle-hardened Warrior. Why not use them in the defense of the caves?" Jabur's brow furrowed in sudden understanding. "It's because you think we've already lost."

"No, it's not the—"

"You've given up before we've even started!"

"Jabur." The steel was back in Mikel's voice. "All these lives are in my hands, and I choose to save as many as I can. Keeping our children safe is the most important task I could entrust to you. Now go and fulfill your orders."

"Yes, sir." Mikel knew Jabur's loyalty. He would follow his orders to death.

A strange sense of calm enveloped Nicho as he heard the sound of the horn echoing through the Grotto. The moment was upon them. The weeks of waiting for the enemy were finally over. Today he would give his all for his people, the Parashi.

On the sleeping pallet next to him, Frintin sat up, momentary confusion creasing his age-lined face.

Gruel, on the other hand, was on his feet, the short blade they had been issued on their arrival already in his hand. "About time too," he growled. "Let's give these Highborn sods what they came for: a fight they'll never forget."

Nicho could not muster the same bravado as the rifter as he snatched up his own knife. He would fight with everything he had, of course, but there was sadness knowing he had to say goodbye to Jed, Rosa, and Simhew. Simhew had argued, rather persuasively, that he wanted to stay and fight. Even Rosa had volunteered to fight alongside the other women, but in the end it was decided that she would take both Simhew and Jed to the Deep Caves. At least there they would be safe.

It took fewer than four minutes for the three men to run down the passage to the meeting place for all those not trained as soldiers.

From here the women and children would leave for the Deep Caves, and the remaining fifty-seven men and women would go to fight under their commander, Jabur.

Most of the women and children were already there, and he spotted Rosa in the crowd, holding a tearful Jed. He pushed his way towards them and, as Jed saw him, the boy stretched out his hands. Nicho lifted him into his arms.

"Hush now, Jed. It's going to be fine. Rosa is going to take you to the safe caves, just like we said."

"What about you?" Jed's words were choked with tears.

"I have to fight the king's army, remember?"

"Will you die? Like Papa?" Sometimes Jed's words pierced as sharply as arrows.

"I don't know, but I'm going to fight as bravely as I can. Will you be brave too?"

Jed shook his head. "I'm not brave. I'm scared."

Jabur stepped onto a large rock, and an instant hush fell over the crowd.

"We have new orders from the High Commander," he said, his voice carrying through the cave and bouncing back in an eerie echo. "The Grotto is under attack but not from the waterfall as we had expected. The king's army is rushing in as we speak . . . from the Burrow."

This announcement met with a rumble of voices that Jabur's raised hand quickly silenced.

"This means that the children and women will not be able to reach the safety of the Deep Caves."

A young mother carrying a baby on her hip let out a single terror-filled cry.

"The High Commander orders that they will instead leave through the waterfall," Jabur continued. "Furthermore, our entire unit will accompany them to protect them with our swords."

This last bit of news was met by shouts of outrage. Nicho could hear Gruel's raised voice over the protests. "No! We will fight the Highborn pigs here. We will not run and hide!"

"Silence!" Jabur's voice bellowed. "We have little time. The waterfall exit is slow. I need volunteers who grew up in the Grotto to accompany the women and children and help them navigate the traps." Several men raised their hands. "Good, you men come with me and the rest go to the kitchens and take as many supplies as you can comfortably carry without being slowed down. Follow us to the exit as soon as you are done."

As Jabur stepped off the rock, panic and mayhem ensued. People pushed towards the passage, and Jabur had to shout again for order. The men who had volunteered to take people through the waterfall herded the children and women into smaller groups and led them down the passage in batches.

"To the kitchens," one of the men, dressed in the thick leather of the armory, shouted. Three other blade-smiths followed him. Gruel, Frintin, Nicho, and two other rifters fell in with them.

"You're from Gwyndorr, aren't you?" one of the blade-smiths said. "We met in the slums."

"Yes. Madoc, right?"

Madoc nodded. "I never really saw you again to say thanks."

"For what?"

"For not telling Commander Pearce I was the one who told you about his brother."

"Ah."

"Would you two stop with the nattering," Gruel growled. "We're under attack here. Maybe you can leave the chit-chat for a better time." Gruel pushed his way to the front of the men and made a sharp right into one of the more dimly lit passages.

"Haia! The kitchens are this way," a man shouted.

"I don't know about you, but I'm staying in the Grotto to fight."

"We have our orders, Gruel," Frintin said. "And a real Warrior would obey them."

"Well, if nobody thinks I'm enough of a Warrior to stay and fight, I guess they won't mind if I disobey an order."

"What we've been instructed to do is important. Noble, in fact," Frintin said. "We are to protect the most vulnerable amongst us. There's nothing shameful in that."

"Fine, that's your choice. I'm choosing another way. Who is with me?"

Gruel's old rifters were the first to push towards him. Then Madoc and two of his companions followed.

"Nicho?" Gruel's eyes bored into him.

Nicho had a sudden recollection of Pearce asking him to come with him and Derry to the Grotto. Would things have been different if he had? Would Derry still be alive? But Jed's words, too, rang in his ears: *will you die like Papa?*

Choices. Nicho had made so many of them. He had chosen to stay in Gwyndorr because it was the responsible thing to do. He had given up Shara to go back for Jed. Always his head shouted one thing, while his heart whispered another. Nicho was tired of listening to his head.

"I'll go with you, Gruel. My blade belongs to the Grotto."

CHAPTER 35

Lucian pushed to where Commander Rillon was overseeing his soldiers' access into the Grotto. It was a narrow entrance that didn't allow more than two men in at a time. The passage sloped down steeply, making entry even more challenging.

"How do your men fare?"

"I'll be honest with you, Lord Lucian." The commander glanced to where the king sat surrounded by his group of young followers, all laughing merrily. "The king doesn't want to hear it, but this is unlike any warfare we've ever undertaken, and every inch of ground we take will cost lives."

"Kings don't count such costs," Lucian said wryly. "To them only the outcome matters. How many men are in now?"

"We got about a hundred and twenty in, but then they encountered opposition, which blocked everything up for a while."

"But now you're sending in more?" Lucian watched the next two men disappear down the passage.

"Yes, the front lines dealt fairly swiftly with that first resistance, but I expect more Warriors will be on the way shortly."

"Keep me posted."

"Yes, Lord Lucian."

Lucian walked away from the throng of soldiers, picking his way across the rocky plateau towards a distant patch of green. He heard the sound of water before he discovered a small stream that sprung suddenly from the ground and rushed towards the edge of the plateau. It was a pleasant and quiet place, far enough from the men he had been forced to be with all these weeks. Lucian craved solitude and quiet. That and a soft sleeping pallet. Not long now, he reminded himself, and almost everything he wanted would be his.

He stared back at the small figures of the king's army milling around the steep Grotto entrance, and his mind drifted to that last time in Shara's mind and the layout of the caves he had moved through. It had been his longest breach into the Grotto—the one that gave him the best sense of the Parashi's lair.

Now, with the men's voices finally stilled, Lucian could finally determine the source of disquiet that had crept over him since they crested the Highlands yesterday afternoon and made their way to the Grotto entrance. They had quickly dealt with the two Warriors posted at the entrance, and Commander Rillon had wasted no time sending his troops into the Caves. Everything was so smooth, so easy. Lucian had expected more opposition.

But Lucian's greatest sense of unease rested on the fact that this entrance looked nothing like the one he had seen through Shara's mind. Where was the giant Chay'ets tree that had stood over the Grotto with such stature and strength?

Mikel heard the sounds of battle long before he stepped into the middle cavern. As he strode up the dark passage towards the flickering lights, he felt the familiar surge of fire through his blood, momentarily pushing away the weakness that gnawed at him. It had been too long since he had wielded his sword. He had almost forgotten the excitement that accompanied the first battle rush. It never lasted long, though. When your friend was cut down next to you, rage and a deep, primal longing to survive replaced any excitement.

Some of Eni's men were congregated around the entrance to the cavern. All the passages leading off the cavern had such "corks" of men in place, stopping the flow of the enemy. The Warriors flattened against the walls of the passage as Mikel squeezed past.

Inside the cavern the battle raged with brutal intensity. The clanging of swords and the angry cries of the living reverberated loudly off the walls, drowning the deeper moans of the dying. Heat pulsed through the throng of men and steel. The air was already thick with the smell of sweat and blood and fear.

"Make way," a voice called out, and the huddle of men parted to let through a Warrior supporting a man whose slashed tunic was red with blood. The wounded man's eyes were large with terror, his face whiter than a snowbarb feather. One look at the wound and Mikel doubted the man would see another morning. He reached out and put his hand on the man's face, drawing close enough to whisper, "You fought valiantly for your people, Warrior. Thank you." Momentarily, his words broke through the man's shock. Gratitude and pride replaced the fear in his eyes. Then they were past Mikel, and the High Commander turned back to the battle.

To his right, a broad-shouldered enemy soldier pulled his sword from the body of a Warrior. His gaze fell on Mikel. The High Commander may have lost speed and agility with age and illness, but he had not lost his finely tuned battle instinct. Before the man charged hungrily towards him, Mikel's own sword was already in his left hand and, as he sidestepped the attack, he blocked the enemy's direct blow. Uncertainty flashed in the man's eyes at the direction of the counterblow, but he was quick to recover, and the next lunge was aimed at Mikel's right side. This, too, Mikel blocked with a double-handed down sweep. This time, pain jarred through Mikel's arms at the strength of his opponent's blow.

The man sneered at him. "Not bad for an old man."

Mikel blocked the third and fourth blows and watched the man's frustration grow. A moment before he charged in with the fifth blow, Mikel changed his sword to his stronger right hand. As he dodged the blow, he plunged his sword into the man's side. The large man dropped his own weapon and crumpled to his feet. Blood gushed from the wound as Mikel pulled his sword free. His first kill in many months, yet there was no sense of victory, only a familiar hollow ache.

Mikel pushed farther into the cavern, slashing down two more opponents before he reached Eni. His commander had just crashed his shield over the head of a king's man, who teetered and stumbled backwards into the tip of another Warrior's waiting blade.

"Sir!" Eni inhaled deep, ragged breaths. "Didn't know you were here." His gaze roved over the battle, alert to opponents who might attack. Mikel did the same, although he was gauging the enemy's strength and numbers.

"How does your unit fare?"

"We've lost men but not as many as the enemy."

"They have more men to lose," Mikel said grimly. "Have any of the passages been breached?"

"No, sir."

Eni suddenly sprang to action as a young soldier barreled towards them. The commander was slightly too slow jumping to the side, for the enemy's blade sliced into his upper arm. With an enraged howl, Eni responded with a fast and fatal blow of his own.

Mikel grabbed Eni's arm and looked at the wound. Not too deep, at least.

"I'd tell you to have that seen to, but that's one order you probably wouldn't obey," Mikel tore a strip from the bottom of his tunic and, as he tied it tightly over Eni's wound, said, "The passages hold, you say?"

"Yes, although the western passage to the kitchen is under threat. If there's going to be a breach, I think it will be there. A few of my men are trying to get over there."

"I'll go take a look." Mikel smiled at the commander. "Strength and courage, Eni."

"To you, too, sir," Eni said as he spun to face his next opponent.

Mikel fought his way across to the western passage and found Eni's words ominously true. The huddle of men at this passage had been drawn forward to fight the crushing and relentless stream of king's men. Only two Warriors now guarded the passage entrance. They seemed relieved to see the High Commander.

"Sir, we need reinforcements," one shouted over the battle din.

"Eni is sending them. I will fight with you till then." One look around told Mikel that they had few men to spare anywhere. "Are there Warriors farther down the passage?"

"Only four, sir. If we don't stop the enemy here, they won't hold the passage for long."

CHAPTER 36

The seven young men who had disobeyed Commander Jabur's orders pushed their way along the western passage towards the middle cavern of the Grotto. One of the blade-smiths, knowing the lay of the caves better than Gruel, took the lead, holding a flaming torch.

The front man stopped and lifted his hand. "Listen."

In the silence, Nicho thought he heard voices. He gripped his blade a little tighter.

They crept forward a little more cautiously, and the voices grew louder. Nicho could now make out the clanging of swords. His blade grip felt slick with sweat, and he had an image of himself losing his grip on the knife as another plunged into his side.

Stop it, he chided himself. *You're a Parashi. Courage flows through your veins.*

Suddenly there was a grunt of pain from their front man. The torch tumbled to the stone floor, where moments later its light extinguished.

A voice hissed, "He's one of ours, Gwian, you idiot."

In the light cast by their remaining torch, Nicho could now see that their front man lay squirming on the ground next to his smoldering torch.

"The fool's lucky I didn't kill him." A Warrior materialized from a dark passage. He bent down and held out a hand to the blade-smith. "Sorry, my friend. Thought you were a king's blade."

The blade-smith took the wiry man's hand and hauled himself to his feet. He rubbed his jaw, tentatively opening and closing his mouth a few times.

Three other Warriors emerged from the passage and studied the seven men.

"You're Commander Jabur's men," Gwian said. "Aren't you supposed to be with the women and children?"

"We thought our swords would be more useful here," Gruel answered defiantly.

"You disobeyed a direct order?" The second Warrior's forehead creased in disapproval. Nicho had seen him before in the dining hall. He was a giant of a man called Midge.

"Fools!" Gwian spat at their feet. "You'll get yourselves killed rushing forward with blazing torches. Do you know nothing of cave warfare?"

The seven remained silent.

"Can you believe this, Pirian? The enemy is close, and now we have to take care of mutinous youngsters."

Surprisingly, the man called Pirian laughed. "I think we might just be able to use these men, Gwian. I've got a plan."

"Not again. You and your plans are going to get us all killed one of these days."

"They haven't yet, have they?" Pirian chuckled. "Why don't we use these fine men as bait?"

Bait? Nicho didn't like the sound of that.

After a moment Gwian let out a single laugh. "I think I see where you're going with this. The long drop?" As Pirian nodded, he said, "Brilliant! Why didn't I think of it?"

"You stay here. I'll show them what to do."

Pirian led them back down the passage until he reached a place where rocks were piled against the wall. "Quickly. Clear away these rocks and use them as best you can to block up the passage to the kitchens."

They quickly followed his orders, uncovering a passage in the wall.

"Where does this lead?" Gruel asked.

"A place we call the long drop. It's a ledge that falls away into a deep cavern. This passage was blocked up a few years ago when three children fell to their deaths."

"So why uncover it?"

"Because you're going to lead the enemy down the passage to their deaths."

Once they had moved away all the rocks, Pirian grabbed the torch. "Come. But watch your step."

The seven followed the Warrior down the cold passage. For a while it was even more dank and musty than the rest of the Grotto, although as the passage began to dip down and they rounded another corner, Nicho sensed a breath of air on his face. Their steps suddenly sounded softer, as if their footfalls had dropped into a large void.

"So when you round this last bend, you need to be particularly careful because you're close to the ledge. Look." Pirian took a few more steps and halted them with his raised left hand. He lifted his right, bearing the torch, high above his head. In the light Nicho could now see the walls of a large cavern ahead of him, but mere feet from where they stood the ground just stopped, falling into dark nothingness. A cold chill swept over his skin.

"How in the abyss do we not fall in ourselves with men chasing us?" Gruel asked.

"There are two places to hide," Pirian said. "The ledge curves a little to the right, so you can stand on it, just around that rock." He swung the torch in the direction. "There's not much room there though. One misstep and you'll fall.

"The other place is here to the left, just before you reach the ledge. A small hollow, probably just large enough for two of you." Nicho could make out the small indent in the cave wall. "It's where I'd hide if I were you."

"This is the craziest idea I've ever heard," Gruel muttered under his breath.

Nicho thought so, too, as he stared down into that deep abyss. His only hope now rested on the fact that no enemy had yet emerged from the battle in the middle cavern. Perhaps the Warriors would stop them there, and Nicho would never need to bloody his sword or act as "bait" in some crazy man's scheme.

CHAPTER 37

Klyden looped the ropes over his shoulder and stepped towards the cliff.

"I had Elxa grind you some rock powder to keep your hands from slipping." His uncle held out a bag of the chalky powder. "Climb to the top and find somewhere to secure the rope. Then throw it down so the men can follow."

Klyden nodded, grimly studying the cliff. "As easy as that."

"Be careful, Kly." The Charabian glanced up at the wall with a small shake of his head. "It's a beast of a cliff."

The men stood around him in silence. One or two slapped him on the back as he passed them. Nyla had not come to see him off. He pushed the thought of her and their last conversation out of his mind. This was no time for emotion.

He took a deep breath, reached up, and placed his fingers into the crack. He pulled himself up, feeling the strain on his shoulders as he did so. Then he placed his feet in the crack and pushed himself forward to the next handhold. Pull. Push. Pull. Push. His body began to feel the rhythm of it as he slowly and steadily crawled up the wall. His hands grew slippery, and he was grateful for the rock powder his uncle had thought to give him.

Klyden had never liked heights. Every now and then, the thought of just how high up he was threatened to overwhelm him. His Charab childhood had taught him to push aside intrusive thoughts, and he did that now with the stomach-clenching thought of how far he would fall if his hands should slip.

He was about halfway up the cliff when his arms and shoulders began to burn. They would soon start to shake from overexertion. Yet he could not rest. The longer he was up here, the greater the strain on his body. He tried to speed up, but this proved dangerous as he lost his footing once or twice, and small rocks plummeted to the ground below. Briefly panic flittered through him.

Push. Pull. Push. Pull. He let the rhythm and the feeling of air all around him, soothe away his panic. The morning light was beautiful, and he pictured the soft light as his father's hand, holding him close and gently lifting him upwards.

Finally, near the top, the cliff arched over him slightly, and he had to cling to it as he leaned backwards. Another wave of fear threatened to consume him.

He focused on one little inch at a time. That's all he needed to do. Push. Pull. Inch upwards. Push. Pull.

Finally with shaking arms, Klyden pulled himself over the edge of the cliff. He lay there for a while feeling his bruised fingers and the ache in every part of his body. He let his breathing slow down and savored the joy of conquering the mountain.

He wished there was somebody here to celebrate with him. Strangely, he wished it could be Nyla.

The cheer from the base of the cliff alerted Nyla that Klyden had reached the top. She hadn't been able to watch, but now she let out a long, pent-up breath and hurried over to join in the celebration, finding the Charabian in the group.

"He did it!" She looked up at the cliff, hoping to see him peer over the edge. He wasn't there. "What now?"

"He'll find something to secure the rope to, and then we'll all follow, safely tied to the rope."

"How far to the Grotto?"

"Half a day, I think."

"I wonder just what we'll find there."

Over the course of the next two hours, Nyla watched intently as, one by one, the men clambered up the cliff. They were strong and agile and made it look easy. Occasionally, a foot or hand would slip, but the rope always pulled taut and held them in place.

Finally only she, Elxa, and the Charabian remained. She watched the rope looping down towards them again.

"Your turn, Your Majesty."

Elxa tied the rope around her waist, pulling it tightly to check the knots. "It will chafe a little, but it's a small price to pay."

"Just take it slowly," the Charabian said. "Hand over hand. The men will help you by pulling you up too. Keep yourself from slamming against the cliff."

Nyla set off slowly. Even through her gown, she could feel the rope burning her. She felt heavier than a grubear trying to pull herself up that cliff wall. She wanted to look down to see how far she had come, but the Charabian had told her to keep looking up. Had the men not been pulling her, she doubted she would have made it on her own strength, but finally she was right near the top.

"Nyla." Klyden smiled at her from above. He reached out a strong hand and pulled her over the last lip of the cliff.

She sat for a moment, light-headed. It might have been from the exertion of the climb or the heady view that opened up to her from up here. But Nyla suspected it had a lot more to do with that single smile of Klyden's, a smile she hadn't seen since they had left Azab Rock.

"Let me untie you." He knelt before her, working loose the knot around her waist. She studied him, aware of just how close he was. There was a streak of dried mud just below his eye. She had an urge to wipe it away with her thumb.

"There you go." As he looked at her, some unspoken emotion stirred in his eyes. He stood quickly. "My uncle and Elxa will be waiting for the rope."

She watched him check the knot that bound the rope to a tree near the edge, before hurling it down. Then all his concentration was on keeping the rope taut as the Charabian climbed up.

The Charab men were scouting out the Highland area. Nyla,

however, stayed where she was near the edge, near Klyden. She looked out over the mountains and rivers and forest stretching far below her. Tirragyl. Her kingdom. Did the fact that it all still looked so peaceful from up here mean the Guardian Rocks had not yet been united? She remembered Mada's ominous warning. *If the Rocks are joined, may Taus protect us all.*

"What are you thinking, Your Majesty?"

Delight fluttered deep in her stomach. Klyden was talking to her again.

"What Mada said about the Guardian Rocks." She shielded her eyes from the glare of the morning light as she looked at him. "I thought we were long past all these formal titles, Klyden. Why not just Nyla?"

"I will call you Nyla again." Her name sounded gentle on his lips. "But I also wanted you to know that I consider you my queen. My words and actions haven't sent you that message lately. I'm sorry."

She nodded, not trusting her voice. The respect was back. Klyden had forgiven her. Now—maybe—she could forgive herself.

Once the Charabian and Elxa had climbed the cliff, the queen and her army set off across the Elam Highlands, heading towards the Guardian Grotto. Nyla knew that she was meant to be here. *Today.* In the weeks she had spent with the Charab, she had heard them speak often of the freedom they had found in the Enderite Forest and how the chains of their past had been broken. The account always filled her with shame. *Her* forefather had brought on their captivity. *Her* tongue was the last to bind them with its curse.

Yet now, walking between the Charabian and Klyden, she felt the joy of their—and her—freedom. These men had forgiven her. She was no longer their enemy. A deep sense of purpose washed over her. Something—or Somebody—had brought her on this journey. A hand much greater than her own.

Help us. The unfamiliar thought pulsed through her and out of her, with nowhere specific to alight. Yet peace settled in the small space it left behind.

CHAPTER 38

The first warning that the middle cavern's defenses had been breached was the flicker of lights on the dark passage wall. The next was the sound of men's boots tramping towards them. Nicho and Madoc, sitting at the entrance to the long-drop passage, scrambled to their feet. Terror surged through Nicho as the first soldier rounded the bend in the passage. The man let out a sharp call as he saw Nicho.

"Now!" Nicho pushed Madoc ahead of him and ran, heart pounding, trying to count the bends before the drop to oblivion. He could hear stampeding feet and men calling behind him. How far back were they? He daren't turn around to look.

Madoc came to a sudden stop, cursing loudly when Nicho almost ran into him.

"Hide!" Nicho whispered, diving for the small indent Pirian had shown them. Madoc followed, dousing his torch as he crouched next to Nicho.

A few seconds later the front man appeared and hurtled towards the ledge. Nicho scrunched his eyes closed at the sound of the scream that followed his fall. The handful of men following right on their leader's heels were running too fast to stop, and Nicho listened to their screams and felt sickened by the silence that followed.

Three men rounded the final bend. The screams had alerted them that something was wrong. They came cautiously, no longer running, and in the flickering light of their torches, Nicho could see their eyes filled with the same fear he felt deep inside him.

What was he doing here? He was not a Warrior used to watching his enemy die. How would he ever silence those screams from his mind?

"Where are they?" the front one asked, so busy looking around that he did not see the gaping chasm near his feet. Nicho almost shouted a warning, but it was the third man's voice that echoed off the walls.

"Careful, Jab!" In two strides the man reached over to the front one and grabbed his arm just as he began to fall. Jab's weight pulled him to his knees, and for a moment Nicho thought they would both fall. But he was a large man and held the weight of the falling man. Now the third man was also on his knees, grabbing for Jab's other arm.

Madoc made his move. He stood up tentatively and reached for his blade.

"No, Madoc," Nicho hissed, but Madoc moved silently towards the trio of men. He stood behind them, uncertainty written on his face as they inched the fallen man back to the ledge. It was Jab who saw Madoc and let out a shout of warning.

Madoc raised his knife above his shoulder and slammed the blade down into the large man's back.

The man plummeted forward, over the ledge, his weight pulling the other two men with him.

In the last light from the falling torch, Nicho could see the whites of Madoc's eyes. Then there was nothing but darkness.

"I'm here, Madoc," Nicho whispered. "Follow my voice."

He heard Madoc shuffling back to him, but the sound of pounding feet drowned Madoc's soft treads. Someone was coming.

"Quickly, Madoc!"

In the light from the approaching torch, Nicho could just make out Madoc scrambling up the slope, but the man hurtling around the bend slammed right into the young blade-smith, and his momentum carried them both over the ledge. This time Nicho pressed his hands to his ears, desperate to drown out the sounds of death echoing through the Grotto.

Nicho was not sure just how long he sat in the deathly silence. No more men came running down the passage. His mind kept replaying the image of Madoc trying to scramble to safety. When he began to imagine the broken bodies lying on the rocks at the bottom of the cave, he knew it was time to move. Only when he tried to push to his feet did he realize how very cold he was.

What had become of Gruel and the others? And the four Warriors in the main passage? Did the battle still rage on?

His left hand trailed over the stone wall as he blindly felt his way to the main passage. His right hand clenched his blade, although after he had seen Madoc thrust his knife into the soldier, Nicho knew he didn't have it in him to kill anybody. He let the knife clatter to the floor at this realization and felt his weakness, his uselessness, to the very core of his being. Pearce had been right all along. Nicho was a coward.

He stumbled out into the dark passage. To his left lay the middle cavern. He could still hear the sound of fighting although it seemed more muted than before. To his right lay the kitchen. For a moment Nicho's urge was to turn right. Perhaps it was not too late to leave through the waterfall and find freedom. Find Rosa and Jed and Simhew. But it was then that he heard a murmur of a voice he recognized.

"Help." *Gruel.*

Nicho felt his way forward in the dark.

"Gruel?" he whispered.

No reply, just a soft groan led him to where the rifter lay crumpled against the passage wall. He dropped down next to him.

"Gruel. It's Nicho. Where are you hurt?"

"Nicho. Bleeding . . . so much."

"Wait, I'll bandage it. Hold on, Gruel!" He began to tear wildly at his robe, but Gruel's ice-cold hand stopped him.

"Just sit with me."

He felt for Gruel's head and shifted position so he could cradle it in his lap. He tried to say something soothing, but his mute tongue stuck dryly to the top of his mouth. Instead he smoothed back Gruel's hair, like his mother used to do when he was small.

"So many men," Gruel whispered. "On us so quickly."

"What happened to the others?"

"Cut down. Even the Warriors couldn't hold them off. So many."

The words punched into Nicho as he sat in the dark, holding his dying friend. The Grotto had been overrun by the king's soldiers. His friends were dead. The legendary Parashi Warriors had not been able to hold back the mighty forces of Tirragyl. They were defeated.

CHAPTER 39

Long after Gruel's breathing had stopped, Nicho still held his friend. Finally, he lifted Gruel's head off his lap and carefully lowered it to the ground. He sat in complete darkness as a profound sense of aloneness gripped him. Only he still lived in this passage.

It was almost a relief when he sensed a rustle of movement from the direction of the middle cavern. Light shimmered onto the walls of the passage as he heard the murmur of approaching voices. But his relief was quickly replaced by a sense of danger. The enemy approached.

Where could he hide? Gruel's body stretched out next to him gave Nicho an idea. He closed his eyes and slumped down on the ground even as he berated himself that Pearce would never stoop to acting dead.

The voices grew louder.

"Lord Lucian is saying the Rock isn't here. Now he wants a Parashi to interrogate."

"By Taus! I wish they'd make up their rotting minds. First they tell us to kill every Lowborn in sight. Now we have to save them?"

They were near him. Over him. Even through his closed eyelids Nicho sensed the torch shining in his face. He held his breath.

"Well, now." One of the men let out a loud laugh, and Nicho felt a searing pain in his upper left arm. He let out an involuntary scream and grasped at his arm, staring uncomprehendingly at the blood dripping from the wound that—a moment before—hadn't been there.

"Just as I thought." The man whose sword had inflicted the cut dragged Nicho to his feet. "The oh-so-brave Warriors are acting dead. This can be our first live one."

They searched him for weapons, laughing when they didn't find any, before tying his arms behind his back. Then they shoved him towards the middle cavern.

As Nicho stepped into the cavern and glanced around, the air punched out of his body, refusing to let him take a new breath. All around him were bodies. Warriors. King's soldiers. Bleeding. Gaping wounds. Groaning. Vacant eyes. He recoiled at the sights and smells and sounds of the battle's aftermath, knowing this would haunt his every remaining dream.

Behind him his captor laughed. "We caught the most cowardly Warrior of them all, Hwin. Look at his face. You'd think he'd never seen a bit of blood before."

Nicho picked his way through the corpses and near-dead men, trying not to look closely into any face. Yet every now and then he would see somebody he had eaten with or laughed with or whose horse he had groomed, and shock would shudder through him.

His captors pushed him towards the far passage, where soldiers were coming and going, bringing provisions, or carrying their slain back to the light. Hatred flashed in their eyes as they saw him, and if Hwin and his other captor had not stopped them, Nicho was sure they would have fallen on him.

"The commander wants him alive," they bellowed. "He's going to tell us where the Guardian Rock is!"

Finally they thrust him out into the light on the Highlands. The last time he had been here, it had been a vast, empty plain, but now it was milling with countless men and horses. Against such a vast army, they had never stood a chance. Perhaps that was why the High Commander had tried to send as many of them as he could through the waterfall.

The soldiers parted to make way for them, although Nicho felt their hostile eyes following him as his captors led him to a large tent.

"Captain Rillon. We have one alive."

The three men seated in the center of the tent, studying a chart, glanced up to look at him.

The youngest of the three men was obviously King Alexor, for he wore a circlet of gold on his thick mane of hair. Nicho recognized another of the men as Lord Lucian. The last of the three men had the bearings of a soldier. This must be Captain Rillon.

It was he who spoke first. "Well done, men. There are a few other Parashi survivors. Go tie him to the chains with the others."

"Wait." Lord Lucian was on his feet. "I know this one." He stepped up to him, and Nicho had to suppress a shudder of fear as he briefly looked into those strange golden-brown eyes. "You're the groom, aren't you?" The lord's voice sounded gentle, and hope surged through Nicho. Perhaps he would let him go when he realized he was only a groom.

"Yes, Lord Lucian." Face-to-face with Gwyndorr's lord, Nicho once more looked down at the ground as he spoke. "I was Master Randin's groom."

"I remember. You and Shara played together when you were younger." Still the voice sounded soothing.

"Yes, my lord."

"And you were one of the men who stole her away on her wedding day?" A dangerous coldness had now crept into the lord's voice. Still, something about the words compelled Nicho to tell the truth.

"I was one of the men."

"Where is Shara now?"

The question, or maybe the way in which he asked it, broke the spell that Lucian's voice had momentarily cast on him. Nicho looked up now, strangely unafraid, into those peculiar eyes. The words of Shara's book, all but forgotten in the battle, flooded back into his heart, filled him with all the warmth and comfort the Gold Breast had brought to them.

"She's where you can never reach her. Back where you stole her from, *Taus*." The name was filled with derision. "She's in Ajalon."

Surprise flashed on Lucian's face. "What do you know about Ajalon, Parashi?"

"I know she'll never be yours. She walked the path Prince E'shua's blood opened up through the Rif'twine. She's home."

Lucian's face twisted into a mask of dark anger. Nicho became aware of the hush that had fallen around them. Lucian, too, seemed to notice it for the first time, for his face contorted back into a practiced smile as he turned to the other men.

"Well, I think I've found the perfect candidate for an interrogation. An hour or so with this young man"—he smiled sardonically at Nicho—"and I should be able to pinpoint the location of the Guardian Rock."

As the men around him murmured their approval, Lucian drew near to Nicho and whispered, "And then Ajalon and its princess will be mine."

CHAPTER 40

They pushed Nicho into Lord Lucian's makeshift tent.

"Leave," Lucian said to Nicho's two captors.

"Commander Rillon told us to—"

"Leave."

Uncertainty flashed on their faces, but Lucian's steely glare convinced them. They let go of Nicho. "We'll just keep guard outside, my lord."

Once the two had backed from the tent, Lucian turned to Nicho. What was it about those eyes that drew you in and repelled you at the same time? Nicho looked away.

"So. You know about Ajalon." His voice sounded pleasant, as if he were merely making small talk. "Who told you about it?"

"It was in the book that Shara found. The one Eliad penned."

"Ah, yes. Eli. Always so *loyal*." He suppressed a yawn. "And this book reveals that I am Taus?" There was a hint of pride in his smile.

"Yes."

"You do realize that I cannot let you live with this knowledge? Perhaps you can say the book, and Eli, signed your death warrant."

The thought was not as fearful as Nicho had imagined. "I should have died in the Grotto anyway."

"I'm sure you're going to wish you had." As he said this, Lucian drew something from the folds of a cloth. "Have you seen one of these before, Nicho?"

Reluctantly Nicho looked at what lay in Lucian's hand. It was a rock, black as midnight, with flecks of white that reminded him of stars. One look and Nicho knew this was no ordinary rock.

"What is it?"

"A Mind Rock. You've heard of it?"

He had, but Nicho suddenly had a strong desire to prolong this conversation. "No."

"A most remarkable rock, really. It's what I used to access Shara's mind. But I was gentle with our little princess. Didn't want to frighten her before I learned exactly where the Grotto was." Nicho clenched his fists at Lucian's words. "Mind you, I was a little rougher with the mind of the Warrior who led me to Waif's Cleft." Lucian smiled as if the memory gave him pleasure. "With you, I'll start gently until I have what I want. Then . . ." he leaned in close to Nicho and his eyes were more black than brown, ". . . I will see just how far I can push the Mind Rock. My anger and the rock's power. I suspect it will be a fearsome combination."

"I don't know where the Guardian Rock is," Nicho said hastily, glancing at the tent flap. If he screamed, would his captors come? Would they stop Lucian?

"I'd like to take your word for that, but I have a much better way to discover the truth." Lucian picked up the rock in both hands. "Let's begin."

"Lord Lucian!" As a soldier came barreling through the tent flap, Lucian secreted the rock into his robe. "The king sends for you."

"You fool!" For a second Lucian's rage pulsed through the tent, tangible in its intensity. "I said no interruptions!"

The man withered under the anger, before recalling his purpose. "Lord, the king sends for you. They have captured the High Commander, Mikel. He is badly wounded, but you might still be able to question him."

"Mikel?" Lucian's eyes flashed with interest. "I have long wanted to meet this infamous Warrior." He looked at Nicho. "I suppose our *discussion* can wait a little while."

Nicho felt a paralyzing sense of relief.

"Bring me the High Commander."

"Yes, my lord. Shall I take this one back to the chains?"

"No. I'm not finished with him yet. Tie him to the center pole. I'll get back to him soon."

The soldier roughly pushed Nicho into a seated position and tied his arms behind the pole. It was Captain Rillon himself who opened the tent flap a moment later.

"Forgive the interruption, Lord Lucian, but we know your interrogation skills. We have captured their High Commander." He waved the unseen men behind him forward. As they stepped into the tent, Nicho's eyes went to the man they half dragged, half carried between them. If he hadn't known it was Mikel, he would not have recognized him, for his hair and face were coated with blood, and one eye was swollen shut. The blood-soaked bandage around his center proclaimed a wound that could well prove fatal.

"My lord, could I have a word with you?" Rillon looked at the men who were busy lowering Mikel to the floor. "Alone?"

"Fine. But let's not delay this too long."

Lucian followed the captain out of the tent. Nicho could hear their low, urgent argument. As he looked over at the High Commander, he was surprised at the lucidity of Mikel's stare.

"Nicho." Mikel's voice was raspier than normal but still carried a steely inner strength. "Did the children get away?"

Nicho was ashamed to admit his rebellion. "I don't know, sir. A few of us younger men stayed to fight."

"Fools." The word carried sorrow, not anger. "The others?"

"Dead."

Mikel groaned as he tried to shift a little closer to Nicho. "Lucian has questioned you?"

"Not yet." Nicho tried to swallow the sudden lump from his throat. "He has a Mind Rock, sir."

"That's how he got into Shara's mind."

"It's also how he learned about Waif's Cleft."

"I underestimated him."

"What can I do, sir?" Nicho was suddenly desperate to hear the answer before Lucian returned. "How do I fight off the Mind Rock's power?"

"You can't. It's too powerful."

"He wants the Deep Caves. I don't want to be the one who gives it up."

"The strongest Warrior is powerless in the face of such magic." Nicho recognized the flat hopelessness in the statement. Hadn't he lived weighed down by such feelings himself before, in Gwyndorr? Before Tabeal.

"The Gold Breast," Nicho said with a surge of hope. "*She* is stronger."

"You have the pipe to call her?" Mikel knew the story of how the bird had appeared when Nicho blew the pipe.

He shook his head. He had given it to Jed. But now Nicho wondered if the faith with which one blew the pipe wasn't more important than the silent call itself. The thought was cut short by the appearance of Lord Lucian.

"Well, what a privilege to have the legendary High Commander Mikel in my tent." His bow was mocking. "We have already met, haven't we? The time I entered the Grotto through Shara's mind? Did you wonder how I did that little trick?" Lucian caught the glance that passed between Mikel and Nicho and laughed. "I see the groom has told you my little, dirty secret.

"You and your predecessors have been a thorn in my flesh for a long time. Longer than most realize." He sauntered over to Mikel and put his boot heavily on the High Commander's wound. Mikel roared with pain. "Yes, I have looked forward to this day. The day I defeat the Grotto and scrape the Warriors off Tirragyl's heel."

Mikel, body arched protectively, was panting with pain long after Lucian lifted his foot.

"So few words from my enemy." Lucian laughed. "The king thinks I should question you, but I think it would be far more interesting for you to watch me interrogate the groom. Very entertaining, a Mind Rock interrogation."

"Leave him be," Mikel hissed, finally able to speak again. "He brushes horses. He knows nothing."

"Perhaps I should enter your mind instead." Lucian seemed intrigued by the idea. "Although pain sometimes obscures memories." He drew the rock from under his robe. "Well, let's try, shall we?"

CHAPTER 41

The Mind Rock drew Nicho's gaze. It looked dark and menacing in Lucian's hands, and as the lord closed his eyes, an ominous power pulsed through the tent. Spiderweb-thin tendrils coiled out of the rock towards Mikel, curling lazily around his head. Then, for a moment, they stopped moving, and Nicho held his breath. In the next instant the tendrils drew together into a single shaft that pierced into Mikel's forehead.

At that moment the High Commander let out a fearful groan. His body convulsed, and his one visible eye rolled back until it was only a frightening white orb.

"Mikel!" Nicho screamed. "Mikel! Come back."

Lucian's rapturous expression faded slightly. The screaming was distracting him. Nicho screamed again. "Help! He has a Mind Rock!"

Any moment now a soldier would appear, and Lucian would have to break the magical connection.

Yet nobody came. Instead, something dark shifted in the tent, and Nicho felt an ice-cold breath on his face. A few tendrils looped out of Mikel and now floated towards him. *No.*

"No. You can't do—" His words were cut short by the flash of light that seared through his head. The light pulsed and grew, pressing outwards till he thought his head would explode. Lucian was here. In his head. Nicho had never felt so violated. He tried to push him back. *Get out. You have no right to be here!*

You should have sat quietly and waited your turn, Parashi. Now I'm going to have to take you along just to shut you up.

Nicho felt the web ensnaring their three minds together. Images that he had never seen before scuttled into his mind. Unknown memories crushed him with longing and regret. And overriding everything was the breath-stealing pain in his abdomen.

No. It's not my pain. Not my memories.

He fought to be free of the mesh of minds, but the more he struggled, the murkier his thoughts became. Where did he begin, and where did he end? Was that thought even his, or was it Mikel's?

Let me go, Lucian. I won't scream again.

His plea was useless. Already their trio of minds was in the Grotto, in Mikel's quarters, rifling through the books and treasures stored there.

Where is it, Mikel? Where is the Guardian Rock?

For a brief moment Nicho sensed he was in a deep cavern lit by a circle of wall-sconces. In front of him was a stone table. Something lay on the table, but before he could see it, the image blurred, and the pain from his abdomen—*no, Mikel's abdomen!*—seared through him again.

Pain and triumph and dark anger crashed together, crippling and confusing.

Laughter. It carried no pleasure, only menace. And a single thought: *the groom won't be so strong, Mikel.*

Now the strands of memories that surfaced in his mind were familiar again. Uncovering the box that held Shara's book outside the walls of Gwyndorr. Shara and he running towards the carriage that would carry them away from her wedding feast. Anger and hatred that he knew were not his own washed that memory away. Arriving at the Grotto. Meeting Mikel. Now he was following the path out of the Burrow onto the Highlands. He walked behind Mikel, going to the Dee—

No! The command crashed into the memory with all Mikel's innate authority. Nicho's memories were overridden by others, ferocious in their intensity. Fighting in the mountains, cutting men down with terrible skill. Studying maps. Training men. A battle in a cavern filled with Warriors: bleeding, dying Warriors. And the leer of the king's soldiers surrounding him. The thrust of his sword as he cut two of them down. The shock and pain as the third drove his sword into his stomach. Regret as his attacker was halted just before he would make the kill-blow. Lord Lucian wanted him alive.

Rage, red as blood, poured into the mind web. *You've lost, Mikel. Your mind may hold, but the groom's won't and neither will your men's. I will destroy each one of them if I must.* Now the images that flashed into Nicho's mind were of men undergoing excruciating torture. Bloodied limbs and terrified faces played to a series of screams and men pleading for mercy.

No. No. Nicho longed to close his eyes, his mind, his ears to the cruelty of the images Lucian conjured, but there was no escape. He sensed Mikel pushing back though. Images of waterfalls and moonlit nights—infused with peace—overlaid the cruel scenes. *Yes, we can defeat him,* Nicho thought, and he let his mind recall the births of foals, the softness of a horse's coat, laughing with Shara.

Fine. The cruel scenes were suddenly gone. *I will negotiate.* The thought was gentle, trustworthy. *The Rock for every one of your Warriors' lives.*

The pain returned and with it tiredness unlike anything Nicho had ever felt before. A heavy, immobilizing, bone-weary tiredness.

You want to rest, Mikel. I will let you rest if you just tell me where the Rock is. I only want the Guardian Rock. Your Warriors will go free.

Uneasiness prickled through the mind web. *He lies, Mikel.* It was his own thought, but it had hardly surfaced when he felt it stifled by a suffocating darkness.

All of them? Men, women, and children? Hope and fatherly love blossomed through the pain.

All. I promise.

They were walking on the Highlands on a day when the sky was a warm, deep blue. Scrambling down a steep incline, they were now in the moisture-laden vale where the Chay'ets, ancient and solid, stood guard. A feeling of anticipation rose in Nicho's mind at the thought of seeing Kella again. *My beloved Kella-girl.* Pushing aside a shrub, they felt their way into the trunk of the tree and down the rope ladder into the Deep Caves, lit by Vulcans.

Nicho sensed the thrill of discovery and desire. Lucian's lust for the Guardian Rock licked through him.

The image of the Deep Caves disappeared instantly. An aching remorse. *We had a deal, Lucian. I showed you where it is. You spare my people.*

Don't you know you should never bargain with a deceiver?

Still that pain, that relentless pain. Nicho felt the precise moment something loosened in Mikel. The struggle to breathe and fight for life waned. The pain eased. Awareness diminished. He was slipping away.

No, Mikel, come back. We need you.

But he was beyond pain, beyond care. One last, bright flash of conscious thought at the sight of a bird with a golden breast flying towards him. Surprise . . . joy . . . peace.

Then it was over.

Heat seared a pulsing pain through Nicho's head. Then emptiness. And a long, stretched-out darkness.

Slowly Nicho grew aware of his surroundings again. He felt sick, like the time he had been thrown off a horse and landed on his head. Confusion and nausea had dogged him for days on that occasion. This was the same feeling.

Tentatively, he opened his eyes. Lord Lucian wasn't there. Mikel lay crumpled on the tent floor.

"Mikel?" Nicho whispered even though he knew. Hadn't he experienced Mikel's death with him?

He thought over everything he had seen and felt as Lucian had had them in the grasp of the Mind Rock. Lucian knew where the Deep Caves' entrance was. He knew where the Guardian Rock was. His promise to spare the Warriors had been a lie, of that Nicho was certain. Grief gripped him at the thought. All was lost.

And then he remembered the last sight Mikel had seen—the Gold Breast—and goose bumps brushed his skin. No. It was not over yet.

"Come. Come soon. We need you," he whispered, soundless as the call of the reed pipe.

CHAPTER 42

Lucian knew his time was short. It had taken a few hours to defeat the Grotto, and he had not forgotten the unit of Warriors that had been on their heels as they climbed up Winter Pass. By his calculations they were probably only an hour or two away.

He pushed into King Alexor's tent.

"Your Majesty, I know where the Guardian Rock is. A deep cave on the Highlands just west of here."

"Wonderful." The king's eyes lit up with anticipation. "We'll set off after the midday meal."

"May I suggest we leave immediately? The Warriors that chased us on our way to Winter Pass will probably be here soon."

"Pff," the king scoffed. "More Warrior blood to spill. We'll annihilate them all today."

Lucian looked to Captain Rillon for support.

"We don't want anything to stand in the way of gaining the Rock," the captain said smoothly. "I see wisdom in riding to these Deep Caves immediately."

The king looked from his captain to Lord Lucian with a petulant glare. "Sometimes I think you two conspire against me."

"Not at all, Your Majesty," Lucian said. "We long to see the joined Guardian Rocks in your hands as soon as possible. With them you will be invincible."

"Fine then." The king pushed himself to his feet. "We set off immediately."

They left their tents and most of their provisions, as well as their wounded and dying, outside the Burrow entrance with a handful of soldiers to care for them. Lucian insisted they take the Warriors who had been captured, forcing the thirty-seven to march behind the army, even though some were in no physical state to do so.

Alexor rode beside Lucian all the way to the Deep Caves. There was a childlike excitement to his questions. "You say the entrance to the cave is through the roots of a tree, Lord Lucian?"

"Yes, Your Majesty."

"Difficult access."

"Indeed."

"There is no other entrance?"

"Not that I know of."

The Chay'ets tree was not visible until they descended into the vale Lucian had seen in Mikel's mind. It stood as majestic and proud as a sentinel, the vast girth of its trunk hinting at its great age. *Your days of hiding the Guardian Rock are numbered*, Lucian thought, smiling. By tonight—if all went according to plan—the tree would be toppled, the Warriors obliterated, and the two Guardian Rocks united.

Behind their leaders the king's army poured steadily into the vale. Despite their losses, Tirragyl's forces were still large and formidable.

"What do you suggest we do now, Lord Lucian?" Alexor asked.

"Now, Your Majesty, we send these last Warriors a message they can't ignore."

Kella grew restless. Her father normally sent a messenger every second day, but by midday nobody had come. Kella's Warriors had been preparing for the women and children to arrive from the main caves. Sleeping pallets lay ready, and extra seating had been prepared in the dining hall. One seldom-used cavern had been painted with bright designs, and chests of lovingly carved toys stood against its walls.

Earlier, the strangest thoughts had beset Kella, adding to her anxiety. Almost as if she daydreamed, her thoughts had taken her to the vale that lay above the Deep Caves. She was walking with her father when he turned and looked at her intently. *Kella-girl*, he whispered, and the forgotten childhood nickname felt wrong on his lips. *When the king's army comes, give them all they want. Give them the Guardian Rock. Don't resist them.*

Now, as she sat down to eat with her unit, Kella tried to shake away the strange words. It was just a daydream, she reminded herself. Just something that sprang from her growing anxiety.

"Commander." One of her young Warriors stood before Kella suddenly, shock on her ashen face. "There is something you should see in the Root Room."

"What is it, Gruna?"

The girl merely shook her head and grasped Kella's hand. It was this last surprisingly tender act that filled Kella with trepidation.

The Vulcans in the Root Room cast their usual soft light. Nothing seemed out of place except that three of her Warriors were kneeling on the floor in the center of the room. They stood up as soon as she entered and stepped away from what Kella thought was a large rumpled sack on the floor.

But not a sack. Shock jolted through her. A body.

She stepped forward, afraid of what—of who—she would find. Something in her knew before she saw the familiar dusky robe and short grey hair. Even though one of her Warriors must have wiped the dried blood from his face, it was bruised almost beyond recognition. Only his lips still held their familiar curve. Kella dropped next to the body of her father, feeling for the large hand that had so often held her own. His fingers felt cold and strange. They would never again grasp her with affection.

A sob shuddered through her body, her throat closing up so tightly it felt difficult to breathe. She wanted to rip her clothes and hair and loudly wail away that tight, painful knot, but instead she closed her eyes and bent over her father and slowly felt her way back to the control she knew he required of her now.

When her breathing had stilled and her thoughts were once more clear, she opened her eyes and let her gaze drop to the knife that pinioned a large piece of parchment to her father's chest. As she rose and pulled the knife out of her father's body, rage flared up at an act so vile and disrespectful. She read the large, arrogant sprawl:

The Grotto has fallen. All but thirty-seven men are dead.

If you deliver the Guardian Rock within an hour, they will live and so will every one of your Warriors.

If not, four of them will be thrown to you every turn of the half-hourglass.

And then we attack.

Not one of your Warriors will be spared.

Her Warriors eyed her nervously. She was the only one who could read.

"The Grotto has fallen," she said. "They threaten to kill the survivors if we don't give them the Guardian Rock."

They said nothing. Seeing the body of their High Commander had told them all they needed to know.

The words of her daydream thrust into her mind. *Give them the Guardian Rock. Don't resist them.* Had her father, with his dying thoughts, reached out to her and told her what to do?

She wanted to believe it was true. How much easier to give them the Rock than to fight. How much easier to spare lives than have bodies plummeting into the Root Room. But she knew the fearsome power that would be released at the joining of the Guardian Rocks. She had to try to prevent that.

Kella-girl. Something jarred at the name and the tone and the message itself.

She knew her father so well. Knew his thoughts. His will. She had spent hours and hours speaking to him about the defense of the caves. *Never choose the easy path over the right path.* That had always been his words to her. Yet in her daydream he was leading her down the easy path. Or could the easy path also be the right one?

Her head ached with suppressed sorrow and confusion. How was she to make a decision at a time such as this?

"Commander?" Gruna's face came into sharp focus. "Shall I tell the others what has happened? And suggest we meet in the dining hall?"

"Yes. Yes, thank you." She was grateful for the gentle nudge. Time was running out.

Pearce pushed into the Middle Cavern, and the bile rose in his throat. It had been a massacre. There were bodies everywhere. Nobody even remained to bury their dead. Behind him, a few of his men stared around with shocked expressions.

This was his doing. All his doing. He had let the enemy slip through.

"Sir, we should bury—" Crif began.

"There's no time. You heard what the Highborn pig said. They've gone to the Deep Caves. We will fight them there."

Pearce and his men had arrived at the Burrow just after midday. Part of him had hoped to see the king's army arrayed across the plain, planning how best to take the Grotto. But they had found only a fraction of the army, mostly injured men. One or two had tried to offer some resistance, but they were swiftly dealt with. Most, Pearce soon realized, were in no state to fight.

One trembling man—busy digging graves for their own dead— had been quick to tell him all he wanted to know. The Grotto had fallen. Tirragyl's forces had marched two hours earlier to the Deep Caves with the remaining survivors. He didn't think there were many more than thirty Warriors alive. Pearce hadn't wanted to believe it, but now, standing in the heart of the Grotto, he did.

Pearce lifted his sword above his head. "We make our last stand at the Deep Caves," he bellowed. "For the Grotto and the Guardian!"

"For the Grotto and the Guardian!" his men echoed fiercely.

Pearce knew that the images of death, seared in their minds, would fuel the fight that day. It would have to be enough.

CHAPTER 43

The original Parashi Warriors had chosen the Deep Caves carefully. The entrance through the Chay'ets tree was impossible to find unless a person knew they were looking for it. Yet those ancient Warriors had known, even better than the Warriors now, that their enemy was powerful and persuasive. They knew of power rocks and mind powers that could reach deep beyond the secret entrances of caves.

This is why the original Parashi had constructed the escape tunnel known to so few. Only Mikel, Kella and two or three others knew of its existence. Only Mikel and Kella had known exactly where it was and how it could be opened. In more than four hundred years, nobody had ever needed to.

Kella stood at what appeared to be the dead end of a musty passage. She swung her torch over the solid wall, feeling for the telltale cracks she knew should be there. Behind her the Warriors stood, silent and solemn. Some of them thought of the hourglass sand falling and the Warrior bodies that would fall with it. Others thought only of the journey—and the possible battle—that lay ahead.

Kella moved to the left slightly, feeling the wall. Nothing. She went down on her knees. *Where the three cracks meet.* Her father had told her the Grotto's secrets when she was blooming into adulthood. Perhaps she had not paid enough attention, believing the Deep Caves to be impenetrable.

The doubts about what they'd left behind still assailed her as well. Should she have stayed and defended the cave? Couldn't they pick off every king's soldier that tried to enter the Root Room before their feet even touched the ground? Or should she have surrendered the Rock as the dream voice had told her?

No. This was the course she and her Warriors had chosen. This was the course they would follow.

Finally her fingers found a fine crack, and she followed it to the place where it met two others. "Pass me the Rock," she whispered to Gruna.

Gruna held the Guardian Rock, lying on a piece of burlap, out to her. Kella picked it up tentatively, knowing its powers. One touch of the wrong person's hand and the Rock could kill instantly. But nothing happened as she lifted it, looking for the striations that matched the cracks on the wall. She rotated the Rock slightly and then aligned it with the wall cracks.

Kella held her breath. She sensed the slight shudder in the Guardian Rock and, on hearing the deep, grinding rumble, she stepped back. Slowly, the solid wall began to move, gliding open from the right to reveal a dark passage of stairs ahead of them.

The Warriors behind her murmured in wonder.

"Lead the way, Gruna. When everyone is through, I will close the wall again," she whispered.

"Where does the passage come out, Commander?"

"West of the vale, I think," Kella said after some consideration. "There is another of these sliding walls at the top of the stairs. I will see you there to open it."

As the Warriors filed past her, she saw her own sorrow reflected on their faces. Perhaps they thought of their remarkable leader, Mikel, lying in a crypt deep in their cave next to some of the bones of their Ancients. How Kella yearned to give him the burial he deserved, but there had been no time.

Shock colored their expressions, too, and regret. This had been their home for a long time, and they had not expected to abandon it in this way.

Yet what Kella saw most on their faces was the fierce determination and pride of their people. They would do all they could to save the Guardian Rock from falling into the hands of the enemy.

When all the Warriors had passed her, Kella found the small indent on the opposite inside wall, which perfectly matched the shape of the Rock. As she placed the Rock into it, the wall slid back into position.

Then Kella followed her Warriors up the stone steps carved by the Parashi of previous generations.

The rope bit into Nicho's wrists so tightly that he could hardly feel his fingers. Two other Warriors were tied to the same post as he was. Next to them, right on the outskirts of the king's army, were more posts with more Grotto survivors. They had been thirty-seven on the march to the Deep Caves. Now they were thirty-three, and if their mocking guards' stories were to be believed, soon the next four would be flung into the Deep Caves.

"Psst, lad," the Warrior next to him whispered. "Move a bit closer and see if you can reach my bonds."

Nicho thought of telling him his fingers were in no state to undo knots, but instead he shuffled closer to the man, keeping an eye on the guard, whose back was turned to him.

"Wait, I can feel yours," the man said. "Let me try to loose you first, and then you can help the two of us."

He sensed the man trying to work the knot, but the rope remained as tight as before.

"Too tight," the man muttered. "I'm going to try Ziran's."

A murmur stirred among the prisoners, and Nicho watched a man push through the cluster of soldiers from the direction of the Chay'ets tree.

"They haven't surrendered yet. We need another four Parashi," he said matter-of-factly.

The guards leered over the Warriors with amusement. "Who's ready for an exciting fall?"

Nicho quickly averted his eyes. *Coward*, he thought, glancing around to see if the others were doing the same. They weren't. Almost all of them were staring straight at the guards with unadulterated hatred.

"I'll go," one voice said.

Then another. "I'll die. For the Grotto!"

"For the Grotto!" other voices echoed.

"Lord Lucian wants the one called Nicho," the matter-of-fact soldier said.

Ice crept into Nicho's blood. *Be brave*, he thought, fighting the urge to press deep into the group of men and deny who he was.

"Where's Nicho?" the guard bellowed.

"I'm Nicho!" a voice cried from a few posts away.

Nicho finally found his voice, buoyed by the bravery of the men around him. "I'm Nicho. I'm the one Lucian wants."

"Fine, I'll take *both* Nichos." The soldier laughed. "And you. And you." He pointed to the two men tied to Nicho's post. "Don't worry, you'll all get your turn today."

The mocking guard knelt down and slashed through Nicho's ropes, before the soldier dragged him to his feet and began to push him towards the Chay'ets tree.

Suddenly, the soldier's steps faltered, and he released his tight grip on Nicho's arms. Nicho turned to see him crumpling to the ground. An arrow protruded from his back.

For a moment Nicho thought one of his fellow prisoners must have broken free and taken the shot, but then he looked up towards the ridge and saw the riders on their sturdy mounts. Parashi horses. As he glanced back around him, he saw that his captor was not the only one struck by an arrow. Another bevy of arrows flew through the air as the cry issued from the king's army. *We are under attack!*

Nicho ducked down and pushed his dead captor onto his back so that he could grab the man's knife. Briefly he considered taking his sword too, but he knew he was not a swordsman and definitely no match against trained soldiers. He ran back to the posts and Warriors, amidst a bevy of arrows. He had expected to die in a humiliating fall. Now he had a chance to die a noble death on the battlefield. The thought took away some of his fear.

He slashed through the bonds of the Warriors with the knife. Those who could, scrambled to their feet.

"It's Commander Pearce and his men!" one shouted, and Nicho turned to see Crypin, Pearce's stallion, pounding down the hill, leading the charge into the king's camp.

"For the Grotto and the Guardian!" He could hear Pearce's shout and see his sword held high. Hope stirred in Nicho.

"For the Grotto and the Guardian!" he chorused with the men around him.

"To me, men!" an older Warrior called Hosra shouted after Nicho cut through his bonds.

"Find weapons!" Hosra called as he bent down to rip a sword from the hand of a dead man. "We will move in arrow formation towards Pearce. Be quick. The enemy's attention is on Pearce right now, but they will soon remember there are other Parashi here."

The men rushed to pull swords and knives from the soldiers slain in Pearce's first attack.

Hosra looked appraisingly at Nicho. "Just the knife, lad?"

"I'm not much use with a sword, sir."

"You're the one good with horses, aren't you? Word is you have the whispering gift."

"I suppose. Won't do me much good here, will it?"

Hosra shrugged "Each of us fights in our own way. Courage has many faces. Plenty of horses on a battlefield is all I'm saying."

The men gathered with their weapons. They silently fell in on both sides of Hosra. Nicho watched as the last Grotto Warriors set off towards the heat of the battle, cutting into the back of the king's army.

Each of us fights in our own way.

Nicho contemplated this as he watched a riderless Parashi horse bolt away. She stopped, pacing nervously a little past the battle line. *Lila.*

Parashi horses were trained to stay where their riders fell. But Lila was young, and she must have lost her unseated rider.

"Lila," Nicho called. His voice did not carry over the sounds of the battle. He whistled sharply and saw her head jerk up. "Come, Lila." He whistled again, and she came towards him.

Nicho pressed his head into her neck, reveling in the familiar comfort of her soft coat and sharp animal tang. "My beautiful girl. You're doing well, Lila," he whispered and felt some of her anxiety seeping away.

Each of us fights in our own way.

He glanced up again to where the last Grotto Warriors battled against the enemy. If he couldn't help them with a blade, perhaps he had something else to offer them.

Nicho pulled himself onto Lila's back. "Let's go, girl."

At the time of Pearce's attack, only a group of about a hundred of the king's soldiers had been mounted on horses, keeping guard on the eastern side of the dale where they expected an attack from the Parashi who had followed them up Winter Pass. The other soldiers had been milling around, their horses tethered at the edges of the camp. Their saddles gleamed in the sun as their riders waited for a response from the Warriors in the Deep Caves.

When the battle started, some had managed to mount their horses, but many had not. It was to these still-tethered horses that Nicho now rode. At the sound of his voice, a gentle nudge or even just a thought-whisper, Lila avoided the pockets of fighting along the way.

When they reached the horses, Nicho leapt from Lila's back and began to untie them, all the time whispering comforting words. He mounted the largest stallion, hoping the others would follow, if not his voice alone, then at least the familiar stallion.

A few balked as he coaxed them to draw alongside him, but the majority—about ten in total—followed on either side of him to where the battle raged. *Just like an arrow formation.* He smiled at the thought, heading to the place where Hosra's Warriors fought. A small group of them still remained, now completely surrounded by the king's army.

"Courage, boy. Courage," he whispered to the large stallion as he pushed him forward, sensing the other horses picking up speed too. At the shaking ground and sound of hooves pounding towards them, soldiers leaped aside, allowing Nicho and his herd of horses a clear passage into the heart of the battle.

He reined in when he reached Hosra's group.

The old Warrior looked up and nodded gratefully before pulling himself onto a stallion's back. A few of the other Warriors managed to mount a horse too. Nicho followed closely behind Hosra as he fought his way to where Pearce's larger group battled. Soldiers thrust swords in Nicho's direction and, without a blade to protect himself, he had to trust in the size, strength, and agility of the horse. Under Nicho's thought-whispers, the stallion became more than just a mount. He became a weapon, one that kicked and reared and knocked over any threats that came their way.

Nicho caught sight of Pearce fighting as fiercely as only he could. He saw the moment when Pearce leaned out to attack the soldier who had just slashed a wound into the Warrior by Pearce's side. The enemy soldier pulled sharply on his reins, causing his horse to rear up. Crypin reacted in fright, rearing too, and Pearce—still off balance from the attack—flew off his stallion's back.

CHAPTER 44

Pearce landed hard, feeling something snap in his left foot. His ankle seared with pain, spreading upwards until he thought it would consume him. *Get up, you fool.* If he lay here a moment longer, he'd have a sword thrust into his chest. But even as he tried to stand, his leg buckled beneath him. Pearce sensed a king's horseman pounding towards him. Grappling for his sword, he pushed the pain aside and again tried to rise to his feet. He was almost upright when the large stallion halted by his side.

A hand stretched out to him. "Pearce."

By the abyss, it was Nicho!

"I can't walk."

"That's fine," Nicho said, grinning. "I'm a particularly fine rider."

Pearce held out his hand and put his right foot into the stirrup as Nicho pulled him up. It was excruciating dragging his left leg over the horse's back. Flecks of black swam into his vision.

"Support it in the stirrup," Nicho said, leaping away from an assailant bearing down on them.

Pearce tentatively put his foot into the stirrup. Again he felt light-headed from the pain, but it eased a little once his foot was secured.

"Pearce!"

Nicho's voice broke through his pain. Pearce looked up just as another soldier rode towards them, sword aimed at Nicho. He lifted his sword and slashed it into the passing man's face.

Nicho pulled the horse around, into the battle again. "If we're going to get out of this alive, we'll need your blade."

And that was how they continued to fight the Battle of the Deep Caves—Nicho riding with unrivaled skill and Pearce dominating with his sword. Together they forged through the enemy line to the Chay'ets tree, with Pearce's men and a handful of the surviving Grotto Warriors following behind them.

The hidden tunnel opened up to the west of the vale in which the Chay'ets stood. Kella glanced back and could just see the very tip of the tree. She heard shouting and clashing of swords from inside the vale.

As her Warriors emerged, she silently pointed westwards. They would head across the Elam Highlands to the place her father had shown her once. Called "The Fissure" in the Old Tongue, it was here that the original Parashi had used their remarkable climbing skills to skirt up and down the mighty cliffs with an ease their enemies could only covet. She hoped some of that innate climbing skill had carried over to her Warriors.

"Commander," Gruna whispered. "Do you think the enemy has turned on itself?"

Kella was curious about the battle sounds, but mostly she was grateful for the distraction it provided to get away. Hadn't her mother told her the story of what had happened at Two Plague Pass? The Ancient One himself had sent the foghounds and the mist to conquer the enemy. Perhaps, in their greatest hour of need, Ab'El had once more come to their rescue.

"I don't know, but we need to get away. Fast."

With every long stride she ran, leading her Warriors away from their beloved home, Kella felt the Guardian Rock, tucked deep into her robe, slapping against her upper leg. The future of Tirragyl lay solely in her hands. If she failed now, the Parashi were lost. All that her father and their forefathers before them had fought to protect would be lost.

With the growing distance the battle sounds dulled, but Kella did not slow her pace. Only when the call of a ram's horn echoed through the air from far behind them did she momentarily stop and glance anxiously in the direction of the Chay'ets. They would be visible to anybody who left the vale.

"Faster!" she called, urging her Warriors on.

But Gruna stood her ground. "Commander." She pointed towards the tree. "I think the ram's call was for us."

Kella looked again. Now she saw the dark mass of riders pouring from the vale towards them. They had been seen. Within minutes the riders would be upon them.

They could not outrun them. They could not outfight them. But Kella would die to protect the Guardian Rock entrusted to her.

She raised her sword above her head. "For the Grotto and the Guardian!" Pride and grief coursed through her as a hundred Warrior voices took up the refrain.

The ground shuddered under their feet as the king's army raced towards them. Kella's Warriors were spreading out in two lines, one to her right and one to her left. About half of them had brought their bows and were solemnly drawing arrows from their quivers. The rest held their swords defiantly in the air. Kella felt for the Guardian Rock, wondering if in this last instant it would protect itself from falling into enemy hands the way it had protected the Grotto for centuries.

"Ab'El, help us," she whispered, looking up at the small white clouds that scudded across the sky as if this was just another ordinary day instead of the day of their destruction.

It was then that she heard the pounding feet behind them and turned to see a group of men running from the west, led by a powerfully built older man. Next to him ran a young, fair woman with a bow in hand.

Who were they? Other than the woman, they did not look like Highborns. Still, perhaps they were another unit of the king's army, which meant that Kella was now under attack from two sides. She sensed the confusion of her Warriors. Many had turned to point their arrows at the running men.

Surprisingly, it was the fair woman who called out. "We come in peace." Her voice carried to Kella across the plain. "I am Queen Nyla, and these are Charab men. We come to defend the Guardian Rock."

There was a stir amongst the Warriors. *The king's assassins were here.*

"Do we shoot them, Commander?" Gruna's arrow was pointed towards the older man.

Kella looked again towards the king's cavalry, now almost upon them.

"No! Turn to the cavalry," she shouted. "Release your arrows."

The Warriors spun back around and within seconds their arrows were airborne, felling many in the first wave of king's men. Behind them the Charab closed the gap, and more arrows—Charab arrows—flew true and far into Tirragyl's forces. She had no time to consider how it was that the assassins of the king now fought by their side.

CHAPTER 45

Lucian had been the one to sense the Deep Cave Warriors trying to make their escape. Since he had brushed into Kella's mind earlier, he had returned to it several times. Her shock and grief at finding her father's body in the Root Room had shuddered through him, and he had known the precise moment she decided to deny him the Guardian Rock. But the arrival of the Warriors who had chased them to Winter Pass had distracted Lucian, which is why Kella and her Warriors were already quite some way across the plain before he realized it. But—he smiled—they were not far enough.

At the news of the Warriors' escape, Captain Rillon had immediately signaled for half his soldiers to leave the vale in pursuit. The rest remained to battle the Warriors who had attacked earlier.

Lucian and the king rode near the back of the soldiers giving chase. They were after all facing Parashi Warriors, and Lucian knew the arrows would fly. There would be time enough to take the Guardian Rock from Mikel's daughter once the Warriors were defeated. King Alexor carried the other Guardian Rock on his saddle in a small chest overlaid with finely carved silver. The thought of it sent a shiver of anticipation through Lucian. If he couldn't have Shara, at least he could have the two Guardian Rocks and all the power that lay dormant within them. Then, finally, Ajalon could be his.

There were shouts from the front soldiers. Lucian watched as a bevy of arrows rained down on the men far ahead of him. Horses veered and men fell. He quickly reined in his horse. Next to him the king did the same.

"Where did the others come from?" The king's voice was puzzled.

"Others?" Lucian looked towards the Warriors and only now saw the new force running behind them. Still, even if Warriors crawled from behind every rock on the Highlands, they would never overcome the king's army. He watched indifferently from his safe distance as these running Warriors lifted their bows and sent their arrows into the air. Yet he startled when one of the arrows thudded into the chest of the man to the king's right.

"By Taus! I thought we were out of range," the king hissed.

"We are," Lucian said. How was this possible? Nobody could shoot an arrow that far. Nobody except perhaps . . . "The Charab!"

"Charab?" The king stared blankly at the running men. "*My* assassins?"

"Their loyalty was never yours, King Alexor." Lucian spun his horse around. "Come, let us retreat until the battle has been won." The king, transfixed, did not move. "Come, Your Majesty. With the Charab here, the battle will be fierce indeed."

"Do you see a woman among them?"

"Many Warriors are women."

"No. Among the Charab."

"Possibly, sire. But come now."

"She is fair." The king was urging his horse towards the battle.

"Sire. It's foolish . . ."

"It's Nyla."

"Impossible!" Yet now Lucian saw her too. Amidst the dark men, her hair shone like the sun on a clear day.

The king was dashing forward, shouting. "Nobody harm the fair woman! I want her alive or I cannot have her soul!"

Lucian considered leaving the king and riding back to safety but, now that he was so close to claiming the Guardian Rocks, he didn't want to be too far away from them. This day was not going as he had planned. He unsheathed his sword and followed the king into the battle.

• • •

Nyla let another arrow fly. It did not go the distance of the Charab arrows, but it still hit its mark. Another rider slumped to the side before tumbling from his horse. Her momentary sense of victory was almost her undoing for she did not see the rider bearing down on her. Klyden stepped in front of her. His sword crashed into the man's blade, unbalancing him. As the man's horse slowed, he leapt up and dragged the man from the saddle, his dagger finding its mark.

Nyla's eyes locked on Klyden's as he leapt clear of the dead soldier. She nodded her thanks as she nocked another arrow into place.

He turned to face the next onslaught. The battle pulsed around her, but always Klyden was by her side, deflecting every sword and blow aimed at her. But the Warriors and even the Charab were falling. Tirragyl's forces were fearsome.

The battle was the fiercest around the female commander of the Warriors. The Charabian himself now fought alongside her, and together they withstood many attacks, but new ones kept coming. It could only mean one thing. *She had the Guardian Rock.*

"Klyden," she shouted. "Your uncle and the female commander need help!" She began to push her way towards them, but his strong grip on her arm stopped her.

"They're in the heart of the battle, Nyla. You can't go in there."

"Since when is a Charab a coward?" she hissed. "Let go of me."

He dropped her arm at the command. "I think she has the Guardian Rock. I can't keep you safe there."

"Stop trying to. This is about far more than my safety."

He nodded reluctantly and followed her. Yet, however hard they tried, they could not reach them. The king's men had now cut off the commander and the Charabian and had them surrounded. Nyla witnessed the trio of blade thrusts that should have killed the woman if the Charabian had not shielded her with his own body. She saw the Charabian stagger back and crumple to the ground—this man who had led his men in giving her their loyalty. Who had given her back so much that Alexor's betrayal had stolen.

The female commander, now completely alone, fought on bravely.

But it was only a matter of time before she fell to Tirragyl's relentless swords.

"We have killed the keeper of the Guardian Rock!" As the voice thundered across the battlefield, picked up, and passed through the combatants, the clash of swords gradually stilled. Then Warriors, Charab, and king's men alike turned to look at the man striding towards the body of the slain female commander. Nyla recognized him immediately.

Lord Lucian.

Nyla began to move forward. And beside her, Klyden.

"No!" she shouted as Lord Lucian knelt down next to the body. "I am Queen Nyla, and I command you to stop. Those Rocks must never be joined!"

She was now mere paces from him.

"Queen Nyla." He looked up at her, his smile not reaching his eyes. "What a surprise."

"Nyla!" Another voice, achingly familiar. "I have found you." Alexor limped towards her, a silver box in his hand. She saw the fervor shining in his eyes as he looked at her and hope flared to life. Perhaps her brother had changed. Could things go back to how they had always been?

"Nyla. I'm so glad you are still alive."

Still alive. The words dulled Nyla's rising hope. He did not care about her. He had not changed. All he wanted was the fragment of her soul that he believed was his due.

The insight gave her an idea.

"Is our half of the Guardian Rock in that box?" She pointed to the small chest in his hands.

"Yes." Alexor did not take his eyes off her. "Lucian is going to join them now."

She slipped the dagger out of her robe and held it against the center of her chest. "Choose now, Alexor. Me or the Guardian Rock. If you let Lucian join the Rocks, I will thrust this dagger into my heart, and you will be a half-soul for the rest of your life."

She sensed Klyden stiffen beside her. "Don't, Nyla."

"Give the silver chest to my protector," she continued slowly, "and I'll come with you into the Adriel River, just like you want me to."

She saw the hunger in her brother's eyes. Behind Alexor, Lucian slowly rose to his feet. "*This* is your plan to save Tirragyl?" he drawled. "As soon as we have you, we will take the box off your protector."

"No. You are going to give it to him, and he and all the Charab and Warriors are going to leave for the west. You will never see the box again. And if you follow them . . ." She flicked the dagger towards her chest. "Decide now, Alexor."

"Fine. Fine." Her brother almost stumbled in his haste to give Klyden the box, although his eyes didn't leave the dagger at her heart. "Don't do anything rash, Nyla."

"Go now, Klyden." Nyla looked briefly into her protector's eyes and saw his desperation. "For me and Tirragyl, and all who died to keep it safe."

"Nyla." His voice was hoarse. "I can die to let you live, but I cannot live and let you die."

"I am your queen." She put every ounce of remaining steel into what would be her very last order. "It is my command."

He stared at her a moment longer as if he was trying to memorize her face. Then he dropped his head. "As you command, Your Majesty." He began to back away with the box. The surviving Charab and Warriors moved in around him.

She caught Elxa's eye. He bowed low before he turned to follow Klyden.

CHAPTER 46

Nicho heard the ram's horn that drew away a large part of the king's army.

"What are they doing?" he called to Pearce, who was plunging his sword into a foot soldier. "Do they retreat?"

"Why would they? We're so few." Pearce killed the next man with an equally swift blow.

Nicho focused only on the battle then, watching all the threats as they approached and sending the stallion thought-whispers to guide his steps. Behind him, Pearce fought every attacker who still reached them.

Only when they had made it to the tree and there was a temporary lull in the fighting did Pearce say, "The only thing that could draw them away like that is the Guardian Rock."

"But it lies in the Deep Caves." Nicho looked towards the entrance of the tree.

"Perhaps Kella had another way out."

"By the abyss." Cold fear rippled through Nicho. He stared at the western part of the vale to which the king's soldiers had ridden at the horn's call.

Pearce's men fought their way towards them and, at a signal from Pearce, spread around the tree. The fight to the Chay'ets had cost them dearly. Less than half his men were here.

"We will hold the Chay'ets entry, Warriors," Pearce called.

"But if what you say is true and the soldiers ride to take the

Guardian Rock, shouldn't we follow them and try to help Kella?" Nicho asked.

"Look around us." Weariness laced Pearce's voice. "We're surrounded. We'll never make it through to her."

As if to prove his words, a fresh wave of king's soldiers already moved towards them. It was hopeless. As valiantly as they fought, they could never defeat an enemy this strong.

The same thought must have gone through Pearce's mind for his next words sounded ominously like a farewell. "I was wrong about you all this time, Nicho. You are the very best of Warriors."

Nyla watched Klyden as he backed away with the silver box containing the Guardian Rock, Elxa and the surviving Charab shielding him. The remaining Deep Cave Warriors had moved in around them, another layer of defense against the king's soldiers who watched them leave with open hostility. Yet the soldiers had little choice but to obey King Alexor's command to let the Warriors and Charab go.

"Touching," Lord Lucian said, coming to stand beside Alexor. "You are indeed the nobler of the heirs of Tirragyl, Queen Nyla. But let's end this right now."

He slid his dagger from its sheath, and Nyla braced herself for the attack. It did not come. Instead she heard the rush of air that escaped from Alexor's lips and saw the shock on his face. He opened his mouth as if to speak, but no sound emerged. The shock on his face crumpled into pain, and he groaned as he fell forwards, thudding into the ground. Only then did Nyla see the dagger sticking from the back of his neck.

"Get the Rock," Lucian said. The soldiers around them, transfixed by what they had just witnessed, moved sluggishly at his command.

Nyla covered the short distance between her and Alexor and sank to her knees.

"Alexor." She grabbed her brother's hand and squeezed it. "I'm here."

"Ny." His eyes fluttered open. "I don't know . . . what . . . ?"

"Hush, hush." She tasted the salt of her tears. "All will be well." She leaned over him. Hints of his familiar scent mingled with the smell of blood. "I am here."

"Queen Nyla." Lord Lucian stood over her, unremorseful and arrogant. "Every one of your Charab and Parashi will die if they do not give up the Rock."

She dragged her eyes away from her dying brother and looked up to see Klyden and the small group of survivors now surrounded by a mass of Tirragylin forces. She heard the violent clash of swords, and even as she looked, she saw a Charab fall. *Not Klyden. Please.*

"Get the Rock and bring it to me," Lucian said coldly.

She rose to her feet, anger coursing through her as she looked into his eyes. "You have just killed the king of Tirragyl. Know that you will pay for this with your life, Lucian."

She walked to the group of Charab and Parashi and, for the second time, the sounds of battle died down. Men stepped to the side, averting their gaze. Finally she stood in front of Klyden, who still gripped the silver box. She held out her hands for it, and he stepped towards her and laid it in her hands, his eyes dark with sorrow. As she turned back to Lord Lucian, she felt Klyden by her side, and she was grateful.

Every step back felt heavy, as if a force were pushing her backwards.

"I can't seem to . . ."

Klyden gripped her by the arm and drew her forward. His brow furrowed as he, too, felt the unseen force.

"The Rocks are repelling each other," Nyla said with sudden insight. She was now only ten paces from Lord Lucian, who still stood over the body of the female commander.

"Don't tarry, Queen Nyla," he said.

"The Rocks don't want to be joined. There's a force pushing me back."

"Help her," Lucian said, and a soldier fell in next to her with two more behind. Only their combined strength pushing against the strange force brought Nyla to Kella's body. By now the force was pushing deep into her.

"Lucian. Don't do this!"

"I'm not going to." He grinned. "You are."

When she didn't move, he shifted his gaze to Klyden. "I sense you care if your protector lives. Do it. Now. Or he's the next man to die."

Nyla passed the silver box to Klyden and bent down, trying not to look at the dead commander's face as her hand roamed around for the Rock. She found it tucked in a pocket against the woman's leg. Tentatively she drew it out, almost expecting it to burn her, but it lay coolly in her hand.

She straightened and met Klyden's gaze, nodding once.

He lifted the latch of the silver box, and his hand shook as he took out the other Guardian Rock. Slowly their hands moved towards each other, soldiers gripping both their arms to overcome the strong repulsive force. Mere inches apart, Klyden shook his head and muttered, "Ab'El help us all," and Nyla closed her eyes, echoing his prayer.

In the last instant, the force fighting to keep the Rocks apart was broken, and they crashed together, louder and brighter than a lightning strike.

CHAPTER 47

Klyden closed his eyes just before the Rocks crashed together. Even so, the bright flash of light—which would blind all of those standing too near—burned with searing intensity behind his eyelids. The deafening crash momentarily stole all other sounds from the air, replacing them with a soft droning in his ears. Power crackled through him, consuming every memory, thought, and desire. Scorching and emptying him of all but one word. *Nyla.*

His instinct was to open his eyes and see if she had survived this initial onslaught of power, but he could not get his body to obey. He was in the grip of something so great and terrifying that it allowed no room for his individual wishes. All he could do was surrender to it.

When he stopped fighting the great force, something happened. Its hold on him lessened. He opened his eyes and saw Nyla still in the grip of its power.

"Surrender, Nyla," he whispered, unsure if she could even hear him. Yet something changed for she finally opened her eyes, white-rimmed with terror, and looked at him. The joined Rocks still lay in their gripped hands. Klyden noticed how dark the day had become. The Guardian's power seemed to be sucking all the light from the day, gathering it from the far edges of the Highlands and drawing it into itself. Klyden sensed how all across Tirragyl the light was being pulled towards the Guardian Rock. Fleetingly he considered if Nyla and he could break the connection and stop the Rock from stealing

Tirragyl's light, but the power flared against the thought. It was useless. He could not stop this thing that Lord Lucian had unleashed.

He glanced across to where Lucian had stood moments before and saw him staggering to his feet, eyes fixed on the Rock. *Give it to me.* Klyden did not hear the lord's words, but they still echoed through his mind. Nyla had sensed them too. Her look of fear confirmed it. They were as powerless to stop the lord, now stumbling towards them in the darkening day, as they were to stop the darkness from encroaching.

Still, they held the Rocks until every ray of light had been sucked from the sky and they could no longer see each other. Perhaps the darkness had stopped Lucian in his tracks for no hand reached out to take the Rock from them.

And still the Guardian continued to devour.

"It has all of Tirragyl's light," Nyla whispered. "What more can it take?"

"Men's breath." Lucian's laughter echoed into the darkness.

Nicho, Pearce and the small group of Warriors surrounded the Chay'ets tree, warily watching the king's soldiers draw nearer.

An enemy voice shouted, "Attack!"

For the Grotto and the Guardian! The call reverberated around the tree and into Nicho's heart. Today he had learned that he truly was a Warrior. He would fight and die courageously side-by-side with his brothers.

The king's men were urging their horses towards them when a bright light and a loud thunderclap flashed in the west. The soldiers reined in sharply, glancing around fearfully.

"What in the abyss was that?" Nicho looked up at the clear sky, but there was no storm in sight.

Pearce said what Nicho feared to admit even to himself. "The Guardian Rocks are joined."

Almost immediately they sensed the light dimming. As he looked up, Nicho watched trails of light pulsing westwards, leaving darkness in their wake. For a while he could still see the king's soldiers a few feet away, could see his own fear reflected in their eyes, but over time a creeping murkiness swallowed them. Soon even the Warriors closest to him were no longer visible. Blackness crept over them all.

"What have they done?" Pearce whispered.

A small breeze wafted over Nicho. There was something unnatural about it, something that made him want to turn the horse and bolt away. The horse had felt the strangeness too. It snorted wildly and tried to pull to the side.

No. We cannot see anything. We must stay here, Nicho whispered to the stallion.

The breeze grew in intensity, whipping at his cloak.

"What is that?" Pearce said. "I . . . I . . . can't breathe." Nicho felt Pearce's weight shifting as he slumped to the side. Nicho grabbed hold of his robe and tried to keep him from falling. But the wind was now a deafening gale in his ears, and it pushed deep into him. Just when he thought his chest would explode from the pressure, the wind rushed out of him. He tried to fight it from taking his own breath with it, but its power was too great. The wind swept away his breath and left him without even a voice to scream for help.

And Nicho began to fall.

Klyden felt the tiny wisps of air rise from across the battlefield, wafting towards them. At first they were as insubstantial as a soft breeze, but as the Guardian's power pushed outwards—reaching ever farther into Tirragyl—the breeze became a wind and then a gale that buffeted against him and Nyla before being sucked into the Rock.

No! He sensed Nyla's aching sorrow for her subjects, falling to the ground as their last breath was stolen away. Yet she was powerless to stop it.

A strange stillness had crept over the land by the time the gale finally died down. *It was over.* Only he and Nyla's breath still filled their bodies.

No. One other man still breathed. Lord Lucian's hands reached out through the darkness, and he finally seized the Rock. As he did so, the power of the Rock thrust Klyden and Nyla backwards, punching them against the hard ground. Klyden rolled around to see that, in Lucian's hands, the Rock glowed red with all the light and life it had stolen. It lit up Lucian's hunger-crazed face. All that power in such evil hands, Klyden thought. Tirragyl was surely lost.

CHAPTER 48

"Sarah."

Just one name—*her true name*—broke into the darkness. It was spoken with a depth of tenderness she had never known before, and every part of her yearned to look on the face of the one who spoke it.

But the darkness held her, refused to relinquish its black hold.

"Sarah, come to me."

The words were commanding and, she sensed, stronger than the darkness. Yet the darkness had her wrapped so tightly in its cold cocoon that she did not know how she could ever be free. She was not strong enough to fight it.

Yet it seemed the words were more than just a call to her. They were also a command to the darkness. She heard, or maybe sensed, a tearing away of the stifling grip around her. A soft breath of warmth seeped into her, and slowly she grew aware of her stiffened limbs. She lifted her smallest finger. It felt as heavy as lead.

"Her finger just moved!" It was a young girl's voice, and it was followed by the deep laughter of a man.

"Did you doubt me, Aislin?"

There was a loud shriek, followed by a chorus of giggles. Sarah couldn't contain her curiosity any longer and, despite their heavy resistance, opened her eyes.

The little girl, darting away from the man tickling her, gave another joyful shriek. "She's awake!"

The man who had called her from the darkness dropped to his knees at her side. He was young and had a mop of dark curls and a short beard, a shade lighter than his hair. His soft brown eyes sparkled with such tangible joy that Sarah felt the thrill of it in her bones.

"Welcome home, Princess Sarah." His smile brimmed with love.

She had known this man once, but for a moment she could not place his beautiful face. And then she knew. The last time she had seen him, he had been bloodstained, his face etched with pain as he hung from the poison tree.

"E'shua?" she asked. "But . . . but you were dead."

"So were you, Sarah." His eyes sparkled with mischief.

"How . . . ?"

"Death is no match for our father's power."

"Father?" The word lodged in her a longing so deep that she knew it must have always, always been there.

"He's waiting for you in the garden," E'shua said gently. "It was your favorite place of all. He always took you there when you were young." A shadow crossed his face. "He has spent a lot of time there since we lost you."

"What of Eliad and Andreo? Did they die too?" She struggled to lift herself up.

"No." E'shua smiled. "In fact, they have just arrived at the palace. But rest a while, Sarah. You have an eternity of garden walks with Father and all the time you wish to spend with your friends. Aislin will show you the path to the garden once you are ready. Won't you, princess?" He tousled the light curls of the girl pressed in close to him, who was watching Sarah intently. She nodded enthusiastically.

"Are you my sister?" Sarah asked.

"Yes. I used to be older, but now I'm not." She frowned. "I don't think that's fair."

E'shua laughed heartily, but the young girl's words brought back the jarring memory of those whispered by The Banished: *Perhaps if you were like his other daughters it would be different. They are worthy of his love. Perhaps even worthy of their brother's sacrifice. But you . . . he will look at you and know you are worth neither.*

"What's wrong, Sarah?" E'shua's eyes creased with concern.

"I . . . I don't think I should go to the garden. I'm not sure the king will want to see me." She couldn't seem to look into *his* eyes now, either.

"Why not? It's been his greatest longing since you were taken."

"I'm not the daughter he remembers. Things have happened since then. Things that . . . change everything."

"The Cerulean Dusk Dreamer, you mean?" She saw no judgment in his eyes.

She nodded. "What you did . . . on the poison tree. I . . . I didn't deserve that, E'shua. I'm not worthy of it. Or you. Or him."

"Sarah." He placed his big, strong hands on her cheeks. Her eyes fell on the wounds the soldiers had inflicted on that dreadful day— now long, raised scars, reminders of his agony. "You are worthy, and I would do it again even if ten power rocks had you in their grasp."

She wanted to believe it, but still the voices echoed in her head. "The Banished said only the perfect can come into the king's presence."

"Those were the lies of the Rif'iends. No one is banished here. You are home, princess." He leaned forward and kissed her forehead. "Sleep a while. I need to leave. There are others to call back to the light."

Home. The word sang through Sarah's heart when she awoke again later, this time alone. She sat up slowly and looked around. The room was large. Light streamed in from three tall windows, draped in breezy cream curtains. Sarah placed her feet on the floor, which was covered with a beautiful and intricately woven carpet, and tiptoed to the window. What she saw took away her breath.

Mountains towered around her against a sky so clear and blue that she wondered if all she had ever seen before were weak, watered-down reflections of skies. Below her she saw parts of the palace: turrets and parapets, paths and courtyards where people milled. Around the side, she caught a glimpse of forests and a field of flowers in a riot of joyful colors. A breeze fluttered the curtains and brought a whiff of perfume, sweeter than she had ever smelled. It pierced through her to a memory of a man lifting her up as her chubby arms reached for a large orange flower.

Sarah quickly turned back, almost dizzy from the assault to her senses. How could there be so much color and loveliness in just one glimpse? How could it be that mere moments in Ajalon felt more alive and more real than all her years in Tirragyl? She took a few deep breaths and glanced again at her room. It was welcoming. Against the far wall stood a dark wood wardrobe and mirror. Opposite it was a bookshelf brimming with books and two plush chairs in which to read them. A large vase of flowers stood on a chest between them, and next to it was a platter of fruit and a tall goblet of water. There was even a fireplace laid out with wood for the cool of evening.

Only then did she notice the gown at the bottom of her four-poster bed. It was simple but beautiful. Made from soft, cream-colored octora silk, the dress had tiny pearls that decorated the bodice and lined the draping sleeves.

Sarah looked down at her own crumpled, stained garment and knew that she could not go to see the king looking like this. Surely the beautiful dress was meant for her? She pulled off her old clothes and stepped into the dress. It fit her perfectly, but she could not close the clasps at the back no matter how much she contorted herself.

"She's awake!" came a loud whisper from the door. She turned to see two young faces peering at her. One of them was her sister, Aislin.

"Aislin! You came at just the right time. Can you help me with these clasps?"

"She's little so it takes her too long," the other, slightly taller girl answered. "Let me do it."

"I've seen you before," Sarah said as the girl came over.

"I'm your sister too. Eloni."

"I remember now. In the book you were dancing with the king."

"We dance a lot with Abba." Eloni smiled. "And E'shua." Her fingers deftly closed the clasps. Then she stood back to admire her handiwork and nodded approvingly. "You look very pretty."

"Do I?"

"You do!" Aislin grabbed her hand and pulled her to the mirror. "See?"

Sarah cocked her head to the side and looked at herself. The dress was indeed lovely, simple in its cut, but intricate in the swirl of hand-sewn pearls that decorated it. Its cream color brought out the warmth of her skin. But there was something else. She stepped closer and examined her face, framed by a tumble of dark curls. She looked . . . radiant. It was there in the glow of her cheeks and the sparkle in her eyes. She belonged to this place and these people, and the joy of this remarkable truth showed on her face.

"I think I'm ready to meet the king," she said.

Eloni nodded thoughtfully. "Yes. Now you're a princess again."

CHAPTER 49

Eloni and Aislin led her down winding passages and curving staircases. Sarah begged them to slow down so that she could take in the marvels all around her: rich fabrics and huge gold-threaded tapestries, intricate mosaic floors and chandeliers as large as rooms, hanging from tall ceilings. She could never have imagined a palace that was both so beautiful yet so welcoming at the same time.

This was probably largely due to the people they met, dressed in rich and colorful robes, who smiled warmly at her. Several of them inclined their heads and murmured words of welcome. Others wiped away tears when they saw her, and a few even broke into a song of joy that lilted down the corridors after them. The children they met were even bolder, coming up to her and hugging her around the knees, reminding her—with a pang of pain—of the Grotto's children.

The palace children trailed behind them as they left the building and entered the formal garden. Sarah recognized this as the place where E'shua had found the crying Yana, the one who had told him Sarah had been stolen away.

The garden was magnificent in its formality. Layers of plants and flowers fringed winding paths. Marble benches provided resting places in the shade of taller trees. The sound of water tinkled from fountains, and every few steps a new sweet aroma delighted her senses. Yet nervousness fluttered in Sarah's belly as she glanced over the faces of people roaming the garden or seated on the benches. Any moment now she would see the king.

Eloni led her briskly down a complicated series of paths, the children still straggling behind them. Sarah sensed they were now near the edge of the sprawling palace garden, for they were approaching a wall of lofty trees. Sorrow bloomed inside her. The king had not been waiting for her as E'shua had promised.

Eloni suddenly stopped and pointed to an old stone archway that stood at the end of their path in the center of a low wall. "There's the Ancient Arch that leads to the wild garden," she said with a fond smile. "Abba's in there."

A fresh wave of anxiety swept over Sarah. "Will you come with me?"

Eloni laughed, a surprisingly light sound, reminding Sarah of the sound of the fountains they had just walked past. "We'd just get in the way. E'shua told us to take you to the arch, no farther."

"Yes," Aislin piped up, "'coz he said Abba can't wait to see you. He's pinning for you."

"Not pinning, Ais," Eloni said sternly. "Pining."

"It means he's got a sore heart," Aislin clarified knowingly.

"I've been pining for him too," Sarah said, and the longing she had felt earlier pulsed through her again.

She threw the children one last smile and then walked—anxiety and longing warring inside her—towards the Ancient Arch. Towards her father.

The archway was covered in moss and a creeper with clusters of purple flowers. As she stepped through the doorway, she paused, glancing back one last time to the children, who gave her a jaunty wave. Then she stepped into the wild garden.

There was something different about this place. Whereas the palace and formal gardens had been magnificent in their splendor, the garden she stepped into was both wilder and more wonderful than anything Sarah had seen so far in Ajalon. An array of trees, shrubs, flowers, and creepers grew in plentiful abundance. Strangely, this verdant disorder created a pleasing loveliness that filled Sarah with childlike wonder.

As she followed the slightly overgrown path, she caught glimpses of strange and colorful birds in the upper canopy of the trees. Never before had she been welcomed by such a joyful chorus of singing. One song—in particular—drew her forward. Had she heard that lilting melody before?

There was movement in the undergrowth, and suddenly a small antelope stepped out of the dappled light and onto the path. Sarah froze midstep and midbreath, not wanting to frighten it away. Yet the small, soft-eyed doe was unafraid. It stepped towards her on reedy legs, lifting its head to nudge at her hand.

Sarah laughed with delight. Even this did not frighten the doe away.

"I don't have any food for you, if that's what you want." Sarah held up her empty hands. Yet the doe nudged at her again. "You want a stroke?"

Sarah stroked the deer's long, elegant neck, amazed at the softness of her coat. The animal leaned in close to her, and Sarah marveled at her trust. In Ajalon even the most vulnerable seemed unafraid. The thought filled her with courage.

The deer took a few steps off the path, then turned expectantly to look at Sarah.

"You want me to follow you?" Sarah was uncertain. "But I have a meeting with the king."

What had E'shua said? *There's no hurry . . . you have an eternity of garden walks with him still.* Her desire to meet Ab'El warred with her curiosity and a lingering sense that she was supposed to follow this animal.

"Oh, fine, show me what you will then."

Sarah stepped off the marked trail and into the very life of the garden. Her fingers brushed against the leaves and stems of plants that boasted more shades of green than she had ever known to exist. She bent over to smell flowers, even picking a perfect yellow one and tucking it into her hair. Her feet crushed grasses that released the smell of life and rain and growth. Joy budded in her and expanded as she walked ever deeper into this garden teeming with life.

Soon she heard water tumbling over rocks and came across a pool lying in the bend of a wide, lazy river. Sarah could see an abundance of life—dragonflies and leaping fish and frogs slipping from rocks at her approach. She giggled with delight at every new sighting. How was it possible that so many creatures lived in such harmony here?

When the deer bent her elegant neck to drink, Sarah realized her own thirst. She perched on a flat rock and cupped her hands into the water and drank deeply. The water was light and sweet and bubbled in her mouth in a way that made her giggle aloud. How could water taste this good? Would Ajalon never cease to amaze?

She sat for a while longer. Slowly the peace of her surroundings penetrated the last hardened knots of failure and regret that remained from her previous life. By the river, her memories of Gwyndorr and the Grotto softened and smoothed, the way riverbed stones are smoothed by water over the course of time.

Time. She wondered fleetingly how much of it had passed as she sat here, but even this thought changed form as she recognized that it was a remnant of Tirragylin thinking. In this place there was none of the urgency and anxiety that accompanied life in her old homeland. Here, time did not drop steadily through the hourglass of a person's life, a constant reminder that death awaited them. Ajalon, untouched by death, was a place where life could be lived fully, moment by moment, with laughter and wonder and joy.

When the doe lifted her head, Sarah saw him. He walked some distance away along the river, dressed in a robe of warmly spun gold, beautiful and dazzling to the eye. So strong and commanding was his stature as he strode towards her, that momentarily Sarah's fear pushed once more to the surface. Suddenly she wanted to run and hide, knowing that she was unworthy to stand in his presence. Knowing, too, that he would look into her eyes and see her every dark deed and thought and all the pain she had brought to the Grotto. The voices she had heard, be they Banished or Rif'iend, had been right after all. None was worthy to stand in the presence of this great king.

Sarah rose to her feet, ready to dart back in the direction from which she had come. He was closer now, close enough for her to see his dark beard and hair, both streaked with grey. Close enough, too, to see the Gold Breast sitting on his shoulder. The bird was singing—the same melody that had drawn her as she stepped into the wild garden.

At that moment the King of Ajalon did something remarkable. Ab'El, the Ancient One, whose breath had created life and whose words had broken the ties of death, began to run.

He began to run towards *her*.

Sarah's lifetime of longing broke wide open at the sight, shattered by the clarity of this fatherly love. The love she had found in Tirragyl was a mere candle to the sun of her Abba's love.

As the dam of longing broke open, a lifetime of tears welled up, blurring her vision. She stumbled towards him. He caught her in his arms and drew her closer, his hand pressing her head gently against his chest. She breathed in the scent of warmth, safety, and strength, of rain-washed soil mixed with rich frankincense. The smell unlocked a flood of disconnected memories. He was holding her high as they chased Aislin across a broad field of yellow flowers. He was bending down and kissing her cheek before stepping up to his throne. He was down on his knees, pointing to a butterfly. He was rocking her to sleep, singing a lullaby.

"Sarah. My Sarah," he whispered.

How long they stood like that she could not tell. It might have been an entire Tirragylin lifetime. But what she did know when he finally drew back to look at her face was that every remnant of her fear and sorrow was gone.

"You are here, Sarah."

She wondered how she could have forgotten his voice, one that resonated with every chord of life. Why hadn't she recognized it in the wind gusting past her room in Gwyndorr or the rush of the Erridale river? How had she missed it in the peals of laughter of the Grotto children? Only Tabeal's song had stirred its memory alive and then only until she let the Dusk Dreamer obscure it.

"I am here, Abba."

"Welcome home, princess."

He threw his arm around her, and they meandered along the river, together marveling at the loveliness of this, the very birthplace of Ajalon. They spoke, not only of E'shua and the poison tree path and of Taus's betrayal, but also of ordinary things. Of friendships and flowers and gowns. And they spoke of deeper things: captivity and fear and grief. Even of love lost.

By the time the king declared it time to go back to the palace, Sarah could hardly recall how it had felt to be apart from him. All her years of pain were remnants of a fast-fading dream. Just one walk with Abba had changed everything.

CHAPTER 50

Nyla watched, by the Rock's glow, as Lucian triumphantly lifted the Guardian into the air. His laughter reverberated into the darkness of the day. Into the darkness of her heart. Tirragyl was lost. She had not been able to save her kingdom.

You couldn't. But I already have.

It was the strangest, softest of thoughts, alighting on her from the black void that had once been the sky. She looked up to see where it had come from but saw only darkness.

Who are you?

She sent the thought back into the dark, not expecting a reply. But still one came, and it sent a shiver of trepidation down her spine.

E'shua, Prince of Ajalon. From the beginning to the end.

"Is this the end then?"

Fear caused her to speak aloud, and Lucian, suddenly remembering that he was not alone with the Rock, looked at her sharply.

"I forget our little queen still lives. You will witness my great victory, Queen Nyla."

"Victory?" She laughed bitterly. "You've destroyed everything. There's nothing left to conquer."

"You small, blinded Tirragylins know so little," Lucian said. He turned and pointed north. "Have you never wondered what lies beyond the Rif'twine?"

"Beyond the Rif'twine?" In the light from the Rock, Klyden had crawled over to her and gripped her hand tightly in his own. "What lies there?"

"A vast, glorious kingdom."

Again Nyla saw hunger in his eyes.

"A kingdom that makes Tirragyl look like a fleck of dust."

"Ajalon." The word slipped from her tongue before she could stop it.

Lucian laughed, surprised. "Very good, Queen Nyla."

"Ajalon already has a king. And a prince," she said defiantly, thinking of the sky voice.

"A weak king and a very dead prince," he said, laughing. "Ajalon needs someone strong to make the kingdom greater still."

"Strong? Like you? Who throws everything into darkness and snuffs out life? How will that make Ajalon any greater?"

His hate-filled eyes turned on her. "How did I end up with such deviant offspring?" He laughed at her expression—a brittle sound. "Yes, indeed. I am Taus, and you, Queen Nyla, are of my line. My very blood pounds in your heart."

"Then I wish I could rip it out of my chest right now."

"If you did, you'd miss my moment of glory." He thrust the Rock back into the sky and began to speak. The words were strange and grating, painful to the ear. They were hatred. Betrayal. Darkness. Death. The Rock glowed ominously.

As the words continued, a loud crack shuddered through the air. Nyla looked down and saw that the ground was breaking open. She felt the tremors rising through her body.

Klyden dragged her to her feet and pulled her away from Lucian. "Run, Nyla!" She stumbled away, but the ever-widening cracks now crisscrossed their path, blocking every escape route.

From the cracks emerged wisps of the same red light as that emanating from the Rock. As Klyden and Nyla were forced to a halt, they saw that the wisps were slowly taking the shape of men.

"He's calling up an army," Klyden whispered.

More and more of the men rose from the cracks. Slightly translucent, but armed and—Nyla didn't doubt—dangerous. They paid no heed to Klyden and Nyla. They continued to rise and spread out until, Nyla imagined, they covered a vast stretch of the Highlands.

Finally, Lucian's grating words halted, and the cracks shuddered closed. Standing in the midst of Lucian's teeming army, Nyla hardly dared to breath. She turned to look into the face of the soldier to her left, but his dead eyes stared ahead unseeingly, or perhaps seeing beyond what mortal eyes could see. She reached out to touch him, but before she could determine if he was made of flesh, her hand was stopped by a force as strong and cold as stone. No matter how she tried, she could not breach it.

"I'm scared, Klyden," she whispered.

Her Charab protector, always so courageous and level-headed, gripped her hand and squeezed it. She felt his fear too.

"We are trapped amongst them," he said quietly, and she saw the truth of his words. The stone-cold soldiers were around them, and they could not push past them. "I can fight men of flesh, Nyla. I don't know how to fight such creatures."

I will fight them.

Klyden's surprise showed that, this time, he had heard the voice too.

"It's Ajalon's prince," Nyla whispered.

"I know that voice," Klyden said. "It is he who spoke to me on the day my uncle almost killed me, the day Taus's curse over the Charab was broken for good."

"If he undid Taus's curse, perhaps he can defeat his army too." Nyla looked across to where Lucian stood at the head of his vast army.

Look to the skies. I arise.

And as she did, she saw a remarkable sight. On the horizon a light dawned. As she kept watching, she saw that it, too, was an army. They rode, not from the eastern or western plains, but from the northern skies. And in their center—on a majestic white horse— rode the Prince of Ajalon. His robe was blood red, and a crown rested lightly on his head. His stallion pounded towards them, fluid in flight. Behind the prince rode a vast army, bedecked in white.

The sound of a ram's horn reverberated through the air from the direction of their approach.

As he drew closer, Nyla could not take her eyes off the prince. She watched as, without slowing, he drew an arrow from his quiver, nocked it into his bow, and let it fly straight at Lucian, who sprang to the side just before the arrow could find its mark.

The battle for Ajalon had begun.

Nyla and Klyden had no choice but to move with the enemy's army. The arrows that flew from the prince's army were not meant to bring down soldiers of flesh and blood. They brought down Lucian's strange soldiers, those creatures called from the dark depths. At first Nyla feared the arrows of Ajalon, but not one of them came close to slaying her and Klyden.

Over and over again, Nyla's gaze turned to the prince. He was a formidable warrior. Every arrow flew true, every sword thrust was filled with power.

"He fights better than the best Charab." Klyden's soft awe-filled voice confirmed her observation.

Only then did she realize that they were free of Lucian's army. Every soldier around them had been slain although strangely no bodies remained.

"What happened to Lucian's soldiers?" Her eyes had been solely on the prince.

"With every arrow or sword-thrust, they just disintegrated into dust."

Only a few of them remained, fighting around Lucian, but the prince's army was too strong for them. Eventually only one man still stood. Lucian.

"Come," Klyden took her hand and drew her towards where Lucian fought, still gripping the glowing Rock with one hand as he parried and thrust with his blade. He, too, was a good fighter, Nyla realized.

Finally Lucian dropped the Rock to the ground and shouted, "Are you a coward, E'shua, that you send your soldiers to fight me? Am I not a worthy opponent for you?"

A hush fell over Ajalon's army as the prince leapt from his stallion's back and strode towards Lucian.

"You had great worth in my father's court, Taus. You lost it on the day you turned against us." He lifted the hilt of his sword to his heart. "But let us finish this today."

Lucian had begun to move, circling the prince. "Look at you. Ajalon's so-called prince of peace. You bring war, not peace."

"You brought the war, Taus. At your defeat, peace will return."

"Perhaps." Lucian glanced down to the Rock at his feet. "But you could not save Tirragyl, could you? You failed, E'shua. Oh, Mighty Sovereign." His words dripped with hatred. "You could not protect your subjects in the southeastern province from the Death Spell. You tried, didn't you? Your sacrificial poison tree death and that silly path through the Rif'twine. But ultimately you lost them. I should know." He glanced down again at the Guardian Rock glowing on the ground. "I stole all their last breaths."

"Who says it was their last breaths?" The prince's voice was soft. "Have you not heard that I am the Giver of Breath. The Giver *and* the Taker."

"I think this time *I'll* be the taker." Lucian bolted towards the prince, his sword arching through the air, aimed straight at the prince's heart. Nyla flinched, and she heard Klyden's sharp intake of breath, both of them sure the blade would find its mark.

Yet the prince was too fast. He shifted his body so that Lucian's sword found nothing but air. At the same time, he thrust his own sword into Lucian's chest. They watched the lord stumble backwards, his sword clattering to the ground as he looked down at the deadly wound and then up at the prince. His last look before he sank to the ground was one of utter disdain.

Prince E'shua stood over his body for a few moments, and there was not a whisper of sound from his army. Defeating his enemy seemed to give him no pleasure.

Then the prince turned towards Nyla and Klyden.

Nyla, Queen of Tirragyl, had never bowed her knee to anybody before, but she sank down and placed her head on the ground, trembling—not out of fear—but out of a sense of her own smallness.

She felt his touch on her shoulder before she heard his gentle voice.

"Rise, Nyla of the House of Tirragyl. And Klyden, son of the Charabian."

She rose slowly, head still bowed, until his large hand reached out and gently tipped her chin up. Only then did she dare look into his eyes. They were filled with laughter and an age-old wisdom. Inside her warred two desires: to fling herself into his arms and to run as far away as she could from that quiet, knowing gaze.

Instead she stood dead-still and, with quivering lips, acknowledged who she was. "My liege, I am a daughter of Taus."

"I know who you are," he said solemnly. "I also know that, like my own, your heart beats with love for your people." He bent forward and picked up the Guardian Rock. "Let us release them from Taus's curse."

"You can do that?"

He nodded solemnly before lifting the Rock to his lips. As he blew on it, the Rock pulsed with light, like a red coal does when exposed to air. And then the same wind that they had felt blowing *into* the Rock began to blow out of it, first softly and then with a gathering strength. As Nyla sensed Tirragyl stirring back to life, she laughed with delight. Klyden's soft chuckles joined her own, and then the prince, too, threw back his head. His laughter was filled with a joy so deep it was balm to Nyla's battered heart.

When all the life and light had returned to the land, the prince turned back to her, his eyes solemn. "Nyla, will you return to the palace in Lydora? Not as a queen but as my representative in the southeastern province of Ajalon."

"It would be my honor, Prince E'shua." Nyla bowed again.

"I will return soon so that we may start restoring the province to all that it was before the Death Spell and Taus took ahold of it. But before I do that,"—he glanced longingly to the north—"there is a celebration I need to attend."

He turned back. "Klyden, would you go with Nyla? Continue to protect her. Be her friend. Not all will embrace these changes."

"I will go gladly, Your Majesty." Klyden, too, bowed after a quick glance at Nyla.

"I'm sure you will do it particularly well." E'shua smiled. "But before I leave, I need to find someone amongst those on the battlefield. Will you help me search for him?"

Nyla looked around. Soldiers and Warriors alike were in various stages of rising from their deathly stupors, dazed expressions on their faces.

"Whom do you seek, Your Majesty?"

"A Warrior. A horse-whisperer named Nicho."

"There are many men. It could take some time."

"We have time. Plenty of it," the prince said.

Nicho opened his eyes, trying to recall where he was and what had happened. Far above, a breeze pushed small clouds across the vast sky. The sight stirred a memory to life. The last time he had looked at the sky, it had been growing ominously dark. And then a wind had blown up, one that had ripped the very breath out of him.

As he rolled onto his side, pain shot into his shoulder. By the abyss. He must have fallen off the horse and slammed into the ground. Fighting the pain, he pushed himself up and looked around.

The ground was strewn with men and horses. Some, bloodied and mortally wounded, were unmoving, but others were sitting or lumbering to their feet. Pearce lay just to the side of him, eyes open but face pinched with pain.

"Pearce." Nicho pulled himself over to him. "Are you hurt?"

"My foot is in agony. And I think I might have a huge bump on my head." He winced as he fingered it. "What happened? I don't remember a thing."

"I think the Guardian Rocks were joined. And it grew dark, and then a wind began to blow."

"I couldn't breathe."

"Yes. But the light is back." Nicho looked around. "And we breathe again."

Pearce was glaring towards the king's soldiers, most still lying or sitting on the ground. "Look at them. They are weak. Now's the time to attack."

"Attack?" Nicho threw back his head and laughed. "Look at *us*. We're in no state to take them on."

"And besides," a deep voice spoke from behind them, "the war is over."

Nicho turned. A man in a deep red robe stood by the Chay'ets tree, a crown resting on his dark hair. Nicho had the strangest sense that he knew this man.

"Over!" Pearce spat. "As long as there are Highborn and Lowborn, this war will *never* be over."

The man moved towards Nicho and stretched out his hand. Nicho used it to pull himself up, all the time looking into the man's eyes, so alight with life and joy. "Do I know you?" Nicho whispered.

"I am Prince E'shua."

"Of Shara's book." Awe—and a touch of fear—swept over Nicho as he sank back to his knee in a bow. "My prince. I thought you were . . ."

". . . dead?" The prince laughed. "A common enough error."

Pearce and the men around him were staring at the prince in open-eyed wonder.

"There are no more Highborn and Lowborn, my friends," the prince addressed the men. "The Death Spell and all the pain and hate it brought with it has been defeated. Together we will rebuild this portion of Ajalon to what it was before."

He turned his gaze to Nicho. "As for you, Nicho. You can stay to rebuild. But I know of someone who would dearly love to be reunited with you and your mother, Marai. So I come to offer you another choice."

CHAPTER 51

"Come, Sarah!" Aislin pulled her forward, her eyes brimming with excitement. "It's the biggest feast we've ever had. There are two hundred forty-eight candles on the tables. Eloni counted them herself." She looked slightly crestfallen. "I can only count to fifty."

Sarah laughed. "I'm trying to hurry, Ais, but I keep tripping on this long train."

When she had come back from her time with Abba in the wild garden, she had discovered a new gown laid out on her bed. This one was obviously an evening gown, and it was the loveliest Sarah had ever seen. Made from a dark-blue satin and embroidered with tiny, sparkling stones, its skirt was long and wide, layered with different hues of blue.

Aislin slowed down only slightly as she led Sarah down several flights of stairs, across a broad marble floor, and towards two tall wooden doors manned by footmen. As they saw the princesses approach, the footmen dipped their heads and slowly—regally—opened the large doors.

Sarah stepped into a large courtyard, under an early evening sky streaked with orange and red. Flowering creepers danced across the courtyard walls and pillars, their sweetness perfuming the air. More flowers bedecked the long tables on which candles—two hundred forty-eight of them—cast their warm glow, reflecting on golden goblets and plates. Voices and music mingled into a comfortable and welcoming hum of humanity. The overall effect was so lovely it filled Sarah with a fresh wave of joy. Would this place never cease to fill her with wonder? Would its remarkable beauty ever fade with familiarity? She hoped not.

"This way." Aislin pulled her through the milling, smiling crowd. Words of welcome drifted across the courtyard as they went. Aislin looked back at Sarah. "You are at the king's table. You're the guest of 'onna. I think that means you're very special tonight."

"Are you there too, Ais?"

"Not this time. I'm sitting with Yana." Her face broke into a smile. "But Eloni and Miriam and Rahel are sitting with me too. And Aron."

Were those the children who had been dancing with the king?

"Are they our sisters and brother?" At Aislin's curt nod, Sarah exclaimed, "Could you take me to meet them?"

"No. Abba said I must bring you to the king's table first."

Of course. Sarah smiled at her own impatience. In Ajalon there would be time enough to spend with her sisters and brothers. Time enough to make up for all the lost years.

Aislin stopped abruptly. "Here's the table, and that is your seat." She pointed to a chair at the center of a table on a raised platform. "Abba is at the head. And E'shua on his right."

At that moment a voice rang out, silencing the music and voices.

"Guests of the king. Welcome to this most joyous of feasts, celebrating the return of Princess Sarah." Aislin spun around and gave Sarah a dazzling smile. "Please make your way to your seats in preparation for the king's arrival."

Aislin squeezed Sarah's hand and darted off to a nearby table, where Eloni and her brother Aron were already taking their seats. With a little flutter of nerves, Sarah stepped onto the platform. The table was set for seven, and she glanced over the crowd, wondering which other guests were to dine at the king's table that night. When she saw the familiar figure stepping onto the platform, she clapped with delight.

"Andreo!"

Andreo's tears and laughter mingled as she flung her arms around his neck. "Sarah. Until I reached the palace, I thought we'd lost you for good. How I grieved for you." He shook his head, looking intently at her. "I still can't believe you are standing here, as alive and beautiful as always."

"The last thing I remember is the arrows. And the pain. But even that is fading from my mind."

"It's Ajalon's way." He nodded knowingly.

"What happened to you and Eliad?"

"The king sent General Ga'abri for your body. Eliad and I made the trip to the palace with men who became dearer to me than brothers."

"Andreo, can you believe this place?" She spun around in delight. "Could you have imagined anything so lovely?"

He shook his head in wonder. "Every corner I turn, I find another treasure. Have you seen the library? In five lifetimes I couldn't read all the books it contains."

"Perhaps in Ajalon one lifetime is more than enough."

"And the herb gardens behind the palace," he said, beaming, "so much variety. And I'm told that there are many more such gardens throughout Ajalon for me to visit, and every region has its own plants."

Just then another man stepped onto the platform. His step was lighter and his back a little straighter than before. *Eliad.*

He bowed in her direction. "Princess Sarah. It is a joy to see you back home."

She ran to embrace him. "Thank you for leading me to the poison tree path, Eliad."

Sorrow clouded his face. "I am sorry I could not keep you from the Rif'iends' lies and arrows."

"We are here now." She looked up at the dusk sky. "Dining under the stars with the king."

"Yes, indeed. No tears here." He pulled out her chair and inclined his head respectfully. "Princess."

At the sound of a trumpet, voices hushed, and chairs scraped against the stone floor as people rose to their feet. Sarah's heart fluttered at the sight of the king making his way to their table. His subjects bowed as he passed them. Even Aislin curtsied, and the other children bowed formally as their father drew near. He paused at their table and said something that sent them into peals of laughter.

When he stepped onto the platform, his eyes sought out Sarah's, and the delight she saw in his expression warmed her to the very core.

He turned to Andreo and Eliad, who both bowed low. "My friends, what an honor to dine with the men who accompanied my daughter on her perilous journey. Eli, it is good to see you again. Thank you for your great courage in accompanying E'shua on his mission and bringing Sarah to his path."

"The choice was easy, my king. You asked me before who I would follow, and I said I was with you and Prince E'shua, even to death."

"Your faithfulness will be remembered, Eli." The king smiled before turning to Andreo. "And I am so glad you broke free of all the lies that bound you in Tirragyl, Andreo. You searched and found the truth, and it led you here. To freedom."

Andreo bowed again, too overcome to speak.

The king sat down and—across the courtyard—the scraping of chairs and hum of voices showed that his subjects followed him. Soon the sound of flutes, lyres, and drums again added their jubilant melodies to the celebration.

It didn't take long before the food arrived, and every bite Sarah took filled her with surprise. The king laughed at her expressions of wonder.

"What is this, Abba? It's so sweet! Why didn't food taste like this in Tirragyl?"

They talked and laughed and basked in the king's attention, but Sarah was also conscious of the three empty seats at their table. Eventually, as their second course platters were being removed, she leaned in towards her father and whispered, "Where are Prince E'shua and the other guests, Abba?"

He smiled at her before glancing over to the far side of the courtyard, where a man in uniform stood. An unspoken question must have passed between them for the soldier nodded.

"They are at the palace gates, Sarah. They will be here shortly."

It wasn't long before the royal trumpet again announced the arrival of an Ajalon Sovereign. The music stopped. People rose to their feet, and a hush of anticipation swept across the courtyard. But as Prince E'shua stepped into sight, loud, victorious cheering broke out.

The king rose too. "E'shua has defeated our enemy," he explained, his face reflecting his deep joy. "Tirragyl, as you know it, is free of Taus's curse. The Rift is no more."

Sarah strained to catch a glimpse of Prince E'shua in the festive crowd. Every one of his subjects wanted to congratulate him. He took time to speak to each of them. When he finally arrived at the king's table, he bounded up the platform and embraced his father.

"It's over, Abba," he said as they pulled apart. E'shua caught sight of Sarah and grabbed her by the hands, twirling her around. "Sarah! You look radiant and joyful. Ajalon agrees with you."

"It's perfect!" She laughed. "Absolutely perfect."

"It's home." Then his eyes sparkled. "I have brought a gift for you."

He let go of her hands and stepped off the platform to the edge of the crowd. He took the hands of two people, who Sarah had not seen standing there, and began to lead them to the king's table.

Sarah stood frozen at the sight of them, her heart pounding in disbelief.

"Father, may I present to you Marai, who was like a mother to Princess Sarah," E'shua said. "And her son, Nicho."

Marai and Nicho had sunk to their knees, their faces to the ground. Sarah could see Marai's large frame trembling as she bowed to the King of Ajalon.

"Rise Marai and Nicho," the king said warmly. "Welcome to my table."

Nicho helped his mother back to her feet, and only then did his eyes find Sarah's. Longing and loss and tenderness pulsed through her in the brief moment before he looked away.

The king extended his arm to help Marai onto the platform. "You have met Andreo, of course. And this is my loyal subject, Eli. It was they who led Sarah back home." Marai exchanged a warm greeting with the men. "And, of course, you know my daughter, Princess Sarah."

Marai's eyes streamed with tears as she looked at Sarah. For a brief moment she seemed unsure how to act, but love compelled her forward. She folded Sarah into a deep, warm embrace.

"A princess. I always said there was somethin' special 'bout you. Didn't I tell you that, my petal?"

"You always made me feel special, Marai." Sarah laughed through her own tears. "Thank you."

As Prince E'shua led Marai to her seat, Sarah grew aware of Nicho standing next to the king, shaking hands with Eliad and Andreo.

The king turned to her with a mischievous smile. "Nicho. I believe you know my daughter Sarah rather well?"

"I do, Your Majesty," Nicho said nervously before bowing to her from the waist. "Princess Sarah. It's so good to see you here."

"You two have much to discuss," the king said, "which is why I have seated you together."

There was so much to say, and yet neither of them spoke for a while after they took their seats. Sarah was glad for the distraction that the new course of food provided. Marai exclaimed in delight that she had never seen a spread as fine.

"Imagine what your mother could do with such fine ingredients," Sarah finally broke the silence.

Nicho nodded with a small smile.

"I didn't know what had happened to you, Nicho. I was so afraid." Her voice wavered. "Did you find Jed?"

"Yes. He, Rosa, Simhew, and I made it back to the Grotto." He briefly met her gaze. "But you had left a few days earlier."

"I used the Cerulean Dusk Dreamer while I was there. They were afraid Lord Lucian would find the Grotto because of it."

"He did." A shadow of pain passed over Nicho's face. "He found it. And destroyed it."

For a while neither of them said anything, the heaviness of this lying between them like a thick veil.

"You two are far too serious for such a joyful celebration." Prince E'shua leaned across the table. "What do you speak of?"

"The Grotto. Nicho says it was destroyed." The old shame washed over Sarah again. *Because of her. Because of her.*

"Yes. There was much lost in the battle. Great pain, which leaves a mark on the heart." The prince took both her and Nicho's hands in a tight grip. "But the peace of Ajalon will soothe it and replace the sorrow with joy." He smiled at Sarah. "Did he tell you, too, that Taus was defeated? That I will return to Tirragyl and restore it as a province of Ajalon?"

"He didn't," Sarah said, feeling her shame wash away at the sight of E'shua's smile.

The prince turned back to a conversation with his father and Marai, and Nicho said softly, "What shall I call you now? Princess Sarah?"

"No!" Sarah laughed. "Do you remember when I told you to stop calling me Miss Shara? And I told you to look me straight in the eye? Do we have to have that conversation all over again?"

He smiled fleetingly but shook his head. "You were already too good for me as a Highborn. Imagine how I feel now that I know you are a princess."

"Nicho." She reached out for his hand, and that first touch tingled right into the center of her. "I'm still me. And . . . and my feelings haven't changed."

He finally looked at her. Long. Deeply. It was all she needed to know that his feelings hadn't changed either.

It was the clapping and cheering that drew her attention. She turned to see that her sisters and brother at the table below them were on their feet, swaying from side to side behind a fiddler playing a joyful jig. She noticed that a new child had joined them. He was laughing and clapping to the tune.

"Nicho. Is that . . . ?"

"It's Jed. I've never seen him so happy." Pride shone in his moist eyes as he looked at the boy. "When E'shua came to present me with the choice of whether to stay or come to Ajalon, I asked him if we could bring Jed. The boy has lost so much. I didn't think he could bear losing me too."

Aislin broke away from the line of dancers.

"Come, E'shua!" She ran up to the king's table. "Come dance with us." She grabbed the prince's hand and drew him to his feet.

He laughed heartily as she led him to the circle of musicians and dancing children.

The king rose to his feet. "Nicho, I believe you will have many chances to dance with my daughter. Can I ask that this first dance be mine?"

Nicho nodded mutely, but she saw by the shine in his eyes that he, too, had sensed the king's approval of the love he and Sarah still shared.

She linked her arm through her father's as they stepped from the platform. Before they reached the group of dancers, the king's voice broke out in song. The words spoke of love and belonging, and she knew that tonight he sang them just for her.

Then Abba pulled her into his arms and led her in a fast-paced, joyful dance.

EPILOGUE

A long procession of people wound its way from Gwyndorr's gate, past her towering walls, and onto the road that skirted the Rif'twine. Nyla, mounted on Skybreeze, sat at the front of the procession with a delegation of elders and statesmen. Klyden, on Skyflame, sat to her right.

More than half of Gwyndorr must have spilled out of the town to witness the remarkable sight. They stood silently staring north. Something had happened to the Rif'twine. Most of the verdant creepers that had slunk over the ground and trees were now brown and brittle. The vines' death had instantly thinned, and brought light to, the Rif'twine. The poison trees, too, were changing. Their branches were beginning to droop, like twisted limbs groaning under an impending death.

"The forest is dying," Lord Briskyl said.

"And with it the rift between us and Ajalon," Nyla said.

From the moment Prince E'shua had defeated Lord Lucian on the battlefield, Tirragyl had been changing. She looked up now at the sky. Was it her imagination, or did it seem bluer and more beautiful than it had ever been before? The faces around her were different too. The weariness and strain on them was gone. There was something quieter in people's eyes, a gentleness, as if they were truly taking in the world—and each other—for the first time.

When Prince E'shua released the light and men's breath from the Guardian Rock, Nyla had dared to hope that Alexor would be returned to her. But he, and all who had died in the battle for the Grotto, had not awakened from their mortal wounds. Nyla's first task as the prince's representative had been to lead the living in burying the dead. The remaining Parashi, Charab, and soldiers of Alexor's army had worked side-by-side in this sorrowful task, often comforting each other. This surprising unity had been the first sign that something had changed in their homeland.

She had urged the surviving Parashi and Charab to come with her to Lydora, promising that they and their families would live a good life there. But the one called Pearce had stepped forward to speak, a woman with short, dark hair and her son, Simhew, by his side. He explained that the surviving men had been reunited with the women and children who had escaped from the waterfall. They would like to stay at the Grotto and rebuild it not—he stressed—as a base for the resistance, but as a celebration of their history and culture.

Elxa, now the new Charabian, had also declined her heartfelt offer with a gentle smile. "We will return to our families with great joy, Nyla. Now that we are free of Taus's curse, we can make something beautiful of our lives again."

She had wept as she bade farewell to him and the men who had served her so faithfully.

Nyla glanced to her right, meeting Klyden's gaze. A surge of gratitude washed over her. He had not returned to his own people but had fulfilled his promise to Prince E'shua to stay by her side. In the warmth of his smile, she read that he would have done so whether the prince had asked it of him or not.

The crowd standing along the road was beginning to stir. Nyla strained her eyes and saw the movement on the eastern road. She watched closely as the small group of figures grew closer. They moved slowly. Many were bent over. Some supported each other. It was the small figures amongst them that loosened the knot of grief from her throat. Nyla jumped off her horse and began to walk towards them. She would have run, but she did not want to startle them.

Behind her the crowd had started to sing and clap in welcome, and a tambourine beat a joyful tune.

The approaching men and women, disheveled and wary, stopped as they saw her. Near the front of their group, a boy of about eight led a younger girl by the hand. Nyla dropped to her knees and opened her arms in welcome. The young girl glanced up questioningly at the older boy and then back at Nyla. Then she tugged her hand away and, despite the boy's protests, started to run. Full of trust and hope, she threw herself into Nyla's embrace.

"Welcome, little one." Nyla's tears fell into the girl's wild tangle of curls.

The rifters and rooters were coming home.

ACKNOWLEDGMENTS

My continued gratitude goes out to Steve Laube and the Enclave/ Gilead team for their commitment to seeing the final book of the trilogy come to life. Thanks especially to Jordan Smith, Katelyn Bolds, and Morgan Busse for their valued marketing support.

Thank you to Ramona Richards for her depth of experience and professionalism in the editing of *Guardian of Ajalon*.

Thanks to Charles Bernard for masterfully designing the cover to tie in with the other covers in the series.

Ashlyn, I love your second map as much as your first. Well done for taking my messy scribbled lines and crafting them into a beautiful illustration.

I want to thank the MAI team—John, Bonnie, and Dawn—for their support and for going out of their way to bring attention to my writing. It means so much to me.

My family have been through all the ups and downs of living with a writer. Thanks to Roy, Nicole, and Ashlyn for bearing with me and for holding space in your hearts for my dreams.

How I have come to value the encouragement of my many friends and readers. I appreciate each and every one of you. Gill Haggis, your belief in my books (particularly this one, of which you read an early version) sustained me when I needed it the most. Thank you, dear friend. Laura Pol, your long-distance friendship is a gift. You have encouraged me over and over again in precious and practical ways. Roma Thompson, thank you for all you did to bring my books to the attention of South African audiences and for your continued enthusiasm regarding this trilogy.

For loving me and singing over me, for telling stories that capture my heart and make me want to tell my own—I am so grateful, Lord. May this story honor you.

ABOUT THE AUTHOR

Joan Campbell is the author of *Encounters: Life Changing Moments with Jesus*, a collection of short stories, reflections, and prayers. Fiction is Joan's first love and she writes intriguing, fantasy adventures with an underlying message of grace. The Poison Tree Path Chronicles includes *Chains of Gwyndorr*, *Heirs of Tirragyl*, and *Guardian of Ajalon*. Joan lives in Johannesburg, South Africa, with her husband, two daughters, and their Labrador, Tabeal, named after one of her characters.

Connect with Joan online:

Website: www.joancampbell.co.za
Facebook: @authorjoancampbell
Twitter: @joancam1
Instagram: @joancampbell_author

The Poison Tree Path Chronicles

JOANCAMPBELL.CO.ZA